COLD IS THE DEEP

GEORGE WALLACE

SEVERN RIVER
PUBLISHING

Copyright © 2025 by George Wallace.

All rights reserved.

No part of this book may be reproduced in any form or by any electronic or mechanical means, including information storage and retrieval systems, without written permission from the author, except for the use of brief quotations in a book review.

Severn River Publishing
www.SevernRiverBooks.com

This is a work of fiction. Names, characters, businesses, places, events and incidents are either the products of the author's imagination or used in a fictitious manner. Any resemblance to actual persons, living or dead, or actual events is purely coincidental.

ISBN: 978-1-64875-638-2 (Paperback)

Also by George Wallace

Operation Golden Dawn

Cold is the Deep

By George Wallace and Don Keith

The Hunter Killer Series

Final Bearing

Dangerous Grounds

Cuban Deep

Fast Attack

Arabian Storm

Warshot

Silent Running

Snapshot

Southern Cross

The Gibraltar Affair

The Tides of War Series

Argentia Station

Never miss a new release! Sign up to receive exclusive updates from George Wallace

severnriverbooks.com

This book is dedicated to the late CAPT John Peters, USN (ret), and CAPT Alan More, USN (ret), my commanding officers on my first two submarines, the USS John Adams SSBN-620B and the USS Woodrow Wilson SSBN-624B, and two of the finest naval officers I know.

PROLOGUE

0100 EST, 17 December 1982, False Cape Beach, Virginia

The pounding surf almost drowned out the hammering of his heart. Somewhere over the eastern horizon, a winter storm was churning the ocean into a confused frenzy. Waves from that storm were crashing far up on the wide, sandy beach. The sky over this lonely stretch was an ink-black dome studded with the bright pinpricks of a million stars.

But nature's beauty was far from Henri DuBois's mind as he pulled his beater Dodge Dart into the empty parking lot. Not surprising that no one was enjoying a beachside stroll this late on a frigid winter night. Not when Virginia Beach's garishly lit nightlife was just twenty miles to the north. It was cold enough that not even the hardiest outdoors enthusiast was interested in beach camping.

This was a perfect location for a drop. Probably why his Russian handler had picked it. The money was good and the work was easy. And there wasn't much risk. Nobody would ever suspect him of stealing secrets. Not with his clearances and years of experience. DuBois figured that was why the handler had first approached him. That had been some fifteen years ago, in a sailors' dive bar just outside Norfolk naval base. Fifteen years of late-night secret drops and envelopes full of cash.

He rolled the window down and sat in the car for fifteen minutes, just watching and listening. It paid to be cautious. If anyone caught him with the roll of film, he would spend the rest of his life in Leavenworth. That is, if they didn't shoot him. Treason still carried the death penalty.

Finally satisfied that he had this stretch of beach all to himself, he slipped out of the car and headed over to the beachside campsites. He buried the film in the sand under the trash can for Campsite 13.

He hurried back to his car and sped down the narrow two-lane road. He was already spending the money in his mind. There was no thought about betraying his country or the submarine sailors whose lives he was putting at risk.

0930 EST, 6 Jan 1983, COMSUBLANT's Office, Norfolk, Virginia

Captain Ted Strange walked into Vice Admiral Rufus Brown's office. He helped himself to a cup of coffee before plopping down in the straight-backed chair at the end of the big oak conference table.

Rufus Brown, Commander, Submarine Force Atlantic, or more commonly COMSUBLANT, looked up from the file he was reading, adjusted his glasses, and asked, "See that you're back, Chief-of-Staff. How was your little vacation?"

Strange suppressed a chuckle. "Well, boss, I'm not sure a trip to Omaha in the middle of winter classifies as a little vacation." He shivered at the thought of the brutal arctic wind whipping across the open fields at Offutt Air Force Base. "This meeting was a bit different from the usual. We all still got together with the Joint Strategic Target Planning Staff and went over all the colored pins on that big wall map of the Soviet Union. Nothing changed there. I don't think we moved more than half a dozen pins."

He flipped pages before he went on. "Then the three of us adjourned to CINCSAC's briefing room for a situational update. Jimmy Nelson, SUBPAC Chief-of-Staff, was there representing CINCPAC. Didn't you serve with Jimmy?"

Brown smiled and nodded. "Yep, he was my Engineer when I commanded *Seawolf*. Good guy."

"And Brigadier General Scot Watson is the new SAC Chief-of-Staff. Being a typical fly boy, he insists on being called by his handle, 'Scooter,' Scooter Watson. Anyway, we got force-fed the latest intel download." Strange shook his head ruefully. "Boss, it ain't good. The Soviets seem to be getting really restless. They're driving big gains across all their programs. They are really pushing deployment of both their road-mobile and train-mobile ballistic missiles. The strategic heavy thinkers are projecting that the Soviets are working toward a first-strike capability, dropping the whole Mutually Assured Destruction idea. The intel estimate is that they have enough launchers for a really credible first strike. The only thing between us and some strong-arm nuclear blackmail is our boomer fleet."

Brown's brow was deeply furrowed with worry, but he nodded and replied, "Yeah, ain't nothing new there."

Strange looked up and scowled. "Intel is saying we have a problem there, too. They are seeing indications that our patrol areas may be compromised. Over the last year, Soviet ASW efforts, especially from their attack submarines, seem to have markedly increased in exactly the areas where we have boomers currently patrolling, and they seem to move between patrol areas at pretty much the same times our boats do. No indication that any of the boats have been detected yet, but it's only a matter of time."

Brown growled, "Does that mean what it sounds like?"

"I'm afraid so, boss. Looks like we have a spy with a pretty high level of access."

1315 EST, 14 January 1983, Building NH-97, COMSUBLANT Headquarters, Norfolk, Virginia

Commander Darren Walsh was intently listening to the young scheduling officer explaining the intricacies of the patrol area management for Walsh's upcoming patrol. Walsh was the skipper of the USS *John Jay*, Blue Crew. He and his command team had flown up from their homeport of Charleston, South Carolina, to the COMSUBLANT headquarters in Norfolk, Virginia, for their pre-patrol briefings just before they all flew over to Holy Loch, Scotland, where they would relieve the Gold Crew who were currently out on patrol. The briefings were meant to give the team all the information they would need on their upcoming deterrent patrol.

Walsh leaned over to Stan Wilkins, his brand-new Executive Officer, and whispered, "XO, pay attention here, but this will all make a lot more sense when we are actually out on patrol. They give us big chunks of ocean, a thousand square miles or more to hide in, but then they rotate us around every couple of weeks, just to keep us awake."

Stan Wilkins chuckled softly. "Thanks, Skipper. This is all new to me. Always been an engineer, back aft, pushing."

Just then Darren Walsh caught movement out of the corner of his eye. He shouted, "Attention on deck!" just as Vice Admiral Brown and Captain Strange strode into the briefing room. Everybody jumped to attention as Admiral Brown walked to the front of the room. He waved everybody back to their seats and then spoke. "Men, you are about to take *John Jay* out on patrol. It will be an interesting and challenging patrol, but you are up to the challenge. Good luck and good hunting." He paused for a second and then added, "Now, if you would give us the room, I need to speak with the skipper and XO for a few moments."

The young lieutenant briefer and the *John Jay* officers filed out and quietly closed the door behind them.

Brown looked up and said, "Darren, Stan, we're going to ask you to conduct this patrol a little differently than normal. We're concerned about operational security. There has been some serious indications of increased Soviet ASW efforts in our patrol areas. This has been especially true for their *Victor II* and *III* nukes. I don't need to tell you what it would mean to our deterrent posture if one of them managed to detect or, heaven forbid, trail one of our boomers."

Walsh and Wilkins exchanged a worried look. "Admiral, the *John Jay* is a really quiet boat," Walsh answered, "and we are very careful how we handle her. So, what do you want us to do differently?"

Ted Strange unfolded a chart of the Norwegian Sea. "Darren, you are patrolling way up north this time. It will be right near Russia's backyard. We're tempting them to come out and play, so you need to stay on your toes all the time. We're going to run a bear-trap operation on you about once a week. That should catch anyone trying to trail you."

Stan Wilkins looked perplexed. "Captain, I'm an attack boat sailor from the Pacific. What's a bear trap?"

Strange answered, "XO, it's very simple. We have you drive through a known point at a known time. We have someone standing off on the sidelines listening for anyone else lurking around. We trap the bear."

Wilkins nodded. "Got it. So you want us to drive through these points at the times indicated. Sounds simple."

Strange replied, "It is. But we are asking that you keep this quiet, even from your crew, until after you are underway. We don't want this info leaking out. Any questions?"

Both Walsh and Wilkins shook their heads. "We got it, sir," Walsh replied as they stood. They shook hands with the Chief-of-Staff and Admiral Brown. As they filed out the door, Brown said, "Good luck. We're looking forward to your post-patrol debrief of a successful patrol."

When Walsh and Wilkins had left, Ted Strange said, "Admiral, we didn't tell them anything about the spy."

"Yes. That was on purpose. The knowledge won't help them, and the fewer people in the know, the easier it will be to catch this son-of-a-bitch."

As Walsh and Stan Wilkins walked out to the parking lot, Walsh checked his watch. "XO, we've got a couple of hours before our flight. I need to run an errand downtown. Want to come along?"

Stan Wilkins recognized that he didn't actually have a lot of choice. The car was Walsh's rental, and it was eight miles to the airport. "Sure, Skipper. Glad to tag along. What's the errand?"

"Wife's birthday is just before we get back from patrol," Darren Walsh explained. "I need to get her gift before we leave. There's a neat little secondhand antiques store down on Colley Ave that has an antique sewing box that Joy loves. Gonna grab it, get it all wrapped up and leave for her to open."

Henri DuBois sat in his car across the street from the antiques store. He stared in utter disbelief as the two officers left the antiques store carrying the sewing box, the very sewing box where he had just hidden his latest film drop. That sewing box had sat on the same shelf for years, just gathering dust. It looked to be a safe place for a quick public drop. Now he had a problem, and it was taking an afternoon flight to Charleston.

1

1730Z, 7 March 1983, Holy Loch, Scotland

The sun dropped below the Cowal Hills, but with the dense drizzly fog, it didn't make much difference. The wet, gray day melded seamlessly into a wet, gray evening. The sodium vapor lights over on Ardnadam Navy Landing, less than half a mile across the water, were a barely visible glimmer through the gloom.

The huge, black submarine slipped silently from its moorings alongside the submarine tender anchored in the center of the Holy Loch. The long, flat missile deck identified it as a *Lafayette*-class fleet ballistic missile submarine. Another FBM, or "boomer," heading out on a routine deterrent patrol, just like they had been doing for more than twenty years.

The wind blowing down the narrow, confined loch drove the sleet-rain mix like bullets, stinging the faces of the men working to stow the last of the lines and secure the cleats on the submarine's main deck. It whipped up whitecaps on the water and caused the red, white, and blue flag to snap crisply. Their work complete topside, the last of the men dropped through the weapon's shipping hatch and dogged it shut as the boat swung into the Firth of Clyde, merging into the outbound shipping lane. They didn't even bother to look up for a last look at the sky they would not see for the next seventy days.

Commander Darren Walsh, Commanding Officer of the USS *John Jay*, hugged his heavy foul-weather coat around him. The dull green Navy-issue jacket had multiple layers and was supposed to be water resistant, but Walsh wasn't convinced whoever designed it had ever been to Scotland. The driving wind was bitter cold on the submarine's unprotected bridge. He sat on the bridge hatch combing and watched as the boat swung around to the southwest. This was his last patrol on the *John Jay*, or *Jayfish*, as the crew sometimes called the boat. He wanted desperately to make it a memorable one.

The 7MC speaker blared, "Bridge, Nav, recommend steady course two-zero-five. Plot shows us twenty yards to the right of track. Recommend ahead standard to conform with PIM."

PIM, or Plan of Intended Movement, was the pre-planned navigational track that the sub would follow.

Walsh had to shout to be heard over the wind. "Officer-of-the-Deck, steer course two-zero-five and come to ahead standard. As soon as the Dunoon ferry pier is abeam to starboard, kick it up to full. Quicker we get out of here and submerged, the better I will like it."

"Captain, XO," the 7MC blasted. This time it was Stan Wilkins, the Executive Officer. "Visibility through number two scope down to two hundred yards. Recommend slowing to steerage way and sounding fog signals."

Walsh grabbed the 7MC mike. "XO, that ain't happenin'. We need to be out of here, underwater, and on alert by midnight. Bobbing like a cork off Gourock ain't gonna cut it. Log your recommendation, and kick up the speed. How is radar behaving?"

Turning to the OOD, Walsh ordered, "Sound fog signals for underway."

The OOD reached down and grabbed the handle that operated the foghorn. He yelled, "Sounding the horn," as he pulled the handle back. The prolonged blast of noise all but deafened everyone in the bridge cockpit.

Wilkins recognized that while Walsh was ignoring his recommendation, by ordering him to log it, he was also assuming full responsibility if anything untoward happened as a result.

"Skipper, the radar is rotating and radiating. We're splitting time with the Nav for radar navigation and my contact coordinating." The XO's voice was clipped. He didn't like risking the boat in a congested area with limited visibility.

Walsh shook his head. It was Wilkins's first run as XO. He was bound to be a little cautious, but now was not the time to play it ultra-safe. "Roger. The channel is nice and wide. Just make sure the Nav is keeping us on the track. You keep an eye out for the ferries. They are damn dangerous around here and don't maneuver for anyone. Send the messenger to the bridge to operate the foghorn."

The boat silently glided down the Firth of Clyde. The only disturbance it made in the Scottish night was a blast from the foghorn every two minutes. The lights of Ayrshire on the port and the more sparsely populated Cowal Peninsula to starboard were invisible, hidden by the fog and rain. The XO passed the range and bearings of all the shipping that their AN/BPS-11 radar detected heading into or out of the busy Port of Glasgow, but up on the bridge, they saw nothing but varying shades of gray and black.

"Bridge, Nav, hold you on track. Hold the Skelmorlie Buoy on radar. Bearing one-nine-seven, range one thousand yards. CPA in two minutes on the port beam, range two hundred yards. Passing well clear of the Skelmorlie Bank." The Navigator, Lieutenant Bob Shippley, was using the radar, fathometer, and the submarine's very sensitive inertial navigation system to keep them in the main shipping channel heading outbound.

"Bridge, XO, recommend coming right to course two-two-five to better clear the Skelmorlie Buoy."

"XO, Captain, won't that take us out of the shipping channel?" Walsh questioned.

"Yes, sir," Wilkins shot back, "but there is more good water there."

"XO, JA," Walsh directed, telling Wilkins to use the JA sound-powered phone handset so their conversation would be private. He then grabbed the JA handset himself.

"Skipper, XO," Stan Wilkins spoke into his handset.

"XO, what is the distance to the dive point off the Mull of Kintyre?" Walsh asked.

"Forty-nine-point-five nautical miles," came the reply.

"And what is our speed over the ground?"

"Eleven-point-four knots."

"And what time is it?"

"Skipper, it's twenty-thirty."

"XO, we have a little over four hours to reach the dive point, get safely submerged, and meet up with our escort. We don't have time to jink around all over the Firth of Clyde just so you will feel a little safer. Now, just keep us in the channel and get us to the dive point on time and without hitting anyone." Walsh's tone was cold and demanding. "Log your recommendation in the deck log and the fact that I ordered you to maintain channel course."

Stan Wilkins gulped. "Yes, sir."

The *John Jay* charged through the night. Fortunately, the combination of heavy seas and low visibility seemed to be keeping seagoing traffic to a minimum. Any sailor worth his salt was moored safely and snuggly in some quiet water if he had a choice. The men on the *John Jay* didn't have the luxury.

Rounding Garroch Head on the south end of the Isle of Bute, the sub lost the protection from the wind that the island's high hills afforded. The full force of the growing gale slammed into them. Salt spray from waves rushing up the rounded deck and crashing into the sail was a constant for the men on the bridge. The powerful submarine shouldered the waves aside, but still the larger ones broke completely over the sail, inundating them and sending a torrent of water down the bridge trunk into the control room below.

The sub skirted around the Isle of Arran and entered the approaches to the Irish Sea. The winds raced down the North Channel and then swirled around the encircling islands, kicking up a dangerously confused sea. More and more bone-chilling salt water was pouring up and over the sail.

"Skipper, Nav," the 7MC speaker on the bridge blasted above the wind. Walsh bent down into the meager shelter of the bridge cockpit to better hear.

"We are thirty-one miles from the dive point," Bob Shippley reported. "We have two hours to get there on time. We are only making eleven knots good. Recommend we contact squadron and tell them we are going to be late."

Walsh thought for a second. His orders were pretty clear. It was vital for him to be at the dive point on time and to make the rendezvous. The whole mission was riding on that. But the reality of the weather conditions was literally hitting them right in the face. Admitting that the weather was just unsafe and then slowing was the prudent course of action.

He shook his head and mumbled under his breath, "No balls, no blue chips." Then he keyed the 7MC mike. "Nav, send the IC man to help rig the bridge for dive. As soon as everyone is below, we will kick it up to a flank bell."

Five minutes later, the bridge was buttoned up with everyone below. The *John Jay* was slamming through the waves at sixteen knots. That was as fast as her S5W reactor plant could drive the mammoth submarine on the surface without over-torquing the shaft and twisting it like a pretzel.

At precisely midnight, Bob Shippley plotted the sub's position and announced, "The ship is at the dive point. Sounding is five-three fathoms. Checks with chart."

Walsh ordered, "Officer-of-the-Deck, submerge the ship."

2031Z, 7 March 1983, off the Mull of Kintyre, North Channel of the Irish Sea

"Conn, Sonar, new broadband contact on the sphere, designate Sierra Three-Five, bearing zero-seven-two," the 21MC speaker announced to the crowded and darkened submarine control room. "Probable submerged contact based on nature of sound. In ATF on the contact, broadband tracker assigned."

The *Sturgeon*-class fast attack submarine *Tigerfish* was steaming submerged two miles south of the Mull of Kintyre, many miles inside British territorial waters. No submarine should be submerged around here unless it flew the White Ensign. Roy Blivens, the *Tigerfish*'s skipper, knew for a fact that the nearest Brit sub was safely bedded down at the Royal Navy's submarine base in Faslane. His Top Secret orders said that he was supposed to have these waters all to himself, at least until midnight. That could mean only one thing.

"Officer-of-the-Deck, man battle stations," he ordered Tom Clemont, the OOD and Navigator. "And come around to course zero-four-five at ahead two-thirds. Let's slip in behind this bastard on our first leg."

Submarine warfare was a cat-and-mouse game played by two dangerous blindfolded cats, each with very nasty claws. The players had to use only their ears to detect the enemy and then to figure out where he was and where he was going. It was a painstaking game of listen, analyze, then maneuver in an underwater game of blindman's bluff. Solving for the other guy's range, course, and speed by measuring the sonar bearing and then seeing how it changed as own ship maneuvered through a series of courses, or "legs," was the heart of Target Motion Analysis. The sub maneuvered to solve the problem and to get into the best shooting position, hopefully without the other guy even knowing you were anywhere nearby. There was no sportsmanship involved. The goal was to shoot the other guy in the back.

The *bong, bong, bong* of the general alarm ended with a 1MC announcement of "Man battle stations." The crew rushed to their battle stations as the sub was made battle-ready. The Executive Officer, Lieutenant Commander George Sanders, stumbled into the darkened control room, rubbing sleep from his eyes.

"Glad you could join us, XO," Blivens said in an aside to the XO.

Sanders half chuckled as he grimaced. "This port and starboard CDO watch sucks. All the action is on your watch, so I get rousted out of my nice warm rack. Nothing happens on my watch, so you get to enjoy your beauty sleep."

"Life ain't fair," Blivens answered with a smile. "But rank hath its privileges. To business. Sierra Three-Five, on the sphere, positive submerged contact, bearing now zero-eight-six. Coming to course zero-four-five for TMA and a lag line of sight."

The Chief of the Boat, Master Chief Machinist Mike Shaw, had barely slipped into the diving officer's chair when he reported, "Officer-of-the-Deck, the ship is at battle stations."

"Steady on course zero-four-five. Get a leg," Sanders ordered into his sound-powered phone mouthpiece.

The fire control party bent to their task of assimilating all the data, then using a combination of the Mark-117 fire control computer system and a series of manual paper-and-pencil plots to determine just where Sierra Three-Five was and where he was going.

"Sierra Three-Five classified Russian *Victor III*." The announcement from the sonar operators wasn't really a surprise, but it was not good news. They were facing the newest and most advanced Russian attack submarine, every bit as capable and deadly as the *Tigerfish*, maybe more so if you believed the Naval Intelligence analysis.

"Skipper, cross-bearing minimum range three-eight hundred yards," Sanders reported. "Best solution from the plots, range six-five hundred yards, course two-zero-six, speed six knots. Ready for another leg."

Blivens nodded and ordered, "Officer-of-the-Deck, come right to course two-seven-zero. I don't want to close him any until we have a shooting solution."

Tigerfish maneuvered slowly back and forth across Sierra Three-Five's wake as the team solved the TMA problem. The painstaking work was slow and tedious, an equal mix of analytical calculation and intuitive guesswork. The team slowly determined that the Russian sub was steaming to the southwest at a range of six thousand yards.

"Possible contact zig," the time-bearing plot analyzer called out. "Rapid increase in bearing rate. Now left four degrees a minute."

At the same time, the time-frequency plotter called out, "Possible contact zig. Upshift in received frequency, now two-point-one knots toward."

Sanders quickly scanned the plots and the computer solution "dot stack" before he announced, "Confirmed contact zig toward. Anchor range six thousand yards. Skipper, we need to maneuver to get off his track."

The problem had suddenly gotten very serious. The Russian sub had unexpectedly turned around and was now rapidly coming toward them.

Had he sniffed out that he wasn't alone in this bit of underwater geography? If so, what would he do?

Blivens ordered, "Officer-of-the-Deck, come to course three-two-zero and ahead standard. Let's open out a little and keep our friend right on the edge of the baffles as we dance around behind him again."

Blivens worked to skirt *Tigerfish* around behind the Russian, back in his baffles where they couldn't be detected by the Russian's bow-mounted sonar. All the while being very careful to stay so quiet that the Russian's sonar would not detect them. It was a very dangerous, slow-moving dance.

Sanders watched the incoming sonar information. "Skipper, he has steadied up. Looks like he is doing some sort of racetrack, essentially toward the southeast and then back around to the northwest."

Blivens thought for a second and then stepped back behind the periscope stand to the navigation chart table. There he hastily sketched in the Russian's track on the chart. "XO, he's running parallel to the shipping channel up the Firth of Clyde. That bastard is waiting to catch a boomer coming out of Holy Loch." He checked his watch. "And we are supposed to meet up with the *John Jay* right here in less than an hour."

Sanders looked over Blivens's shoulder. He muttered, "That can't be a coincidence. Whatta we do now?"

"We get rid of him," Blivens said as he stepped back around to the periscope stand. "Make tube one ready in all respects. Firing point procedures, tube one, on Sierra Three-Five, set submerged tactics."

Sanders glanced questioningly at Blivens. "Skipper, that tube has an exercise fish loaded."

Blivens half grinned. "Yeah, I know. Watch this."

Lieutenant Bill Andrews, the Weapons Officer, passed the order down to the torpedo room, where tube one was flooded, equalized with sea pressure, and the outer door opened. He then checked that the weapon was powered up and receiving inputs from the fire control system before he reported, "Weapon ready."

Sanders checked to make sure that the best target solution was set in the fire control system and reported, "Solution ready."

Tom Clemont made sure that the ship's course, speed, and depth were within the limits for a torpedo launch and announced, "Ship ready!"

"Shoot on generated bearing!" Blivens ordered.

Andrews grabbed the large brass handle in the center of the weapons launch panel and yanked it to the left. "Stand by." He yanked all the way to the right. "Shoot!"

Down in the torpedo room, high-pressure air was ported into a cylinder that rammed a piston down a long water-filled cylinder. Ports opened behind the torpedo in tube one. High-pressure water escaping from cylinder flushed the torpedo out of the tube. When the torpedo sensed that it had been shoved out into open water, its otto-fuel-powered swashplate engine started. The weapon sped toward its target.

"Weapon launch, weapon running at pre-enable speed," Andrews announced.

"Normal launch. Weapon running normally." Sonar could hear the outbound torpedo, and it sounded normal.

The fire control party shifted to tracking the weapon to make sure that it was going where it was supposed to. The weapon ran out on an almost straight line at better than sixty knots until it was a couple of thousand yards short of Sierra Three-Five, or at least the fire control team's best estimate of where the Russian was. It then slowed and turned on its active sonar. The torpedo became an undersea bloodhound, snaking back and forth, using its high-frequency sonar to sniff out its target.

"Sierra Three-Five is speeding up." The 21MC from sonar announced that the Russian sub was now trying to evade their torpedo. "Three-Five is cavitating." The Russian was going fast enough that low-pressure steam pockets were forming around the edges of his screw and planes. The pockets collapsed with an ear-shattering bang, like machine-gun fire, that could be heard for miles. He was running for his life.

"Detect, detect, acquisition," Andrews called out in quick succession. The torpedo had found its target, confirmed that it actually held the target, and was rushing in at high speed. With the torpedo racing in at better than sixty knots, the Russian had less than a minute to evade.

Andrews watched the drama play out on the CRT screen in front of him. The icon showed the torpedo intersect with Sierra Three-Five and then steam away.

"Turn away!" Andrews called out.

Then the weapon turned back around and attacked the Russian again as Sierra Three-Five raced out into the Irish Sea as fast as it could go.

Blivens chuckled. "That exercise fish will keep him busy and crapping his drawers for a while. With a half tank of gas, should be good for at least another fifteen minutes' entertainment."

Sanders shook his head. "Skipper, how did you know he wouldn't counter-fire?"

"I didn't for sure. That's why we had a warshot in tube two ready to go." Blivens checked his watch. It was midnight. "Just in time. We should be detecting *John Jay* right about now."

"Conn, Sonar, loud transients bearing zero-three-five. Sounds like high-pressure air venting. Possible submarine submerging."

2

0900Z, 8 March 1983, USS John Jay, *North Atlantic*

The *John Jay* threaded its way up the North Channel and out into the Atlantic. The *Tigerfish* stayed close behind, keeping on the edge of the *John Jay*'s baffles while it swept the seas for any other unwanted intruders.

The rough, confused inshore waves gave way to the long rollers of the broad open ocean. Life on the two submarines rapidly returned to the normal underway routine.

The *John Jay* was not scheduled to go on alert until noon, so Darren Walsh gave his crew a few hours of uninterrupted rest. After noon, they would be required to be in continuous communications with the National Command Authority and to keep all systems ready to launch their load of Poseidon ballistic missiles on a moment's notice if the president ordered it, a state of readiness called Condition 2SQ. They would need to stay in Condition 2SQ for every single minute until their patrol ended some seventy days from now. That was the reason for the *John Jay*'s existence, to provide a very real deterrence so that anyone foolish enough to think about launching a nuclear strike against the US knew for sure that the *John Jay* was out there, safely hidden in the broad expanse of the Atlantic, ready and able to launch a devastating retaliatory strike.

Stan Wilkins, the XO, called for a department head planning meeting in the wardroom for 0900. At precisely 0900, Darren Walsh stalked into the wardroom, filled his coffee cup, and plopped down in his seat at the head of the table. He tossed a large manila envelope out onto the red Naugahyde-covered table. The envelope was marked in large red letters "Top Secret, Special Handling Required."

Walsh glanced around the table. "XO, where's the Eng?" he growled. All the department heads and the Chief of the Boat were seated around the table. All except the Engineer. Lieutenant Commander Pete McKay was not among the gathered assembly.

"He's back aft," Wilkins answered, "nursing the lithium bromide. Says the thing has rocked up again. They are searching for an air leak. Eng said he would come forward in a couple of minutes."

Almost as if on cue, the door burst open, and Pete McKay charged through. A big guy, and slightly overweight, McKay seemed to charge headlong into everything.

"Skipper, sorry I'm late," he announced in a voice that was a little too loud for the room. "Think we've fixed the bromide plant. Small air leak on the absorber outlet. M Div is unrocking the plant now." He shook his head. "That thing still mystifies me. You dump steam in and get cold water out. Pure magic."

Darren Walsh, very familiar with Pete McKay's feigned ignorance, knew full well that the MIT graduate in mechanical engineering could easily give a graduate-level course on the thermodynamics of a lithium bromide air-conditioning system, but right now they had a patrol to plan.

"Gentlemen," Walsh began as he pulled a sheaf of documents from the manila envelope, "this patrol is going to be a little different from previous runs. We're heading up into the Norwegian Sea. Most of our alert time will be at the ice edge. If we can maintain comms, we will try to operate some under the ice.

"This document will stay in radio. I expect each of you to read through it and be intimately familiar with it." He pulled out a section of the larger document and skirted it down to Bob Shippley. "Nav, you will note in Appendix N that we are directed to pass through a whole series of what they are calling 'tie-points.' We need to be at each one precisely on the date and time specified."

Bob Shippley looked perplexed. "Skipper, isn't that a little bass-ackwards from normal doctrine? You know, the one where we stay hidden and no one off the boat has any idea where we are?"

Walsh nodded. "Yep, Nav. It sure is. But Admiral Brown's signature is at the bottom of this page. If COMSUBLANT tells us to be at these tie-points, we will be at the tie-points. Now, let's get the *John Jay* on a warship footing."

He turned to Lieutenant Brett Burns, the Weapons Officer. "Weps, get the target packages all verified, and get the system over to Condition 2SQ. We'll run a Weapons System Readiness Test right after lunch. And get the BQR-15 towed array streamed. It's time for the *Jayfish* to play submarine again and go fishing for Russians.

"XO, I want the ship fully rigged for sea. Let's run angles and dangles right after the WSRT. Make sure that everything we shake loose gets properly stowed. COB, we'll start tomorrow morning off in true patrol fashion, with a field day."

1000 EST, 8 March 1983, Building NH-97, COMSUBLANT Headquarters, Norfolk, Virginia

Captain Ted Strange, COMSUBLANT Chief-of-Staff, ordered, "Attention on deck!" as the conference room door swung open and Vice Admiral Rufus Brown strode in.

The half dozen men seated around the conference table jumped up and snapped to attention as the short, gruff man wearing three stars on his collar ordered, "As you were," and took his seat at the head of the table. A coffee cup and steaming carafe were already waiting at arm's reach. He poured a cup. After tasting the brew, he sighed and turned to Strange. "All right, Chief-of-Staff. Let's get this brief on the road. What happened out there last night?"

Strange nodded to Captain Jay Lawton, the N-3 Operations Officer, who stood behind a small lectern and clicked the first slide. The screen showed a chart of the west side of Scotland out to the continental shelf. He slapped his pointer at the chart. "Admiral, the *John Jay* got underway from Holy Loch last night on schedule. She submerged south of the Mull of Kintyre and proceeded out the North Channel into the Atlantic. Her dive message reports everything normal."

Brown grumped, "What about *Tigerfish*?"

"Commander Blivens reports encountering a *Victor III* south of the Mull just before the *John Jay* arrived," Lawton answered. "He chased it off with an exercise Mark 48. The *Victor* ran south, into the Irish Sea. We notified the Brits. They are out conducting an ASW search and retrieving our weapon."

Brown chuckled. "Exercise Mark 48, huh? That Russkie must have crapped his drawers. Damn smart maneuver, but Blivens is real lucky the Russkie didn't counter-fire."

Strange nodded. "Yeah, I'll have discussion with Commander Blivens when he gets back about provocative maneuvers and taking unnecessary risks. But it looks like our spy got through and the Russians are at least nibbling at the bait."

Brown nodded but was noncommittal. "Probably, but we won't know for sure until the *John Jay* gets to the first tie-point. Wish we could have told Walsh that he was the bait in this little trap."

2114Z, 8 March 1983, USS Tigerfish, North Atlantic

The *John Jay* headed to the south, out toward the deep waters of the Rockall Trough, while Roy Blivens steered the *Tigerfish* well to the north, skirting the north side of the Stanton Banks. Blivens and Tom Clemont, the Navigator, stood in the aft port side of the control room, studying the chart laid out on the chart table.

The quartermaster, QM-1 Eric Swarton, swung the parallel motion protractor around and plopped it down. The line he laid out connected their current position with a mark labeled "TP-1." Reading the PMP scale, he reported, "Skipper, recommend course three-three-two, then around to due west after we clear the Banks to get to the first tie-point. Distance two hundred forty-three miles."

Swarton grabbed his nautical slide rule. This special-purpose circular slide rule was developed just to solve time/distance/speed calculations quickly and accurately. No competent Navigator would be caught without one somewhere within arm's reach. He spun the wheel around so the speed arrow pointed at 12 and the distance arrow at 243. "At twelve knots, it will take eighteen hours. That gets us there at fifteen-fifteen tomorrow."

Clemont opened the binder that he clutched and read from it, "Rendezvous time TP-1 0800Z, 10 March. *Tigerfish* is to arrive in area at least twenty-four hours before rendezvous and is to conduct an ASW sanitization of the TP. *Tigerfish* is to remain undetected at all times. If hostile submerged contact is detected, *Tigerfish* is to conduct trail ops against contact." He looked up. "Skipper, we need to be at TP-1 no later than 0800Z tomorrow."

Swarton played with the circular slide rule for a second. "Skipper, that means we will need twenty-two knots."

Blivens shook his head. "I ain't racing in there blind at a flank bell and telling every Russian for miles around that we are on our way. Nav, plot a track at a flank bell until we are ten miles short of TP-1. Then drop it to a two-thirds bell. We'll slip in a little more unannounced."

Blivens stepped around to the periscope stand. "Officer-of-the-Deck," he said, addressing Bill Andrews, "Make your depth four hundred feet, come to ahead flank, steer course three-three-two, and deploy the towed array."

Bill Andrews grabbed the 21MC microphone ordered, "Sonar, Conn, take stations to deploy the towed array."

Then he turned to Eric Swarton. "QMOW, sounding?"

Swarton keyed the fathometer and then read the sonar return. "Depth five-six-zero fathoms beneath the keel."

"Diving Officer, make your depth four hundred feet, ahead flank."

The submarine nosed down into the depths. The boat shuddered as four of the massive main coolant pumps shifted to fast speed, slamming shut check valves for the idle pump in each main coolant loop. Steam roared into the main turbines as the throttleman spun the throttles open.

The boat leaped ahead, accelerating until the reactor power meter hovered right at the one hundred percent power mark. *Tigerfish* was racing through the depths at better than twenty-six knots.

1845Z, 9 March 1983, USS John Jay, *North Atlantic*

Darren Walsh pushed back from the wardroom table. The remnants of the evening meal had been cleared away. The junior officers had disappeared to attend to whatever business needed attending before they would reappear in a few minutes for officer training. He and Stan Wilkins, his new XO, had the wardroom to themselves.

It felt good to be settling into the patrol routine again. Wednesday evening. That meant an hour of wardroom training from nineteen hundred to twenty hundred, and then the evening movie. Walsh loved the predictability of boomer life. He knew, with pretty good certainty, just what they would be doing for each Wednesday for the next seventy days, just like they did for every other day of the week.

More than the predictability, Walsh loved the camaraderie, especially in the wardroom. The evening training sessions followed by the movie went a long way toward forging those bonds.

Walsh reached over to the buffet and grabbed the coffeepot. He topped off his cup and offered to do the same for the XO. Stan Wilkins shook his head. "Thanks, Skipper, but I'm going to beg off. Already had too much coffee today." He pushed back his chair and rose to leave.

"XO, grab the cribbage board," Walsh directed. "It's time for you to be introduced to one of the great traditions of the submarine service, the tradition of the XO being routinely vanquished by the superior skills and experience of the CO."

Wilkins started to protest that he had work that needed to be done. Walsh held up his hand. "XO, accept your fate. Cut for the deal."

The two senior officers sat and played out their hands, slowly pegging their way around the board. Wilkins won the deal and then managed to peg halfway down the first street on the first hand. Walsh struggled to keep up but was five pegs back after Wilkins counted the crib.

Walsh dealt the next hand. After discarding to the crib and turning up a six of clubs for the start card, Wilkins threw down a six of diamonds. "See one, play one."

Walsh immediately played a nine. "Fifteen for two," he called out, moving his peg two places.

The 1MC blasted, "Alert one! Alert one!"

Both officers threw down their hands and dashed toward the control room. The boat had just received an Emergency Action Message. An EAM was the method that the National Command Authority communicated to a boomer with orders to either launch their missiles or to stop launching if that order had previously been authorized. So far, in all of the many patrols that boomers had made, the EAMs had always been practice messages, a test to hone the crew's skills. But there was no way of knowing if the message was practice or for real until the code had been broken and the message authenticated. And they only had a precious few minutes to find out if it was a practice EAM or the start of World War III.

They had to dodge a pair of lieutenants junior grade, Will Morris and Tony Stagnetti, as they all crowded toward the ladder to upper level. Morris and Stagnetti both ducked into radio while Wilkins and Walsh ran on aft, into control. As Walsh stepped up onto the periscope stand, Brett Burns, the on-watch Officer-of-the-Deck, handed him several printouts of the EAM. He already had OPORD 2134, the pub that had the instructions, laid out on the desk and open to the right page.

Walsh and Wilkins read through the message together. Each copy was from a different broadcast source, and they all had some sections that were unintelligible. Walsh pulled out a pen and started to piece the different messages together with Wilkins's help in an attempt to get one clear message. To be valid, they had to have an EAM that was properly formatted. That is, it had to contain all of the right information in the right places. There could be no ambiguity in the message.

They were halfway through piecing the message together when Morris and Stagnetti stepped into the control room. They both clutched a small piece of brightly colored foil, keeping it clearly visible and above their heads as they walked. The piece of foil contained a set of Sealed Authentication System codes. The sealed foil packets had been delivered to the boat before the *John Jay* departed on patrol and had been stored in a double-locked safe ever since. Each of the two officers had one of the combinations. This way, no one person had access to the codes by himself. If the codes in the foil packet matched the codes on the EAM, they knew for sure that it was a real message, that it was valid.

Morris clutched the message in his other hand. Stagnetti held another copy of the OPORD.

"Skipper, we have a properly formatted message. Request permission to authenticate," the two said together.

Walsh replied, "Let's see how you pieced it together." Both the CO and XO watched as the two junior officers explained each step in how they put together the EAM. Satisfied, Walsh ordered, "Authenticate the message."

The pair broke open the foil wrap and pulled out the card. Together they read off, "Romeo, Bravo, Four, Seven." It matched exactly with the code on the EAM.

"Captain, message authenticates," Morris said.

Stagnetti nodded and said, "Agreed, message authenticates."

Walsh turned to Brett Burns and ordered, "Officer-of-the-Deck, man battle stations missile for a WSRT. Pressurize all tubes."

The Weapons System Readiness Test was an unannounced drill initiated by COMSUBLANT that tested the entire submarine ballistic missile system all the way from generating the launch message at the command center up to pressurizing the missile tubes on the submarine for launch. And the clock was ticking. Thirty minutes from the time the message was released in Norfolk until the first bird was simulated away. This one was unusual. The boats seemed to always receive WSRT messages in the wee dark hours of a Saturday night. Probably from a SUBLANT watch officer who was bored and needed something to keep him awake. A Wednesday evening test seemed just too easy.

The Chief-of-the-Watch grabbed the 1MC microphone and announced, "Man battle stations missile for a WSRT." He then pulled the handle for the general alarm, which bonged loudly. He quickly followed with a repeat of the 1MC announcement, "Man battle stations missile for a WSRT." It took thirty seconds for the crew to man battle stations. The COB, Master Chief Steuben, was sliding into the diving officer's chair as the Eng ran into control to relieve Burns, the Weapons Officer, as the Battle Stations OOD. Burns disappeared, heading to the Missile Control Center. The "trigger" to launch the Poseidon missiles was in MCC, and the Weps was the guy who pulled the trigger.

"Battle stations missile is manned, the ship is ready to hover," Steuben called out.

"Very well," Pete McKay answered. "All stop, commence hovering at one-two-zero feet."

John Jay slid to a stop. A system of tanks, some pressurized so water could be blown off the boat and some vented so water could be flooded in, automatically kept the big submarine at exactly 120 feet deep even though it was stationary in the water so the missiles would not be bent over by the force of flowing water as they shot up to the surface.

Walsh pulled a key from around his neck and inserted it in a panel that hung above the periscope stand desk. The lock had three positions: Locked, Strategic Launch, and Exercise. He turned the key to the Exercise position. Grabbing the 1MC mike, he announced, "This is the Captain. Set Condition 1SQ, this is an exercise. Pressurize all missiles for a WSRT."

He handed the mike to Wilkins, who announced, "This is the XO. Set Condition 1SQ, this is an exercise. Pressurize all missiles for a WSRT."

The clock ticked twenty-nine minutes when the first bird was simulated launched.

Walsh checked his watch as the last of the sixteen missiles was simulated away. It read nineteen thirty. "Well, XO," he said to Wilkins, "I guess the Admiral effectively canceled tonight's wardroom training. Let's get set up for the movie. I need a popcorn fix. What's on the agenda?"

Wilkins pointed to the plan of the day posted on the conn. "POD says tonight's feature is *Swamp Thing*."

"Oh, goody," Walsh answered, not even trying to hide the sarcasm in his voice.

3

0800Z, 10 March 1983, USS Tigerfish, *TP-1, North Atlantic*

Roy Blivens stepped into the sonar space. CRT screens glowed green in the darkened room. He stood behind the passive broadband operator and watched the waterfall display develop. Nothing out there but a bunch of sea noise, biologics, and a tanker way off to the south, probably delivering Norwegian oil to the US. The passive narrowband operator's screens weren't any more informative.

Senior Chief Al Zwarlinski was the sonar supervisor for this watch, and in Blivens's mind, the best sonar operator in the Atlantic. "Skipper, same thing as when you stepped in ten minutes ago. We ain't got nothin'."

He clutched his earphones to his ears and held up a finger. Then he smiled and handed the phones to Blivens. "Hear that slow 'thump, thump'? That's a fin whale calling his friends to dinner. That sucker is probably seventy feet long and weighs fifty tons. Not many of them left out here anymore."

Blivens nodded and handed the headset back to Zwarlinski. "Let's hope this guy doesn't get amorous and decide to mate with the biggest, blackest fish he can find. That would take some explaining back in Norfolk."

Al Zwarlinski was noted for his love for marine life. He loved studying anything that made a sound in his ocean and loved talking about them. "Skipper," he started. "Did you know that a whale's penis might be eight to ten feet long and a foot in diameter? And they mate belly to belly, so he is upside down in the water."

Now Blivens laughed. "That's more information than I wanted to know. If we find a ten-foot sausage stuck in a ballast tank grate, I'm blaming you."

Blivens stepped out of the sonar shack. The XO's stateroom was directly across the narrow passage, and the door was open. George Sanders looked up from his unending stack of paperwork. "Any luck finding a party crasher?"

Blivens shook his head. "We have sliced and diced this whole area seven ways to Sunday. Not even a sniff of any Russian submarines. Either they have come up with a very quiet ghost boat or SUBLANT is barking up the wrong tree. I need you to draft a message to SUBLANT telling them that we came up empty here. We'll send it as soon as we rendezvous with the *John Jay*."

Before Sanders had a chance to reply, Al Zwarlinski stuck his head out of the sonar shack. "Skipper, just starting to pick up a real faint sixty-point-two-hertz tonal on the towed array. Not strong enough to assign a tracker yet, but reciprocal bearings are one-six-five and zero-one-five. Sounds like the *John Jay* is leisurely strolling in from the southeast."

1530 EST, 10 March 1983, COMSUBLANT, Norfolk, Virginia

Captain Ted Strange clutched an aluminum clipboard marked "TOP SECRET" on the cover as he stepped into VADM Rufus Brown's office.

"Admiral, latest report from *Tigerfish*," he said as he slid into one of the leather chairs across the desk from Brown. "They came up empty. Roy Blivens says that they scoured the area for twenty-four hours without a hint of a Russian sub. Maybe they didn't take the bait after all."

Brown stroked his chin for a second and then answered, "Possibly. But, on the other hand, maybe the *Victor* that Blivens scared the bejesus out of might have been assigned to TP-1. Brits have been beating the dickens out of him for three days solid. They're somewhere off the southern Irish coast by now."

He slid a folder across the desktop. "The intel weenies were just in. Take a look at the latest satellite imagery from Polyarny. Looks like our friend Admiral Golubev is sending a bunch of boats to sea. Intel counts four *Victor III*s, a pair of *Victor II*s, and an *Alfa* all deploying in the last four days. Haven't heard a sniff of any planned spring exercise up there in the frozen north. That's a lot of firepower all at once to be just local training."

Strange leafed through the photos, studying them as he thought. "Coincidence?" He shook his head. "Probably not."

He then looked at the SOSUS report. The SOSUS network of undersea hydrophones was vital in detecting and tracking Soviet submarines coming out of the Barents Sea and trying to sneak through the Norwegian Sea into the Atlantic.

"The North Cape array picked up the *Alfa* heading outbound," he read. "Not surprised. That seagoing sports car makes more noise than a garbage truck. Not seeing the *Victor*s."

He put the reports back in the folder and glanced over at the large map of the North Atlantic hanging on the wall.

"If our Russian friends were smart and sneaky, they might send the *Alfa* out to grab our attention while they slip the *Victor*s up around Svalbard real quiet like and then down the Greenland Sea. Let's not throw in the towel yet. I'm betting we'll be a lot luckier at TP-2."

"Anything new on our spy?" Admiral Brown asked.

The spy seemed to have gone quiet. They hadn't seen any positive information since the dead drop at Sandbridge a couple of months ago. Only guesses and intuition out of the NIS and FBI field officers. That didn't bode well for the plan to entrap the traitor.

Strange answered, "Nothing concrete. FBI is looking to see if they can work back up the chain, maybe find a link to the Russian embassy."

"And the NIS?" Brown asked. "Are they still keeping tabs on our suspect?"

Strange nodded. "From what they are telling me, our guy is going about his normal day-to-day duties. Except he has made several trips down to

Charleston, burning up Interstates 95 and 26 on the weekends. And he has made several calls to Charleston from his house."

"They gotta have his phone tapped," Brown interjected. "What did they get?"

Strange shook his head. "They can't get a warrant. New judge at the Eastern District Federal Court. He keeps reciting some legal gibberish about the Church Committee and saying NIS hasn't shown probable cause. If you asked me, he has the ACLU on speed dial."

Brown slammed his fist onto his desk. "God preserve us from lawyers!"

"It gets worse," Strange went on. "Grey Mole has met several times with a guy named Leland Samson. Works at NAVELEX. NIS thinks he may be part of Grey Mole's spy network."

"So now he has a spy network?" Brown choked out. "When did we get that little tidbit? What do we know about this Samson guy?"

Strange looked at his notes. "Not a whole lot. Like I said, he works at NAVELEX. Some kind of senior tech. Raised on one of the sea islands. His Gullah is a lot better than his English. Nothing in the records to draw any attention, no politics, no money problems. Nothing that really ties him to Grey Mole. NIS is looking closer."

"There's got to be something," Brown insisted. "I don't see our Grey Mole driving all the way to Charleston just to enjoy a beer and barbeque with a stranger."

"It seems that Grey Mole has shown an extraordinary interest in the Walsh family," Strange continued. "He was spotted cruising their neighborhood in Goose Creek several times, including parking across the street for several hours when no one was home."

"Where did you get that information?"

"Apparently NIS kept a loose tail on our spy while he was cruising the South," Strange answered. "They just got around to telling us."

"Nothing like good, solid teamwork." Brown's voice dripped sarcasm. "If Grey Mole is interested in the Walshes, we need to find out what he is looking for. And we need to make sure that the Walsh family is safe. Notify the local authorities with as little information as possible, but enough to get their interest that they need to keep an eye out."

"What if we had NIS stake out their house?" Strange replied. "That's pretty much in their wheelhouse, and it makes it a whole lot easier to keep a lid on the security."

"That works. Set it up."

1130 MSK, 11 March 1983, K-324, GIUK Gap

Captain Second Rank Boris Novikov prowled the control room of his submarine, the *K-324*. Known as a *Victor III*–class submarine by NATO, his boat was officially a Project 671/RTM as far as the Soviet Navy was concerned. But what was important to Boris Novikov was that he commanded the most advanced, most capable warship at sea anywhere in the world. It was his duty to the Soviet Party to ruthlessly employ his submarine in carrying out whatever order the Northern Fleet High Command tasked him with.

His tasking today was both simple and incredibly dangerous. He was to search a ten-kilometer square area halfway between Iceland and the Faroe Islands. He was to search it for twenty-four hours starting precisely at twenty-one hundred Moscow time. His prey was an American *Lafayette*-class Poseidon missile submarine. When he found the American, he was to trail it for as long as he could and then report back to the High Command. He didn't even think to question why Northern Fleet High Command thought that an American missile submarine would be in this little bit of water at this precise time. What he did know for sure was that this area, known as the GIUK Gap to the Americans and their British allies, was the most intensely patrolled bit of water in the entire world. Keeping his submarine hidden would be extraordinarily difficult.

Novikov leaned over the navigation table to check the chart. The Navigator had plotted their position ten kilometers to the east of their search box. He checked the clock. They had three and a half hours to make sure that they were fully ready and to arrive in the search area. It was time to start.

Novikov turned to the watch officer. "Dmitri, deploy the *Barrakuda* towed array and energize the *Sistema Obnarujenia Kilvaternovo Sled*."

Dmitri Vinogradov, *K-324*'s watch officer, snapped to attention. He responded, "*Da, ser.*"

Turning to his watch team, the young captain lieutenant ordered the passive towed array sonar sensor to be reeled out of the pod mounted on top of the submarine's rudder and the *SOKS* non-acoustic wake detector system on the submarine's sailed energized. The *K-324* was ready to search out and find its prey.

4

1030Z, 11 March 1983, USS John Jay, *North Atlantic*

LCDR Pete McKay dropped down the after ladder into auxiliary machinery room two lower level. He was in the middle of his normal morning routine, walking through all the engineering spaces on the *John Jay* and surveying his domain. The ballistic missile submarine was a tremendously complex piece of equipment, and McKay knew that it was his responsibility to make sure it ran like a fine Swiss watch. Like the rest of the famous *41 for Freedom*, the *John Jay* had been launched back in the early sixties. She was now coming up on her twentieth birthday. In those twenty years, she had seen a lot of hard service, or in McKay's words, "She had been ridden hard and put away wet." The ship's systems had years of hard usage; bearings were worn, valves leaked, pipes corroded, and there was little time for deep maintenance. Constant vigilance was the only way to find the next problem before it reached up and smacked them in the face or bit them on the posterior.

On the *John Jay*, AMR2 separated the reactor compartment from the engine room. The upper-level space housed the complex electronics that controlled the reactor and the switchgear necessary to distribute electrical power around the boat. It was the domain of the electronics technicians, the ETs. AMR2LL, auxiliary machinery room two lower level, belonged to the machinist mates. Down here was everything from high-pressure charging pumps for adding water to the reactor to the emergency diesel generator, their only source of power if the reactor broke. The AM2LL watch had to be an expert in operating many varied systems, but mostly he had to watch. It was usually tediously boring.

McKay was expecting to find MM2 Ross Stanley sitting by the steam generator sample sink at the bottom of the ladder, but Rosebud, as Stanley was known onboard because of a tattoo on his posterior, wasn't there. McKay ventured forward on the narrow metal walkway along the starboard side. He stepped through the narrow space between the diesel and the valve-operating water flasks, over to the port walkway.

He was almost all the way back aft when he heard the high-pitched trill of a piccolo. He looked up and spied Rosebud sitting in a lotus position on top of number four main feed pump, almost completely hidden in a maze of piping.

"Rosebud," McKay growled. "What the hell are you doing?"

Stanley lowered his instrument and smiled. "Practicing, Eng. The Charleston Symphony is playing Shostakovich's Number Ten Symphony right after we get back, and I got a solo. This is the only place in lower level where I can hear myself."

McKay fought to repress a chuckle. He harrumphed, "Get your tattooed butt down out of there. You can practice on your own time."

"Station the fire control tracking party!" the 1MC speaker above McKay's head blasted.

His ears ringing, the Engineer rushed forward to take up his station as the plot coordinator. He charged through the back of the control room, past the Mark-113 fire control computer, and grabbed a JA sound-powered phone headset conveniently waiting for him at the Mark-19 plot table.

He clapped the earphones over his ears just in time to hear Stan Wilkins say, "Sonar contact on the BQR-15, Sierra Two-Six, bearing three-five-seven, and Sierra Two-Seven, bearing one-four-three degrees. Three-hundred-hertz tonal equates to that *Alfa* that was on the last intel update."

McKay quickly got his team at work with a time-bearing plot and a time-frequency one. Bearings received from the towed array tended to be scattered. The only way to get any kind of accuracy was to plot them and then smooth a curve through all the scatter. This at least minimized enough of the data scatter to start to determine target motion.

It took twenty minutes of plotting dots on the paper, but finally Pete McKay could make some sense out of the splatter. He took a straight edge and slapped it up on the graph and, using a wide magic marker, drew a line through the mess. Really, two separate messes and two separate lines since they didn't know yet which was the real sub and which was the ambiguous one. "Coordinator, I have a curve," he said into the headset while muttering under his breath, "Or at least something that looks like a curve. I could fit a bowl of spaghetti through that blob."

Just as soon as McKay finished, Walsh ordered the *John Jay* to a new course to the northwest. The big sub swung around slowly and steadied up on a course of three-two-zero. Five minutes later, the towed array was again a straight line far behind the boat and sending sonar information.

"Conn, Sonar, regain Sierra Two-Six, best bearing three-four-nine. Drop Sierra Two-Seven," the 21MC blasted. They had resolved the bearing ambiguity. The contact to the north was the real sub.

McKay played with his plot for a while. The only solution that he could make fit the fan of bearing lines was for someone heading to the southwest, going really fast.

Darren Walsh and Stan Wilkins stepped over to the plot table and watched over McKay's shoulder. He looked up and grunted before drawing a line across the chart. "Skipper, XO, my best guess on this guy is that he is out in excess of fifty thousand yards, on a course of two-four-zero, plus or minus ten degrees. He is making something better than forty knots. My guess is that he is heading for the Denmark Strait."

Walsh looked at the plot and nodded. "Makes sense. He is no problem for us. Time for us to remember the boomer motto. 'We hide with pride.'"

Turning to Wilkins, he added, "XO, secure from fire control tracking party. Let the section tracking party keep tabs on our speedy friend while we saunter off to the next tie-point."

1421 EST, 11 March 1983, COMSUBLANT, Norfolk, Virginia

Captain Ted Strange burst into VADM Rufus Brown's office without knocking. Brown was accustomed to these sudden interruptions and immediately knew that this one was important. He looked up from the report he was reading and waited for the flood of information that was about to come.

"Boss, SOSUS is reporting a new track in the GIUK Gap," Strange reported as he came to a halt in front of the big walnut desk. "They are reporting contact on both the Stornoway array and the Jan Mayen one. Gives us a probability ellipse with a seventy-five-mile major axis and a seventeen-mile minor one. Looks like a *Victor III* trying to be real covert. And it's right over the second tie-point."

Brown took off his reading glasses and placed them carefully on his desk. "That's still a pretty big chunk of ocean," he offered. He scratched his chin. "A little over four thousand square miles. They can't do any better?"

Strange shook his head. "Not until they develop the track for a while. We can get a couple of P-3Cs out of Reykjavik on top of this guy pretty quick."

Brown shook his head. "Nope, don't want to alert Ivan that we are on to him. Might queer the whole op. Just get an Op Immediate message out to Blivens. Let him do his job."

1530 EST, 11 March 1983, Goose Creek, South Carolina

The yellow school bus ground to a stop at the corner. When the door swung open, Pug Walsh, Darren Walsh's son, charged off and ran right down the center of the street. Thoughts of a glass of milk and Mom's warm cookies after a hard day in third grade filled his eight-year-old mind.

Ten-year-old Samantha, Sam for short, was far more reserved than her younger brother as she descended from the bus and strolled down Jasmine Lane. That was probably why she spotted the dark green Chevy panel van with the tinted windows. Her mother had repeatedly admonished the pretty, young girl to be wary of strangers. This panel van was certainly out of place. Nobody on their tight-knit little cul-de-sac drove anything like it.

Sam was about to call a warning out to Pug, but he was already past the van and running up their walk. She hugged the left side of the sidewalk as she skirted around the vehicle. She glanced inside to see two men sitting in front, looking out the windshield and not paying her any attention. It took her a few seconds to realize that their attention was riveted on the Walshes' little brick ranch house.

The young girl shivered and ran up the walk. She slammed the door behind her and yelled, "Mom! Come quick!"

Joy Walsh emerged from the kitchen, wiping flour from her hands with a dish towel. "Sam, dear, what's the matter? You all look like you've seen a ghost." The Walshes had lived in the Low Country long enough that her New England accent had been softened with a bit of Charleston drawl.

Sam peeked out between the curtains. "Mom, look at that van. There are two men in there, watching our house. I'm scared. I wish Dad was here."

Joy hugged her daughter. "I wish he was home, too. But we have a couple of months yet. Until then, we have to take care of everything on the home front." She looked out the front window, but the combination of the van's tinted windows and the sun glare prevented her from seeing anything.

"Maybe the Johnstons got a new van," she ventured. Sarah Johnston and her family lived next door, and the van was parked right in front of their house. Just like most of the people on this cul-de-sac, the Johnstons were a submarine family. Sarah's husband, Wilbur, was out on patrol on the *Lewis and Clark*.

Sam shook her head. "No, Timmy would have been bragging about it in class. He can't keep a secret about anything. Besides, there were a couple of men sitting in it."

Joy grabbed the phone off the stand and dialed Sarah Johnston's number as she watched out the window. Sarah answered on the second ring. It took only a few seconds to determine that the strange van did not belong to the Johnstons and that it had been parked out front all afternoon. She was just as worried about it as Joy now was.

"Sarah, the Berkeley County Sheriff will just blow us off. Bunch of hysterical housewives," Joy Walsh determined. "I'm going to call the Sub Group Six Chief-of-Staff. I'll let you know what he says."

Joy looked up the number in her patrol briefing package and dialed the number.

Captain Brian Houston answered on the second ring, "Sub Group Six Chief-of-Staff. This is not a secure line."

"Captain Houston, this is Joy Walsh, Darren Walsh's wife."

Houston was jocular. "Yes, Joy, I remember you from the Submarine Christmas Party at the O' Club. What can I do for you?"

Joy Walsh explained the situation and asked what she should do.

Houston's demeanor changed to serious. "Mrs. Walsh, the men in that van are Navy Investigative Service agents. SUBLANT has requested protection for you and your family."

"Protection? Why?" Joy Walsh asked. "Why do we need protection? Is Darren okay? Is he doing something dangerous?" This was decidedly not normal. Fear and worry were just below the surface.

"Mrs. Walsh, I can't discuss that," Houston answered. "SUBLANT has reason to believe that protecting you is warranted. Let me remind you, this is not a secure phone line. Why don't you come into the Group Six building tomorrow morning and we can discuss it."

0320 EST, 12 March 1983, Summerville, South Carolina

Henri DuBois swung the beat-up old Dodge Dart into the parking lot. He stepped out of the car and stretched. The drive down to Summerville from Norfolk was long and boring. Other than stopping for gas somewhere south of Rocky Mount, North Carolina, he had driven straight through for almost eight hours, never getting above fifty-five, even with the truckers trying to blow him off the road. And his back felt it.

He stepped into the Waffle House. Leland Samson was sitting in the last booth, back in the corner, nursing a cup of coffee.

DuBois scooted into the seat and said, "Evening."

The big Black man smiled as he answered, "Mister Henri, *gin ya see, it done three thirty inna da mawnin', evenin' ain't sou'un' right.*" He pushed over the laminated menu for DuBois. There was a small envelope tucked under the menu.

Born and raised on one of the remote sea islands that dotted the South Carolina coast, Samson spoke Gullah, the creole language that the isolated Black communities had developed over the centuries. It was an amalgamation of their native African languages mixed with Southern English. As the islands became less isolated over the years, the Gullah language slowly evolved more toward English, while it also became more common off the islands, even in major southern cities like Charleston. Even though more common, Gullah was still exceedingly difficult for non-Gullah speakers to discern.

DuBois chuckled and answered, "Don't think I need one. Pretty much have *l'menu grave dans la memoire.*" DuBois unconsciously slipped into his native Cajun as he pocketed the envelope.

The waitress arrived and hovered over the table, waiting for his order. After ordering a pecan waffle and side of country ham, and after the waitress had returned to the counter, he turned serious. "What's in the *escouepe?*"

Samson waved his hands as if the envelope contained nothing of value. "*Jes de plan fuh* that new radio, the RO-1039, *ef oona axed fa.*"

DuBois's smile brightened. "*C'est bon, tres bon.*" He slid a fat envelope across the table.

Leland Samson didn't bother to open it. He knew it was filled with cash. Should be enough for a new dock behind his place on Horlbeck Creek. The old one was falling into the marsh. He had learned early on in their relationship that Mister Henri didn't negotiate. He paid whatever he paid, and that was the end of the matter. But Leland had always been more than satisfied with whatever the envelope held.

DuBois handed Samson a piece of paper and said, "Leland, I need for you to break into this house and grab a package. Call me when you have it. *Comprends?*"

"*What da package hol'in?*"

"It's not important that you know. Just get it, *rapido*. Hire someone if you must, but *soyez prudent.*" DuBois turned his attention to his meal. *"Scusez-*

moi. I need to eat my meal and then get some sleep. It's been *une longue nuit,* and I have much to do in *la matin.*"

0920 EST, 12 March 1983, Charleston, South Carolina

Joy Walsh pulled their two-year-old Ford van into a parking space at the Navy Exchange. It was a beautiful spring day in Charleston. Puffy white cumulus clouds flitted across the cerulean-blue sky. The azaleas were in bloom, painting the Low Country in pinks and reds. A great day to be out, even for the short drive down to the Navy base. Maybe after meeting with Captain Houston she could look for a new Easter dress for Sam. The little girl was growing so fast it was impossible to keep her in clothes. And new pants for Pug.

She locked the van and strolled down Holland Street to the Submarine Group Six building. It was exactly 0930 when she stepped into the cement structure. Brian Houston was waiting for her at the quarterdeck. This caught her by surprise. The normal procedure was for her to speak with the quarterdeck watch. He would check her ID card and call back to the Chief-of-Staff's office. Some junior sailor would then arrive to escort her to Captain Houston's office, where she would wait until the Captain was ready to meet with her. But here he was on the quarterdeck. Something was definitely up.

He held the door open for her and led her down the drab hallway. His office was at the far end on the right. The door on the left was a little fancier, with a wooden placard that read "Commander, Submarine GROUP SIX."

"Coffee?" he offered, waving toward a coffeepot on a low side table. The office was spartan, obviously furnished out of a GSA catalog, but only if GSA handled used and battered furniture.

"No, thank you," she said, taking a seat in one of the chairs across from Houston's gray, government-issue steel desk. "Now, Captain," she began as she demurely arranged her skirt, "maybe you can explain why I have NIS agents sitting outside my house. This is Darren's fourth patrol in command, so don't tell me that this is normal."

Houston sat and looked at his hands for a few seconds before he answered. "Ma'am, what I am about to tell you cannot leave this room. The information is very highly classified, and lives may very well be at stake."

Joy Walsh looked to see if he was joking. The look on Houston's face was serious.

"Mrs. Walsh, we have reason to believe that there is a spy in SUBLANT. Your husband's patrol may have been compromised. We don't have any idea where or who the spy is. We don't know what their game is. The agents are guarding you as a precaution." Houston shook his head. "I'm sorry, but that is all I can tell you."

Joy Walsh's mouth dropped open. This was unbelievable. It was a warm springtime morning in Charleston, but a cold chill ran down her back, making her shiver. Her husband was out on patrol, but here she was caught up in some Soviet spy novel. But it was for real.

"Can't tell me any more, or is that all you know?" she shot back. There was a sharp edge on her voice. She had a family to protect and wasn't interested in playing secret squirrel games.

Houston held up his hands, palms facing outward. "That's all I can say." He rose and said, "Let me walk you out. Please call me immediately if you see anything that bothers you. I don't care how trivial it is."

Joy Walsh walked out onto Holland Street. Clouds rolled across the sky, promising a rainy evening. The spring day was not nearly so bright as when she'd walked in.

5

1930Z, 12 March 1983, USS **Tigerfish,** *GIUK Gap*

The buzzer caused Roy Blivens to jump. He just could not quite get used to its demanding tone. It always seemed to hit just when he was deep in some other thought, or deep in sleep. He grabbed the handset and growled, "Captain."

"Captain, we are in the search area around TP-2." Lieutenant Commander Steve Dunn, the *Tigerfish*'s Engineer, was standing the Officer-of-the-Deck watch. "We are at the southern boundary. I have come left to course three-zero-five and slowed to ahead two-thirds to commence a sonar search. Sonar reports no new contacts. The only sonar contact is Sierra Four-Seven, classified merch, bearing one-six-two, range in excess of forty thousand yards, past CPA and opening."

"Thanks, Eng. I'll be right out," Blivens answered.

He stood, stretched his aching back, and stepped through the head that he shared with the XO. George Sanders was seated at his desk, buried deep in the admin paperwork that Blivens remembered as the bane of an Executive Officer's existence. But while Blivens remembered hating and avoiding it when he served his time as XO, Sanders seemed to relish the journeys into the minutia of bureaucratic trivia.

Sanders looked up from the pub he was studying. "Skipper?"

"XO, the Eng just reported we are in the search box for TP-2," Blivens said. "I'm heading out on the conn to observe. Why don't you step into sonar and watch them work for a bit, at least until we get the search routine settled out."

Sanders put a slip of paper in his pub as a bookmark, closed it, and stood.

"Roger, Skipper. Want to set up a CDO watch routine again?"

Blivens nodded. "Sure. Just as soon as we get all coordinated. I'll take the first watch. Give you the midwatch."

Sanders grinned, but there was a sarcastic tone in his voice. "Gee, thanks, boss." He headed across the passageway and disappeared into the sonar shack. Blivens headed forward, into the control room.

Blivens stepped up onto the periscope stand and carefully evaluated the electronic scribbles on the BQR-21 DIMUS repeater. Every little blip appearing on the screen represented a noise heard by the big spherical sonar array that filled *Tigerfish*'s bow. The "waterfall" display represented bearing on the horizontal and time on the vertical, building from the top. That way, if something was out there making a constant noise, like a ship, it would show up as a solid white line going down the screen. Normal biological noises just showed as random blips. Blivens wasn't seeing any patterns that he could equate to his quarry, a Russian sub.

He looked over to the BQH-1 and glanced at the ink display of sound velocity graphed against depth. "When was your last depth excursion?" he asked Dunn.

"We went to six hundred feet at the start of my watch," Dunn answered. "Pretty much isothermal all the way down. Not seeing any sound channels."

Blivens nodded. "Yep, Eng, pretty much what I see, too. But let's check now, just to be sure. Drop down to six hundred feet and then back up to one-fifty. Let Senior Chief Zwarlinski and his sonar wizards tell us what the best search depth is. And I want to shoot a BT every watch while we are in this box."

An SSXBT, expendable submarine-launched bathythermograph sensor, was a small probe launched out of the submarine's three-inch signal ejector. The probe floated to the surface and then dropped a temperature sensor into the depths. A hair-thin copper wire that connected back to the sub sent temperature versus depth as the sensor sank. In seawater, temperature, depth, and salinity were the major variables in sound velocity. If salinity was assumed constant, then the BT was giving a direct plot of sound velocity against depth. And it could sense to a much deeper depth than the submarine could go. The drawback was that the sub could only be going a couple of knots during the process.

"Conn, Sonar, picking up a faint one-fifty-hertz tonal on the towed array." The 21MC speaker blasted out Senior Chief Zwarlinski's voice. "Designate Sierra Four-Nine and Sierra Five-Zero. Best bearings zero-three-five and two-one-five. Signal too weak to assign a tracker, sending buzz bearings to fire control."

Because the towed array was a single line of hydrophones towed far behind the sub, its beams formed a series of cones around the array. A sonar contact could be anywhere in a specific cone, or more realistically on either side of the array on reciprocal bearings. The sub would need to maneuver to determine which bearing was real.

Blivens grabbed the 21MC mike. "Is this our friend?"

Zwarlinski immediately answered, "Can't be one hundred percent certain, but one-fifty-hertz tonal equates to motor rotational lines on a fifty-hertz system. Most probably a *Victor III*–class Soviet submarine."

Blivens smiled. Senior Chief Zwarlinski was the uncontested expert on all things sonar, especially as related to Soviet submarines. He was mildly surprised that the Senior Chief had not provided a hull number and the CO's favorite vodka.

"Eng, let's resolve bearing ambiguity and work in behind this guy," Blivens said. "As soon as you have a leg, come around to course north. If he's really to the northeast, that will let us close him some on the next leg. And station the fire control tracking party."

The initial approach, while contact was still tenuous and the contact's range, course, and speed were only a guess, was the most dangerous time. It was the time for the first team to be playing. The fire control tracking party was the first team.

As *Tigerfish* swung around to the new course, the towed array, a two-hundred-foot-long line of hydrophones pulled by a cable over half a mile long, acted like it was playing a big game of crack-the-whip. The array was useless until it had settled out, straight and stable on the new heading. That meant no information for ten minutes or so. Contacts could, and frequently did, disappear during these turns, never to be seen again.

Finally, Senior Chief Zwarlinski called out, "Array is stable. Regain Sierra Four-Nine. Best bearing zero-two-eight."

George Sanders, now the Fire Control Coordinator, looked around at his team crowding the control room. He spoke into his sound-powered phone, "All stations, drop Sierra Five-Zero. Track Sierra Four-Nine. Sierra Four-Nine is the contact of interest."

Solving the problem of where the other submarine was and where it was heading using only passive sonar was a long, slow, iterative process. The only truths were bearing and received frequency. Everything else, like course, speed, and range, had to be assumed, and then the assumption had to be tested. Slowly, after several maneuvers and testing many trial solutions, the target's actual course, speed, and range would eventually fall out. The trick was to maintain sonar contact during this whole process without being counter-detected by the target. In that case, the hunter quickly became the hunted.

Finally, George Sanders was satisfied. His solution for Sierra Four-Nine was tracking. He turned to Roy Blivens and smiled. "Skipper, I have a shooting solution. Range one-three thousand, course three-one-zero, speed nine. Recommend we close to broadband range to track on the sphere."

Steve Dunn looked up from the navigation plot that he had been studying. "Hey, Skipper," he called out. "Look at this." He took a ruler and extended Sierra Four-Nine's track forward. "He is heading straight for TP-2. And with a speed of nine knots, he will get there an hour before our friend is scheduled to arrive."

Blivens looked at the track that Dunn had laid down. "Good work, Eng," he said. "Pretty much nails it. This guy has information on where to go to catch our boomers." Then he smiled. "Let's screw up his day a bit. Weps, have the torpedo room load a MOSS in tube one. Load the boomer tape."

The MOSS, or Mobile Submarine Simulator MK70, was a ten-inch-diameter, electrically powered sonar decoy. It was designed to swim out of a torpedo tube and then to follow a pre-programmed track. A pair of hydrophones played a pre-recorded tape. To a passive sonar, it sounded and acted just like a real submarine. The tape on this fish was a recording of the *John Jay* made several months ago.

"Eng, I want you to work us up so that we are just on the edge of Sierra Four-Nine's baffles and out about six thousand yards."

0215 MSK, 13 March 1983, K-324, GIUK Gap

Captain Second Rank Boris Novikov stood in the back of the control room of the *Victor III*–class submarine *K-324*, sipping a cup of tea while he watched his team operate. Dmitri Vinogradov, the watch officer, was very good, and the rest of the team seemed to be performing their duties as prescribed. He checked the digital clock above the fire control station. The American submarine should come lumbering through in a little over an hour. He had steered the *K-324* to be exactly where he wanted to be, ready to fall in behind the unsuspecting American so that he could trail it for as long as possible.

"Captain," Vinogradov called out, his voice tinged with excitement. "Sonar has detected the American. Bearing is two-nine-six. Estimated range is two thousand meters. We are seeing all the parameters we expect for an American *Lafayette*-class missile submarine."

Novikov came alert. This was not good. The American was an hour early, but he was also too damn close. Exchanging paint samples underwater was never a good idea.

"Come to all stop!" Novikov ordered, a little louder than he wanted. It was not good to betray worry to your crew. "Let the American pass in front of us and then maneuver into trail of him."

The Soviet submarine slid to a halt, hanging stationary one hundred meters below the surface. Novikov held his breath as the American drew nearer. He sensed that this was going to be very close, but he knew the Americans should be up at about fifty meters so they could communicate back to their command center. The American press made a very big deal that the Yankee missile submarines were always in communication with their Pentagon.

He watched the sonar screen. The bearing did not waver, but the trace got progressively brighter. Then he could hear the heavy beat of the American submarine's screw. It must be passing nearly overhead.

Then it started to slowly recede away. Miraculously, they had not collided, and there was no indication that the American knew that the K-324 was anywhere in this ocean.

Novikov took a deep breath and slowly let it out. Then he said, "Comrade Vinogradov, fall in behind the American. And energize the SOKS system. Let's see if the engineers back at the Rubin Design Bureau have worked out the kinks in our wake detection system."

The Russian submarine captain sat back and watched as his crew maneuvered behind the American. Sonar was tracking him easily, heading off to the northeast at ten knots. Lieutenant Vinogradov steered the K-324 back and forth across the American's wake, even coming shallow to make sure they were going through the very heart of the submarine's turbulence. The SOKS stayed silent. There was no indication that it was detecting anything.

Novikov was drafting the message back to the Rubin Design Bureau in his head when Lieutenant Vinogradov called out, "Captain, we have lost contact with the American!"

Novikov's head shot up. That was impossible. The sonar track had been very strong, burning into the screen. He looked. Sure enough, the brilliant display had suddenly ceased. It just disappeared.

Novikov stared in disbelief. Sonar contacts faded out. They didn't suddenly disappear. This was very unusual. He had the sonar operator replay the tapes. One second, the missile submarine's noise is burning K-324's sonar screens. The next, it is gone. He had the sonar system checked out to make sure everything was operating properly. Nothing was amiss. There was only one possible explanation. The Americans must have some new toy, a cloaking device like in those silly American movies. Now he really had something to report. And he had the proof, right there on his sonar tapes.

0115Z, 13 March 1983, USS Tigerfish, GIUK Gap

"Conn, Sonar, new sonar contact on the sphere, bearing two-nine-six. Designate Sierra Five-One," Senior Chief Zwarlinski's voice boomed over the 21MC. "Classified US *Lafayette*-class based on nature of sound. Sounds like she is developing a rub on a main seawater pump bearing."

Roy Blivens looked down at the navigation plot. "Looks like the *John Jay*, right on schedule. Where is our Russian friend now?"

George Sanders smiled. "When last seen, he was chasing the MOSS off to the northeast. Should be about twenty miles out by now and scratching his head, trying to figure where that big, juicy American boomer disappeared to."

6

1330 EST, 13 March 1983, Goose Creek, South Carolina

Joy Walsh cleared away the lunch dishes and called the kids in from the backyard. When Darren was out on patrol, the family had established a routine. Sunday afternoon they gathered around the kitchen table and wrote a weekly family-gram to Dad.

Each family was allowed to send their sailor seven family-grams per patrol. Joy figured that seven messages for a nominal seventy-day patrol worked out to one per week. It was their only link, however tenuous, to Darren. And she knew how much these messages meant to her husband, isolated out there somewhere under the Atlantic with 150 of his closest friends.

Family-grams were short, forty-word-max radio messages. The messages were strictly one-way. And they were not the least bit private. Joy would deliver the bit of paper to the Gold Crew off-crew office on Monday morning. The Gold Crew radiomen would screen it, type it up on the right form, and send it downstairs to the Sub Group Six Communicator. He would make sure it met the rules: only good news, nothing that could possibly upset the recipient. Then it would be sent out on the regular submarine radio broadcast. Every boat in the fleet would copy the message. Although there was no privacy in a family-gram, some could be quite original and humorous. Most boats would post the best, most embarrassing one as the "Family-gram of the Day" as long as it wasn't addressed to anyone on that boat.

The whole process usually took several days, but that depended on how much official traffic was filling the airwaves. Family-grams were near the bottom of the priority list and were frequently bumped for higher-priority traffic. Sometimes it could take a couple of weeks before the gram was delivered.

Pug Walsh rushed through the screen door, pulled out a chair, and plopped down at the table. Sam sauntered in at a pace she considered more sophisticated, at least for a ten-year-old girl.

Pug grabbed a thick pencil and the family-gram form. "It's my turn to write first," he stated. "Sam started first last time." He scrawled, "Dad, hit homerun, T-ball, Love Pug." He shoved the form over to his older sister.

Sam Walsh bit on the eraser and diligently thought about what she wanted to write. Just what should a young lady say to her father. She pondered long and hard. There were just too many possibilities. She wanted to tell him all about the van parked out front, but she knew that was off-limits. Maybe she could say something about her best friend's birthday party next week. She decided to wait until after the party to talk about that. Finally, she shook her head and wrote, "Dad, love you, miss you, come home soon. Sam."

Some of the wives simply wrote family-grams to their sailor-husbands themselves and didn't get the rest of the family involved. Joy felt that it was important that the kids have a direct link to him, even if it meant that she had fewer words. Joy read what the kids had written. Their fifteen words were important. It left her twenty-five. Twenty-five words weren't anywhere near enough to tell Darren how much she missed him and needed him home. But she had to be very careful not to even hint how very scared she was right now. She finally decided a white lie and a plain, innocuous message was the best.

"Dearest, all is good at home. Kids fine. Spring beautiful here. Show you pictures. Miss you. Love you. Stay safe. See you soon."

2330Z, 13 March 1983, USS John Jay, *GIUK Gap*

The control room on the *John Jay* was dimly lit with red fluorescent bulbs, giving everything a darkened, almost foreboding cast. Since it was nighttime up on the surface, the control room and adjacent passageways were "rigged for red" to allow the Officer-of-the-Deck to quickly adapt to the darkness if they suddenly needed to go to periscope depth and he needed to look out of the periscope.

Darren Walsh and Bob Shippley stood around the nav plotter in the forward starboard corner of *John Jay*'s crowded control room. The "bug," or lighted marker, on the Mark-19 plot table showed that they were about 150 nautical miles north of the Faroe Islands and about an equal distance from Iceland to the west. They were leaving the GIUK Gap and entering the Norwegian Sea.

"Okay, tie-point two is in the rearview mirror. Off to tie-point three," Shippley said. "Skipper, what is supposed to be happening at these tie-point things? It sure seems to violate our boomer motto, 'We hide with pride.' Whatever happened to the old, 'you own this big patch of ocean, just stay somewhere in it' idea."

Darren Walsh looked up from the message board that he was perusing. "Nav, nearest I can figure out is that SUBLANT is worried the Russkies might have figured out some way to trail us on patrol. The tie-points are probably a chance for them to delouse us."

Bob Shippley shook his head. "But, Skipper, we haven't seen a hint of any other submarine since we left the *Tigerfish* back in the Irish Sea. If they are delousing us at these tie-points, I sure don't know how they are doing it."

Walsh answered, "Ours not to reason why. Nav, how far to tie-point three?"

Shippley pulled out his dividers and walked off the distance across the chart. "Four hundred nautical miles. Twelve miles due east of Jan Mayen Island." He pulled out his nautical slide rule and spun it around. Reading off the cursor, he said, "OPORD has us there at midnight eighteen March. Skipper, recommend we make five knots by log so we can get a little ahead of PIM."

PIM, or Plan of Intended Movement, was the sub's planned course and speed as it moved from one point to another. If the boat followed the plan, or stayed on PIM, it would arrive just where it wanted to be just when it wanted to be there. It was the Navigator's job to make the plan and then to make sure that it was followed.

The growler for the 2JV sound-powered phone handset on the periscope stand whooped. Brett Burns, the on-watch OOD, grabbed the handset and listened for a second, then he handed it to Walsh. "Skipper, it's the Eng. He wants to speak with you."

Walsh held the handset to his ear. "Captain."

"Captain, Engineer. We have a problem with number two main seawater pump. Its mechanical seal is running hot," Pete McKay reported. "I've increased the leak-off, and that helped some. Recommend we limit number two pump to super slow speed and operate main seawater cross-connected."

The two main seawater pumps each normally supplied cooling water to one of the two main condensers. The two systems could be cross-connected so that either pump could supply both condensers, but that put a limit on the sub's top speed, depending on how cold the outside water was. At four or five knots, it wouldn't be a problem, particularly in the cold wintertime Norwegian Sea. But it could be a real problem if they suddenly needed to go fast.

Darren Walsh was exasperated. The *John Jay* was getting to be an older boat. These equipment failures were happening more and more often as the gear wore out. You had to plan ahead and make sure your backups were ready to go.

"Okay, Eng. I concur on reduced status for number two main seawater pump. What is your plan for fixing it?"

"Skipper, right now I have a watch stationed at the pump monitoring temperature and adjusting leak-off. If the seal fails, we'll engage the emergency flax packing. If that fails, we'll have to operate with one main pump. No way I know of to fix it at sea."

Walsh shook his head, although he knew Pete McKay could not see him. He was just unwilling to give up and admit something couldn't be repaired until all possible options had been explored and rejected for good, sound reasons. That was just not the case yet.

"Eng, give the problem some careful study. Don't be afraid to think outside the box."

The quiet in the control room was disturbed by a loud chirping emanating from the starboard side of the periscope stand. Brett Burns turned to the Chief-of-the-Watch and said, "Find the Aux Electrician Forward. Sounds like the french fries are done."

The COW sent his messenger out to find the AEF. One of the AEF's more important routine duties was to rewind the timer on the BST-1 Submarine Emergency Communications Transmitter Buoy, commonly called the Beast Buoy. The buoy was designed to alert the National Command Authority in the event an FBM submarine was sunk. Then it floated to the surface and broadcast a coded radio message. It could be launched manually or automatically if its sensors indicated that the sub had been sunk. It also would automatically launch if its timer was not rewound every two hours. It was the AEF's duty to wind the timer. If he was late, an alarm that sounded very similar to a McDonald's french fry machine would start to chirp. If he did not rewind it within five minutes, a very loud horn would blast. After another five minutes without being reset, the buoy would launch, under the assumption that everyone onboard was incapacitated for some reason.

ICFN Horace Faris rushed into the control room and over to the BST-1 control panel. He fumbled with his key but finally got it inserted in the rewind slot and wound the timer. The chirping stopped and quiet was restored. Faris looked up and saw Darren Walsh standing on the periscope stand, watching him.

"Sorry, Skipper," Faris stammered, "I was down in the library aligning tapes on the entertainment system. That Sundstrand is a pain to align."

Walsh nodded as he replaced the 2JV handset. "Faris, that Beast timer is a whole lot more important than making sure the crew has fresh music. You don't want me to have to send an emergency message back to the admiral telling him that we're okay, ICFN Faris just forgot to rewind the Beast because he was changing tapes, do you?"

Faris shook his head. "No, sir, I sure don't. Sorry, sir. It won't happen again." He grabbed his logs and hurried out of the control room.

Walsh turned and studied the BQR-21 waterfall display for a few seconds. At least according to their BQR-2 passive sonar, they were all alone in this part of the ocean, but the traces were showing a lot of sea noise up on the surface. Anyone on a surface ship up there would be having a rough night, typical weather for March in the Norwegian Sea.

He yawned and looked at his watch. It was well after midnight. It was time to end a long day. Tomorrow would be another long day, and he needed his rest. Turning to Brett Burns, he said, "Weps, I'm going to hit my rack. Have the messenger wake me at 0530."

He turned and headed down the passageway toward his stateroom. He noticed that the light was still on in the XO's stateroom and that Stan Wilkins was at his desk, writing. But he didn't see the stateroom door.

Walsh was chuckling when he stuck his head into Wilkins's stateroom. "I see the patrol has officially begun," he related to Wilkins. "The crew has already stolen your door. What do you plan to do about it?" Pranks played on the XO were the subject of many a sea story. As long as they were all in good fun and didn't get out of hand, they were good for crew morale.

"I'm getting the COB to start a search. Can't be that many places to hide a door on a submarine."

Walsh shook his head. He leaned against the now empty doorway. "Back when I was XO on old Ustafish, the crew got my door. They actually hid it under my mattress. Took a couple of weeks to finally find it."

"What did you do?" Wilkins asked.

"I just hung a blanket over the door and pretended like nothing was going on. It drove the crew nuts." Walsh laughed at the memories. "They thought they really had one over on me, but then nothing happened. Oh, when I did zone inspections after field days, I made sure that I covered the likely spots, up over the main turbines, under the torpedo ram, places like that. Nothing overt. When I finally found it, I never let on. Just left the blanket hanging. It drove the pranksters nuts."

Wilkins started to laugh. "Skipper, that's great. Think I may do the same thing."

Forward of the XO's stateroom was the Equipment and Electrical, or E&E, space, a small room that housed the capstan, the towed array handling gear, the mechanical compensators, the BQR-2 and BQR-7 sonar beamformers, and a host of other equipment jammed into a small space, even further restricted by the submarine's hull necking down toward the bow. Among its other functions, it served as a workshop for the Interior Communications Division. The IC men kept all of the phone systems and the various position indication systems onboard working.

On the *John Jay*, the IC Division also was home to the boat's chief pranksters, although the radiomen disputed that title.

IC-2 Delvin Brimley looked around carefully to make sure no one could overhear his conversation, as if someone could hide in the cramped space. His voice was barely above a whisper. "Anyone see you?"

Interior Communications Fireman Horace Faris harrumphed. "Del, it's a friggin door. Of course people saw me. Farley is the Aux Forward. He ran interference. It's in the frame bay outboard the missile control center. The missile techs have been sworn to silence."

Brimley chuckled. It sure looked like they had gotten clean away with the prank. Now to sit back and watch the fun.

0430Z, 14 March 1983, USS **Tigerfish**, *Norwegian Sea*

Roy Blivens's eyes shot open. Some sixth sense had told his subconscious that he needed to wake up. Something in the subtle noises and vibrations of his submarine was different. Different was not a good thing.

He reached above his head and grabbed the JA handset. With his other hand, he pushed the buzzer button as his eyes tried to focus on the clock. 0430, damn! He had only been asleep for two hours and had another hour before he needed to be up.

"Yes, sir, Officer-of-the-Deck." Bill Andrews's nasal New England accent came through.

"Weps, what are you doing? What's going on?" Blivens knew that he sounded groggy. But he hadn't taken the time to get fully awake.

"Nothing, Skipper," Andrews answered warily. "Just steaming toward the next tie-point in accordance with the night orders. Speed twelve, depth three-five-zero feet, course two-nine-two. No sonar contacts. Everything hot, straight, and normal."

"Well, something has changed," Blivens almost growled. His sixth sense was on full alert. "Find out what."

He swung his legs out of the bunk and grabbed his rumpled poopie suit. No sense trying to go back to sleep. He was just jamming his feet into the poopie suit when the 1MC announced "Fire! Fire in the fan room! Rig ship for fire!" That was followed by the *bong, bong, bong* of the general alarm.

There were two things that a submariner dreaded above all others: flooding and fire. Unlike on a surface ship, there was no going topside to escape either one. You had to stay and fight. There was no other option. And, of the two, fire was worse. At least with flooding, you could still breath and still see. With fire, the boat would quickly fill with smoke so dense that everything was done by feel.

Blivens grabbed his emergency air breathing mask and dashed out to the control room. He could smell smoke. There was enough in the air to make his eyes sting. He was plugging his EAB into the air manifold on the periscope stand when Bill Andrews, already wearing an EAB, reported, "Skipper, Auxiliary Electrician reported fire in the fan room. Fire in fan two. Fan two is deenergized."

QM-1 Eric Swarton, wearing a JA sound-powered phone headset, reported, "XO is in charge at the scene. Fire jumped to boxes of chem wipes stored in the fan room." His voice was muffled by the EAB. He had to shout to be heard over the near continuous sound of air being sucked from the manifolds through the EAB regulators.

Smoke was building to where everything was in a gray cloud. As soon as the fire was out, they would need to emergency ventilate the boat to clear it. Only then could they overhaul the fire to make sure it was really out and begin the repairs.

Blivens turned to Andrews. "Weps, get us up to one-five-zero feet and clear baffles. We'll take care of fighting the fire. And rig control for black. You need to be able to see out the scope."

The Chief-of-the-Watch lined up the pressurized auxiliary trim tank to the trim header and announced, "The fire main is pressurized," just as Swarton reported, "The XO has ordered the mess decks fire hose to the scene and pressurized."

The Engineering-Officer-of-the-Watch, back in Maneuvering, announced on the 7MC, "The AMR2 upper-level fire hose is pressurized and standing by in the tunnel."

Andrews tapped Blivens on the shoulder. The smoke was so thick that Blivens could barely see the OOD, even though he was only a couple of feet away.

"Skipper, at one-five-zero feet. Made a baffle clear to the left. Hold no sonar contacts. Speed twelve knots. Request to go to periscope depth."

Blivens put his nose up against the BQR-21 sonar repeater and read the traces through the smoke. Even with a flashlight, he had to strain to see the screen. As best he could tell, it looked like Andrews was right. He couldn't see any contacts, either. He shouted, "Officer-of-the-Deck, proceed to periscope depth."

Going to periscope depth was the most dangerous evolution that a submarine did routinely. Even with the most modern, sensitive sonar systems, there was always the very real possibility that a ship was up there, hidden by a thermal layer, incorrectly analyzed, or just plain quiet. For this reason, going to periscope depth was a carefully choreographed procedure. Nothing else happened, and the control room was kept silent except for specific necessary reports. Doing all of this during a fire, with everyone in EABs, coordinating fighting the fire, and in near total blackness, was several orders of magnitude more difficult.

Andrews reached up into the overhead and rotated the lifting ring for number two periscope. "Raising number two scope," he called out. "Dive, make your depth six-two feet."

"Speed twelve," the COW called out.

As the scope emerged from the well, Andrews slapped down the training handles and pushed his masked face up against the eyepiece. He began to walk in a slow circle, on the lookout for the underside of a ship, hopefully to be seen in time to drop back down and avoid hitting it. But with the EAB air hose, he could make a revolution in one direction before the air hose wrapped tight, then he had to reverse directions.

Finally, the scope broke the surface. Andrews found himself looking out at a clear, cloudless night sky. A quick look around confirmed that he had the whole ocean to himself.

"No close contacts."

Everyone breathed a sigh of relief. They could go back to business as normal. Or at least as normal as you could get on a submarine at sea fighting a fire.

Swarton reported, "XO says the fire is out, reflash watch is stationed."

Blivens ordered, "Weps, slow to ahead one-third and emergency ventilate the ops compartment with the blower."

It took ten minutes to clear the smoke out of the ship as the main induction fan sucked in cold, clean air through the snorkel mast while the low-pressure blower sucked out the smoke and sent it overboard through the snorkel exhaust.

Finally, the atmosphere was back to normal. The EABs were gratefully removed. George Sanders was wiping sweat from his brow as he stepped into the control room.

"Skipper, the fire is overhauled," Sanders grunted. "Electricians are starting an investigation of fan two. Looks like the controller is toast. Not sure what other damage we have. I'm going to have a heart-to-heart with the Engineer. The ELTs know better than to store chem wipes in the fan room."

Andrews pulled off his EAB and shook his head. "Skipper, how the hell did you know? You woke up from a sound sleep and warned us before anybody found anything wrong."

Blivens laughed and answered, "Weps, it's a special implant they give you at Prospective Commanding Officers School."

7

0900 EST, 14 March 1983, Goose Creek, South Carolina

The phone startled Joy Walsh. She was sitting on the screened porch, enjoying a leisurely cup of coffee and listening to the news after getting the kids off to school. The azaleas in the backyard were in full bloom, and the birds were chirping merrily. The weekend had been a nonstop marathon with soccer, swimming, a Scottish Highland dance contest, and it seemed a dozen other activities. Now she needed a quiet hour before facing the laundry, housecleaning, and grocery shopping.

Joy played with the idea of letting the call go to the answering machine, but she remembered that she had forgotten to replace the tape. She grumbled but got up and traipsed into the kitchen and grabbed the offending phone. "Walsh residence."

Joy did not recognize the gravelly voice on the other end. "Mrs. Walsh, good morning. Excuse me for interrupting your day. This is Vice Admiral Rufus Brown at SUBLANT."

"Could you repeat that? Oh. Yes, sir, Admiral," she stuttered out a surprised reply. "What can I do for you?"

"I need to discuss some concerns with you, things that we can't discuss over the phone."

Joy knew that Admiral Brown had a reputation for eschewing small talk. He jumped right to the heart of the matter. "If I send a plane down to Charleston for you today, can you come up to Norfolk for a couple of days? You will be our houseguest at West Virginia House."

"Can you tell me what this is about? Is Darren okay?" Joy Walsh's voice quavered. She was on the edge of panic. A call like this, from COMSUBLANT himself, could not be good news. He wasn't inviting her to Norfolk for teatime with his wife.

"Commander Walsh and the *John Jay* are fine," he reassured her. "There is no cause for any concern about them. I really can't talk over an open line, though. I'm afraid this is going to sound like a James Bond movie, but this is for your eyes only. I don't want anyone else in Charleston to even know that we are having this discussion, let alone what we might be talking about. My C-12 can be at Charleston Air Force Base in an hour. Those NIS agents outside will run you over there. Can you be ready?"

Joy was shaking her head, although she knew that Admiral Brown could not see her. "I have two little ones in school," she countered. "I can't just up and run out the door. I'll have to arrange for them to be picked up from school and stay with the neighbors. That means at least the neighbors will know where I've gone."

Brown chuckled. "Why don't you bring Pug and Sam along with you. The plane can pick you up at eighteen hundred to give you plenty of time to pack for the kids. That is a major advantage of having your own plane. My wife will play babysitter and tour guide for a couple of days. But please be very careful in who you tell anything about my call or this trip."

Joy Walsh was already planning the logistics for the kids and for the trip when she realized that she was listening to a dial tone. Brown had delivered his message and had gone off to some other task.

2215Z, 14 March 1983, USS John Jay, *Norwegian Sea*

Ross "Rosebud" Stanley shot awake. The pain was excruciating. He had never felt anything like it before. He groaned loudly as the hot knife shot through his abdomen. He banged his head into the middle bunk. Then he curled up into a ball, crying out.

Delvin Brimley had the middle bunk. He leaned out and looked down into the lower bunk. "Hey, Rosebud, you okay?" he asked.

Rosebud answered with a groaned obscenity.

Brimley jumped out of his rack, pulled back the curtain on Rosebud's, and snapped on the reading light. He found his shipmate curled up, moaning, and sweating heavily. He ran out of the bunkroom and grabbed the 4MC Emergency Phone. He shouted, "Injured man in crew's berthing! Injured man in crew's berthing! We need the corpsman!"

He had barely put the handset down when the 1MC blasted, "Injured man in crew's berthing. Corpsman lay to crew's berthing."

"Doc" Morrison, *John Jay*'s hospital corpsman, leaped down the ladder to Ops lower level. Delvin Brimley grabbed him and dragged him to Rosebud's rack. Rosebud was lying on the deck, moaning and groaning incoherently. Several crewmen stood around trying to figure out what they could do.

Doc stretched the ailing sailor out and tried to assess what the problem was. Rosebud was sweating heavily, and he had a fever. When he attempted to palpate Rosebud's abdomen, he screamed out in pain and forcefully shoved Doc away.

Doc looked up. "Get me the stretcher. We need to move him to the wardroom."

Just as he was speaking, Stan Wilkins pushed his way through.

"What's going on, Doc?"

"XO, it's Rosebud. He's in bad pain. Whole bunch of possibilities. I can't tell until I get him where I can do an exam. We need the wardroom set up."

"The Chop is already working that," Wilkins answered. "Let's get him up there. I'll go talk to the Captain."

By the time Doc and the stretcher team managed to carry Rosebud out of berthing and up the ladder to Ops middle level, Ensign Sam Lowe and his team of cooks had turned the *John Jay*'s wardroom into an emergency operating room, complete with surgical lights hanging from the overhead and an array of medical equipment laid out on the buffet. They slid

Rosebud onto the table and stood back to allow Doc room to conduct his examination.

He was just finishing the exam when Darren Walsh walked in. "How is he, Doc?"

"Skipper, he is in real pain," Morrison answered. "Pain seems to be centered in his abdomen on the right side. Could be kidney stones, could be appendicitis. I don't have a test out here to tell them apart."

"Well, what do we do?" Walsh asked.

"I've put him on a one-fifty ml per hour saline drip with three grams of ampicillin antibiotic. I need the XO to get into the controlled medicinals safe and break out the morphine."

Rosebud moaned loudly.

Doc continued, "That's all I can do. We need to medevac him as soon as possible. If it's appendicitis and it ruptures, we could lose him."

Walsh nodded. "We're about four hundred miles away from the nearest medevac point. Can you keep him stable for twenty-four hours?"

Doc Morrison nodded. "I'll do my best."

Walsh turned to Wilkins. "XO, get the message drafted to SUBLANT. Tell them we need an emergency medevac. Heading to Iceland at best speed. Request helo transfer from Keflavik. Our ETA twenty-four hours."

Wilkins dashed up to the radio room as Walsh headed to the control room.

2015 EST, 14 March 1983, Naval Air Station Norfolk

The C-12, the Navy version of a Beechcraft Super King Air, pulled off the main runway at Naval Air Station Norfolk and taxied directly to its hangar on the north side of the field. As the plane came to a halt, a gray Navy van pulled up alongside. The twin turboprops had barely spun to a stop when the passenger door swung open and the steps dropped down.

Pug Walsh, full of eight-year-old energy, charged down the steps and bounced right into Admiral Rufus Brown.

"Wow! Did you see that?" the little boy enthused. "I got to fly the plane! I'm going to be a Navy pilot when I grow up!"

Brown was still chuckling but maintained a firm grasp of Pug's hand as he helped Sam and Joy down the ladder. An active Navy airfield was no place for an eight-year-old to run free. Far too many spinning propellers, moving airplanes, and jet engine blasts.

"Mrs. Walsh, I am so glad that you could come up," Brown said as he extended his hand. "Let's get you all settled over at West Virginia House. Ann is holding dinner for you."

"Joy, please, Admiral," Joy Walsh answered as she took his hand. "What can I do to help?"

"We'll discuss all that tomorrow, after we have briefed you," Brown answered as he guided the family to the waiting van. "Tonight, let's get the children fed and maybe have a cocktail."

They all piled into the Navy van. The driver snaked through a confusion of hangars, repair shops, and official-looking buildings before turning onto a tree-lined boulevard. The street was lined with large Victorian mansions, completely out of character from the industrial aviation area they had just left.

Brown, sitting in the front passenger seat, turned around and said, "The houses on Dillingham were all built as part of the Jamestown Exposition in 1907. Several states competed to build the finest mansion that reflected their state. They were far too nice to tear down when the Exposition ended. The Navy purchased them when it expanded onto Sewells Point at the end of the First World War. After the Second World War, they became flag officer housing. West Virginia House is sort of the unofficial residence for SUBLANT."

The van pulled under the portico of a large buff-colored house. A nicely dressed lady stood on the broad porch at the top of the steps. Admiral Brown introduced his wife, Ann, as he guided the group into the house.

Joy Walsh didn't realize how tired and hungry she was until Ann Brown ushered them into the dining room. Her mouth was watering from the delicious smells, but her eyes were drooping. She was quite happy that she made it through the meal without falling headfirst into the dessert. It was time to beg off the after-dinner cocktails and head up to her room.

Tomorrow promised to be a very full day, and she needed to be alert and at her best.

0745Z, 15 March 1983, USS Tigerfish, *Norwegian Sea*

The boat still stank of smoke and burnt insulation, even after emergency ventilating for six hours. The atmosphere samples were all well within normal bands, but she still stank. Roy Blivens knew that the smoke had permeated their clothing, their bedding, and everything else that could pick up the smell. They would just have to live with it. At least until they got back home and could give everything a really deep cleaning and air out the boat.

Blivens stuck his head into the fan room to see Steve Dunn hunched over the controller for fan two as he and Chief Paul Anders, the Electrical Division Leading Chief, surveyed the damage. The chief was shaking his head as they poked through the charred remains.

"Ain't gonna be able to fix this one," he lamented. "The main contactors welded, and I'm getting a zero ground on the motor's primary. So it's not just the controller. The fan is gone, too."

Blivens looked toward Dunn. "You going to be able to fix it, Eng?" He was pretty sure he knew the answer already, but, just maybe, E-Div could pull a rabbit out of their hat.

Dunn shook his head as Anders answered, "Skipper, we can fix the controller, but the current surge and fire took out the fan motor, too. We ain't got no way to fix that. That's a tender job, for sure."

Blivens carefully backed out of the fan room to find QM-1 Eric Swarton waiting for him in the passageway.

Swarton checked his watch and came to attention. "Captain, the Navigator sends his respects and presents the 0800 position report." He handed Blivens a small slip of paper on which the Nav had recorded the ship's position as well as the status of the navigation equipment.

Blivens read the slip before pocketing it. He dismissed the quartermaster with a "Very well," and turned aft, entering the reactor compartment tunnel and then AMR2UL. It was time for his daily tour of the boat.

0930 EST, 15 March 1983, COMSUBLANT, Norfolk, Virginia

Joy Walsh shivered as she stared up at the gray monolithic structure. Building NH-95, a six-story solid slab of concrete uninterrupted by a single window, housed COMSUBLANT's highly classified operations center. The armed Marine guard standing behind a bulletproof glass window sternly demanding her ID did nothing to ease Joy's sense of foreboding.

Rufus Brown slid his ID through the slot and said, "Check the access list that my office sent over this morning. You will find Mrs. Walsh on it. I will be escorting her."

The Marine scanned Admiral Brown's ID card, grabbed a notebook from under the counter, and read down the list. He then slid both IDs back, snapped to attention, and said, "You both are cleared."

The heavy bronze door unlocked with an audible click. The pair stepped into a small vestibule. There was a heavy, locked door on either side and a single elevator on the far wall. Brown punched a passcode into the elevator's controls. The door promptly slid open. They stepped inside and were immediately whisked to the sixth floor. There they were greeted by another pair of armed Marines guarding another heavy, locked door. This door was labeled with several signs attesting to the high classification of the work on the other side and the dire consequences of unauthorized entry.

Once again, Brown escorted Joy Walsh past the guards, through the door, and into a bustling space with people hurrying about with files and clipboards. Several of the walls were covered with maps of the Atlantic and Arctic Oceans. People were moving little silhouettes around on those charts.

Brown waved a hand generally around the expansive room. "Joy, this is the Operational Control Center. We call it the OPCON for short. From here, we track and direct all our submarines operating in the Atlantic and up north. Those charts show generally where our subs are and the areas that we have given each to operate. If you look north of Iceland on that chart," he pointed to one showing the GIUK Gap and the Norwegian Sea, "you will see a chunk of ocean where *John Jay* is now steaming."

Joy Walsh stared at the chart for a second, wondering where Darren was and if he was safe. This was all overwhelming, exciting, but intensely worrisome.

Brown directed Joy toward a conference room that opened off the central operations center floor.

Ted Strange met them at the door. Two other men, both dressed in dark gray business suits, stood back on the far side of the broad conference table. Once everyone was inside, and before any introductions were made, Strange carefully shut and locked the door.

He then turned to Joy Walsh. "Mrs. Walsh, these gentlemen are Special Agent Chad Johnson and Special Agent Jeremy Baldwin from the Naval Investigative Service. They are here to brief us and to answer any questions that you might have."

Besides dressing nearly alike, charcoal-gray suit, white shirt, muted blue tie, the pair were almost twins. Both were about five foot ten, late twenties or early thirties, probably about one-eighty. The only differentiator was that Johnson was a blue-eyed, blond White man while Baldwin was Black.

Agent Baldwin jumped right in. "Admiral, Captain, Mrs. Walsh." He nodded toward each as he spoke. "Agent Johnson and I are going to brief you on what we know about the suspected penetration of SUBLANT by a Russian agent and where we are with the investigation." Looking toward VADM Brown, he asked, "Admiral, has Mrs. Walsh been cleared for access to this information?"

Brown nodded. "Yes, she is cleared and definitely has a need to know."

"Very well, sir," Baldwin answered. "In that case, we will continue. As you already know, we have established that known KGB assets out of the Soviet embassy have turned an individual in the SUBLANT OPCON. We think that we have isolated that individual so that he only has access to information that we want him to feed to the Soviets. That seems to be working for right now, but we aren't sure how soon the KGB will start to get suspicious that they are being fed tailored info."

Agent Johnson picked up the brief without a noticeable break. "We have code-named our spy as Agent Grey Mole. We have found that Grey Mole has been contacting someone in Charleston pretty regularly. He has called two different numbers, one at Naval Communications Station Charleston and the other at the Naval Electronic Systems Engineering Center, Charleston. As a little background, all submarine radio traffic is routed through NAVCOMSTA Charleston, so people there would have access to everything going to and from our boats at sea. NAVELEX Charleston maintains the command-and-control systems and the ocean surveillance systems in the Atlantic. An unknown spy in either place would be very bad."

"Couldn't you just tap this spy's phone and listen in?" Joy asked. It seemed so easy.

Agent Johnson shook his head, more in frustration than to express a negative. "The local federal judge won't issue a warrant. Says we don't have probable cause."

Agent Baldwin picked up the story. "Grey Mole has made at least two trips to Charleston over the last couple of months. We have seen him loitering in your neighborhood. There is a strong possibility that you either know something that threatens him, or you have something that he wants."

A perplexed look flitted across Joy Walsh's face. She held her hands palm up. "I have no idea what it would be. I have never heard of this Grey Mole character. There is nothing in our house that would be a threat to anyone, except maybe Darren's dress sword."

Baldwin nodded. "That's about what we figured. We're just going to have to keep watch on your house and intercept Grey Mole if and when he makes a move."

Joy Walsh nodded, but she was very worried. The agents had just described a trap that they were setting for this Russian spy. She and the children were the bait in the trap. She didn't like it, but what was the alternative?

8

2300Z, 15 March 1983, USS John Jay, *twelve nm off Iceland*

The navigation plot said that they were fourteen miles due south of Iceland's Grindavíkurbaer Peninsula when the *John Jay* popped to the surface. It took almost twenty minutes to rig the bridge for surface operations.

Darren Walsh stuck his head out of the bridge cockpit and was immediately slapped with a drenching ice-cold saltwater spray. He looked out to see the waves running six to eight feet. Every couple of minutes, a larger wave would well up and completely submerge the missile deck. There was no way that they could safely do a medevac from there. It would have to be the much riskier and more difficult transfer from the bridge.

Walsh grabbed the 7MC mike and spoke, "Control, bridge, XO, set up for a bridge transfer. Way too rough for a main deck one."

Wilkins grabbed the 7MC mike by the nav stand. "Captain, XO, aye. We are in radio comms with the helo. Brit SAS bird. Call sign John Bull Seven-Six. They are five minutes out."

Walsh answered, "Roger. Tell them to come up on channel sixteen. When we have them there, lower all masts and antennas. Tell the COB and

Doc to start moving Rosebud up here. Make sure he has plenty of blankets. It's damn cold out."

Wilkins answered, "John Bull Seven-Six is on channel sixteen. We are Navy Unit One. All masts and antennas coming down."

The helo's flashing red light was just visible on the horizon, coming toward them fast.

Walsh grabbed the ship-to-ship walkie-talkie and keyed it. "John Bull Seven-Six, John Bull Seven-Six, this is Navy Unit One. We hold you visual. On course two-seven-zero, speed three."

The answer came back with a heavy Brit accent. "Roger, Unit One. We see you. Request verify all masts and antennas lowered."

Walsh answered, "Seven-Six, all masts and antennas lowered. Wind is from two-seven-zero. Estimate ten knots. This will be a bridge transfer."

"Roger, mate. Bridge transfer it is."

The Westland Lynx helicopter made a pass over the *John Jay* and then slowly approached the surfaced submarine along its starboard side. When the helo was matching speed with the sub, it lowered a line on a winch and carefully moved over so that it was directly above the sail.

The COB used the grounding wand to reach out for the hook, but each time he tried, the combination of the helo's downwash and the wind blew the hook out of reach. Several attempts proved fruitless. The COB had tears of frustration in his eyes.

"Unit One, Seven-Six. This isn't working, mate. Let's try something else. Request you come to all stop."

Walsh ordered all stop and keyed the bridge-to-bridge. "Unit One at all stop. What do you have in mind?"

As the *John Jay* slid to a stop, the Lynx moved a few yards off the sub's starboard side. A swimmer dropped out of the bird, into the frigid water. He swam over to the sub, rode a wave up onto the main deck, and then climbed the ladder up the sail.

"G'day, mate," he said as his head appeared at the bridge combing. He handed Walsh a waterproof bag and then handed the COB a rope that had been tied around his waist. Together, they pulled in the rope until the winch hook was in hand. Seconds later, the SAS swimmer and Rosebud were safely lifted away and headed back to dry land.

"Unit One, your passenger is safely aboard. Smooth sailing, cheerio."

"Seven-Six, much thanks. Next round is on us."

Darren Walsh was down in the warm control room and the *John Jay* was once again safely submerged when he remembered to open the waterproof bag. Inside, he found the latest issue of *Playboy* and today's issue of the *Sun*, already turned to page three and the scantily clad young lady featured there.

Walsh laughed. "Damn SAS. They are certifiably crazy. Jump out of a perfectly good helicopter in the middle of the night into freezing cold water, fifteen miles from the nearest shore. And he delivers the *Sun*. Gotta love 'em."

0845 EST, 16 March 1983, Goose Creek, South Carolina

Joy Walsh finished washing the breakfast dishes, stacking them neatly in the dishrack to dry. She poured herself a cup of coffee, emptying the coffeemaker in the process. She pulled back a chair and sat down at the kitchen table. There was time to sit back and relax for a few minutes while she decided if she was going to work planting the vegetable garden this morning or take the van in for its routine oil change.

She sipped her coffee and sat back as the FM station moved from some easy-listening jazz to the morning traffic report. They were reporting major delays on I-26 South at the Remount Road exit. Joy shook her head, glad that she wasn't going to the Navy base today. But that also decided her morning plan. The car dealership was on Rivers Avenue, just off Remount Road. No sense in fighting traffic if you didn't need to. So gardening it was.

She looked out the bay window behind the breakfast nook, planning out the garden plot in her mind. The little patch of dirt backed up against the low fence and azalea bushes that separated their backyard from the Rodriguez one. Only enough room for some tomatoes, the inevitable zucchini, and the hot habanero chilis that Darren loved.

A flash of movement across the Rodriguezes' backyard grabbed Joy's attention. That was very odd. The Rodriguez family was vacationing, visiting relatives in Corpus Christi. But someone was sneaking across their yard, using the azaleas and gardenias for cover. Two men, but she couldn't see their faces.

The cold tendrils of fear gripped Joy Walsh. A week ago, she would have dismissed it to some maintenance men fixing a phone line or tracing out some buried pipes, but Admiral Brown's briefing had left her nerves on edge. She grabbed the kitchen phone and punched in the emergency number that the admiral had given her.

It seemed like hours passed, but in reality, it was less than five minutes until the two NIS agents stationed out front dashed into the backyard with guns drawn. They quickly cleared the yard and checked the neighboring yards, too.

The lead agent tapped on the kitchen door. Joy cracked it open.

"You okay, Mrs. Walsh?" he asked as he looked over her shoulder, into the room behind. "Everything safe inside?"

Joy's voice quavered as she answered, "Did you see them? There were two men in the Rodriguez backyard." She was trying very hard to stop shaking and to hide the tears. Panic was right around the corner.

The agent was using his most calming, reassuring voice. "No, ma'am, we didn't see anyone. Agent Jones will stay in your backyard for a couple of hours while I go around to check out the Rodriguez place. See if anyone saw anything over on Canebrake Lane. Just stay inside and stay calm. There is nothing to worry about. You're safe now."

Joy knew that the agent thought she was imagining the whole thing, but she had really seen a couple of men sneaking toward her house. Or at least she thought she had. Hadn't she? She wished Darren was home and that this whole nightmare was over.

1730 MSK, 16 March 1983, K-324, Norwegian Sea

Boris Novikov was mystified. Northern Fleet headquarters had made no response to his message reporting the discovery of the new cloaking technology on the American missile submarine. Surely even the old, hidebound admirals could grasp the implications of such a technology.

Novikov sat back and scratched his chin. He flipped open the message boards and riffled through the stack of radio traffic once again. Maybe he had missed something. Maybe hidden in with instructions to report the weekly political indoctrination of all crew members and the notice of tainted *tushonka* canned stew meat. Nothing.

But it was still only two days. The admirals were just being cautious. None of them would make a decision until they had all come to a common outlook. Until then, he would just have to act on his own while carrying out his orders. The very thought of taking any action, any initiative, without specific direction from higher command was totally at odds with all his training and very much out of character. But Novikov knew that, at least this once, he would act on his own. He slapped his hands to his knees, jumped up out of his chair, and stormed out of his tiny stateroom.

The *K-324*'s control room was quiet as the nuclear submarine cruised through the depths. Nothing was happening as they steamed toward their next assigned search area. And they were not scheduled to arrive there for another two days.

Dmitri Vinogradov reported that they had no sonar contacts except for a very noisy distant merchant ship. They had not seen anything that could possibly be classified as a submarine since the American had mysteriously disappeared two days ago.

Novikov stepped back to the navigation table and studied their planned track. He grabbed a pair of dividers and walked off the distance to their next search area. Their current speed was calculated based on arriving in the search area on time, a leisurely fifteen kilometers per hour. Increasing speed to thirty kilometers per hour would get them there in a day. That day would allow them to very carefully search out the area, to be ready and waiting when the American arrived.

"Dmitri," Novikov ordered, "increase speed to thirty kilometers per hour. I want to be in the search area by 1200 tomorrow. And energize the SOKS. Use it for continuous search, just in case we cross the American's wake."

1900Z, 16 March 1983, USS* Tigerfish, *66 degrees 34 minutes north, 10 degrees 5 minutes west, Norwegian Sea

"Conn, Sonar, close aboard contact," Senior Chief Zwarlinski's voice blared across the 21MC. "Sounds like a pod of narwhals."

Enrique Ortiz, the JOOD, laughed and said to no one in particular, "Senior Chief sure loves his whales, don't he?"

Steve Dunn, the OOD, nodded and answered, "Yep, but he doesn't normally announce them over the 21MC."

He was just reaching for the 21MC microphone when Zwarlinski announced, "Receiving underwater comms from the bearing of the narwhals. Sounds like 'All hail Boreas Rex, King of the North. *Tigerfish*, stand by to receive his majesty.'"

Ortiz looked at Dunn. "Eng, what the heck is going on? Senior Chief can't be serious."

"Did you check ship's position when you relieved?" Dunn asked.

"Of course."

"And?"

"Sixty-six degrees thirty-four minutes north by ten degrees west. So?" Ortiz responded.

"Well, Nub," Dunn explained. "We just crossed over the Arctic Circle. I expect you are about to get inducted into the Royal Order of the Blue Noses."

George Sanders and Tom Clemont strolled into the control room. Sanders stepped up onto the periscope stand and grabbed the 1MC microphone. "Eng, mind if I make an announcement?"

Dunn smiled, nodded, and said, "Go ahead, XO."

Sanders announced, "Blue Noses, relieve the on-watch Nubs. All Nubs muster on the mess decks, now!"

Clemont turned to Dunn. "Okay, Eng, what you got?"

Dunn was mystified. Why would he be relieved for these shenanigans? He answered, "What are you talking about, Nav? I'm a Blue Nose. We patrolled North when I was on the *John Adams*. I don't need a relief."

Sanders shook his head. "Sorry, Eng. It ain't in your service jacket. My records show that you're a Nub."

"Of course it ain't in my service jacket," Dunn shot back. "Boomer patrol areas are classified. But we were up North."

Sanders answered, "Eng, you know the Navy way. If it ain't in your jacket, it didn't happen. Mess decks as soon as Nav relieves you." He turned and headed for the ladder to the middle level.

Dunn grumbled, "Shit! This ain't going to be fun." Turning to Ortiz, he ordered, "Scoot, Nub. I'll be down in a minute." He then spoke to Clemont. "Nav, why do I smell you behind this? You had to be the one who put the XO up to checking my service jacket."

Tom Clemont just smiled and said, "I relieve you, sir."

Steve Dunn walked down to the mess decks, only to find it transformed into the regal court of His Majesty, Boreas Rex, Master of Polar Bears, Emperor of All Reindeer, King of the North. Even arrayed in the royal robes and wearing the imperial crown, the King bore an uncanny resemblance to Chief Anders. And the throne, securely clamped to the aftermost table, looked like it might have been liberated from the Chiefs' head.

The seasoned Blue Noses were delegated as attendants to his Imperial Majesty. When Dunn stepped into the mess decks, the COB threw him a sheet and shouted, "Nub, to enter the Imperial Realm of the North for the first time, you must be properly dressed as the Nub that you are. Strip and don the Nub diaper."

Dunn looked around and saw that Enrique Ortiz and the other Nubs were indeed wearing sheets wrapped around them like massive diapers. He followed suit.

"Now, Nub, you must perform a noble task to prove yourself worthy," Boreas Rex intoned. He held up a plastic bottle normally used to sample the steam generators and a long checklist. "Nub, you will obtain a baffle sample from the aftermost point on the *Tigerfish*. You will have the sample approved by the regal chain of command, and you will present it to the Imperial Custodian of Baffle Samples. You have ten minutes. Depart."

"Who is the Imperial Custodian of Baffle Samples?" Dunn asked.

The COB snorted, "Must you be told everything, Nub? Figure it out. Now get to it."

With that exchange, Steve Dunn decided that he had some thinking to do. This was not simply filling the sample bottle and running it around to the various people on the checklist. Too simple. First, he needed to determine what exactly a "baffle sample" was. The baffles were the area behind the sub that sonar could not hear, but what did that have to do with a water sample? Didn't matter. He would simply grab some seawater drawn from as far aft as he could get it. That would be the leak-off from the shaft seals. No problem. He grabbed the bottle and headed aft.

It only took a few seconds to fill the bottle from the leak-off. He duly dated and timed the sample and headed to Maneuvering for the first review. He found Bill Andrews sitting in the Engineering-Officer-of-the-Watch chair. Andrews grinned when the Eng asked to enter Maneuvering. He then took the sample bottle and held it up to the light. He shook his head and then opened the bottle. He dipped his finger in the seawater and tasted it.

"Totally unsatisfactory, Nub. This sample has the essence of polar bear piss," Andrews announced. "Get another sample." He dumped out the bottle.

Dunn glowered at Andrews. "You are in on this, aren't you, Weps?"

Andrews glanced at the clock above the throttleman's head. "You've got seven minutes, Nub. Better get a move on."

Dunn saw how this was going to work. He filled several spare bottles before heading forward. The OOD, Tom Clemont, was next on the list, and he already deduced that Clemont would send him for another bottle. He was down to two minutes when he got to the CO.

Blivens smiled, took the sample, and studied it. After reviewing the paperwork, he shook his head and said, "Sorry, Eng. This simply will not do. I'm afraid you need another sample."

When he had finally satisfied the CO, Dunn noted that he had thirty seconds left, but he still needed to find the Imperial Custodian of Baffle Samples. Then it hit him. It had to be Senior Chief Zwarlinski. It only made sense. The whole thing smelled of something the sonar senior chief would think up. He had been up north too many times and had seen too many Blue Nose initiations.

With just seconds to spare, Dunn crashed into the sonar shack and announced, "Oh, Great Imperial Custodian of Baffle Samples, here is your approved baffle sample."

Zwarlinski laughed as he signed and dated the checklist. "Now, Nub, you need to pay homage to His Majesty, Boreas Rex. If he finds you worthy, you may become a Blue Nose yet."

Steve Dunn dropped down to the mess decks/Imperial Throne Room and presented His Majesty, Boreas Rex, with the completed checklist. The King of the North reviewed the checklist before he ordered Dunn to kneel before him. He dubbed the Eng on both shoulders with his trident and announced, "I declare you worthy to be a Blue Nose."

With that, the COB swabbed the Eng's nose with a big dab of Prussian Blue. It would be several weeks before that wore off.

9

0030 EST, 17 March 1983, Deep Creek, Chesapeake, Virginia

The night was pitch black. Thick, low clouds hid the stars. The moon had long since disappeared over the western horizon. The few cars hurtling down I-64 toward the Elizabeth River Bridge into Norfolk offered the only illumination on this stretch of Deep Creek. Other than the elevated freeway, swampy marshland, dark and uninhabited, was all Henri DuBois could make out. The only sound was the gentle wave slap against the boat's hull and the low burbling of the idling outboard motor.

The little float was easy to find. Probably someone's crab pot, lost and forgotten from last year's crab season. But it was exactly where he was told it would be. Fifty feet off a narrow spit of land when he had the two big swamp oaks on the spit lined up. Once again, his handler had found a truly isolated location for a drop. As long as no one accidentally saw him, it was ideal. But, DuBois had to muse, if he was spotted, it would be suspect. Why would anyone be out here in the middle of a dark night unless they had something to hide.

DuBois reached out with the boat hook and quickly yanked the float aboard. He pulled out a message from the weighted watertight bottle and replaced it with his latest rolls of film. Nothing really earthshaking to report, just boats leaving and returning from patrol, some message traffic from boats out on their missions. And the key lists for the submarine broadcast cryptology that would allow the Russians to decipher the submarine radio communications. Enough to keep the money flowing from his handlers into his growing offshore bank accounts.

Dropping the float back into the dark waters, DuBois turned the boat around and idled back down river. He had several hours to kill. Arriving back at the boat landing before daybreak might cause some curious glances. Plenty of time to read the crumpled note. After a few seconds, he was scratching his head. He was supposed to find whatever he could about something his handler was calling a 'cloaking device.' Something he had never heard of, and with his position and clearance, an unknown secret would be very unusual. Still, the promised money was very good. He would find something about a cloaking device even if he had to make it up. The reward was just too good.

1420Z, 18 March 1983, USS John Jay, *Norwegian Sea*

Pete McKay was making a tour of the engine room. There was always something back here that demanded his attention. The easiest and quickest way to find a problem before it bit him in the butt was to spend time observing how the plant was working. The *John Jay* was a finely crafted, highly complex machine that normally operated with smooth precision. But she was over twenty years old, really old for a nuclear submarine. Pete McKay had to stay at the top of his game to make sure that the engineering department "kept the lights burning and the screw turning."

He stopped outside the Maneuvering room door and looked in. The sign over the door read *"Jayfish* Power and Light Company." From inside this tiny cubicle, barely larger than a closet, the complex reactor, steam, and electrical systems were monitored and controlled.

Four men crowded into the space. The throttleman stood just inside the door. Using the big chrome plated handwheels, he regulated the amount of steam flowing into the main turbines and thus controlled how fast the sub was going. The steam plant control panel in front of him was festooned with gauges and meters that measured pressures, levels, and flows to tell him how the steam plant was running.

Next to the throttleman, the reactor operator sat at the reactor plant control panel. The RO operated the reactor plant. The switch that moved the control rods in or out of the reactor core, the shim switch, sat right in the center of his desktop. The massive main coolant pumps that forced water through the reactor core were controlled by switches on his panel. The RPCP had even more meters and gauges to tell the RO what was happening in the reactor.

All the way outboard, the electrical operator controlled the electrical distribution system from the electric plant control panel. From the EPCP, the EO could operate the turbine generators, the motor generators, and remotely open or shut various breakers to provide the submarine with reliable and safe electrical power.

Sitting on a stool behind the three enlisted men, the Engineering-Officer-of-the-Watch supervised everything they did and provided direction to the watch standers outside Maneuvering who directly operated equipment. Bob Shippley, the Navigator, was standing his monthly proficiency watch as EOOW. The Nav's duties were almost always in the forward part of the ship. He clearly disdained all things engineering and was not comfortable around machinery. The only reason he had to venture back into the engine room was for his proficiency watch to maintain his standing as a nuclear-trained officer, and this only reluctantly and with much complaining. But if he ever wanted to be in command and keep his nuke pay, he needed to at least keep up minimum requirements.

Pete McKay felt it prudent to be close at hand with the Nav in Maneuvering, so he would usually schedule some evolution that required him to be in the engine room during that time. Today he was conducting a material inspection that should take just about as long as the Nav would be on watch.

Chief Josh Rosecrans, the Engineering Watch Supervisor, stuck his head through the hatch to engine room lower level. Along with being the EWS, he was also the Machinery Division Leading Chief, the enlisted man responsible for maintaining all the mechanical systems that made the boat go.

"Hey, Eng," he called out. "Got a minute? Need you to look at number two main seawater pump." Without any further discussion, he dropped back down the ladder.

McKay found the Chief squatting down and looking at the MSW pump coupling. Water was spraying out of the upper seal and cascading down over the pump into the bilge. It was fortunate that they were operating at only a 150 feet. At deeper depths, the increased sea pressure would turn the leak into a major problem.

"You tighten down on the flax packing?" McKay asked.

"Yep, but it ain't workin'. 'Spect packing is cocked," the machinist drawled. "We could fix that. But listen to that knockin'." He put his ear up against the pump motor.

When McKay did the same, he could hear a very distinct knocking noise, and he could feel a vibration. Neither should be there. There was something seriously wrong with this pump, more than just a failed seal.

He grabbed a 2JV handset, spun the growler handle, then spoke. "Maneuvering, Engineer. Cross-connect main seawater. Secure number two main seawater pump. Inform the Captain and tell him that I want to put number two MSW pump out of commission."

When the pump was turned off, he heard a loud clunk. The pump would not turn by hand when it should spin easily. They had a problem, and he needed to figure out how to fix it. But at least the water quit pouring out when the pump was off.

1740Z, 18 March 1983, 830 kilometers above the Greenland Sea

The NOAA-6 satellite was in a sun-synchronous polar orbit, 830 kilometers above the Earth's surface. It crossed the North Pole and headed down across the Arctic ice and then the Norwegian Sea. This orbit followed the five degrees west longitude line as it circled the globe north to south. The weather satellite's Advanced Very High Resolution Radiometer sensors searched out the sea surface and atmosphere temperatures. The information was downloaded to the Global Atmospheric Research Program to develop enhanced weather forecasting from remote sensors. Because the system supplied forecasting for remote, little traveled areas of the world's oceans, one of GARP's major customers was the Navy Meteorology and Oceanography Command and from there on to COMSUBLANT.

NOAA-6 sensed sea-surface temperature anomalies and developing high winds in the Greenland Sea north of Svalbard. The Navy meteorologists, sitting in their comfortable offices in Stennis, Mississippi, forecast a high probability of severe winter storms over the Greenland and Norwegian Seas. The information was relayed to Norfolk for broadcast on the 19 March North Atlantic weather forecast message.

0720Z, 19 March 1983, USS John Jay, *Norwegian Sea*

Darren Walsh sat at his stateroom desk, enjoying a cup of coffee while he read through the drafts for lieutenant fitness reports that Stan Wilkins had put together.

Reviewing FITREPs was one of those tasks that wasn't fun, but it had to be done and it was best done early in the morning, before the hectic day demanded attention. All of the lieutenants in the Navy were evaluated annually by their commanding officer. Those evaluations were racked and stacked by NAVMILPERSCOM to figure out who got the choice assignments for their next tour and who got promoted or not. Because none of the COs had any insight on how good anyone else's lieutenants were and each CO had a different approach to evaluating his officers, a common, equitable approach was impossible. While Walsh was writing about how great his handful of lieutenants were, the Carrier Air Group Commander was ranking a couple of dozen pilots under his command, and a Rear Admiral in the Pentagon might be ranking a hundred or more FITREPs for his signature.

It was enough for Darren Walsh to tear his hair out. How did he make sure that great officers like Brett Burns, his Weps, or Dale Horton, the MPA, moved ahead in this man's Navy? The only way was to rank them all the way to the left, the highest scores, and embellish the narrative with as many fancy adjectives as he could think of. A tour as a submarine CO writing officer FITREPs certainly should prepare someone to successfully write fiction.

And, once the lieutenant FITREPs were done, the lieutenant junior-grade ones were next month.

He was wielding his red pencil with full force when he heard a tap at the door. Walsh grunted, "Enter," as the door slowly swung open.

RM3 Milt Schoneman peeked around the door and meekly said, "Skipper, this morning's message boards, and we got our first bunch of family-grams. There is one for you."

He handed Walsh the aluminum clipboards and a small slip of paper. Walsh set the slip aside to savor later and flipped open the boards. The top message was the North Atlantic weather forecast. A cursory glance told him that they were due for a blow in the next twenty-four hours.

"Nav see this?" he asked, tapping the forecast.

"Yes, sir," the radioman answered. "He said to tell you that he would brief you as soon as he lays down the storm track."

Schoneman backed out and quietly closed the door.

Walsh unfolded the slip of paper. He read "Dad, hit homerun, T-ball, Love Pug. Dad, love you, miss you, come home soon. Sam. Dearest, all is good at home. Kids fine. Spring beautiful here. Show you pictures. Miss you. Love you. Stay safe. See you soon."

Suddenly, everything was right with the world.

10

1030 EST, 22 March 1983, COMSUBLANT, Norfolk, Virginia

Ted Strange walked into Vice Admiral Rufus Brown's office carrying a file. The gray folder was heavily embossed with security classification codes several layers above Top Secret and dire warnings of the consequences of the wrong eyes seeing the contents. He opened the folder and slid it across the desk.

"Boss, you need to read this. Latest SIGINT from the Polyarny area. Seems their submarine command is all in a tizzy. We have a phone intercept between a submarine flotilla commander there and some senior officer from the Northern Fleet over in Severomorsk," Strange explained as Brown scanned the pages. "Seems one of their sub COs is reporting us using some kind of stealth device."

Brown read down to the paragraph Ted Strange was talking about and started to chuckle. "This character has quite an imagination, doesn't he. He's calling it a 'cloaking device.' Any idea what this Novikov is talking about?"

Strange nodded. "Nearest we can figure, this is the guy at the second tie-point that Roy Blivens sent off chasing a MOSS. Way I figure it, Novikov was all hot and bothered trailing what he thought was the *John Jay*. You gotta picture the woody he would have, actually thinking he was in trail of an American SSBN. Probably could taste the Order of Lenin. Then the MOSS runs out of gas. As far as he could tell, it just disappeared. Voilà, cloaking device."

Brown looked up and rubbed his chin, then his face twisted into a devilish smirk. "Ted, get Dr. Former at the Naval Underwater Sound Lab up in New London on the horn. I think Comrade Novikov just handed us the tool to draw our spy out again and to throw a real monkey wrench into their ASW plans. We just need a couple of plausible-sounding research papers out of NUSL, and I think Dan Former is just the egghead to write them."

1200Z, 23 March 1983, Greenland Sea

The Gulf Stream, a river of water flowing through the Atlantic Ocean across the Norwegian Sea, delivered a steady flood of warm Caribbean waters all the way to the Arctic far north. Between the northernmost reaches of Norway and Bear Island, the Gulf Stream split. Some of the flow headed due east into the Barents Sea while the remainder curved north and west, around Svalbard and into the Greenland Sea. In this icy environment, warmer was a relative term. In March, waters in the current were typically only a couple of degrees above freezing, while waters nearby were twenty-eight degrees Fahrenheit, freezing for seawater. But that warmer flow was enough to feed an incredibly rich fish population while it warmed Norway's rocky shores.

Just a few miles further north and west, air temperatures over the ice pack fell to minus forty degrees Fahrenheit. When this bitter cold air blasted out over the warmer water, the temperature differential built a massive heat engine, much like a tropical hurricane in reverse.

Olaf Svenson stood on the bridge of his trawler, the *Torsk Fisker*, watching the dropping barometer with concern. It had been a thousand millibars, signifying a low-pressure area but still in the normal band, when he first checked a couple of hours ago. Pressure had already dropped twenty millibars. The frigid Arctic air was crystal clear, but the north-western horizon had developed into an ominous dark cloud. The anemometer mounted high up on the *Torsk Fisker*'s mast was bouncing back and forth between a steady twenty knots and gusts up to fifty. Temperature didn't seem to be dropping much, but the seas were picking up, regularly breaking over the *Torsk Fisker*'s broad, high bow. Too late to get the crew out with the axes to chip ice off the deckhouse and rigging before the seas really kicked up.

The gray-black cloud raced across the water directly at the little trawler. Svenson could see lightning flashes in the roiling mass of clouds. It was time to turn his stern to this sea and run.

The barometer was hitting 960 millibars and the wind was at sixty-five knots when the crew of six fishermen huddled in the tiny wheelhouse. The ten-meter seas were crashing up over the stern, threatening to poop the fishing boat. But the larger concern was the ice rapidly building on any exposed surface.

The barometric pressure plunged as the temperature rose. It didn't make any sense to Olaf, but he didn't have time to ponder mysteries of the meteorological question. He was far too busy trying to stay alive and keep his boat afloat. It would be safer if he could turn so the *Torsk Fisker*'s bow could plunge into the on-racing waves and shoulder them aside, but he would be broadside to them while he turned. The seas would push them over, capsizing the already top-heavy boat.

The ice on the deck outside the bridge house was at least a meter thick when the mast came crashing down, a victim of the accumulating ice and the roaring wind. The last reading Svenson saw on the anemometer was over a hundred knots.

He began to mumble a prayer when he saw the pooping seas totally submerge the main deck. The *Torsk Fisker* shook off the first wave and bobbed back up again. The second wave was just as bad, but the third wave was much larger. It slammed down on the fishing boat, caving in the hatches and smashing the windscreen. Olaf Svenson's last sensation was a realization of how terribly cold the seawater was.

The sudden Arctic storm raced on south across the Greenland Sea, churning up the waters as it went.

1600 MSK, 23 March 1983, Olen'ya Naval Air Base, Murmansk, Russia

The big four engine Tupolev Tu-142 taxied to the south end of the 3,300-meter-long main runway at the Olen'ya Naval Air Base. The lumbering, heavily laden ASW aircraft, code-named BEAR-Foxtrot by NATO, would need every meter to claw its way into the frigid Arctic air. As the plane lined up at the runway threshold, Captain Lieutenant Leonid Pavlov ordered the flight engineer to shove the four throttle quadrants to full military power. The four big Kuznetsov NK-12MV turboprop engines drove the contra-rotating four-bladed propellers that pulled the bird down the runway and into the air. Pavlov pulled back on the yoke, causing the Tu-142 to rotate and leap into the air.

Twenty minutes later, Captain Lieutenant Pavlov's BEAR-Foxtrot passed over the Murmansk coastline at Polyarny with an altitude of six thousand meters and an airspeed of three hundred knots. In accordance with Soviet naval aviation standard doctrine, to which the senior captain lieutenant would not and could not deviate, he ordered sensors activated to commence a high-altitude ASW search.

When the Tu-142's anti-submarine Korshun surface-search radar lit off, it caused immediate alarms at the Norwegian Air Force Control and Reporting Center. The powerful air-search radar implanted high on a mountaintop above Hammerfest looked deep into Russia. It detected Pavlov's aircraft shortly after it took off from Olen'ya and tracked it on its northward flight to the coast. But the radar could only tell that the aircraft was large and slow. The plane's dedicated ASW radar told the Norwegians that this was a BEAR-Foxtrot and it was most probably heading out to hunt submarines. Within ten minutes, the Norwegian Control and Reporting Centre Sørreisa had passed the information on to their American allies. Two hours later, a Flash intel message went out to all submarines in the Atlantic and Norwegian Sea. There was a "Bear in the Air." From now on, as far as NATO was concerned, Pavlov's plane was identified as Case 031165.

Soviet air control vectored Pavlov due north, well to the east of Spitsbergen Island. That isolated, ice-bound bit of rock marked the split in the

Gulf Stream. To the west, the warmer waters from the south extended the sea ice edge another five hundred kilometers further north. To the east, the cold Arctic waters sent the ice edge another hundred kilometers south of the islands, into the Barents Sea.

The vector to his turn was almost two hours of flight time and over three hundred kilometers north of the sea ice edge. Leonid Pavlov was a product of the Soviet naval aviation training pipeline. That training hammered into him an automatic response to unquestioningly follow any orders. But this order made no sense. No ASW aircraft, even the finest product of the vaunted Tupolev Design Bureau, could detect a submarine through two meters of sea ice. But still, he steered the big plane northward. Air Control had access to information that he didn't have.

"Comrade Captain," the squeaky voice of Yevgeniy Grekov, the Navigator, filled Pavlov's headset. "The meteorologic report is showing a heavy storm developing over the Greenland Sea. Winds at over two hundred knots up to ten thousand meters. Our flight plan routes us right through the center of it."

Yevgeniy Grekov and Leonid Pavlov had flown together since they had entered naval aviation school as classmates. From there, Leonid went down the pilot-engineer pipeline while Yevgeniy was shunted off to the navigator-engineer one. They crossed paths again at the Yeysk Higher Military Aviation School. Over much vodka and pickled herring, they developed an unlikely friendship. Pavlov was a true child of the Revolution, a disciple of Marx and Lenin. Grekov, born and raised in Crimea, always questioned the party line and was frequently in trouble with the school political officer. Pavlov finished his training at the head of his class. Grekov, with his low political evaluation, barely managed to graduate. But they found themselves assigned to the same aircrew when they arrived at the 73rd Long Range Aviation Squadron. In Grekov's words, "He managed to balance the political correctness on their spanking-new Tu-142M so it could maintain level flight."

Pavlov glanced down between his feet to see Grekov seated at his tiny navigation table in the Tupolev's glass-enclosed nose. The Navigator was poring over a text message spread out on his plotting table. He glanced at the air chart and keyed his microphone. "Comrade Pilot, mark time to turn.

Fly heading two-five-five to compensate for winds. Increase airspeed to four hundred knots to make three hundred over the ground."

Pavlov chuckled. "Comrade Navigator, don't you mean speed over the water? I don't see any land out there."

The retort was quick, "Speed over the ice. That isn't water out there either. Now, if the loyal apparatchik pilot would excuse me, I have to piss."

Pavlov saw Grekov remove his headset, grab a bottle, and head aft. When it came to crew comfort, the Tu-142 was primitive. Even though designed for sixteen-hour-plus missions, the aircraft had no toilet facilities. Crew members brought a bottle along for that function.

Norwegian air-search radars on Spitsbergen tracked Case 031165 as it passed north of the island and then headed south across the Greenland Sea. Shortly after Case 031165 passed over the sea ice edge, its radar return merged into the Arctic hurricane raging over the open water. Shortly after Case 031165 disappeared from Spitsbergen's radar screens, the Korshun surface-search radar disappeared as well. Case 031165 had disappeared.

2142 MSK, 23 March 1983, 73 degrees 5 minutes north, 8 degrees 47 minutes west, Greenland Sea

The giant aircraft bucked and pitched as it fought winds in excess of two hundred knots. Captain Lieutenant Pavlov used all his strength to keep his Tu-142M on some semblance of level flight and nearly on course. He peered down to see Yevgeniy attempting to plot their position when his head was not buried in a bucket, heaving the contents of his stomach.

The pasty, greenish Navigator turned and yelled, "Comrade Pilot, we are at the patrol point."

Pavlov gulped. According to his patrol orders, this was the point where he was supposed to descend to two hundred meters above the raging sea and begin their ASW search. Flying that low in this weather was courting suicide. One blast of wind from the wrong direction could easily slam them into the frigid sea. But orders were orders. They could not find an American submarine if they stayed safe up here at altitude.

He pushed forward on the control yoke. As the big plane started its descent, Yevgeniy Grekov looked back at him, his eyes as large as saucers. "Leonid, you certainly are not going to do a standard ASW search, are you?" he pleaded.

"Comrade Navigator," Pavlov answered, "those are our orders. We will descend to two hundred meters, deploy our sonobuoys, and then orbit at four hundred meters. Hold on tight."

Pavlov flew the plane as low as he dared. The hurricane-force winds kicked the plane around the sky like a leaf. He fought the controls with all his strength. Even with his copilot adding additional muscle, it was all they could do to keep the plane in the air.

They dropped one line of RGB-26 passive sonobuoys and came around for a second pass. An unexpected two-hundred-knot downdraft slammed the plane down into the raging sea. Both wings broke off on impact. Icy-cold water flooded into the cabin. Leonid Pavlov barely had time to unstrap and grab the emergency life raft stowed behind his seat. His copilot was slumped over his control yoke, not responding to his yelling. He kicked open the cockpit hatch, shoved out the raft, and then grabbed the copilot just as the wrecked plane slipped beneath the waves.

He grabbed the raft and pulled the lanyard to inflate it. Getting the unresponsive deadweight of the copilot into the raft was a struggle, but Yevgeniy popped to the surface, sputtering and spitting seawater. Together, they managed to get all three men into the pitching raft and then searched for any other survivors. In the storm-tossed sea, the search was fruitless.

Pavlov dug around in the life raft's zippered pockets. Among the flares, emergency water supplies, and some candy bars, he found a Cospas-Sarsat Emergency Locator Transmitter buried in one pocket. He energized it in the meager hope that someone could locate and rescue them before they froze in this watery wasteland. Even the covered life raft was meager shelter, at best.

1415 EST, 23 March 1983, COMSUBLANT, Norfolk, Virginia

The orbiting LEOSAR satellite received and stored the Cospas-Sarsat ELT's signal and then downloaded it as it passed over the receiving ground station in northern France. Within minutes, an emergency Notice to Mariners was transmitted, alerting mariners that someone needed rescuing in the frigid Greenland Sea. COMSUBLANT copied the notice and rebroadcast it to all submarines at sea.

11

2120Z, 23 March 1983, USS John Jay, Norwegian Sea

Darren Walsh stepped into the control room. Since the medevac just over a week ago, the patrol had been routinely boring. Their patrol area was now up on the western edge of the Norwegian Sea. At this time of year there was very little surface traffic in this inhospitable part of the ocean. Everyone with any sense stayed over near the Norwegian coast, on the warmer side of the Gulf Stream, although warmer was relative. At least the seawater didn't freeze in the bilge over there and the seas were normally a lot calmer.

Even at 150 feet below the surface, the *John Jay* was pitching and rolling uncomfortably. Walsh was very glad that they were down here in a nice warm, dry submarine and not up on the surface at the mercy of a major late-winter storm.

He stopped at the quartermaster station and reviewed the chart taped down on the Mark-19 plotter. Iceland was three hundred miles astern. Jan Mayen Island, a mostly uninhabited bit of volcanic rock and ice, lay fifty miles to the northwest. Other than that, they seemed to have the ocean entirely to themselves. Their next tie-point, TP-3, was almost two hundred miles due south. They were scheduled to be there in three days. Plenty of time at patrol speed.

Bob Shippley, the Navigator, looked up from the chart where he had been busily plotting a position.

"Skipper, you see the message board?" he asked. When Walsh shook his head, he handed him an aluminum clipboard. "There's a message on top that you should look at."

Walsh took the clipboard. The top message was COMSUBLANT's rebroadcast of an emergency Notice to Mariners about the downed aircraft. He read the message and looked down at the chart.

"Nav, you plot these coordinates?" Walsh asked.

Shippley nodded. "Just finished." He took a pair of dividers and measured the distance between *John Jay*'s current position and the crash site location. "Forty-two nautical miles. Almost due north."

"Mighty lonely stretch of ocean to need an Emergency Locator Beacon," Walsh mused. "We have to be the closest ship."

Shippley replied, "Suspect you are right, Skipper. Nothing on sonar, and we haven't seen anything all watch."

Walsh thought for a second, and then he ordered, "Nav, come to course north, increase speed to a full bell. That should get us over there in about three hours. If someone really is in the water, let's just hope they can hold out that long."

The big FBM submarine came around and came up to speed. It was near midnight when the boat reached the message's reported position. Walsh and Stan Wilkins had used the three hours to brief the crew on what might be required for an at-sea rescue in this storm. Walsh knew of only one time when a submarine rescued plane crash survivors during a hurricane. Six years previously, the *Barb* had plucked the crew of a downed B-52 from a typhoon-tossed sea off Guam. He hoped the lessons learned from that adventure would help the *John Jay* on this rescue. That effort had required a swimmer to go in the water to rescue the downed fliers. The waters off Guam were a lot different from the northern Norwegian Sea in late winter. Walsh really did not want to order any of his crew to jump into the frigid Arctic waters.

The Chief of the Boat, Master Chief Max Steuben, worked with the deck gang to check that all of the rescue gear was there and operating.

Having a piece of gear missing or inoperable when they needed it just would not do. Not when people's lives were at stake.

Brett Burns, the Weps and the Officer-of-the-Deck, steered the *John Jay* up to periscope depth. The heavy swells sweeping across the fairwater planes and the broad, flat missile deck immediately sucked the submarine up to the surface, where it pitched and heaved in the towering waves.

Walsh grabbed the Type 15 periscope and looked around. From what Walsh could tell between the wave tops, they were all alone in the dark night. There was no sign of anyone floating in that dark stormy water.

"Officer-of-the-Deck, conduct a normal surface," he ordered.

They were already on the surface, but to stay up there, they needed to blow the main ballast tanks dry and to align systems for operating on the surface. With the ballast tanks blown dry, men raced to the bridge. IC-2 Delvin Brimley lugged the bridge bag, laden with the ship's heavy spotlight, up the long ladder to the bridge. Walsh threw on his foul-weather jacket and grabbed his binoculars before following Brimley on the long climb up.

They emerged into the night just as a wave crashed over the sail. As the water drained out of the sail, they surfaced, sputtering and shivering in the cold. The pair was tossed around in the confined bridge cockpit, battered against the hard steel, promising a host of bruises in the morning.

Brimley managed to plug in the searchlight and get it energized. He used the narrow saber of light to sweep the horizon, but they saw nothing except pitching seas and spume blown across the waves. Heavy cloud cover blotted out the moon and stars. Everything, even the angry sea, was shades of gray and black. This could prove to be an impossible search.

A wave washed up and sent a wall of water down the trunk. Many gallons of ice-cold seawater flooded into the control room, washing over the crew and vital electrical equipment down there.

Walsh called down, "XO, shut the lower hatch." That would at least keep the seawater out but also would isolate Brimley and him up on the bridge.

Walsh knew that they couldn't stay up here for long. It was just too dangerous. There had to be a way to quickly find whoever was lost out here. He called down to the control room, "XO, load a white flare in the signal ejector and launch it."

A minute later, a bright white streak erupted out of the signal ejector, lofting high into the sky and then drifting slowly back toward the sea surface.

"That should alert anyone within a hundred miles that we are here," Walsh mumbled. "So much for hiding with pride."

Suddenly Brimley called out, "Skipper, I have a red flare. Two points off the port beam."

Walsh swung his binoculars around and looked in the direction Brimley pointed. Sure enough, there was a red light rising and then disappearing in the waves.

"Conn, Captain, track the red flare, bearing three-zero-zero. Steer us over there. Have the man-overboard party stand by in AMR-1."

The *John Jay* swung around until it was pointed directly at the flare. Ten minutes later, it slid to a stop a few yards from a bright orange inflatable life raft. Walsh could just make out a couple of men in the tiny raft.

"Conn, Captain, lower the outboard. Test and shift to remote," Walsh ordered.

Back in AMR2, the lower-level watch punched a couple of buttons. An electric outboard motor lowered out of number five main ballast tank. The little 325-horsepower motor could push the *John Jay* home at a couple of knots if something happened to the main shaft, but more importantly, it was turnable so that it could push the submarine's stern around. This allowed the normally very ungainly boat to maneuver with fine precision.

The watch stander tested the motor and then transferred control to the helmsman in the control room.

"Captain, Conn, outboard is lowered, tested, and shifted to remote."

"Very well. Get the man-overboard party topside. No one goes topside without a harness and deck traveler engaged," Walsh ordered. The deck traveler was a clip that slipped into a track topside. It kept the wearer firmly attached to the sub and prevented them from being swept off the deck and lost into the sea.

"Man-overboard party lay topside," the 1MC blared.

Walsh carefully swung the submarine around so that the life raft was on the lee side, somewhat protected from the wind and waves. He looked aft just in time to see Master Chief Steuben's big, burly frame emerge from the weapon's shipping hatch. He was followed by three other sailors. Then ICFN Horace Faris, the ship's swimmer, emerged, dressed in a wetsuit and clutching his fins and mask.

A wave washed over the missile deck, dumping tons of seawater down the hatch and knocking the COB off his feet and sending him over the side, banging into the steel submarine and then plunging into the cold sea. Fortunately, his harness jerked him to a stop and kept him from being swept away. The deck crew heaved and pulled Master Chief Steuben back up on deck. He stood, shook himself off, and went on supervising the rescue, apparently little worse for the dunking.

"Captain, XO," the 7MC speaker on the bridge blasted loud enough that Walsh could hear it above the howling wind. "Recommend we give up on this and get back down before we hurt someone!"

"XO, I can see three men in that raft! We quit now and they are dead for sure," Walsh answered. "We'll give it a try."

Walsh used the outboard to maneuver the submarine until the life raft was only ten yards from the sub. Steuben threw a line over to the raft. Even in the wind, the line fell right across the raft, but the men were too weak and hypothermic to catch it.

Faris tied the line to his harness, took off his deck traveler, and leaped over the side. He swam over to the raft. He clutched it while the deck crew pulled both him and the raft back to the sub. In the pitching and heaving sea, the party spent several minutes trying desperately to pull Faris and the three airmen up to the main deck. A wave conveniently washed the raft up and dropped it on the deck. The team pulled the three men and Faris from the raft and lowered them down the hatch before following them down and shutting it.

With everyone aboard and the weapon's shipping hatch once more shut, Walsh and Brimley rigged the bridge for dive and dropped back down to the control room. Minutes later, the *John Jay* slipped back beneath the waves.

Walsh headed straight for the wardroom, now converted to an emergency aid station/operating room. There he found Doc Morrison attending to his patients. Faris was sitting on the couch, draped in blankets and clutching a cup of coffee. He was shivering so hard that the coffee sloshed onto the deck. The COB was being treated for minor cuts and bruises by one of the cooks. He would be sporting a massive black eye tomorrow.

"You okay, Faris?" Walsh asked. He clapped the sailor on the back.

With his teeth chattering, the swimmer answered, "Skipper, that water is damned cold. It's going to be a couple of weeks before my balls come back down out of my belly."

Walsh chuckled. He hadn't taken the time to change out of his soaking-wet poopie suit. "I know exactly what you mean." He turned to Doc Morrison. "How are our guests?"

Morrison shook his head. "One didn't make it. Broken neck. I'm guessing he died in the crash. The other two are severely hypothermic. Core body temperatures are below the scales on all my thermometers. The nukes are bringing me one of theirs. Neither can talk right now, but I'm guessing they are Russian from the badges on their flight suits."

"We going to be able to save them?" Walsh asked.

"It's going to be tough, but I think so. I've got hot water bottles in their armpits and crotches. Chop has the cooks heating a bunch of blankets, and I am setting up a couple of warm saline IVs. We'll just have to see how it works out."

Walsh turned to find Stan Wilkins stepping into the wardroom.

"Skipper, that was some fun up there. We're still cleaning up control. We were pretty lucky. The Mark-19 plotter took a real soaking. The quartermasters and IC men will be spending some time fixing it. Other than that, it's just wiping stuff down and washing away salt water. We weren't so lucky back in machinery one. That wave that washed the COB overboard sent a lot of water down the hatch. Looks like the number one sixty-four-kilowatt motor-generator is out of commission until the electricians can fix it. That might take a while."

"XO, draft up a message to SUBLANT," he ordered. "Tell them that we have two Russian survivors onboard and one that died in the crash. Work with Doc to see if he needs anything from them. And tell them that we will be a day late in making tie-point three. And give them a status report on the damages. I'll be in control, making sure we clear this area without picking up any unwanted company."

0910 EST, 24 March 1983, COMSUBLANT, Norfolk, Virginia

VADM Rufus Brown read the message, took a healthy swig of coffee, and read it a second time. The words hadn't changed. He breathed deeply and let out a sigh, visibly working to control his anger, or maybe it was anxiety. Brown couldn't be sure, but he knew that he had to come up with a good answer to this latest twist, one that would not result in an international furor and at the same time not undo all his efforts to manipulate their spy.

He shouted at the closed office door, "Hey, Chief-of-Staff, we need to talk."

As he expected, the door swung open almost immediately. Ted Strange had been standing just outside, anticipating his summons. "You need something, boss?"

Brown pointed at the Top Secret message board. "Yeah, you read this one from Darren Walsh on the *John Jay*? I swear he is out fishing for trouble."

Strange nodded. "Yeah, I saw it. Playing search and rescue on an alert patrol. Not exactly a typical boomer response. By the book, he should have turned tail and slunk out of the area."

Brown gave Strange a quizzical grin. "Suspect there are a couple of Russian fliers who are mighty glad that Walsh is not typical and didn't read that part of the book. But what do we tell him to do?"

Strange replied, "I spoke with the medical people. They are drafting up a protocol for the corpsman on *Jay*. Bunch of stuff about external warming and warmed intravenous fluids. When they started talking about warm body cavity lavages and warm-water enemas, I decided that it was more information than I needed to know. Bottom line, if the corpsman can stabilize those Russians over the next few days, they will be good to go."

Brown grunted. "Yeah, but what do we tell Walsh to do about the patrol plan? I sure as hell don't want to bail on that when we are just getting things going our way. And he is going to be a no-show at TP-3. How do we handle that?"

Strange was quiet for a second, then he smiled. "Why don't we use this to our advantage and play with their heads some more? Tell Walsh to stay well clear of TP-3. Then have *Tigerfish* send another MOSS through the tie-point at just about the right time. When it shuts off, that should just about seal the deal on their 'cloaking device' idea. Don't ya think?"

Brown smiled. "I like it, but let's add a little twist. We know how much Ivan likes to use active sonar. Set up the MOSS so that if he goes active, it gives one positive return and then shuts off. He will think that the cloaking device responds to active pulses, too."

Strange grinned and nodded. "I'll draft the message to *Tigerfish*. But what do we do about the Russian fliers? The weather guessers are forecasting another major winter storm moving into the GIUK Gap and most of the Norwegian Sea and lasting for the next week or so. Sea state six or higher, sustained winds above forty knots, and waves to twenty feet. A medevac would be somewhere between really risky and downright impossible."

Brown rubbed his temples. "Damn it, Chief-of-Staff, you're giving me a migraine. No sense risking either our crews or those Russians unnecessarily. As long as those fliers are stable and okay, tell Walsh that the medevac is on hold until the weather clears, but keep him within twelve hours of Iceland."

Brown popped an ibuprofen into his mouth and washed it down with a slug of coffee. Then he went on, "But this has all kinds of political ramifications. Way above our exalted pay grades. All we need is some Russkie claiming we kidnapped their aircrew and are holding them illegally. I'm calling over to CINCLANTFLT. Let the four-star earn his keep and run this up the Pentagon and State flagpoles. The heavy-duty Washington brass can argue it out and then tell us what to do. I'm betting that will take several days. By then the weather will have cleared."

12

1629Z, 24 March 1983, USS **Tigerfish,** *Norwegian Sea*

Bill Andrews stared out the periscope at a gunmetal-gray sea. The storms had blown out, and the seas had calmed some. The *Tigerfish*'s gentle rocking at periscope depth served as a mild reminder of the sea's power. The sea surface was empty all the way to the horizon. They had this piece of the Norwegian Sea all to themselves.

"Conn, Radio, one minute to copy the sixteen thirty ZBO." The radio room 21MC interrupted his musing. "Request the BRA-34 be raised."

Andrews ordered, "Chief-of-the-Watch, raise the BRA-34."

Andrews swung the scope around and watched as the sea-green antenna emerged and rose into the sky.

"BRA-34 indicates raised," the COW announced. Almost immediately, the 21MC called out, "In sync on the broadcast," followed quickly by, "All new traffic aboard and receipted for."

Their job up here on the surface was done. It was time to return to the deep. Andrews called out, "Chief-of-the-Watch, lower all masts and antennas. Number two scope coming down. Dive, make your depth one-five-zero feet."

As the deck angled down and the *Tigerfish* returned to the safety of the depths, Roy Blivens stepped up on the periscope stand. He held up the Top Secret message board and flipped it open. "Weps, load a MOSS in tube one. Flood down tube one and open the outer door."

As Andrews was ordering the MOSS loaded, Blivens stepped back to the navigation table. QM-1 Eric Swarton was just plotting the latest navigation fix. He smiled at Blivens. "That worked out well. Managed to get a Transit pass while we were up."

When the Transit, or NAVSAT, satellite passed overhead, a computer on the submarine would calculate its position by using the measured Doppler shift and the known satellite position. This gave the submarine a very accurate position even far out to sea.

"Good," Blivens answered. He checked the chronometer right above the QM's head. "What is the course and speed we need to make good to reach ten thousand yards short of TP-3 by 2300?"

Swarton swung the parallel motion protractor around, jotted down the course, and then walked off the distance with his dividers. "Captain, recommend course zero-four-six, speed ten."

Blivens turned and called out, "Officer-of-the-Deck, come to course zero-four-six and ten knots by log."

1845Z, 24 March 1983, USS John Jay, *Norwegian Sea*

Doc Morrison adjusted the IVs for his two patients. The "lounge" area that made up the forward part of the wardroom was set up as a temporary ICU with the benches on the port and starboard bulkheads rigged out as bunks. The patients were each strapped into one of the beds.

The low, kidney-shaped coffee table that normally occupied the space between the benches had been removed and a curtain hung to separate the ICU from the rest of the wardroom. The forward bench cushion was removed, and the pan was littered with medical gear.

Doc had spent the last twenty hours solid with his two patients. Since the only ID that either carried was the Cyrillic lettering on their flight suits and Doc couldn't read a name from that, he had arbitrarily named them

Ivan and Igor. Not that it mattered. Both were unconscious when he got them to the wardroom.

A night and day filled with warm IVs, warm-water lavages, and a constant flow of warmed blankets. Ivan's and Igor's body temperatures slowly started to climb back toward normal, and their skin tone lost the pronounced blue-gray color that it had been. Their breathing and pulse, both extremely slow and shallow when they first were brought onboard, was also returning to normal.

Doc saw the flicker of Ivan's eyelids as the stricken Russian returned to the edge of consciousness. The flier tried to move, but he was strapped to the bunk. He mumbled something that Doc didn't understand, but Doc soothingly answered, "Easy, easy. Just lie back and take it easy. You're okay now."

The flier relaxed and laid back, shivering. Doc piled on more warmed blankets just as Darren Walsh popped his head through the curtain.

"Doc, how are the patients?" he asked.

"Skipper, one is starting to come around," Doc Morrison answered. "The other one is still in a coma."

"Amerikanets?" the flier asked, his eyes now wide open. *"Gde ya?"*

"You are on an American submarine," Walsh answered. Then he translated that to Russian. *"Vy nakhodites na amerikanskoy podvodnoy lodke."*

The Russian attempted to laugh, but it came out as a weak cough. "Your Russian is horrible," he said with a heavy accent. "Let's speak English. How is Yevgeniy? How is my Navigator?"

Doc Morrison answered, "Igor is still unconscious, but his vital signs are improving."

"Igor?"

"I'm sorry. I couldn't read your names, so I called you Ivan and Igor," Doc answered, waving at each of the two Russians.

The Russian answered, "I am Captain Lieutenant Leonid Pavlov of the Soviet Naval Air Force." He nodded toward the other bunk. "He is Lieutenant Yevgeniy Grekov, my Navigator." He lay back and took a couple of breaths, regaining his energy. "What happened? We were flying in a really bad storm. We were trying to drop a pattern of sonobuoys when we got blown down. I remember being very, very cold. That's the last thing I remember."

Darren Walsh shook his head. "Damn! You tried to drop buoys in that? That was a full-blown hurricane you were flying in. Damn!"

He pulled up a chair and took a seat. "I'm Darren Walsh. I command the American submarine *John Jay*. We pulled three of you out of the water, but one of your crew didn't make it. Broken neck. He was dead when we pulled you all aboard. We are now down deep, riding out the storm up there. We've told our command that we have you aboard. We'll evacuate you when the storm lets up."

Walsh turned to Doc Morrison. "Doc, let's get these straps off Captain Lieutenant Pavlov. I don't think he's going to roll out of the rack now."

Morrison removed the straps, but when the patient tried to sit up, he firmly pushed him back down. "Captain, you are in no condition to sit up yet. I want you to stay lying down and covered up until we get all your vitals back to normal."

Pavlov lay back. "Yes, doctor," he replied. "But please call me Leonid. Much easier than Captain Lieutenant Pavlov, isn't it?" Then he added, "I am hungry. Is it true that food on an American submarine is almost as good as on a Russian one?"

Walsh looked at Doc, who nodded and answered, "Warm soup only. Nothing solid yet."

Walsh rose and turned to Pavlov. "I have to get back to the control room. I'll have the cooks rustle you up some soup. Afraid we don't have any borscht, but they make a really mean chicken noodle soup."

0247 MSK, 25 March 1983, K-324, Norwegian Sea

Captain Second Rank Boris Novikov stood in the control room of his *Victor III*–class nuclear-powered submarine, *K-324*. He was frustrated, and it showed as he paced the deck. Still no response from Naval High Command to his message warning them of the American *maskiruyuscheye ustroystvo*, the cloaking device. It seemed that they were purposely ignoring him.

He was left only with his orders to intercept the American missile submarine at the next point and then to track it. The chart showed that they were three kilometers to the east of the point. The American was due to arrive at 0300 Moscow time.

He glanced at the clock. He had less than fifteen minutes. This time he would see just how effective the *maskiruyuscheye ustroystvo* really was.

It was almost precisely 0300 when the sonar michman yelled out, "*Kapitan*, I have contact on the American submarine on the passive sonar. His bearing is three-four-one. His bearing is drawing right."

There he was. Right on schedule and once again, he did not have his cloaking device energized. Now to get in behind him before he was alerted. Novikov deftly maneuvered his submarine around and danced into a position off the American's starboard quarter. The American's own noise should hide the *K-324* from detection.

He glanced over at the SOKS wake object detection operator. At this range, the system should be locked on to the big American submarine's churning wake, but the operator shook his head. There was nothing out there.

"Go active with the seven-kilohertz sonar," Novikov shouted. At this close range, the American submarine should fill up the screen. He could easily hear the high-pitched blast of acoustic energy, nearly 250 decibels, emanating from the hydrophones in the *K-324*'s bow-mounted sonar array. Two seconds later, the sonar operator called out, "Positive return, range three thousand meters, bearing zero-two-seven. Definitely an American missile submarine."

Novikov smiled. So the Americans did have a weakness, after all. Active sonar was the answer. "Track the American with active," he ordered.

The active operator shook his head. "*Kapitan*, I got one positive return, and then he disappeared. There is nothing out there."

The passive operator reported, "Lost signal on the American. It was like he turned off a switch."

Novikov kicked a locker in frustration. The American was getting away again. "Come to course zero-two-seven, ahead full," he ordered. He would prove the American was out there by taking a paint sample off the side of the hull if he had to.

The *K-324* ran right through where the American was supposed to be. Novikov turned around and ran through the point again. Nothing. He slammed his fist against a bulkhead and stalked off to his stateroom.

0030Z, 25 March 1983, USS **Tigerfish,** *Norwegian Sea*

Roy Blivens and George Sanders watched the plot of *K-324* chasing the MOSS. The little evasion device had performed flawlessly, imitating *John Jay* as it steamed through the third tie-point right on schedule. When the Russian submarine had gone active, the MOSS's tiny hydrophones, one in the bow and another towed a couple of hundred feet behind, had recorded the active sonar signal and then played back a return that looked just like the *John Jay* to the Russian sonar operator. And then, just as Blivens had programmed it, the MOSS turned off and sank into the deep after the first ping. To the Russians, it had just disappeared.

"That Russian skipper has to be pulling his hair out," Sanders chortled. "Look at him go back and forth through the datum. It looks like he is trying to ram the MOSS."

Blivens nodded but was more serious when he corrected his XO. "He is trying to ram the *John Jay*. That boy is playing for keeps. Get a message ready for SUBLANT. Tell him what happened. We'll pull back a few miles before we send it and then head for TP-4."

Senior Chief Zwarlinski stepped out of the sonar shack and over to where Blivens and Sanders were conferring. "Excuse me, Skipper, XO," Zwarlinski said, his south Jersey accent sounding almost like Southern drawl. "I cut a tape on our friend. Nothing particularly identifying about him, except he does have a noticeable shaft rub. We picked it up real clear when we were on his port quarter. I checked against the *Victor III* at TP-3. I'm pretty sure that this is the same guy, Sierra Four-Nine."

"Good work, Senior," Blivens acknowledged. "One more data point for the intel base."

0930Z, 25 March 1983, USS John Jay, ***Norwegian Sea***

Commander Darren Walsh stepped through the hatch into the engine room. He stopped just outside the Maneuvering room door and watched for a few seconds. Lieutenant Dale Horton, the EOOW, nodded toward the skipper, but the three enlisted watch standers kept their eyes firmly glued to their panels. Normally when the skipper was spotted in the engine room, drills were about to go down. They had no way of knowing what devilishly tricky "casualty" was about to happen, but the gauges and meters on their panels would provide the first indications. Then it was their task to deliver the correct and timely response to "keep the reactor safe, the lights burning, and the screw turning."

Walsh smiled and stepped into Maneuvering. The watch standers sat up even more erect. They were sure that bells and sirens would be going off momentarily. Walsh asked, "You seen the Eng?"

Horton replied, "He dropped down into lower level a few minutes ago." He reached up and grabbed the 2MC microphone. "You want me to page him, sir?"

Walsh shook his head. "Naw, I suspect that I'll find him in the vicinity of number two main seawater pump." He stepped out of Maneuvering, lifted the hatch to lower level, and dropped down the ladder.

Pete McKay was squatted down on the narrow portside catwalk. He and Chief Rosecrans were staring at a tech manual lying open on the metal deck. Various tools and parts filled the deck around them.

"What you got, Eng?" Walsh asked.

"It's not looking good, Skipper," McKay answered, shaking his head. "We broke the pump coupling. The motor spins free, but the pump is frozen. Locked solid. Tech manual says that it might be packing too tight or a failed mechanical seal. We loosened them both all the way. Still froze solid. Gotta be something with the impeller or impeller nut."

Walsh looked at the manual for a second, then at McKay. "Well, what's the plan to fix it?"

McKay stared at Walsh for a second, then he answered, "Skipper, a main seawater pump repair like this is a tender job. We'd have to rig the motor out of the way, and that thing weighs better than a ton. Then we'd have to crack open the pump casing to get to the impeller. Unless we shut down the whole engine room, we'd only have one valve between us and a whole lot of really cold seawater."

Walsh smiled. "All right, Eng. So far, I've heard some really good excuses for living with this. What I want is your best plan to fix the pump out here. Once you have your plan all worked out, then we can decide whether or not we do it. Now I gotta get back to the conn. Let's see what you have this evening."

As Walsh was climbing the ladder to upper level, Chief Rosecrans chuckled and looked at McKay. "Well, Eng, I guess we'd better figger out how we gonna do this." He grabbed the tech manual and piping drawings. "Why don't you work on keepin' the water outta the people tank, and I'll figger out what we need to fix the pump."

13

1525 MSK, 25 March 1983, Soviet Northern Fleet Headquarters, Murmansk, Russia

Fleet Admiral Dmitri Golubev, commander of the Soviet Red Banner Northern Fleet, sat at his broad, ornately carved desk and glanced out the large window toward the bustling piers below. An icy wind was sending heavy gray clouds scudding across the sky. A storm was forecast, and the sky certainly held the portents of one. But for now, the weather was clear. A pair of tugs were pulling the brand-new *Slava*-class missile cruiser *Marshal Ustinov* away from the pier. Golubev shook his head, wishing that he was standing on the bridge of the cruiser, heading down the Murmansk Fjord and out into the Barents Sea. Even facing a storm-tossed winter sea on the pitching deck of a cruiser was better than being strapped to this desk and listening to interminable briefings.

"Admiral, shall I continue?" the weaselly little man asked peevishly. Although he was dressed in a rumpled gray civilian suit, Sergi Baranov was a Vice Admiral on the General Navy Staff and the head of the Navy Intelligence Directorate. But more importantly to Golubev, he was also the Deputy Director of the Main Intelligence Directorate, the dreaded GRU.

Such a man needed to be handled carefully and treated with the utmost respect.

"I apologize, Sergi," Golubev replied quickly as he turned back to the briefing. "I was watching the *Ustinov* stand out to sea. Let's continue."

Baranov chuckled drily. "Always the sailor, Dmitri. You can take the man away from the sea, but you can't take the sea away from the man. Unfortunately, there is no time for idle daydreaming, we have work to do, decisions to make. The commander of the *K-324* has sent us a second message about this American *maskiruyuscheye ustroystvo*, this cloaking device. Either he has a very vivid imagination, or the Americans have a new secret weapon that we are totally unaware of. We discussed this with our acoustic experts, and they say that such a device is theoretically possible but years ahead of anything we have developed."

Dmitri Golubev nodded and grunted. "Sergi, you are not telling me anything we don't already know. What is it that you want?"

Baranov unlocked and opened his briefcase. He removed a file and slid it across the desk to Golubev. The buff-colored file was emblazoned with the words "*Samyy Sekretnyy*" in large red Cyrillic letters at the top and bottom of the cover. "Most Secret" was the highest security classification in the Soviet Armed Forces. Only documents of extreme sensitivity were classified "Most Secret," and distribution outside intelligence channels was very rare.

"Dmitri, you have asked how we know where the American missile submarine *John Jay* is patrolling," Baranov explained as Golubev gingerly opened the file. "We have a very deep and very valuable asset inside the American submarine command. It has taken us years and a great deal of money to get him in a position where he has the access and willingness to give us eyes there. He gave us this information. Now we have tasked him to find this cloaking device. I want you to vector two more submarines, ones with experienced, reliable commanders, to the next so-called 'tie-points.' We will see if the Americans actually have a cloaking device or if Captain Second Rank Novikov is imagining things."

Golubev read through the file with interest. It described the American missile submarine operation very differently than he understood it. He had always been told that the American submarine commanders operated pretty much on their own, going wherever they liked. In the American vernacular, "like a bunch of cowboys." But this described an operation order that was very tightly controlled, with the submarine required to be at certain specific locations at very specific times, almost like how the General Navy Staff controlled the Soviet missile submarines.

He reluctantly slid the file back to Baranov, who snatched it and locked it securely in his briefcase. Then the spymaster smiled. "Interesting reading, isn't it?"

Golubev grunted. "If we could get the same orders for each of their despised missile boats, it would be almost too easy. We simply wait at a tie-point and suddenly the American missile threat is no more."

Baranov nodded. "Dmitri, you hit on exactly the problem. It is almost too easy. Are the Americans playing with us, setting us up by feeding us false information? We need to find out for sure."

Golubev shrugged. "Sergi, I am a simple sailor. I know nothing about the spy business. That is your game. What are you suggesting we do, and why are you telling me?"

A sly smile slid across Baranov's face. "Well, Admiral, I'll answer your second question first. I am telling you because we may need the assistance of your fleet, more specifically a couple of your submarines." He pulled a chart out of his briefcase. "I need them moved so that one of them is here." He pointed to a spot in the ocean off the Virginia coast. "It is a hundred miles off of the naval base at Norfolk. I need that submarine to be very noisy getting there." He pointed at a second spot only thirty miles off of Charleston, South Carolina. "And that boat needs to be very quiet. The success of this mission depends on it not being detected. And I need them both in position by the night of ten April."

Golubev stared at the chart for a few seconds. He did some quick calculations in his head. Then he smiled. "It will be cutting it pretty close, but I think we can make that happen. What will the mission be for these boats?"

Sergi Baranov rose and snapped his briefcase closed. He grabbed his heavy top coat and fur hat. "You will receive the mission in good time, Admiral. Just get the submarines in place." He turned and went out the door.

1305Z, 26 March 1983, USS John Jay, 65.2 degrees north, 9.8 degrees west, southern Norwegian Sea

A hundred miles north and east of Iceland, a brutal storm whipped the sea surface into a maelstrom. Fifty- and sixty-knot winds roared down from the Arctic, ripping the tops off the thirty-foot waves. A thick, dark cloud cover completely blotted out the sun.

The black submarine cruised along smoothly three hundred feet below the roiling surface. Only its BRA-8 communications buoy, a big, black collection of radio antennas in a body resembling a miniature submarine, floated a few feet below the surface. Connected by a thick cable to the submarine, the buoy's very low frequency loop antenna kept the *John Jay* in constant communications with COMSUBLANT, over two thousand miles away to the southwest. A reel, housed just aft of the submarine's missile deck, pulled the cable with a constant tension, allowing the buoy to pitch and heave with the waves while the submarine cruised along, undisturbed by the storm.

Pete McKay knocked on the Commanding Officer's door. Darren Walsh looked up from the file he was reading and grunted, "Eng, what you got?"

The big engineer stepped into the little stateroom, followed closely by Dale Horton, the Main Propulsion Assistant, and Josh Rosecrans, the nuclear Machinist Chief. Both Horton and Rosecrans were carrying a stack of manuals. They plopped the books on the little fold-down table.

"Afternoon, Skipper," McKay said as he slid onto a small bench seat on one side of the table. "We want to brief you on our plan to repair the seawater pump."

Horton slid onto the bench on the other side of the table while Rosecrans opened a folding chair and sat. Walsh spun his chair around so that he was facing the table. "All right, so what's the plan?"

Horton opened a tech manual to a cut-away drawing of the pump. "Skipper, the pump impeller has seized. Something has caused it to drop inside the casing. The only thing we can figure is that the impeller nut has come loose for some reason. Ain't no other way it could drop like it did."

Walsh glanced over at Rosecrans. The chief machinist was nodding and smiling. He had obviously carefully briefed the young officer before they came here but was keeping quiet now. Walsh knew that Rosecrans would only speak up if Horton got in over his head somewhere. It was all part of the tradition of an older and much more experienced chief training his young division officer.

Walsh studied the drawing for a second and then asked, "How do we repair it?"

Horton opened a file. "This is our work procedure. After we set plant conditions, we will have to rig the motor up off the pump and out of the way. Then we crack the casing and lift the upper half out of the way. That gives us access to the impeller. Hopefully, we just need to tighten and torque the nut."

"What if the nut is damaged?" Walsh asked. "Do we have a spare?"

Horton wasn't prepared for that question. He didn't have a good answer. Rosecrans chimed in, "Skipper, supply doesn't carry a spare. It's not something that would normally be needed at sea. We'll have to make one on the lathe. It'll take a day or so. We got all the other materials we'll need. We'll have to turn it out of carbon steel, so it won't last as long as a Monel one would, but it will last plenty long enough to get us home."

Horton picked up the briefing again. "We figure it will take two days to rig everything out, do the repairs, and rig everything back and reassembled."

"Retest?" Walsh asked.

Horton flipped pages on the procedure. Then he went on, "We op-check the pump as soon as we finish and clear the danger tags. Then we need to make a controlled dive to test depth to clear the SUBSAFE departure from spec."

SUBSAFE was a process, implemented after the loss of the *Thresher*, that made sure that all the material and work performed on systems that were subjected to sea pressure met very specific requirements and were tested to prove they were adequate. The number one rule of submarining was to keep the water on the outside of the people tank. The SUBSAFE process was one significant way of ensuring that rule was observed.

"What about plant conditions?" Walsh queried.

McKay took over the brief. "I want to stay down here at a depth where it is nice and calm. That pump motor weighs over a ton. I don't want it up in the air, swinging around in any kind of sea state. Too dangerous." McKay shook his head. "We'll have to operate the engine room with a single main engine on the starboard turbine and a single turbine generator. We'll windmill the port turbine. That'll limit our speed to about twelve knots. Then we danger tag out the port main seawater system and drain it to the bilge. When we don't see any water coming from the vents, we will know the valves are holding and not leaking by. Only when we are sure everything is stable, we put Chief Rosecrans and his boys to work."

Walsh grabbed the work procedure and signed the approval statement. "Chief, draw the parts from supply and get your boys making the new nut. When that is all done, we'll look for the right time to do the work."

2107 MSK, 26 March 1983, K-373, Norwegian Sea

The Soviet *Alfa*-class fast attack submarine *K-373* eased out from under the Arctic pack ice. The small, very-high-speed submarine had drawn the incredibly boring duty of playing nursemaid for the *K-408*, a *Yankee*-class ballistic missile submarine, as it ventured into the North Atlantic on a thirty-day patrol.

Captain Second Rank Sergey Vyalitsyn, skipper of the *K-373*, considered these patrols an incredible waste of assets. The *K-373* was the fastest, deepest diving, most dangerous submarine in the world. His titanium craft was more than a match for even the new *Los Angeles*–class submarines just rolling off the American building ways. But the crusty old admirals back in Murmansk had decided that it was more important for the *K-373* to putz around at three or four knots, escorting an ancient missile boat on a tour of the Sargasso Sea.

Sergey sat back and surveyed the boat's small, compact control room. The *Alfa*-class submarines were unique in many ways, not the least of which was centralizing all the sub's controls into one space. Indeed, the third compartment, where the control room was located, was the only normally manned compartment out of the boat's six watertight compartments. The crew only visited the other compartments rarely for maintenance. From his seat, Vyalitsyn could easily see the *Akkord* combat information displays, the *Sozh* navigation terminal, and the *Okean* sonar outputs. Turning in his seat a little allowed him to monitor the reactor, the sub's weapons, and just about every other function on the boat. He could operate his entire undersea fighter from right here in this one seat. It must be how his brother Mikhal felt flying his spanking-new Su-27 fighter jet.

"Comrade Captain," Senior Lieutenant Belikov called out. "It is time to copy the broadcast." The young officer was the *K-373*'s Navigator and Communications Officer. With a crew of only thirty officers, it was necessary to double up on many duties.

Vyalitsyn glanced at the clock hanging just above the *Ritm* panel. It read twenty-one-zero-nine Moscow Standard Time. They had one minute to get up to periscope depth and raise the radio antenna. There was no time to waste. Submarine command back at Polyarny expected every boat to copy their broadcasts precisely on time.

At Vyalitsyn's order, the *K-373* angled up toward the surface, leveling off just as the periscope broke through the churning waves. He raised both the *Vint* and the *Tissa* radio antennas. That way, he could copy both the HF broadcast and the satellite UHF signal at the same time. The two printers started clacking away almost immediately. Twenty minutes later, the printers finally fell silent. A bell rang, signifying the end of the broadcast.

The *K-373* dropped back down to seventy-five meters. Sergey ripped the paper off the printer and began to read through the messages. He had just read the second one when he turned to Belikov. "Comrade Lieutenant, make your depth one hundred meters, come to ahead flank."

The submarine rocketed ahead as the lead-bismuth-cooled reactor fed steam to the main turbine. Forty-thousand-shaft horsepower pushed the little sub to forty-three knots.

Belikov looked questioningly at his captain as Vyalitsyn spread a chart on the plotting table. The submarine commander walked his parallel rule across the chart. Then he called out, "Steer course one-nine-seven." His voice was almost happy when he added, "We are going to America to patrol off of their Norfolk naval base. An American aircraft carrier is heading out, and we are to shadow it."

The *K-408* was soon far behind and all but forgotten. It would patrol the Sargasso Sea by itself.

14

1930Z, 26 March 1983, USS **Tigerfish**, *Norwegian Sea*

Saturday night was pizza night on the *Tigerfish*, and tonight the chiefs' quarters were doing the baking. The crew was taking great delight in ordering their custom-made pies and then berating the chiefs if the order took too long or was not up to the crew's standards. But the chiefs were returning the barbs with equal gusto.

The Chief of the Boat, Master Chief Mike Shaw, was presiding over the galley as the master chef. His apron was covered with flour dust and spattered with tomato sauce. He had even manufactured a tall *toque blanche* out of a heavily starched tablecloth, but that had gotten splattered, too.

Senior Chief Zwarlinski, as sous chef, supervised the sauce making, which was why the COB's apron was so splattered. The sonar senior chief did not fully appreciate *Tigerfish*'s temperamental mixer, which had switched itself to high speed just as he dropped it into the bowl of sauce. This resulted in most of the galley, including the chiefs, receiving a tomato-sauce baptism.

EMC Paul Anders was wiping sauce out of his hair when the mess decks Dial-X telephone rang. He answered it, held out the phone, and yelled at Zwarlinski, "Al, sonar. They got a contact they want you to look at."

Zwarlinski wiped his hands, removed the apron, and dashed up the mess-decks ladder to the upper level. He stepped into the dimly lit sonar shack to find everyone huddled around the BQR-20 spectrum analyzer in the aft corner of the shack. He had to elbow his way into the shack and up to see the BQR-20 readout.

Stan White, the on-watch sonar supervisor, spied Senior Chief Zwarlinski and announced, "Make a hole. Let the pizza king through. Senior, you get tomato paste in my shack, I ain't field daying it."

"Funny, White," Zwarlinski retorted. "I'll make sure to save an anchovy pie just for you. Now, what do you need that demands me to leave my culinary responsibilities?"

Stan White turned serious. "Senior, we are getting hits on the towed array. Contact is designated Sierra Seven-Six. Best bearing is somewhere to the north. Fifty-two-point-seven-hertz received frequency. Something don't correlate. Speed in the line of sight is better than forty-five knots. I ain't never seen a sub move that fast."

Zwarlinski shook his head. "White, were you sleeping through all those ACINT briefs? What you are looking at is an *Alfa* going balls to the wall and coming pretty much right at us. Tell the Officer-of-the-Deck and start cutting tapes on this guy. I'll go and tell the skipper."

2230 EST, 27 March 1983, Chesapeake, Virginia

Henri Dubois sat at the counter and nursed his coffee. The smiling waitress had already filled the cup a couple of times. The plate of hash browns "all the way" sat barely touched. The Waffle House was nearly empty. Not very many people with a hankering for waffles late on a rainy Sunday night. A trucker gnawed on a T-bone at the other end of the counter, and a young couple cozied up together in a booth for an inexpensive night out on a budget.

DuBois glanced at the clock above the grill. It was time. He stood and sauntered toward the restrooms but stopped at the pay phone. He punched in the well-remembered number and dumped several quarters in the slot.

Leland Samson answered on the second ring. To Dubois, his singsong Gullah greeting was totally unintelligible. Even when Samson spoke English, Dubois found understanding him challenging.

"Leland, speak English and speak slowly," Dubois commanded.

Leland Samson laughed heartily. "That'a be a preety good 'un," he chortled, slowly enunciating each word. "A' considerin' ya'll be talking Cajun, Mister Henri."

DuBois smiled ruefully. The big Black man had a point. His family had called southern Louisiana home for over two hundred years. He considered Cajun English to be normal. Everyone *else* spoke with an accent.

"That's *assez* idle chitchat," he said, unconsciously slipping into Cajun English. "Did *vous* get the stuff?"

Samson answered in a Gullah-English mishmash. "*Us waited b'hin de house until the chillum leaved. Figgered us'd go in dayclean when missus done gone ta fetch dem papuhs. Dee see we inna de gyaa'd'n. Sheriff be gyaa'd de house. Us sees um un mak'ace head'um fore day ketch us.*"

So Samson had tried to break into the house and steal the box when the house was supposed to be empty but had been seen by the wife. Evidently the house was guarded and Samson had to run. DuBois was amazed that he could almost understand what Samson said. He was even more amazed that anyone with such a rudimentary grasp of English was employed in a Navy electronics research lab, although he knew that Leland Samson was a senior technician at the NAVELEX facility in North Charleston.

"Thank *vous*," DuBois answered. "*On'll* have to try *quelque chose* else. J'll be in touch with a *nuef* plan."

He hung up the phone knowing that he needed to find someone else, a professional, to break in and steal the package and the film hidden inside. Samson was a good source for information, but he clearly could not be used for operations like this.

2330Z, 28 March 1983, USS John Jay, GIUK Gap

Delvin Brimley pulled the movie rewinder from behind a locker and plopped it down on the workbench. Horace Faris walked into the cramped E&E space, lugging a flat, dark green paperboard box. He put it on the workbench next to the rewinder and proceeded to open the straps that held the box closed.

"That the flick?" Brimley asked.

"Yep," Faris answered. "Something called *The House Where Evil Dwells*. A real gagger. From what the torpedomen told me, it's worth two punches on your hacker card."

On a boat, the IC men were responsible for the reel-to-reel movies that the crew watched for entertainment during a patrol. The Navy contracted for every movie that Hollywood put out rated PG or higher. That meant the system was flooded with a lot of bad movies with only a limited few gems. Really bad movies were the order of the day, and a crewman who sat all the way through a bad movie was said to get his hacker card punched. A movie had to be exceptionally bad to rate two punches.

Faris pulled the sixteen-millimeter reels out of the box and mounted reel number two on the rewinder. "There is supposed to be skin in reel two, about halfway through, real quick like."

The pair started slowly feeding the celluloid from the first reel to the second while watching the images slide by. It took the better part of an hour, but finally, there it was. No more than a dozen frames, at standard movie speed of twenty-four frames per second, barely a flicker. But there it was, honest-to-goodness skin. Female skin.

Brimley snipped out the section while Faris grabbed the film splicer. They were busy splicing the reel back together when Stan Wilkins stepped out of the ship's office. The office door was only a foot or so aft of the E&E space door. The XO saw the two IC men industriously working late on a Sunday evening. He walked into the space to see what was going on.

Brimley looked up and smiled. "Evening, XO. Out for a stroll?"

Wilkins answered, "Just keeping up with the admin. What are you two working on that's so important?"

Faris held up the splicing tool. "Nothing very exciting. Just catching up on fixing the movies. This reel broke last time. Splicing it now."

Wilkins nodded and wandered off in the direction of his stateroom.

Brimley wiped his brow. "That was close." He held the short segment of film up to the light. "Yep, skin. Even some nipple on this one."

Faris pulled a reel out from its hiding place in the locker below the workbench. The reel was less than half full. Together, the pair spiced the segment onto the reel.

"Yep," Brimley chortled, "by the time we get through all the films we're carryin' this run, should have half hour or so of some good skin."

0815 EST, 29 March 1983, Goose Creek, South Carolina

Joy Walsh had just successfully gotten Pug and Sam out the door in time to catch the school bus when the phone rang. She sighed, realizing that long-awaited second cup of coffee would have to wait a few more minutes. She grabbed the handset from the wall phone and said, "Walsh residence, this is Joy."

"Mrs. Walsh, this is Annie May Faris." The voice was almost squeaky. Joy thought that she sounded very young, with an accent that she would describe as "sorghum molasses and biscuits." And Joy noticed that the caller sounded like she was fighting off tears.

"You probably don't remember me. We met at the family pre-patrol meeting. You said to call you if we ever had a problem." With that, Annie May Faris broke into full-on sobs.

Joy Walsh didn't remember Annie May, but that wasn't surprising. There had been over seventy wives at that meeting, and almost half were first-timers. But she had dealt with plenty of sailors' wives in crisis before.

"Take it easy, Annie May. Take a deep breath, and let's see what we can do. Tell me what the problem is."

Annie May sobbed some more, blew her nose, and then sniffled. "It's the bank. They just called and said my checks bounced for insufficient funds." This brought on the tears some more. "That just ain't right. They hafta be wrong. I still got checks inna my checkbook. How am I supposed to pay ma rent? The landlord, he gonna kick me out inna ta street."

Joy assumed a calm, soothing voice. "Annie May, nobody is going to kick you out in the street. We'll get this all sorted out."

Annie May calmed a little. "Horace and me just got married right after Horace finished sub school. He drove home to Haywood. That be in Arkansas. Just so we could get married. When Horace left for patrol, he left me a hunnert bucks cash and the checkbook full a checks. He said there was enough there to tide me over until he got back. That hunnert went fer groceries already. The checks are all I got."

"I'll call Navy Relief," Joy said. "They will help you out with a loan. They will also help you make a budget and teach you some things about family finance. They are down on the Navy base in the same building as the Exchange. Can you drive down there this afternoon?"

Annie May started crying again. "I can't drive. I ain't got no license. I'm only fifteen."

Joy Walsh gulped. Now that was a new twist to an old, familiar problem. "I'll call the COB's wife. Her name is Camille, Camille Steuben. She will set up some of the wives to help you out with transportation. You good with that?"

Joy heard what sounded like retching. "Annie May, you all right?"

"Guess I et something that ain't agreein' with me," Annie May answered. "Been havin' trouble keepin' breakfast down."

"Annie May, any chance you are pregnant?"

"Don't know," Annie May answered. "Maybe."

"All right. We'll get you to the Navy clinic, too. And maybe figure out how we can get your high school finished while we're at it."

1300 MSK, 30 March 1983, K-373, 30 nm east of Norfolk, Virginia

Sergey Vyalitsyn checked the navigation charts. The chart showed that the entrance to America's Chesapeake Bay was only sixty kilometers over the western horizon. The Norfolk Navy base, the home of the American Fleet, was just inside the mouth of that bay. The long, high-speed run down from Spitsbergen was done. Now it was time to carry out the rest of his orders and bait the American bear.

"Comrade Belikov," he said to Daniil Belikov sitting at the *Boksit* course control system, "slow to ahead one-third and come to periscope depth. It is time to tell our masters at Northern Fleet headquarters that we arrived for our mission."

The submarine's periscope had barely broken the surface when a P-3C ASW aircraft came out of the sunrise and flew directly overhead. Vyalitsyn involuntarily ducked as it roared by, less than a hundred meters above the ocean. The American plane circled around and dropped even lower. He could easily see the bomb bay doors swing open as the big bird lined up directly at his periscope.

Vyalitsyn lowered the periscope and shouted, "Go deep, three hundred meters! Ahead flank! American P-3C coming in to drop a torpedo!"

The *K-373* arched steeply down and rocketed ahead. All thought of stealth was abandoned. They had to outrun the American torpedo! Fortunately, it was an air-dropped torpedo, so it would be short-ranged and not nearly as sophisticated as the American Mark-48 submarine torpedo or their own TEST-71 torpedoes.

Vyalitsyn watched as the sub's speed leveled out at forty-three knots. The forty-knot American Mark-46 torpedo would have a very difficult time catching up with the racing submarine, but the noise of the water across the *K-373*'s hull prevented them from hearing the torpedo. The only way to know that it was no longer chasing them was to keep racing away until it had exhausted its fuel. He waited fifteen minutes. By that time, they had run nearly twenty kilometers, well beyond the range of the American weapon.

"Slow to ahead one-third," Vyalitsyn ordered. There was no sign of the torpedo. The ocean was quiet. "Come to periscope depth."

The *K-373* smoothly rose until just the periscope peeped above the rolling waves. Vyalitsyn put his eye up against the eyepiece and rotated the scope around.

Impossible! There it was again. The American P-3C down at wave-top height coming right at them with the bomb bay doors open again.

Vyalitsyn lowered the periscope and again shouted, "Go deep, three hundred meters! Ahead flank! American P-3C coming in to drop another torpedo!"

Once again the *K-373* raced away. Vyalitsyn could not believe his bad luck. How could the Americans be right on top of him when they had raced almost twenty kilometers away. No one could be that lucky.

15

0617 EST, 30 March 1983, P-3C Tail Number 161124, 30 nm east of Norfolk, Virginia

The Lockheed P-3C, tail number 161124, pulled up at the end of its low-altitude run. Scott "Blunt" Sharples laughed as he pulled back on the yoke and watched his bird climb back up to a thousand feet, where he leveled off. He glanced over at his copilot.

Tom "Birdman" Byrd was grinning from ear-to-ear. He chortled, "Ivan must be crapping his pants. Every time he pops up, we're right on top with the doors open. He can run, but he can't hide."

Sharples keyed his throat mike. "TACCO, we still hold our friend on the buoy pattern?"

The Tactical Action Officer, Wilbur "Wee Willy" Weston, sitting a few feet behind the flight deck, looked up at the acoustic display and said, "He'll pass right through the third DIFAR line in five minutes. He keeps on this course and speed, we'll need to lay another pattern out ahead of him in ten minutes. This guy is a real trash bucket. He's blasting the passive buoys."

Sharples chuckled again. "This is almost too damn easy. We should be back to Oceana in time for happy hour at the club. Does the SpruCan still hold him?"

Weston answered, "The *Oldendorf* is up on the link. They report they have him on the TACTAS. This guy is well and truly screwed."

The Link 11 tactical data communications link passed the track information between P-3C 161124 and the *Oldendorf*, a *Spruance*-class destroyer, fondly called a SpruCan. From there, it could be passed to anyone else "up on the link" to ensure that everyone had the same information.

"Blunt," Wee Willy Weston called out, "*Oldie* reports their LAMPS is in the air. Maintaining below angels five hundred, squawking IFF Mode Four."

The *Oldendorf* had launched their SH-2 LAMPS helicopter to do an airborne prosecution of the Russian sub. The SH-2 would stay below five hundred feet altitude and was using its IFF, Identification Friend or Foe, beacon to highlight its radar return. It could copy the data from the P-3C's sonobuoys or drop its own pattern to track the Russian.

Sharples looked out the windscreen but couldn't sight the small Seasprite helicopter. Birdman Byrd, looking out the right-side windscreen, pointed and called out, "Got 'em. Two o'clock, down low. Looks like he's planting a pattern out in front of ours. TACCO, you coverin' the freqs for their buoys?"

"Not yet, but I will before they go live." Wee Willy Weston was busy inputting the data-link frequencies into the AN/ARR-72 sonobuoy receiver. Each buoy had its own frequency, and there were twenty-four buoys in this pattern. It would take a few minutes.

Then Wee Willy keyed the intercom. "The *Oldie* just went active. Positive return on the Russian at a range of fourteen thousand yards. Poor guy is going to have a persecution complex."

Blunt Sharples laughed. "Just wait. Norfolk control is reporting three SH-3s outbound to practice dipping sonar on our friend down there."

1415 MSK, 30 March 1983, 200 kilometers east of Charleston, South Carolina

The Soviet *Victor III*–class submarine *K-314* cruised silently, one hundred meters below the surface of the churning North Atlantic. The *K-314* was the newest and most modern of the Soviet submarines. It was also the quietest, benefiting from the secrets that John Walker had betrayed to the Russians about American submarine technology. At slow speeds, the Russian boat disappeared into the noisy ocean.

Captain Second Rank Ilya Agapov, commanding the *K-314*, knew that his boat was the stealthiest submarine on the planet as long as he kept the speed below ten knots and kept the crew mindful of the threat that any inadvertent noise created.

At his command, the submarine had crept down the coast of Greenland, hugging the icy shore the whole way. Going through the Denmark Strait was the most nerve-racking. The Americans had sown this narrow bit of water with acoustic sensors to find submarines just like his that were trying to sneak out into the open Atlantic. It made for an anxious day, but when nothing happened after twenty-four hours, Agapov knew that they were undetected. He made for the southernmost tip of Greenland and then followed the west wall of the Gulf Stream all the way down to the American coast.

With the Gulf Stream heading north at four knots and his silent speed being less than ten knots, progress was excruciatingly slow. Seventeen days of dodging in and out of the oceanic river's north wall, using the extreme temperature changes between the frigid Arctic waters of the Labrador current pouring down out of the Davis Strait and the warm gulf waters to hide and confuse the sonars of any possible pursuer.

Finally, they arrived, two hundred kilometers east of the South Carolina coast, right on the edge of the Gulf Stream. Agapov reviewed his orders again. The orders were very simple. He was to stay hidden here and watch for what the American Navy did. He was to tell the Northern Fleet headquarters if any American submarines, particularly their missile submarines, left port. He was to remain here until he received further orders. He was not to allow the *K-314* to be detected by anyone.

1800 EST, 30 March 1983, COMSUBLANT, Norfolk, Virginia

Rufus Brown closed the dun-colored file and sat back. He smiled as he contemplated what he had just read. Dan Former, or Doctor Dan as he was known in the submarine community, had written a masterpiece, made up out of whole cloth. He had come up with something called "active noise cancellation." The idea was so simple that it would probably actually work. Just sample the noise source and then broadcast a signal exactly 180 degrees out of phase. This rebroadcast signal would then cancel out the original noise. For the listener, the noise simply went away. Doctor Dan's imaginary system captured the noise from the submarine and then rebroadcast the anti-signal to cancel it out. He even included a couple of real patents for reference. Thus, the submarine cloaking device was born.

"Well, what do you think, boss?" Ted Strange asked. "Think this is good enough?"

"Ted, I'm ready to go buy this ANC system for our boats," Brown laughed. "Set up some very hush-hush briefs, with just enough noise that our spy gets wind of something being up. Get this file doctored up with all the right classification jargon. Then store it in a safe where he can find it."

"You got it, boss." Strange took the file and marched out of Brown's office.

1203Z, 1 April 1983, USS Tigerfish, Norwegian Sea

The buzzer for the JA phone jumped to life. The buzzer and handset were hidden under the wardroom table by the captain's seat so the Officer-of-the-Deck could instantly talk with the skipper, even if he was eating a meal. Roy Blivens had just sat down for lunch. He was hungry and particularly looking forward to sliders and fries, today's noontime repast.

He reached under the table and grabbed his handset. "Captain," he growled.

"Captain, Officer-of-the-Deck," Bill Andrews said. "On course zero-seven-five. We are on the five-mile circle from TP-4. Sonar is reporting two new contacts, both on the TB-16. One hundred-hertz tonal, either Sierra Seven-Six bearing three-five-five or Sierra Seven-Seven bearing one-five-five. Probable *Yankee*-class submarine. Fifty-two-hertz tonal, either Sierra Seven-Eight bearing one-eight-zero or Sierra Seven-Nine bearing three-three-zero. Probable *Victor I*–class submarine. Coming right to course one-three-zero to resolve bearing ambiguity on both contacts."

Blivens nodded even though the OOD couldn't see him. Andrews had taken just the right actions and had then made a concise report about a confusing situation. "Very well," Blivens said. "Station the section tracking party. Get a leg on both contacts. I'll be right up."

Roy Blivens carefully folded his dark green napkin and fitted it into the heavy napkin ring. The lunch meal was gone for now; it was time to get back to work. He pushed back from the table and, waving at the other officers not to stand, rose. Grabbing his notepad from the sideboard, he headed toward the door.

George Sanders pushed his chair back to follow the skipper out, but Blivens said, "XO, I'll take care of this. Finish your lunch. Weps is reporting a couple of Russkie subs on the Sixteen. By the time you've enjoyed your ice cream, we'll have it sorted out and ready for the fire control tracking party. Should give you a fun-filled afternoon."

As he was walking out the door, the skipper turned to the supply officer. "Chop, have Cookie put together a plate for me. I expect I'll be hungry when we get done playing."

Blivens bounded up the ladder to the upper level. He stuck his head into the sonar shack to see what Senior Chief Zwarlinski's team was up against. The shack was, as normal, dark, with the various CRTs providing the illumination necessary to see what was happening. Zwarlinski, wearing a headset and a harried expression, was alternately keying through the displays on the BQR-23 narrow-band analyzer, listening to his headset, and playing with the self-noise monitoring system.

He pulled off the headset when he saw the skipper standing there. "Skipper, we got a couple of things happenin'. Resolved ambiguity on Sierra Seven-Eight to the south. Developing a good bearing on him now.

Haven't regained Sierra Seven-Six yet. Still searching. As we were turning, I was listening to the broadband hydrophone for self-noise. Thought I heard something real quick like but couldn't be sure. Checking on the self-noise monitoring system to see if we have developed a problem. Sounds like a bearing squeal back aft. Working with Maneuvering to narrow it down."

The self-noise monitoring system was a network of hydrophones placed at key locations around the *Tigerfish* to listen for any noises that the submarine might be putting out into the water. By regularly monitoring the system, they could determine how much at risk the boat was to detection, and if a hydrophone suddenly showed a marked increase in noise, the sonar team and the engineers could work out what the offending component was by shifting pumps and motors around until the culprit was isolated.

"How bad?" Blivens asked.

"Ten dB above baseline," Zwarlinski responded. "Enough to be concerned about detection if anyone gets inside a couple of thousand yards." He paused for a second to listen over the headphones, then he added, "And if it don't get no worse."

"Let me know what you find. In the meantime, we'll try our level best to keep the Russkies outside a couple of thousand yards."

Blivens ducked out of the sonar shack and headed forward to the control room. As he walked into the space, QM-1 Eric Swarton, the Quartermaster-of-the-Watch, called out, "Captain's in control."

Bill Andrews met him as he stepped up onto the periscope stand. "Skipper, resolved ambiguity on Sierra Seven-Eight. Current best bearing one-eight-three, drawing left. Lost Sierra Seven-Six. Still searching. Sonar reports a self-noise spoke, probable motor-bearing problem. Working with Maneuvering to isolate it."

"You have a leg on Seven-Eight?"

"No, sir. Not yet. Narrow-band bearings are really scattered. Time-bearing plot looks like someone splattered it with paint. Working to get a best fit through the scatter, but best guess is going to be plus or minus ten degrees."

Blivens nodded. Trying to pull bearings, particularly at lower frequencies, from the towed array was a real art. The array beams were broad, causing the operator to do a "best guess" of what bearing within a beam had the strongest signal. The only way to get any kind of accuracy was to take a lot of data and assume that the errors canceled out over time. Lieutenant Junior Grade Enrique Ortiz, standing watch as OOD Under-Instruction, was plotting the bearings against time on a large roll of chart paper hanging down from the overhead just forward of the fire control consoles. He slapped a straight edge through the splatter of dots, trying to balance the number of dots above and below the line. When he was happy, he drew a line and pronounced, "I have a curve."

Andrews turned to Blivens and reported, "Skipper, I have a curve. Coming to course two-two-zero to close Sierra Seven-Eight."

Blivens nodded. He looked at the possible solutions on the computer screen and at the bearing data. "Very well. This could be an over-lead situation. Keep a close eye on which way the bearings are drawing. I don't want to get out ahead of this guy." He glanced at the clock above the number one Mark-117 fire control console. It had been almost half an hour since Andrews had called him from lunch, just as his growling stomach was reminding him. "Bill, let's get this leg and then call away the fire control tracking party."

The *Tigerfish* slowly worked its way around behind the submerged contact. The fire control tracking party, the first team, relieved the section tracking party from the task of working out the target's course, speed, and range.

George Sanders arrived in the control room, working a toothpick and patting his stomach. "Those were really good sliders," he chuckled as he relieved Roy Blivens as the Command Duty Officer. "And Cookie made a really good chocolate cake for dessert. I think there was a piece left, but you never know with those chowhound junior officers."

"Glad you enjoyed lunch," Blivens harrumphed, but with a grin. "Time for you to get to work before I waste away from starvation. Sierra Seven-Eight is a probable *Victor I*. We're holding him on the TB-16. He currently bears two-six-three. Best base frequency is five-two-point-one hertz. Range is about fifteen thousand yards, course something around two-eight-six, speed roughly ten knots. Solution has tracked reasonably well through the last couple of legs. We're going to need to get within hull array range to refine it much more. Let's see what we can do to close into about ten thousand yards. I don't want to get any closer until we have nailed his solution better."

Sanders nodded. "Got it. Anything else?"

"Yeah, Zwarlinski and Maneuvering are chasing down a self-noise back aft. Bearing squeal, but they haven't located it yet. I'll be in the wardroom eating my reheated lunch," he said ruefully. "Call me if anything changes."

Blivens had just sat down with his warmed-over lunch when the JA phone buzzed. He grabbed the handset and growled, "Captain."

"Captain, XO," George Sanders said, "Sierra Seven-Eight has zigged. Looks like he is heading straight for TP-4. And we have two new contacts on the TB-16. One is a one-hundred-hertz tonal, either Sierra Eight-Zero bearing three-four-seven or Sierra Eight-One bearing two-zero-three. Classified a Soviet Type II nuke. He might be a regain of Sierra Seven-Six. The other is a fifty-five-hertz tonal, either Sierra Eight-Two bearing one-two-five or Sierra Eight-Three bearing zero-five-five, classified Soviet Type IV nuke. We have a leg on all three. Coming to course two-three-zero to resolve ambiguity on Sierra Eight-Zero and Sierra Eight-Two while we get another leg on Sierra Seven-Eight."

Lunch again forgotten, Blivens was busy visualizing all the information, moving his hands in the air to picture all the relative bearings. With what was, in essence, five different submerged contacts, three real and two ambiguous, and adding in *Tigerfish*'s own movement, it could easily become confusing.

"Two-three-zero opens TP-4," he challenged Sanders. "I have a feeling TP-4's where the party will be."

The XO had his answer ready. "Yes, sir. I only plan to stay on two-three-zero long enough to resolve ambiguity. This keeps everyone out of end-fire. It allows me to come around to the northwest for the next course and get in behind everyone."

Because the beams on the towed array were conical and the array was a straight line, bearings taken from right angles to the array were reasonably accurate, but the closer the bearings got to the ends of the array, the less accurate they became. For low frequencies, it was like waving your hand across a broad arc and saying, "He's out there somewhere." Consequently,

George Sanders was working to keep all the contacts out of the end-fire beams.

"Sounds good, XO," Blivens said, pushing back from the table and ignoring the gnawing in his stomach. "I'll be right up."

Roy Blivens walked into control just as George Sanders announced, "Resolve ambiguity Sierra Eight-One, bearing two-one-one, drop Sierra Eight-Zero. Resolve ambiguity Sierra Eight-Three, bearing zero-five-two. Drop Sierra Eight-Two." Sanders held the sound-powered phones to his ears. After a couple of seconds, he added, "Sierra Eight-One classified *Yankee*. Sierra Eight-Three classified *Victor III*. Assign Sierra Seven-Eight to Analyzer One, assign Sierra Eight-Three to Analyzer Two. Analyzer One, run Sierra Eight-One in background."

Blivens shook his head. "Damn, XO, you've even got me confused," he said. "Let's try to make this as easy as possible. First off, I'm not really concerned about the *Yankee*. He's a Russian boomer, so he is just going to try to slink out of here. Put Sierra Eight-One in CHURN and let the computer worry about him."

CHURN was an algorithm in the fire control system that automatically generated a best-fit solution for the target's range, speed, and course without any operator inputs. It was useful for keeping track of secondary targets when there were too many for the operator to handle.

The laughter following his boomer comment helped ease the tension of dealing with a slew of Soviet submarines.

Blivens nodded to Enrique Ortiz sitting in front of the screen for Analyzer One. "Mr. Ortiz, the *Victor III*, Sierra Eight-Three, is your little problem. You stack dots on him and get me a solution."

The young junior officer smiled and answered, "You got it, Skipper."

Blivens then looked toward LTJG Brad Bishop sitting in front of Analyzer Two. "Mr. Bishop, the *Victor I*, Sierra Seven-Eight, is yours."

Bishop, a non-qualified officer on his first run, was too busy twirling knobs and punching buttons to do more than acknowledge Blivens. "Yes, sir."

Blivens moved over to the Mark-19 plotter in the forward starboard corner of the cramped control room. Steve Dunn held court there as the plot coordinator. His team was working out the target solutions the old-fashioned way, with paper and pencils.

"Eng, I see that the blue has almost faded." Blivens smiled and pointed toward his nose. He then tapped the chart right at TP-4. "Draw a circle around TP-4 at five thousand yards. Plot the best solution for both *Victor*s every minute. As soon as one of them gets inside that circle, yell at me. That's when we need to put the MOSS in the water."

Dunn drew the circle and then stepped off the distance from it to the current position for each of the Russian subs. "Skipper, Eight-Three is two thousand yards from the circle and headed right at the tie-point. Looks like Seven-Eight is sorta loitering out to the west at ten thousand yards."

"Weps, make the MOSS in tube four fully ready to launch." Blivens checked the time and looked at their current position. "We're six minutes away from launch. Get the MOSS course from the Eng." Turning around to the OOD, he ordered, "Nav, come to course north and increase speed to standard. We need to make sure the MOSS arrives at the tie-point on time."

Blivens knew the risk with this maneuver. This little patch of the Norwegian Sea was getting very crowded, and it looked like everyone was heading for the same spot. Even if the *Tigerfish* wasn't counter-detected, there was a real risk of going bump in the night with one of the Russians. He was speeding up and heading right for the tie-point. To top it off, he was about to add another player to the mix. He really had no idea how the Russians would react.

Blivens watched as the clock ticked down. He needed the *Tigerfish* to be two thousand yards short of the tie-point position when Eight-Three crossed the five-thousand-yard circle. That way, the MOSS would arrive at the tie-point precisely on time.

Time seemed to stand still. Tension mounted in the tightly packed control room as all eyes were glued on the clock. Finally, Steve Dunn called out, "Skipper, Eight-Three is at the five-thousand-yard circle. We are two thousand yards from the tie-point."

Roy Blivens glanced at the plot for a second, then at the fire control solutions on Sierra Seven-Eight and Eight-Three. Everything was working as planned. "Slow to ahead one-third. Launch the MOSS in tube four," he ordered.

Bill Andrews grabbed the big brass lever on the Mark-75 launch panel and pulled it to the left as he called out, "Stand by." He held it there until he saw all the interlock lights come on, then he pulled it to the right and announced, "Shoot tube four."

Down in torpedo tube four, the battery in the little ten-inch-diameter metal fish energized and started the screw spinning. The MOSS swam out of the tube, came up to its ten-knot programmed speed, and headed directly for TP-4.

The MOSS had barely cleared the torpedo tube when Blivens ordered, "Nav, come left to course two-nine-zero, make your depth one thousand feet. It's time to sneak out of Dodge." The *Tigerfish* quietly sank deeper into the sea and came around to head away from the tie-point.

When the MOSS had traveled a thousand yards, the transducer system turned on. To any listening sonar, the MOSS became the *John Jay*.

"Hold the MOSS going active," Senior Chief Zwarlinski announced. After a pause, he reported, "Shark Gill active sonar from Sierra Eight-Three. SPL plus thirty-five. Less than thirty percent chance of detection."

At the same time the WLR-9 Active Intercept Receiver behind the periscope began alarming. The Navigator reached up and shut off the alarm. The readout agreed with what Senior Chief Zwarlinski had just reported. Sierra Eight-Three was using a seven-kilohertz active sonar to track the MOSS.

"Loss of the MOSS. The MOSS has shut down." As it was programmed to do, as soon as the little submarine simulator heard an active sonar signal, it shut down and sank to the bottom.

"Torpedo in the water!" the 21MC blasted. "Torpedo from Sierra Eight-Three! Bearing zero-four-two!"

The Officer-of-the-Deck was reaching for the 1MC mike to initiate the actions for torpedo evasion when Blivens reached up and swatted his hand away. "Hold on a second, Nav. He isn't shooting at us. Let's not tell him we're here."

"Torpedo bearing zero four-zero!"

"Receiving forty-three-kilohertz active sonar. Torpedo has gone active. Torpedo classified Soviet SET-80."

"Torpedo bears zero-three-five."

Steve Dunn had been slapping down the bearing lines to the torpedo as fast as he heard them from sonar. He looked at the fan he was drawing. It went right toward where the MOSS had been. "Skipper, he's shooting at the MOSS!"

Roy Blivens smiled and nodded. "That's what I figured, Eng. But now we know these guys are serious. Let's keep real quiet and see what they do next."

16

1330 EST, 1 April 1983, Goose Creek, South Carolina

Joy Walsh heard the car pull into the driveway. Glancing out the front window, she saw three ladies walk toward the front door. She recognized Camille Steuben leading the way and Donna Braxton bringing up the rear. The very young girl in the middle, looking lost and out of place, must be Annie May Faris. She couldn't be more than four or five years older than her own daughter, Sam.

Joy ushered the three into the living room, where she had already laid out coffee and cookies.

Camille Steuben started the conversation while Annie May Faris stirred cream and two scoops of sugar into her coffee. "Joy, we got Annie May all set up with Navy Relief. They have given her a loan to tide her over until the boat gets back." She nodded toward Donna Braxton. "Donna and I are helping her put together a budget."

Annie May Faris smiled and looked up. Her Arkansas accent was thick. "Miss Joy, these ladies have been real nice to me. They done got me money to tide me over." She patted her stomach. "I guess I need to be sayin' 'us over.' An' I gonna be studyin' for my GED. Hopin' ta have my deeploma by the time Horace is home."

Donna Braxton added, "Since Annie May can't drive yet, we've set up a carpool to get her to her appointments. Three of the wives live in the same trailer park, and I'm just down the road a piece."

To Joy, it sounded like the crew wives had come together to take care of Annie May. The four ladies nibbled on cookies, sipped their coffee, and made small talk.

0912 MSK, 2 April 1983, Soviet Northern Fleet Headquarters, Murmansk, Russia

Fleet Admiral Dmitri Golubev read the message reports from the two submarines out in the Norwegian Sea. Captain Second Rank Novikov described how he had maneuvered his submarine, the *K-324*, to be within two thousand meters of the tie-point position at precisely the required time. He had detected the American submarine as expected. He used his seven-kilohertz active sonar to obtain a firing solution. As had happened previously, the American submarine simply disappeared. Novikov explained that he had shot a torpedo at the American in the belief that either the advanced USET-80 torpedo's sensitive sonars or its wake homing device would locate the enemy submarine. The torpedo had not seen any target. The American cloaking device proved effective against the USSR's most sophisticated ASW weapon.

Golubev scanned the second message. Captain Second Rank Kudryavtsev reported that he maneuvered the *K-53* to observe the encounter and to intercept the American submarine as it tried to evade. His report pretty much coincided with Novikov's. He had detected the American with his passive sonar, but as soon as the *K-324* used active sonar, the American submarine disappeared. He heard the *K-324*'s torpedo run right through the American's position without even wavering. It ran until it expended its fuel and sank.

Golubev slammed the file holder down on his desk in disgust. Either he had two incompetent submarine captains or the Americans really had some secret new weapon. What did Novikov call it? A *maskiruyuscheye ustroystvo*, a cloaking device.

He grabbed the secure phone and dialed a well-remembered number. As soon as the phone was answered, he growled, "This Fleet Admiral Golubev. Get me Vice Admiral Baranov."

"Immediately, Admiral," the female voice answered. "The Deputy Director will be right with you." Whoever the assistant was, she had not so subtly reminded Golubev that he might rule the Northern Fleet, but Sergi Baranov ran the dreaded GRU and was not to be trifled with.

A minute elapsed before the phone crackled. "Dmitri," Baranov's voice boomed. "How is life in the frozen north?"

"Sergi, I didn't call to get a weather report on how balmy it is in Moscow today," Golubev harrumphed and then chuckled. "For your information, today is the first day we have been above zero degrees Celsius since last October. At this rate, the snow may melt by July. I have put the *ushanka* and *varezhka* in the closet."

"I'm glad that you are enjoying a fine spring day," Baranov answered. His voice turned serious. "To what do I owe the pleasure?"

"Sergi, I just saw the message reports from our submarines looking into the American *maskiruyuscheye ustroystvo*. The reports are conclusive. The cloaking device even worked against our most advanced torpedo. We need all the information we can get if we are going to develop an effective counter."

Sergi Baranov listened quietly. Then he answered, "Dmitri, we have tasked our agent in the American submarine headquarters to find whatever he can. We hope to hear from him in the near future."

Golubev growled, "Hope will not defeat this new American weapon. We need information."

1530Z, 2 April 1983, USS John Jay, GIUK Gap

LCDR Pete McKay made the long climb down the ladder into the main seawater bay in engine room lower level. The cavernous space was a maze of piping, valves, and pumps sucking in seawater to cool the main condensers and various auxiliary systems before pumping the heated seawater back out into the ocean. The two main seawater pumps normally sat side-by-side at deck level in the center of the space. Currently, the motor for number two MSW pump had been disconnected, hoisted off the pump, and lowered onto the diamond-tread steel catwalk. A chain fall was already rigged to a pad eye-high in the overhead and hooked to a couple of lifting bolts screwed into the pump casing.

Dale Horton, Josh Rosecrans, and a couple of machinists waited at the bottom of the ladder. McKay looked around and noted that everything appeared in order. The shiny new pyramidal-shaped impeller nut, freshly fabricated on the metal lathe, sat on the deck amid an array of large wrenches and sockets.

"We ready?" McKay asked Horton. "How is the leak rate from the condenser drain?"

"Eng, the port main seawater system is isolated and drained," Dale Horton reported. "We're getting about ten drops a minute, so the isolation valves are holding."

The port main seawater system's ten-inch-diameter pipes were designed to pump thousands of gallons per minute of seawater through the main condensers to cool and condense the steam after it exited the turbines. Massive hydraulically operated hull and backup valves, as well as the single cross-connect valve that separated the port from the starboard main seawater system, were now shut to keep the water out of the system and to protect the submarine from uncontrollable flooding when they disassembled the pump. The only way to make sure the valves were holding back the sea was to watch the drains. A few drops of water per minute was fine. A steady flow was not.

McKay turned to MM2 Jack Harrigan, standing at the forward end of the bay and wearing a pair of sound-powered phones. "Phone talker, to control," McKay said crisply. "Conditions are set and verified. Request Captain's permission to break open the pump casing."

Harrigan mumbled into the phone's mouthpiece, listened for a few seconds, and then said, "Control reports that ship is stable at three hundred feet. You have the Captain's permission to break open the seawater pump."

The two machinists grabbed wrenches and started loosening the casing bolts while Chief Rosecrans snugged up the chain fall. They were all well aware that when they lifted the pump, there would only be a single valve protecting them from the sea. If it failed, water would rush in at a pressure of more than a hundred pounds per square inch. Tons of ice-cold seawater would flood in, and there would be no way to stop it. The sub would become a crushed tomb at the bottom of the Norwegian Sea. When the bolts came loose, they were committed.

The last bolt dropped out. Chief Rosecrans ratcheted the chain fall to lift the upper casing. The casing suddenly popped free. A wall of ice-cold seawater welled up out of the pump and flooded out onto the catwalk. Jack Harrigan threw down his phones and scrambled up the ladder. He was clawing at the escape trunk hatch, trying desperately to leave the sub, when the upper-level watch managed to catch him and calm him down. In his panic, Harrigan didn't stop to question where he was going with three hundred feet of water over his head.

McKay shook his head while Chief Rosecrans bent over laughing. They both knew that the pump casing was full of water. When they lifted the upper half of the case, all the trapped water rushed out. Several gallons fell into the bilge, where it was pumped overboard. All was now calm. It was time to fix the pump. The machinists struggled to lift the impeller up onto the shaft. They cleared away the corroded remains of the old impeller nut and screwed the new one on the shaft, securing the impeller. Rigging the casing back in place, bolting it securely down, and replacing the shaft seals took another couple of hours.

It was midnight before the repairs were completed and the pump was fully tested. McKay was dead tired when he finally came forward to tell Darren Walsh that the *John Jay* was once again fully operational.

"Captain," McKay reported, "the pump is running like a fine Swiss watch. All we need now is a controlled dive to test depth to clear the SUBSAFE work package."

"Eng, let's hold off going to test depth until after we off-load our Russian guests," Walsh responded. "Give your team a big attaboy for this work. I really don't think anything like this has ever been tried before. And I hear that the crew has bestowed a new nickname on Petty Officer Harrigan.

After his attempt to climb out the escape trunk, he is now 'Ho-ho-ho' Harrigan."

Part of every crew member's initial submarine training was to learn to do an emergency ascent from a sunken submarine. To prevent their lungs from embolizing while they rocketed to the surface, they were trained to yell "Ho ho ho" on the way up. Submariners were noted for their humor, which could be merciless at times.

17

0930 EST, 4 April 1983, COMSUBLANT, Norfolk, Virginia

Ted Strange was enjoying a cup of coffee as he read through the Top Secret message boards. The report from Roy Blivens on *Tigerfish* was the fourth message down in the stack. The Chief-of-Staff chuckled as he pictured the Russian commander's frustration. Having an American boomer in his sights, then having it just disappear for the fourth time had to be driving him nuts. Knowing that there was a second Russian sub just to witness what was happening must have been the height of embarrassment. But having the Russian actually shoot a torpedo was extremely worrisome. They had upped the ante considerably. Strange realized that he would need to warn both the *John Jay* and the *Tigerfish* that the Russians were playing for keeps.

The last sentence in the report spurred Ted Strange into action. Blivens reported that *Tigerfish* had expended the last of her MOSS. Strange grabbed his secure phone to the SUBLANT OPCENTER. "Watch Officer," the Chief-of-Staff ordered, "mod the *Tigerfish*'s OPORD and bring her into Holy Loch ASAP. Get a load out of a half dozen MOSS on her as soon as she arrives, then send her right back out again."

Strange had just refilled his now cold coffee cup when the red phone jangled. "Captain Strange, this is Special Agent Baldwin. I'm calling to inform you that we have been ordered by NIS headquarters to remove the protection detail that has been watching the Walsh house. There has been no activity for over two weeks. Headquarters is saying that they need those assets elsewhere and that they are just being wasted twiddling their thumbs in Charleston. Sorry."

Strange started to splutter an enraged protest, but then he recognized that Jeremy Baldwin was only the messenger. This was a fight better carried out between flag officers. He needed to get Vice Admiral Brown to have a short, sharp discussion with the Rear Admiral who commanded the Naval Investigative Service. He hung up. VADM Brown was scheduled to return from briefing Congress in the late afternoon. He would brief him then.

1140 EST, 4 April 1983, Goose Creek, South Carolina

Joy Walsh finished putting away the laundry. She was still mystified as to how two young kids could generate such a large pile of laundry over a weekend. Pug was the undisputed champion at finding mud, no matter where he went. Saturday's soccer match had certainly contributed to the pile, but so had a Sunday afternoon romp at the playground. And Sam seemed to have left her entire wardrobe piled in the middle of her bedroom floor. It was all done and back in the closets now, at least for a couple of days.

Joy moved to the next item on her list, cleaning out the office closet. There were boxes in there still unopened from their move down here from Norfolk, three years ago. Now that she had a few free minutes, there was time to sort through them and see what needed to be trashed and what should be kept. Six large shipping boxes of old files; tax records, old receipts, letters, all the assorted detritus that seemed to accumulate in the home office. Sorting through it all was a job that she had been avoiding, but one that needed done. Probably nothing in there worth saving, but you could never be sure until you actually sorted it.

Joy had just pulled the first box out of the closet and heaved it up on the desk when she spied movement out of the corner of her eye. She looked up to see the big green van pull away from the curb. That was strange. The NIS guards usually swapped out at 0800 and 1600. One van always would pull in before the other would leave. Not seeing a green van out front was unusual and, somehow, disturbing. She shook her head. If anything was happening, the NIS agents would call and let her know. Joy returned to sorting through the boxes.

Joy moved two full boxes out to the trash bin and was rewarding herself with a cup of coffee and piece of pecan pie when the phone rang.

"Mrs. Walsh, this is Ted Strange at SUBLANT. I called to tell you that NIS has removed your protection. We are working to get it restored as quickly as we can. In the meantime, we can move you and the children into the BOQ on base."

"Thank you, Captain," Joy Walsh answered, "but we'll stay here at the house. I'm sure everything will be fine."

She hung up, thanking her lucky stars that Darren had bought her a pistol when they were first married and then taught her how to use it. She immediately went into the bedroom and searched the high shelf to find the little Beretta. She gingerly took the tiny pistol and clip out of the box, checked both that the pistol was unloaded and five rounds were in the clip, just like Darren had taught her, and put them both in the hidden drawer in the antique nightstand beside their bed. At least now she could get to it in a hurry if she needed to, but just as important, it was some place where Pug wouldn't find it.

Speaking of Pug, it was time to get the kids' afternoon snack ready. They would be home from school in a few minutes.

1715Z, 4 April 1983, USS **Tigerfish***, Norwegian Sea*

Roy Blivens was just finishing up his daily tour of the boat. No better way to actually find out what was working and what wasn't than to go out into the spaces and talk with the crew. The lower-level watch would often tell the skipper something was just not quite right when he had not yet reported it to his chief, usually simply because Blivens was actually in lower level and showing a real interest when the chief was not.

Blivens pushed up on the grate that served as a hatch from the shaft lube-oil bay up to engine room upper level. He quickly scooted up the short ladder and carefully lowered the grate back into position. Dropping it would have caused a loud clang, which was not a good idea on a submarine.

"Afternoon, Skipper." Stan White was working up a sweat on the exercise bike strapped down in the narrow space between the spinning main shaft and the boat's hydraulic plant. The bike barely fit in the confined space and had to be disassembled and stowed after use. But, as inconvenient as it was, riding the exercise bike was one of the few chances the crew had to try to keep fit on a long and usually boring deployment.

"Afternoon, Petty Officer White," Blivens responded. "You going to need a guide to find your way back forward? I can make sure the EWS helps you out," he joshed. It was a standing joke that non-nukes were lost as soon as they passed through the reactor compartment hatch.

"That would be mighty kind, sir," White laughed. "Senior Chief Zwarlinski was making noises about cleaning and restowing all the lockers in sonar. Figure he will never find me back here."

"Your secret is safe with me." Blivens winked.

Just then the 2MC speaker blared, "Captain, contact Maneuvering."

Blivens grabbed the 2JV sound-powered phone handset from the holder at the emergency propulsion motor station and answered, "Captain."

"Captain, Engineering-Officer-of-the-Watch," Brad Bishop answered. "The Officer-of-the-Deck requests that you go to control. He reports that we have received a mod to the op order."

"Very well," Blivens responded. "Tell him I am headed forward."

He replaced the handset in the holder and skirted around the reduction gears and main turbines as he headed forward. He found George Sanders and Tom Clemont huddled around the Mark-19 plotter in the aft port corner of control. They had a small-scale chart of the Norwegian Sea spread out on the table. Clemont had laid down a line connecting their current position down to the North Channel, gateway to the Irish Sea.

Sanders slid the message board across to Blivens. "Skipper, we are ordered to Holy Loch to reload MOSS. We have three days to get there, a day to load out, and then three days back to here, actually to TP-5."

Blivens nodded and scanned the message as he mumbled, "Thanks, XO." Looking over at Clemont, he added, "Can we do it, Nav?"

"We'll have to scoot," Tom Clemont answered. "I measure just a little over thirteen hundred nautical miles to the tender at Holy Loch. I come up with a twenty-knot speed of advance overall. It'll take a couple of hours to get the charts all laid out and ready to go."

"Well, let's get moving in the right direction while you get everything fine-tuned," Blivens answered. Turning to Steve Dunn, the Officer-of-the-Deck, he ordered, "Eng, come to course south, depth four hundred feet, and ahead flank."

0630Z, 5 April 1983, USS John Jay, *GIUK Gap*

Darren Walsh stepped into the wardroom, expecting to get a late breakfast. He had just spent the last hour observing Tony Stagnetti take the boat to periscope depth to ventilate and get a NAVSAT pass. The long-lasting winter storm was still whipping up the seas. Successfully managing the boat safely had been a real challenge for the junior officer. Walsh had to smile. The young A-Weps was turning into a pretty good Officer-of-the-Deck. By the time they got back from this patrol, Walsh felt certain that he could recommend to the Squadron Commodore that Stagnetti receive his gold dolphins.

Walsh found one of their Russian guests, Captain Lieutenant Leonid Pavlov, seated in front of a plate heaped high with scrambled eggs and sausage. The Russian spied Walsh and started to jump to his feet. Walsh waved him to stay seated as he greeted him, "*Dobroye utro, Kapitan-leytenant.*" He looked around the wardroom but did not see Lieutenant Yevgeniy Grekov, the Russian Navigator. "Where is your shipmate?"

Pavlov laughed. "Captain, your Russian pronunciation is much improved. By the time we leave your fine ship, we will have you sounding like a Muscovite. I'm afraid Yevgeniy has not found his sea legs as of yet. Just the thought of food sent him to the *vannaya komnata*. As Doc Morrison so colorfully phrases it, 'Yevgeniy is praying to the crapper sea god.' Such a shame. Even if the eggs are powdered, the *zavtrak*, the breakfast, is excellent."

"Speaking of your time onboard," Walsh replied, "I'm afraid you are going to be our guests a bit longer. The meteorologists are forecasting that this storm will likely be with us for another week. Our higher command won't approve evacuating you at least until the weather clears."

Pavlov shrugged. "Why should we complain? Doc Morrison and Ensign Lowe are keeping us well fed and comfortable." He took a sip of tea. "Even your cooks are trying to brew a proper Russian tea. But without a real samovar, it will take some trial and error to get the right balance."

Walsh poured himself a cup of coffee and ordered a plate of eggs and sausage. He looked down the table at Pavlov and said, "Leonid, now that you two are up and about, I'm afraid that I am going to have to ask that you and Yevgeniy restrict yourselves to the operations compartment and only the middle and lower levels. I'm sure you understand that there are classified systems and operations on this boat that I can't allow you to have access to. I don't want to put you on a leash and assign guards, so I'm relying on your word. The spaces are all manned around the clock, and my crew has been briefed. We understand each other?"

Leonid Pavlov waved his hands and nodded. "Of course, Captain. We understand. In the words of your James Bond, 'We could see it, but then, you would have to kill us.'" He laughed heartily. "Captain Walsh, we have no wish to die. Not after you pulled us out of the sea. Just think of the stories we will have for our grandchildren." He laughed again. "That is assuming either one of us can find a *Russkaya devushka* foolish enough to marry us."

2230 EST, 5 April 1983, COMSUBLANT, Norfolk, Virginia

Henri DuBois sat up and carefully looked around the room. For the last hour, he had been mindlessly typing away, filling out order forms for admin supplies. It was busywork that he could do with his eyes closed. But he needed to look like he was being harried and overworked, so every few minutes he would angrily rip the form out of the typewriter, ball it up, and fling it into the overflowing trash can. Then he would grab the phone and call a number for an office that he knew was empty. After listening to the phone ring for a few minutes, he would angrily slam it down and then start the whole show over again.

The last officer in the SCIF closed the file he had been studying and locked it away. He wished DuBois a good night and left the vault. At last DuBois had the place to himself. He carefully opened the Chief-of-Staff's Top Secret safe. The file he wanted was right in the front, just where Captain Strange had jammed it when he was getting ready to leave for the day an hour ago.

DuBois spread the file flat on his desk and carefully adjusted his desk light so that it raked across the paper. He pulled his Minox C camera from its hiding place in his sock. He had found that with this camera, a shutter speed of 1/250th of a second and a focus distance of forty centimeters worked best for these documents.

He took a deep breath to calm his nerves. No matter how many times he did this, controlling his shaking hands was always a problem. Any slight tremor would cause the photo to be blurred. He certainly didn't want to risk his life and freedom only to take a blurry picture. Finally calming the shaking, he worked through the entire document, all twenty pages, taking two pictures of each page just to be sure.

DuBois had just put the camera back in his sock and returned the file when the heavy steel SCIF door swung open.

"You still here, Henri?" Ted Strange asked as he walked into the secure space.

"Yes, sir," DuBois answered, absent-mindedly slipping into his native Cajun dialect. "*Droite finishing up and fixing to barrer up pour the night*, I mean I was just finishing up some admin and fixing to lock up for the night. Can I help you with something, Chief-of-Staff?"

Strange held up the Top Secret message board that he clutched in his hand. "Just need to lock this away. Sure glad I caught you before you locked up for the night. This SCIF is a pain in the ass to get opened after hours."

The pair walked out together. DuBois swung the door shut and spun the tumbler dials to engage the dual locks before he followed Strange down the long hallway toward the door.

DuBois headed out toward the parking lot, jumped in his car, and drove away. He had a two-hour drive to make it to the drop point to get rid of this film.

Ted Strange went up to his office and grabbed his phone. He dialed a number. When it was answered, he reported, "He bit. I'm betting Grey Mole is heading out to make the drop even as we speak."

18

0930 EST, 6 April 1983, COMSUBLANT, Norfolk, Virginia

Vice Admiral Rufus Brown sat at the head of the small conference table with Ted Strange on his right and Jay Lawton, the SUBLANT Operations Officer, on his left. The door to the SCIF conference room was shut and locked from the inside, with a guard outside to block anyone from intruding on the trio as they sat listening to the speaker of the red secure telephone. This was probably the most select conference call on the most secure phone line in the Western World. The line connected the National Military Command Center, deep in the bowels of the Pentagon, with SAC in Nebraska, COMSUBPAC in Pearl Harbor, and Brown's own OPCON in Norfolk.

"Gentlemen," the Secretary of Defense began the call, "I called you together this morning to make you aware of some rather disturbing intelligence that we have just uncovered. Colonel Murphy from the DIA will brief us."

"Thank you, Mr. Secretary. Gentlemen," a gruff voice replaced the Secretary's mellifluous Midwest accent, "our analysis has uncovered some recent movements by the Soviets that are raising considerable concern. We are seeing the Soviet Strategic Rocket Force generating significantly more deployments of their rail mobile and road mobile strategic missiles than normal. Additionally, we estimate that ten squadrons of Tu-95 Bear bombers and five squadrons of Tu-22 Backfire bombers are currently on strip alert, evenly distributed between air bases on the Kola Peninsula and bases in Far East Russia. Satellite imagery has been spotty, but we have not detected any unusual sorties from their *Delta-* or *Yankee*-class missile submarines or their one *Typhoon*. HUMINT sources are reporting a significant increase in tension. Additionally, they are reporting a general recall of military personnel from leave and rumors of an anticipated reserve call-up."

"Do you postulate any reasoning behind these developments? While our relationship has not exactly been cordial under détente, we haven't seen them saber-rattling in quite a while," Brown asked.

Colonel Murphy cleared his throat and answered, "Admiral, we can only guess at their reasoning and intentions. Our best guess is that this is an attempt to force our policies away from direct confrontation. Beyond that, we really do not want to venture a guess."

The Secretary of Defense picked up. "Couriers will be delivering hard copies of this information to you today. I have conferred with the Joint Chiefs, and we find this information very disturbing. Accordingly, we will be releasing an order to raise our readiness posture for all nuclear forces to DEFCON FOUR today. You can regard this as a warning order to start immediate preparations. Thank you."

The conference line went dead. Rufus Brown looked around the small room. "Well, damn, that came out of the blue! Jay, get your people briefed up and get the DEFCON 4 orders prepped. Ted, give the group commanders and squadron commodores a heads-up. And both of you, make real sure that you keep a tight lid on this. I don't want this to leak out and find ourselves out ahead of the Secretary in the press. Understood?"

2245Z, 6 April 1983, USS John Jay, *GIUK Gap*

It was a routine quiet evening for the *John Jay*'s wardroom. Darren Walsh and Stan Wilkins sat at the table, playing cribbage. Yevgeniy Grekov and Leonid Pavlov were finishing up their third bowl of popcorn. The two Russian fliers had developed a real appetite for American popcorn and American movies. Will Morris and Sam Lowe were busy rewinding the reels from the evening movie while Pete McKay and Dale Horton were arguing about the merits of the evening's entertainment, a particularly bad flick titled *The Last of the Wild Bunch*.

"Damn it, Eng," Horton complained. "I sat through a whole lot of really dusty scenery and sleeper of a plot just because you said there was skin in it. I'm demanding two punches on my hacker card."

McKay laughed as he reached over and smacked Horton on the arm. "Glad to give you two punches." He then shook his head. "I don't understand. I saw this flick last off-crew. There was skin in it. I would remember something like that. What happened to the skin?"

"Alert one! Alert one!" the 1MC blasted, interrupting the discussion. McKay and Morris crashed into each other at the door as they rushed out, closely followed by Dale Horton. All three rushed up the ladder and then ducked into the radio room.

Walsh waited for the melee to leave and then slowly stood. Looking over at the pair of Russians, he said, "Leonid, Yevgeniy, you two stay here with the Chop. Looks like we have business to attend to, probably just another drill." He and Wilkins followed the other three up the ladder to Ops upper level, then continued straight, on to the control room.

They had just stepped up onto the periscope stand when McKay and Horton charged in from radio holding a page of print.

"Captain," McKay said solemnly, "we have a properly formatted alertment message. Sir, this is not an exercise message." He handed the page to Walsh.

Walsh and Wilkins read the formatted message.

TOP SECRET -- SIOP
Fm: CTF 144
To: TF 144
Subj: Establish DEFCON FOUR
DTG: 2153Z, 06 APR, 1983
Ref: A. Op Plan 2134.6
BT

1. All units are advised that DEFCON FOUR is established. All units are directed to take actions to set DEFCON FOUR IAW Ref. A. All units are directed to review security posture and take appropriate actions. No change in ROE is authorized.
2. Disc: Heightened state of readiness warranted by increased activity from units of Soviet strategic forces.
3. No further dissemination of this information is authorized.

BT

Horton handed Wilkins a copy of the Op Plan, already open to the section for DEFCON FOUR. They read through the list of required actions. Most of the Op Plan actions were directed toward getting boats that weren't already on alert patrol ready as quickly as possible. And for heightened security around bases. Whole sections talked about Air Force bombers on strip alert, more communications systems being activated, and command center procedures. Not much changed for the *John Jay* other than realizing that the world was a whole lot more dangerous.

"Skipper," Wilkins reported, "*John Jay* is set for DEFCON FOUR." He hesitated for a second and then added, "We need to figure out what to do with our Russian guests. If things heat up any more, they could be a real problem."

Walsh nodded. "Just thinking the same thing. Not much chance that SUBLANT is going to order a HUMEVAC now. I don't want to lock them up. Tell the COB that I want a round-the-clock watch manned to escort them any time they are out of the wardroom."

Walsh then grabbed the 1MC microphone. "This is the Captain. We just received an alertment message that raises the DEFCON to DEFCON FOUR. I don't have much information on why, other than the Soviets have increased activity with their nuclear forces. It should not be something to lose sleep over. DEFCON FOUR is just a level of heightened alert and more security. It doesn't mean that missiles are about to fly. We are going to do what boomers do best. We are going to quietly sit out here and hide. Our job is to be ready if things get worse."

He put the mike down and turned to Wilkins. "XO, feel like another game of cribbage before we call it a day?"

0900Z, 7 April 1983, USS John Jay, *GIUK Gap*

Master Chief Max Steuben reached over and filled his crusty coffee cup from the goat locker coffeemaker. The COB bragged that his cup had not been washed since he first pinned his dolphins on in 1958 on an old *GUPPY II* diesel boat, and the layers of brown crud added validity to his claim.

Taking a healthy swig of the dark, bitter brew, he looked around the chiefs' quarters lounge and counted faces. The only chief missing was Isadore Braxton, the IC division leading chief. Steuben was not surprised. Izzy Braxton had a reputation for being late.

"Izzy was probably late for his own birth," Steuben harrumphed and took another swig. Might as well wait for the tardy chief. That way he wouldn't need to repeat himself.

The passageway door swung open. Izzy Braxton bounced in and tried unsuccessfully to burrow into a hidden corner behind Josh Rosecrans. "Sorry, COB," he blurted out. "Late getting a relief as Chief-of-the-Watch."

Steuben laid a baleful eye on Braxton, cleared his throat, and said, "Wasn't Harrison your relief? He is one of your people. I would expect that you could control your own division and work out your watch relief. Doesn't look like anyone else had a problem making this meeting."

Turning to the rest of the group, he continued, "Now that Izzy has graced us with his presence, we can begin. You all heard the skipper announce last night that we are now at DEFCON FOUR. Sounds really scary, and I am sure your troops are worried. The XO and I went over the instructions this morning. Really doesn't affect us a whole lot. Just increased emphasis to be ready. Don't suspect that we will be doing many engineering drills for a bit."

This brought smiles to the group.

"I want you to sit down with your troops and tell them that all this stuff means is that the Russians have made some moves that bother the brass hats in the Pentagon. DEFCON FOUR only means that we are keeping a closer eye on them. Nothing to worry about."

Josh Rosecrans interrupted Steuben, "COB, you ever been to DEFCON FOUR before?"

"Yep, twice that I recall. First time was when I was still on *Pickerel* back in '62," Steuben answered. "At the end of the Cuban Missile Crisis, we went from DEFCON THREE to FOUR as things wound down. Same thing in '73 during the Yom Kippur War. Went straight to THREE and then back to FOUR as things wound down."

"Well, that gives me a warm fuzzy," Braxton snorted.

Steuben stared at the IC chief for a second and then went on, "What I don't want is a bunch of shook-up sailors, so worried about things back home that they mess up. Talk to your guys, find out what they are thinking, and reassure them." He looked over at Braxton. "There is one final thing. The XO wants a round-the-clock guard on our Russian guests. That means an extra watch station we need to man. Izzy, you and your group of miscreants win the lottery."

Braxton started to protest, but Steuben held up his hand. "And, Izzy, I want your guys to stop with the practical jokes. We know who stole the XO's door. A little mouse told me that they are now planning to screw with the missile techs. No more. Understand?"

2100Z, 7 April 1983, Holy Loch, Scotland

The sun was just slipping behind Dalinlongart Hill, to the west of Dunoon, as the *Tigerfish* rounded Hunters Quay. As usual for early April, a gale-force wind blasted down the Holy Loch, churning up the confined waters and drenching the line handlers just laying topside. Several ball caps blew away and didn't hit the water until they were well on their way to Gourock, a couple of miles across the Firth of Clyde.

Roy Blivens drove the submarine up the Holy Loch beyond where the *USS Hunley*, the submarine tender, was anchored in the center of the Holy Loch. He swung the *Tigerfish* around until it was parallel with the tender and allowed the wind to drive the boat down toward the tender. He then used the main engines to stop and hold the boat alongside the tender. It took a minute to get lines fore and aft over from the tender and taken to the capstans. The two capstans made short work of snugging the submarine up against the tender. Blivens had to smile as he watched the COB, Mike Shaw, alternately cajoling and prodding the line-handler teams as spring lines and then the night riders were fed across and secured. The lines had just been doubled when the torpedo loading hatch swung open and the torpedo loading skid was raised up into position, ready to receive the first MOSS.

Roy Blivens made the long climb down from the bridge, descending into the control room to find what looked like bedlam. In the passageway just beyond his stateroom, both the upper- and middle-level decks had been removed, leaving a chasm all the way down to the torpedo room in lower level. The below-decks torpedo load-line had been set up as the submarine was coming up the Firth so that all would be ready immediately when the *Tigerfish* was tied up. With the load-line in place, the interior of the boat was essentially cut in half. There was no way to safely move fore and aft except to climb topside through the forward escape trunk and walk around, then drop down through the after escape trunk.

Roy Blivens climbed up through the forward escape trunk just in time to see the tender crane swing the first bright green MOSS over to the *Tigerfish*. He watched for a minute as it was lowered to the torpedo loading skid and then strapped to the loading tray before being lowered into the boat.

Satisfied that his crew had the load well in hand, Blivens walked up the gangway onto the *Hunley*. Finding himself in a machine shop, it took a few seconds to get oriented before he began climbing ladders up to the O-4 level and then forward to the squadron commodore's cabin.

He was surprised to find Ted Strange sitting there, sipping a cup of coffee. Strange looked up and smiled. "Welcome back, Roy. Fine bit of ship handling tying up. Looks like you have had an interesting run so far."

"You could say that. Interesting is the right word."

Blivens grabbed a cup of coffee from the pot sitting on the sideboard and joined Strange at the conference table. "I'm a little surprised to see you here. What brings the Chief-of-Staff out to the far reaches of his realm?"

Strange pulled a file out of his satchel and slid it across the table to Blivens. "This may help explain, a little," he answered with a smile.

Blivens glanced at the title and then read the abstract. "Is this 'active noise cancellation system' for real? Reads like it would make a boat disappear."

Ted Strange laughed. "We certainly want our Russian friends to think it's real. It looks like they heard a couple of those MOSS you shot. When they shut down, as far as the Russians were concerned, the target just disappeared. It wasn't very long before we started hearing rumblings from our Russian sources about a 'cloaking device' that those wily Americans were using."

"So that's the reason for the hurry-up in getting back here and reloading those MOSS," Blivens exclaimed. "Now I'm beginning to understand. But what I don't understand is how the Russians know where to look. They seemed to be lurking right at those tie-points just at the right time to intercept the boomer who is supposed to be coming through. Where are they getting that information?"

Strange looked around the empty stateroom, almost like he was making sure no one was listening. In a low voice, he said, "Roy, this is very close-hold. It looks like information is leaking out of SUBLANT somewhere. We think we have a spy. We are using him to feed bum dope to the Russians. So far, they are biting. Now we need you to feed them more bait. But, based on your last encounter, it looks like they are shooting first. Not very sporting of them. The boss wanted me to remind you of your rules of engagement.

Self-defense is authorized. If you think a Russian is shooting at you, you are to take him out. Don't use an exercise fish this time. Any questions?"

Roy Blivens shook his head. "No, sir. Sounds pretty clear to me."

Ted Strange pulled a sealed envelope out of his satchel. "Good. Here are your orders for the rest of this run. Open them once you are underway and submerged." He stood and offered his hand to Blivens. "Good luck and good hunting."

Blivens shook Strange's hand and then headed back down to the *Tigerfish*. The MOSS should be just about loaded by now. They needed to stow all the handling gear and get underway as soon as possible. He needed to be submerged off the Mull of Kintyre before sunrise. It promised to be a very long night.

19

2100Z, 10 April 1983, USS Tigerfish, *Norwegian Sea, 100 nm south of Jan Mayen Island*

QM-1 Eric Swarton marked the 2100Z estimated position on the chart. The little penciled *X* just touched a red circle drawn around a point in the ocean marked "TP-6." He looked from the nav plot and called out, "Nav, our EP plots twenty miles from tie-point six. Recommend we slow to patrol speed."

Tom Clemont, the Navigator on *Tigerfish* and the on-watch Officer-of-the-Deck, stepped around the periscope stand to where he could see the chart. Turning to the helmsman, he ordered, "Ahead two-thirds," while he was reaching for the 7MC microphone. "Maneuvering, Conn. Shift main coolant pumps to slow speed," he ordered.

As the boat slowed from its charge northward, Senior Chief Zwarlinski and his sonar team scoured the nearby seas for any sounds from another submarine. Other than the plaintiff grunts, groans, and barks of a horny male humpback whale looking for a mate, and the sea noise from a dying storm, the ocean was quiet. No sign that they shared this patch of water with anyone else. Zwarlinski started a tape of the whale to add to his ever-growing collection.

Clemont started a slow circle of the tie-point, always staying at least ten thousand yards away from that imaginary spot. Just slowly spiraling, watching and waiting. The *John Jay* was not scheduled to steam through the tie-point for another twenty-four hours, so it was not surprising that no one had slipped into the area to snoop around.

0930 MSK, 11 April 1983, Soviet Northern Fleet Headquarters, Murmansk, Russia

Fleet Admiral Dmitri Golubev listened quietly as Sergi Baranov, the Deputy Director of the GRU, flipped through the prints of an American document titled "Active Noise Cancellation System Operations." The prints were very obviously made from photographic film. The lighting and focus were not the best, but the text was readable. It looked like the work of someone trying to surreptitiously make a copy of a document, quickly, quietly, and without being detected.

"Admiral, our asset delivered this file less than a week ago," Baranov explained. "As you can see, it would appear that Comrade Captain Novikov was correct. The Americans do have a *maskiruyuscheye ustroystvo*, a cloaking device. Our best engineers have reviewed this paper and have determined that the concept is valid. They do stipulate that the computer processing would need to be very complex and near instantaneous for the system to work. Otherwise, it would broadcast a very strong signal out into the water, making the submarine very detectable rather than invisible. This *maskiruyuscheye ustroystvo* is well beyond our current capabilities, and the best assessment was that it was beyond the West's abilities as well. But that seems to be an incorrect estimate."

The pair flipped through pages covered with complex vector diagrams and incomprehensible equations. Finally Golubev removed his reading glasses, grabbed a cloth, and started to rub them clean. "Sergi, this Active Noise Cancellation System seems to require a tremendous amount of electrical power. And some very careful synchronization. Is it possible that these are the reasons the Americans seem to operate without the system and only turn it on at these so-called 'tie-points'?"

Baranov nodded. "That is a possibility that we are investigating. We think that the 'tie-point' may mark the initiation of something more. Perhaps they cloak at the tie-point before going off to do something else."

"Like what?" Golubev grunted.

"We don't know, but we are working to find out."

Golubev rubbed his chin. "My friend, I fear that this new American toy has upset the careful balance that we have developed over the years. If they can really make their ballistic missile submarines disappear, they could move in close to our coastline to launch a devastating surprise first strike. The first warning we would have would be nuclear warheads falling on the *Rodina*, the motherland."

Baranov nodded. "That very fact is being considered in the Kremlin. Remember, only last month the American president, that cowboy, announced what he called the American Strategic Defense Initiative. The Kremlin fears that the Americans are working toward winning a nuclear war. They have abandoned their so-called MAD policy. They are calling us the 'evil empire' and mean to destroy us."

"If that is the case, I worry for our children's and grandchildren's future," Golubev responded. "I never liked the mutually assured destruction idea, but at least we could count on sane men making responsible decisions. It appears that is no longer the case."

"*Da*, our engineers and scientists will struggle valiantly to defeat these new weapons," Baranov stated. "But I fear that they may not have the time before the Americans strike. Our only hope may be an immediate first strike before the Americans are ready. This is what the Secretariat is discussing even as we speak. Comrade, I urge you to move the Northern Fleet to a full war footing. I fear that we will be at war before summer."

1230 MSK, 11 April 1983, K-324, Norwegian Sea, 100 nm south of Jan Mayen Island

Dmitri Vinogradov stood in the control room of the *Victor III*–class nuclear submarine *K-324* and watched as the submarine slowly circled. Their orders had specified that *K-324* be at this location at precisely 1230 Moscow Standard Time today and to search the area for twenty-four hours. Just as Comrade Captain Novikov had directed, he had arrived on time and slowed the submarine to begin a careful search. Vinogradov ordered that the *Barrakuda* towed passive sonar array be deployed from the hydrodynamically shaped pod atop the *K-324*'s rudder and the *MGK-503 Skat-KS* sonar suite to be fully manned. With the *SOKS* non-acoustic wake detector system on the submarine's sail energized and the towed array listening, the *K-324* was ready to find any American submarine that was foolish enough to venture anywhere near them. This time he would be ready and would find the Americans before they could turn on their cloaking device.

Vinogradov prowled the control room, looking over the shoulders of his *michmen* as they stared at their screens and fine-tuned their instruments. The atmosphere was heavy with silent tension. The Americans had beaten them four times already, and Vinogradov had made it very clear that a fifth time was not going to happen while he was in charge.

Captain Second Rank Boris Novikov put down the report he was reading and glanced at the clock that hung on the outboard bulkhead of his tiny stateroom. It was time for him to check on the watch section and to see that all was in order to finally catch the Americans. He placed the report back on his desk and slowly rose. It was only a couple of steps out to the submarine's control room, but there was no urgency. If anything important was happening, Dmitri Vinogradov would have summoned him.

Novikov had just stepped into the control room when the emergency announcing system blasted, "Fire! Fire in the fifth compartment! Fire in the switchboards!" The alarm blasted for a few seconds. Then the announcement, "An emergency shutdown of the reactor has been completed."

Novikov shouted, "Isolate the fifth compartment! Initiate fire suppression in the fifth compartment!"

The *Nachal'nik Vakhty*, the Chief-of-the-Watch, flipped one of the switches in a row on his panel, replying, "The fifth compartment is isolated." Then he flipped another switch that flooded the compartment with freon gas to suffocate any fire in there.

Vinogradov protested, "Captain, there are men in the compartment. Give them time to evacuate."

Novikov replied without hesitation, "Comrade Vinogradov, the men were trained to evacuate immediately. If they are slow, they will die. Better a few men than the entire submarine. Now, get the *K-324* to periscope depth and start the diesel." He glanced at his watch. "It will be five minutes before you can send men back into the fifth compartment."

Vinogradov used the little forward momentum that the submarine still had to plane up to the surface. When the last of the momentum was used, he ordered that ballast water be pumped overboard from the trim tanks to lift them toward the surface and that the slow-speed spinner propellers on each stern plane be energized. The tiny electric motors could drive the submarine forward at one or two knots. They were useful when the sub needed to be very quiet or when the reactor wasn't dumping steam into the main turbines. They provided a little forward speed, but not nearly enough to make the sub manageable in a heavy winter sea.

It was futile to try to stay at periscope depth. The seas grabbed the submarine and flung it to the surface, where it bobbed helplessly. By the time the crew started the emergency diesel generator, the fire was extinguished, and the fifth compartment air temperature had returned to normal. Nothing was visible through the tiny dead-man viewing window. Heavy smoke obscured anything inside the compartment. Men with emergency air-breathing systems rushed in to make sure that the fire was out and to evacuate the men who had been trapped. Miraculously, only five men had been trapped, but none of them survived. With the compartment opened, the diesel made short work of ventilating it with clean sea air and discharging the smoke and freon overboard.

It took the crew a little over an hour to restart the reactor. With extensive fire damage to a couple of switchboards, Novikov was ordered to point the *K-324* north, back toward Mother Russia.

1015Z, 11 April 1983, USS **Tigerfish***, Norwegian Sea, 100 nm south of Jan Mayen Island*

ST-1 Stan White held the headphones tightly to his ears. Something weird was happening with Sierra One-Seven-Six. They had detected their old friend, the Soviet *Victor III*, at the beginning of his watch, and followed it as it sneaked into the area around TP-6. Same shaft rub that they had heard before. The guy was predictable. Always seemed to show up twelve hours before the scheduled rendezvous time, then sneak in real slow like while circling the tie-point. Probably thought that he was so stealthy that he was invisible, but Stan White had him dead to rights.

Everything had been going real smooth. They had detected the guy when he first arrived and then maneuvered around him for a bit, just to make sure they had a handle on what Sierra One-Seven-Six was doing. Now the *Tigerfish* was settled in a safe six thousand yards back on Sierra One-Seven-Six's port quarter, just watching and waiting.

White sat up and said, "Chief, One-Seven-Six is going bonkers. I'm hearing all kindsa crap from him."

Senior Chief Zwarlinski grabbed a spare headset dangling down from the overhead and listened for a second before he reached for the 21MC mike. "Conn, Sonar, Skipper, One-Seven-Six is having some sort of problem. He's slowed way down. Looks like all-stop, and I'm hearing all kindsa transients. Sounds like alarms and hatches slamming. But we lost the shaft rub, so I don't think he's on the main engines." He held the headset tight against his ears. "Skipper, he is coming shallow."

Blivens's voice came back over the 21MC. "Sonar, Conn, aye. Senior, get this on tape."

"Yes, sir. You got it."

Tigerfish slowly circled the Russian submarine, staying six thousand yards away from where the boat bobbed on the surface.

"Skipper, One-Seven-Six has commenced snorkeling. He definitely has a problem," Zwarlinski reported.

Roy Blivens turned to Bill Andrews, the Officer-of-the-Deck, and said, "Weps, let's get to periscope depth. I want to see what is happening with our Russian friend. Let's stay outside six thousand yards. We know he has a tendency to shoot first and ask questions later."

As Bill Andrews was bringing the sub up to periscope depth, Blivens turned to George Sanders. "XO, get into radio and draft up a message to SUBLANT. Tell them what we are hearing and ask them to get a P-3C out here to monitor. We don't know if One-Seven-Six will need assistance or not, but we will be standing by."

The *Tigerfish* came up to a gray, heaving winter sea. The Russian sub, only three miles away, was invisible in the pitching, tossing waves.

20

1705Z, 12 April 1983, **USS** John Jay, *GIUK Gap*

Darren Walsh was exploring lower-level missile compartment. He liked to explore every compartment on the *John Jay* at least weekly. His explorations weren't a simple walk-through of the space. A nuclear submarine, particularly a boomer, had a lot of out-of-the-way, hard-to-get-to spaces. He climbed into the overheads or down into the bilges, poked around in frame bays, and squeezed behind switchboards. It was all an effort to really know his boat, to know its condition, and make sure that there were no hidden surprises. The officers and crew were familiar with Walsh's explorations and worked to make sure that they found and corrected any hidden surprises before the skipper did. And, in the process, they got to know the boat better.

He slipped down into the bilge alongside the gas generator for missile tube twelve. The gas generator was really a rocket motor bolted to the missile tube with its exhaust aimed to dump into a chamber under the missile. When the missile was launched, the gas generator ignited, pouring a flood of hot exhaust gas under the missile. The missile was then shoved up to the surface by the gases while it was also enveloped in a cloud of those same gases. The missile never got wet in its journey to the sea surface, where its own rocket motor ignited and thrust it up into space. But right now, each gas generator was just a maze of piping around the base of its missile tube.

Walsh climbed around the piping, finding a crescent wrench and a couple of screw drivers lying in the bilge. More tools for his growing collection. The chiefs' quarters knew to ask the skipper when they ran low on tools. He probably had the wrench they needed in his collection.

Then he looked up. Something looked different about the underside of the deck grating between tube ten and tube twelve. He climbed through the bilge until he could clearly see it. Chuckling to himself, he carefully retraced his path and emerged out of the bilge.

Walsh glanced at his wristwatch, the Seiko that Joy had given him for Christmas. It was ten minutes until dinner. He climbed up out of lower-level missile compartment, up the ladder all the way to upper level, and then forward through control. He stopped for just a second, observing the watch standers, before heading to his stateroom. He stuck his head in the XO's door. Stan Wilkins was just closing a report before heading to the wardroom for dinner.

Walsh smiled as he said, "XO, you might want to take a tour of lower-level missile compartment. Make sure you climb down between missile tubes ten and twelve. I suggest that you carefully inspect the underside of the deck grating down there. You might find it interesting. Take a couple of missile techs with you. They can help carry your door back. Anyway, it's Halfway Night. Let's get dinner and then steel ourselves for the celebration."

Halfway Night, signifying that the patrol was half-finished, was a time for celebration on the *John Jay*. The crew would perform skits, normally ribald and suitable only for submariners. Those with musical talent, however meager, might be induced to perform. There was a "beauty contest" and several raffles. Gambling was forbidden on board, but the money raised by the Halfway Night raffles went directly to a ship's recreation fund for post-deployment activities like family picnics. The most popular ones were to choose someone to perform the dirtiest, grossest mess crank duty for the evening, manning the deep sink to initially scrape and spray off the dishes before they went into the sanitizer. The other popular event was to raffle cream pies to be squashed into an unsuspecting victim's face.

The pair walked into the wardroom together. Bob Shippley and Brett Burns stood at the foot of the table, carrying broad, conspiratorial grins across their faces. Stan Wilkins was just too curious to refrain from asking, "Nav, Weps, which one of you two Cheshire cats ate the canary?"

Weps grinned even wider and answered, "Eng won the raffle. He's the Halfway Night Mess Crank. Cookie has him manning the deep sink."

Wilkins shook his head. "I thought you two were leading that raffle. Neck and neck last time I heard, a hundred bucks ahead of the Eng. He was a real dark horse."

"Yeah, that's what everyone thought," Nav chuckled. "It's amazing what a couple of hundred bucks can do at the last minute. Judicious and timely bet placement and the dark horse surges to the lead at the wire. Stick your head in the scullery and you'll see our quiet, unassuming Engineer at his finest."

"Gentlemen, let's eat, and then we can go down to the mess decks," Walsh said as he sat down.

The meal proceeded uneventfully. Walsh carefully folded his napkin and slid it into its ring before standing. "Shall we see what the crew has dreamed up?"

As the officers walked out of the wardroom, Faris and Brimley met them, pushing cream pies into both the Weps's and Nav's faces. Then they handed the two notes before disappearing back to the mess decks.

Wiping the whipped cream from his eyes, Shippley read his note.
Two can play at this game. I only paid twenty-five for these pies.
Love from the deep sink,
Eng

1800 EST, 12 April 1983, Goose Creek, South Carolina

Joy Walsh turned onto the unfamiliar street lined with new homes still under construction. Tall Pines was a sprawling new neighborhood, situated alongside a freeway giving easy access to the Navy base and to downtown Charleston. It was being built to house the burgeoning population created by the expanding military presence in the Low Country. But right now, the new construction meant more half-finished houses and new streets to get lost on every time she ventured over here.

Joy pulled to the curb and read the driving directions that she had scratched on a notepad.

Exit I-26 onto College Park Road – Check.

Left onto the Frontage Road – Check.

Right onto Eastern White Pines Road – Check.

Right onto Ponderosa Pines Drive – Check.

Now what? She saw nothing but houses under construction on a muddy, unpaved road. Where were the street signs? She was supposed to make a right onto Pinecone Way. Where was it? She eased the car forward, skirting a pothole, before coming to an unmarked intersection.

Joy Walsh admitted to herself that she was lost. The instructions didn't say anything about this. Mentally flipping a coin, Joy turned right and headed down the street, trusting her luck. The unmarked road curved around to the left and then, a block down, she was back on a paved street sporting new brick bungalows on either side.

There was Pinecone Way. Luck was with her this evening. Turning onto the street, she saw that parked cars lined both sides. 410 Pinecone Way was the fourth house on the block, but she had to drive past two more houses before she found an empty parking space. She eased the Ford van into the space and walked back to 410, enjoying the warm evening breeze.

Camille Steuben's living room was crowded with wives. Some were seated on the couch or several chairs arranged around the room, nibbling on pastries and sipping coffee. Joy found a crowd in the kitchen, enjoying glasses of wine. She decided that a glass of chardonnay would be nice and poured herself one.

"Excuse me, Miss Joy." Annie May Faris was standing nervously, crumbling a cookie. "I wanted to thank ya'll fer helpin' me out. Miss Camille done got me enrolled fer my GED. The other wives is helpin' me get groceries and getting me to my doctor's appointments."

Joy Walsh smiled and answered, "Annie May, the wives have to stick together and help each other when the men are out. That's what it means to be part of a submarine crew. What did the doctor have to say?"

Annie May smiled and rubbed her tummy. "He said I was pregnant fer sure. Best he could figger, I was four ta five months along. He said everthin' looked normal." She suddenly gulped and looked startled.

"You okay?" Joy Walsh asked.

"That felt funny," Annie May responded. "I think the baby just kicked."

2355 EST, 12 April 1983, NAVELEX Compound, North Charleston, South Carolina

Leland Samson hated the night shift at the big NAVELEX compound. He would far rather be sitting on his back porch, nursing a beer and listening to the night sounds from the marshes. His little place over on Horlbeck Creek wasn't exactly his mama's place up by Pawley's Island, but the night sounds were the same, and the sweet grass growing in the marsh was almost as fine as the pliant stems his mama used in the traditional sea-islands weaving technique. The baskets that his wife wove were very popular with the tourists in the old City Market. They added a little extra spending money, and she enjoyed the ancient craft.

Henri DuBois had insisted that he take the night shift at NAVELEX for the next couple of months. The Cajun up Norfolk way was *heet-yed*, but his money was good. Samson tried his best to stay on DuBois's good side, so here he was, cooped up in his office and not out net casting for shrimp in the marsh. And with the bare sliver of a crescent moon, his Coleman lantern would attract shrimp like a magnet, a full net with every cast and some fine shrimp and grits for *day startah*.

The phone on his desk buzzed. Samson grabbed the receiver and said, "Hello, *dis yah* Leland Samson."

Henri DuBois's voice boomed through the phone. "Leland, let's be quick. I have a job that I want you to hire out and oversee. We need the package from that Walsh woman's house. You screwed it up last time. This time, hire some local yokels and break in. Kidnap her and the brats if you have to. But find the box and make sure that there are no witnesses. I want it done within the week. Understand?"

Samson started to protest but realized he was talking to a dial tone. The Cajun spy had hung up.

He stared at the phone for a few seconds before putting it back in its cradle. He rubbed his temples. His head was pounding with a tremendous headache. What was he going to do? DuBois had his hooks way too deeply embedded to just turn away and ignore him. He had been on the spy's payroll for too many years and had fed him too much incriminating information. If he turned on DuBois now, the best he could expect would be to spend the rest of his life in some maximum-security federal prison staring at a cement block wall. No more sunrises over his beloved marshes, no more tangy salt breezes. Just a lonely cell.

He cradled his head in his hands. Prison was the best possible outcome. More likely, someone would find his body floating facedown in the Cooper River. Henri DuBois played for keeps.

He slapped his fists down onto his desk. Kidnapping and murdering an innocent woman and her *pickney*, children, was something that he just couldn't do. Samson stood up and paced around. He headed out and down the long hallway toward the door. He would have to think of something. He had seven days to come up with a plan.

0300 MSK, 13 April 1983, Soviet Northern Fleet Headquarters, Murmansk, Russia

Fleet Admiral Dmitri Golubev stood by the window where he could look down on the piers. He fingered the newly arrived report from the Okolnaya submarine support base saying that missile load-out was completed on the *TK-208*, called a *Typhoon* by the West, with twenty R-39 Rif ballistic missiles loaded in her launch tubes. The mammoth submarine had just departed Guba Okolnaya, heading out to the patrol bastion. *TK-208* was the last of the strategic missile submarines able to answer the emergency deployment order.

One *Delta I*–class boat, the *K-279*, had experienced a reactor casualty and could not leave the pier. The *K-279* joined the two *Yankee*-class boats that were also unable to deploy. The *Yankees*' R-31 ballistic missiles were too short in range to threaten the US while the subs were tied up, but they could still hold Western Europe at risk. *K-279* was an entirely different matter. Her R-29 missiles could easily reach their assigned targets in the US while she was tied up to the pier.

Golubev's masters in Moscow might not be happy that three of his submarines were unable to seek the protection of the Arctic ice, but Golubev calculated that counting the *Typhoon* and eighteen *Delta* submarines in the icy bastion, plus the four *Yankee*s out in the Atlantic, he had deployed over three hundred nuclear-tipped missiles aimed at the heart of America. Even the foolhardiest saber-rattling American politician would pause at ordering a nuclear strike knowing that utter destruction from these missiles would be the result.

Admiral Golubev shook himself and stared out the window. The valiant Northern Fleet was sortieing away from the piers of Murmansk. They would form the battle line that defended Golubev's Arctic missile submarine bastion from the American aircraft carriers and attack submarines. The mighty *Kirov*, the world's only nuclear-powered battlecruiser, slipped her moorings and backed away from the pier. Two smaller *Slava* cruisers followed the *Kirov* down the fjord toward the open Barents Sea. Dozens of destroyers were steaming away from various piers along the Murmansk Fjord.

Golubev longed to feel the sea swell under his feet once again, but he knew that his place was here in the Northern Fleet command center where he could oversee the operation of all of these ships and submarines. He took a sip of tea and formulated his fleet orders in his mind. The fleet would form an impenetrable barrier from Norway's North Cape north to the ice edge at Svalbard, six hundred kilometers of Soviet steel and muscle. If only the Americans gave him enough time to get his ships in place.

21

0335Z, 13 April 1983, USS **Tigerfish**, *Norwegian Sea, 100 nm south of Jan Mayen Island*

George Sanders paced the tiny space between the fire control computers and the periscope stand. As usual, he was the midwatch Command Duty Officer, overseeing the crew while Roy Blivens slept. It promised to be a quiet night watching Sierra One-Seven-Six, the stricken Soviet submarine.

Bill Andrews, the OOD, had his eye glued to the eyepiece on the number two periscope. Sanders glanced over at the perivis monitor. A video camera in the Type 18 periscope fed the perivis monitor so that Sanders could see what Andrews was looking at out the periscope. The monitor was one of the few things illuminating the darkened control room and even it was dimmed down and covered with red plexiglass. Sanders could just make out the grainy black-and-white image of Sierra One-Seven-Six on the TV monitor. With no moon on a dark night, the Russian submarine was little more than a darker smudge against a dark background.

Sanders looked over at the solution on the Mark-117 fire control system console. Sierra One-Seven-Six was still on a course of zero-seven-zero at three knots. The Soviet submarine had been very slowly heading east since it popped to the surface two days ago. At this rate, it would take two weeks for it to return to Mother Russia. Sanders had to feel for the poor sailors on the stricken sub, stuck bobbing like a cork on a damaged boat steaming through a choppy sea. Not fun.

"Conn, Radio, request you raise the BRA-34 to copy the 0340 SSIX broadcast," the 21MC blared. Without pulling his eye away from the scope, Andrews reached out to grab the 21MC microphone and answered, "Radio, Conn, BRA-34 coming up." He then ordered, "Chief-of-the-Watch, raise number one BRA-34."

Seconds later, the 21MC announced, "Conn, Radio, ZBO onboard. One new message of interest." The SSIX, or Submarine Satellite Information Exchange, was a satellite-based digital UHF communications system for rapid and secure submarine communications. Although capable of two-way communications, submarines normally just copied whatever messages that SUBLANT sent them. They only sent outgoing messages if absolutely necessary. The ZBO was a listing of messages on the broadcast. The submarine would wait around only to copy messages addressed to them.

"All traffic onboard. Lowering the BRA-34 from radio. Request the Command Duty Officer come to radio."

George Sanders headed back to the radio room and read the new message fresh off the printer. He took the message board and knocked on Roy Blivens's door before sticking his head in to find the skipper just rousing. "What you got, XO?"

"Skipper, just got the 0340 broadcast onboard," Sanders replied. "We received an OPORD change. We're relieved from hopping around those tie-points. We're to trail Sierra One-Seven-Six back to the Barents. If we detect any missile boat activity, we are to report immediately and then switch to trailing them. OPORD has new areas assigned. Haven't plotted them yet."

Blivens swung his legs down to the deck and sat up. "Okay, XO. You go and get them plotted. Get the boat headed in the right direction. I'll get dressed and be out in a minute."

Sanders headed forward just in time to hear Stan White over the 21MC, "Conn, Sonar, possible contact zig, Sierra One-Seven-Six. Increasing bearing rate and we are detecting the shaft rub again. Looks like he is back on the main engines."

"Lost visual on Sierra One-Seven-Six," Bill Andrews announced. "Looks like he's gone deep." Andrews reached up into the overhead and grabbed the periscope control ring to lower it. "Dive. Make your depth one-five-zero feet, all ahead two-thirds. Rig control for red."

Tigerfish slipped back down into the deep and moved to stalk the now submerged Russian submarine.

1015 EST, 13 April 1983, Goose Creek, South Carolina

Joy Walsh had just finished the breakfast dishes and was wiping down the counter when the phone rang. She didn't recognize the deep, booming male voice, but the accent sounded a lot like the Gullah ladies down at the market where she bought baskets.

"Mis Walsh, ya ain know me, but I da call fuh warn ya. Bad foke da lookin' fuh one package ya got. Dey gonna bresk een yuh house fuh tek um. Dey wan fuh hurt ya. Ya need fuh git from yah quick and hide somewhere safe."

The line went dead before she could even ask the caller to repeat the message. She wasn't exactly sure what he had said, but she understood enough to be scared. She caught the word "package" and sort of got the gist that someone was planning to break into her house to steal it. And that they, whoever "they" were, planned to hurt her and that she needed to run. A shiver of dread ran down her back as she looked out into the empty backyard. She could almost see the pair of thugs that had tried to break in a month ago. Her hand started shaking so badly that she dropped the phone when she tried to hang it back on the wall.

Joy sat at the kitchen table, put her head in her hands, and tried to think. What was she going to do? She had to get Sam and Pug someplace safe, but where? Maybe her parents' farm, back in Ohio? No, that would only put her parents in danger, and she would have to drive all the way to Ohio.

In desperation, Joy grabbed the phone and dialed Ted Strange's number. The submarine force had caused this problem. They could fix it.

Ted Strange answered his phone on the second ring. "SUBLANT Chief-of-Staff. This is not a secure line. Captain Strange."

"Captain, this is Joy Walsh. I need help and I need it now!" Joy was almost hysterical.

"Calm down," Strange said soothingly. "Tell me what the problem is and what you need."

Through the tears, Joy Walsh described the threatening phone call, something about breaking in to steal a package. The only package she knew anything about was the birthday present that Darren had left for her to open on her birthday. It was sitting, all wrapped up, on a shelf in the office.

The line went silent. Joy was at the point where she thought they had been disconnected and was about to hang up when Ted Strange came back on the line. "Mrs Walsh, the local police are on the way. They should be there in a few minutes. They will stay with you until NIS gets there."

She could faintly hear the sirens in the distance as she thanked Strange and said goodbye.

1130 EST, 13 April 1983, SUBLANT Compound, Norfolk, Virginia

Henri DuBois was nervous. Something didn't feel right. He couldn't quite put his finger on it, but something, some subtle difference, was prodding his inner sense of danger. Maybe it was the tension with the world situation. It seemed that everyone, all his office mates, were much more diligent. Maybe it was when he realized that the spying game was now a lot more serious. In wartime, spies were shot, not traded across some European border crossing. Whatever it was, his senses were screaming that he needed to run, and run now.

DuBois forced himself to appear calm as he grabbed his hat and coat. The only thing he took from his desk was the tiny Minox camera, which he slipped into his pocket. The roll of film in the camera had images of the latest effective crypto key lists. Those were just too valuable a bargaining chip with his Soviet masters to leave behind. They would help ensure a luxurious, if quiet, retirement somewhere behind the Iron Curtain.

Mumbling to the Marine guard about getting lunch at the CINCLANT

Compound cafeteria, DuBois left the bleak cement pile of NH-95 and the SUBLANT headquarters for the last time. He walked toward the cafeteria but then circled around the block to scurry to his car. Leaving the Norfolk Navy base complex, he hit traffic on Interstate 64.

He stopped at his house only long enough to grab some clothes and the satchel full of cash. Over the years, he figured that he had squirreled away somewhere north of a million dollars in that leather satchel, stashed and ready for an emergency just like this one. That, and another couple of million in numbered offshore accounts, was his retirement plan. If he needed to, he could simply disappear to some South Pacific Island. They spoke French in Tahiti. That sounded good, but the French had extradition treaties with the US.

He entered the traffic flow back on I-64, but northbound this time. Traffic ground to a halt when he hit the Hampton Roads Bridge Tunnel. He suffered terrible visions of the FBI dragging him out of the car while he was trapped in the tunnel.

By the time he had driven through Newport News, DuBois knew what he needed to do. It was time to call the emergency contact number and institute the escape plan. He pulled off the freeway and into a gas station. The pay phone was outside, right next to the restroom door. He fumbled with his pocket change, then dialed the memorized number.

The phone was answered on the second ring. "Yes."

DuBois stammered nervously as he answered, "This is Henri. *Ah got dat feelin' dey done caught onto me, cher*. We need to implement the *plan d'echappement*."

DuBois was expecting to be told to race to the Soviet embassy in Washington or to an airport where tickets would be waiting. He was very surprised when he was directed to drive down to an address on Johns Island, just south of Charleston. He had no idea what kind of escape he could be making from that marshy sea island, but he would be told where to go from there once he arrived. And to take the back roads, staying off the interstate. DuBois wasn't sure if the "voice" was merely being cautious or if they expected trouble. It didn't really matter. He was worried enough for both of them.

DuBois fished his old Colt Cobra .38 revolver from its hiding place under the spare tire in the Dodge's trunk. It would ride next to him on the front seat for the rest of this trip. He eased out of the gas station, onto US 17. The two-lane highway would take him all the way to Charleston while winding through every little town all the way down the coast. He was anonymously safe as long as he watched the speed limits and the feds didn't issue an APB for him. The local cops were too busy grabbing speeding tourists and drunk college kids on spring break to bother with a beat-up old Dodge steadily making its way south.

2010 MSK, 13 April 1983, K-314, 100 kilometers east of Charleston, South Carolina

The *Victor III*–class Soviet nuclear submarine *K-314* was making random circles, maneuvering to avoid the coastal traffic and fishing boats that littered the crowded waters one hundred kilometers off the South Carolina coast. Captain Second Rank Ilya Agapov was way past bored. They had spent the last two weeks in these warm shallow waters, steaming in endless, mindless circles. His orders were explicit and hadn't changed. He was to keep his submarine within a hundred kilometers of the American coastline off the city of Charleston. He was to stay here until ordered otherwise. And, most importantly, he was to expend every effort to remain undetected. Avoid any contact with American ships and practice absolute radio silence. No messages back home under any circumstances.

So far, he had been successful. None of the freighters and barges moving up and down the coast had spied the submarine. He had avoided the few warships that he had seen racing in and out of the busy port city. It had been all too easy. The Americans were amazingly lax about their security. No one was looking for a submarine lurking just off their beaches.

Agapov looked at the clock hanging on the control room's forward bulkhead. It was 2010 MSK, time to go to periscope depth and copy the submarine broadcast. Maybe there would be new orders, possibly ordering them home, or even better, a port call in Havana. Agapov knew he was dreaming. If there were any messages for the *K-314* at all, they would be useless administrative taskings to prepare reports of his crew's political reliability to be submitted immediately upon return to port.

Turning to Anatoly Balakirev, the current watch officer, he ordered, "*Vakhtennyy Ofitser* Balakirev, take the submarine to periscope depth and copy the broadcast. Use the passive sonar only." Normal practice, particularly in areas where there was considerable surface traffic, was to use the active sonar to search out the area and make sure it was safe to come up. But this was hardly a normal area. This was the Americans' front yard. If they energized their active search sonar, every American Navy ship within a hundred miles would hear the *K-314*. They would be at the very center of a massive ASW search. Better to risk the slight possibility of bumping into some small fishing boat.

The *K-314* angled up. Anatoly Balakirev raised the periscope. A big bear of a man, the watch officer seemed to envelop the periscope as he peered out its optics and danced a slow circle. Agapov watched the depth gauge as they ascended. When it leveled off at eighteen meters, he knew that the periscope was out of the water and Balakirev should be gazing at blue skies as he made his slow clockwise circles.

Suddenly Balakirev stopped his circling and then swung back a little. He flipped the optics to high power and then said, "Comrade Captain, you need to look at this."

Ilya Agapov put his eye to the periscope and found that he was staring at an American submarine running on the surface. He quickly estimated that it was about three thousand meters away. As it swung around so that it was broad to him, Agapov could clearly see a missile deck. It was an American missile submarine, one of their *Lafayette* class, probably heading out on patrol.

"Sonar, do you have any contact on bearing three-four-seven?" Agapov growled. How could an American submarine, even if they were known to be very quiet, get so close without *K-314* detecting it?

Agapov could almost hear the scurrying in the sonar room as they trained their passive flank array sonar to the bearing he had given them. Was it guilt or fear that he heard in the sonar *michman*'s voice when he reported, "Captain, we have a passive contact on that bearing. We had classified it as a distant merchantman."

Agapov roared, "*Nekompetentnyy* idiot! That is an American submarine, and he is only three thousand meters away. How can you let him get so close? Were you sleeping in there?"

The American submarine steamed right on past the *K-314* without any sign that they had detected the Soviet boat lurking beneath the surface. Agapov watched intently as the missile boat slowed and then huge plumes of mist blew up from around the bow and the stern. It slowly sank lower in the water until the long missile deck was awash and then the sail dipped below the surface. He realized that he had just watched it dive and that he was in the perfect position to slip in behind and trail it. It would be a tremendous coup to trail an American missile boat from the first day of its patrol. It was the chance of a lifetime dropped in his lap.

But then Agapov reluctantly remembered his orders. He turned away and headed back toward the coast while the American slipped out to sea. He needed to get away to send a message back to Murmansk to warn them.

Vakhtennyy Ofitser Balakirev protested, "But *Kapitan...*"

"Orders, Anatoly. We must follow our orders."

0220 EST, 14 April 1983, Mount Pleasant, South Carolina

Henri DuBois eased off the road, into the all-night convenience store's well-lit parking lot. He bought a bag of chips and a Coke to ease the gnawing in his stomach before feeding a quarter into the outside pay phone. He dialed Leland Sampson's phone number, but the voice answering his call didn't have the familiar Gullah accent. In fact, it sounded more like a Yale accent.

DuBois immediately hung up. The strange voice could only mean that Samson had been caught. But where was the package? Had he managed to retrieve it before he was caught? Did the FBI have it already? What about the Walsh woman? Too many questions. But one thing was clear. He had to figure out where the package was and how to get it. There was no way that he was leaving the country without it safely tucked under his arm.

DuBois made a second phone call. This time the heavy Southern accent was exactly what he expected. If Leland Samson couldn't do the job, these people could. Way more ruthless and violent than the Gullah spy, the Anderson boys specialized in armed robberies and hurting anyone who got in their way.

He pulled out of the parking lot and eased back onto US 17. It was a short ten-minute drive over the Cooper River Bridge into Charleston and then another twenty minutes up Rivers Avenue to his destination.

22

0430 EST, 14 April 1983, Goose Creek, South Carolina

Leland Samson sat in the car. He parked in the back of the Baptist church parking lot, around the corner and down the street from the Walshes' cul-de-sac. He figured that the big live oak tree would conceal the car better than parking out on the street, and, even if it was spotted, no one would question a car left in the back corner of a church parking lot.

He didn't really care that Amos and Willie had to walk a couple of blocks. He had no idea what their last names were and didn't want to know. They were just two toughs that he had picked up from a dive bar off Spruill Avenue, not too bright and willing to do just about anything for a few bucks. He figured that it would take about an hour for the two dimwits to break into the Walsh house, steal the package, and sneak back to the parking lot. Hopefully the Walsh woman was smart enough to run when he warned her. If not, then she would suffer for not listening.

Samson glanced at his watch. Amos and Willie had been gone for half an hour. He heard loud pops that sounded like gunshots. The pair weren't carrying guns as far as he knew. Something was up, and it didn't sound good. He reached for the ignition. It was time to leave. Amos and Willie were on their own.

Samson was jolted when he heard the tapping on his window. He looked over to see the business end of an automatic and a badge. He switched off the ignition and raised his hands above the steering wheel. Leland Samson's career as a spy was finished.

Henri DuBois had just pulled into the housing development when he saw the flashing police lights down the street. The whole area was alive with police cruisers. The cul-de-sac was blocked off with a crowd standing outside the Walsh house. He could just make out Mrs. Walsh standing on the lawn as he eased by. Then he saw another crowd of cops in the church parking lot. They had someone in handcuffs, marching him to a wagon. Leland Samson's tall figure was unmistakable. DuBois eased on down the street and around the block.

If Samson was in custody, it was only a matter of time before they would be looking for him. It was vital that he clean up this problem and get over to Johns Island. It was his only way out of here now. But where was the package? He was not going to leave without it.

Circling the block, DuBois made one more pass by the cul-de-sac, one last chance to see what was happening. The woman, Walsh, was herding a couple of *p'tits* into a van while several plainclothes cops stood around watching. He could feel their eyes boring in on him as he cruised past. The decrepit Dodge Dart would normally just blend into the background, but cruising a crime scene at five in the morning with the Anderson boys, three big rednecks, filling it to overflowing, just stood out too much. It was time to leave the development and figure out what his next move would be.

DuBois pulled out onto Route 52 and then immediately into a gas station. He didn't have to wait long. The gray van pulled out of the development and headed south on 52. DuBois allowed a couple of cars to get between him and the van and then pulled out onto the highway.

Even this early in the morning, the traffic was building as people headed to work, either over to the Naval Weapons Station or down toward Charleston and the busy Navy base. Staying a couple of cars behind the gray van was easy as long as they didn't get caught by any traffic lights. That wasn't a problem until they reached the outskirts of North Charleston where Route 52 became Rivers Avenue. From there on downtown, it was a traffic light every couple of blocks. DuBois was forced to stay closer to the van and risk being seen. There really was no option. He couldn't afford to get caught by a red light and lose the van.

The van eased over to the center lane as it came up to the light for Ashley Phosphate Road. When the light changed, the van turned left and then immediately into a motel parking lot. DuBois cruised on by, crossed over the freeway, and then turned back. He pulled into an office park across the busy Ashley Phosphate Road from the motel and slipped into a parking place.

DuBois carefully scoped out the motel. It was one of those older, low-cost ones that had an individual outside door for each room. They were common in the South and made these kinds of break-ins much easier. It only took a few seconds to outline his plan to the Anderson boys. The plan was simple. Storm into the room, shoot anyone who tried to stop them. Grab the package and run. Meet back at the car and then disappear into the morning traffic.

Slipping the Colt Cobra into his jacket pocket, DuBois headed across the street, followed by the Anderson boys. The empty van was conveniently parked right outside the door to the motel room.

The biggest Anderson boy simply smashed the wooden door open and rushed in, followed by the other two, with guns drawn. Two of the three agents sitting in the room were caught by surprise, gunned down as they groped for their weapons. The third agent managed to slam shut the door to the adjoining room and get off a couple of rounds. One of the boys slumped to the ground with a third eye bleeding in the middle of his forehead. Another one took a slug in the shoulder as he gunned down the agent.

DuBois slipped into the room with his gun drawn. He pointed toward the adjoining room door and said, "Get it open."

The one Anderson still standing emptied a couple of rounds into the lock and then kicked the door open. The room was empty, save for the suitcases still lying on the bed. The outside door was swinging open.

DuBois rushed outside just in time to see Joy Walsh herding two children and running toward the motel office. He raised his gun as Joy turned and saw him. She fired her little Beretta as DuBois tried to aim. The bee sting on his leg knocked off his aim enough that his shot hit her in the shoulder. Walsh fell to the ground and tried to crawl behind a parked car.

DuBois looked down and saw blood streaming from his right thigh. He jumped back into the room. He could hear sirens screaming in the distance. There wasn't time for a shootout with the Walsh woman. She probably didn't know anything useful, anyway. Right now, he needed to run. Grabbing the suitcases, he dumped them on the floor. The package, still wrapped in brown paper, fell out of the second one and onto the floor. He grabbed it and limped toward the door. The one uninjured Anderson boy was tending to his wounded brother. DuBois couldn't leave anyone behind who could identify him. The Colt Cobra barked twice.

DuBois limped back across the street and climbed into the Dodge Dart. He caught a glimpse of police cars, lights flashing, screeching around the turn off Rivers onto Ashley Phosphate Road. He turned onto the I-26 entrance ramp and disappeared into the morning traffic.

1245Z, 14 April 1983, KH-11 OPS-2581, 160 nm above Murmansk, Russia

As the KH-11 OPS-2581 Keyhole spy satellite's sun-synchronous orbit passed over the North Pole, it maneuvered to aim its Cassegrain reflecting telescope down at the target path, a two-hundred-mile-wide swath down across western Russia. As it then passed down across the Kola Peninsula, the KH-11's vast array of tiny charged-couple diodes began sensing light reflected from the Earth's surface, 160 nautical miles below. The satellite's CCDs converted the light into electronic signals that were then encrypted and relayed to a communications satellite in a geosynchronous orbit twenty-three thousand miles above Greenland.

By the time the KH-11 had passed east of Moscow, printers at the National Reconnaissance Office were already printing out images of the docks in Murmansk. The images were so clear the brow signs on the few ships still in port were clearly legible. But the cameras were still on, photographing a broad swath of the Russian steppes west of the Ural Mountains. Hidden in plain sight across these dry, barren grasslands were dozens of SS-18 ICBM silos. The belt of silos constituted the major portion of the Soviet heavyweight ICBM force aimed at the US. Tanker trucks littered the maze of roads surrounding the silos, delivering dangerous and highly toxic hypergolic fuel for the liquid-fueled missiles. The nitric acid and hydrazine were so toxic and volatile when mixed that they were stored separately and away from the silos. Tankers delivered the fuel shortly before a planned launch.

By the time the KH-11 was passing over the Caspian Sea, phones were ringing in the National Military Command Center, deep under the Pentagon.

The watch officer, an Air Force brigadier general, glanced at the images and immediately called the Secretary of Defense. "Mr. Secretary, we have the latest images from KH-11 OPS-2581. The piers at the ballistic missile base in Polyarny are empty. The *Typhoon* and the *Delta*s that are normally tied up there are all gone. And we have clear images of tankers fueling the SS-18 sites. We have never seen this type of coordinated activity before."

The Secretary of Defense thought for a second. The last satellite pass by KH-11 OPS-3984 over Petropavlovsk had shown similar results for the Soviet Pacific Fleet. The FBMs homeported in that icy and isolated base on the Kamchatka Peninsula were also missing. What were the Russians up to, and why?

"What in the hell is happening? We have Russian submarines shooting at what they think are American submarines. Then we have them deploying all their boomers and fueling their ICBMs. Looks like we are staring into the abyss." He paused and took a deep breath. Then he said, "By the president's authorization, I am declaring DEFCON THREE. Immediately release the messages to all strategic forces to establish DEFCON THREE."

0930 EST, 14 April 1983, Johns Island, South Carolina

Henri DuBois tried to appear calm. There was no sense in getting frustrated now. It would only draw unwanted attention. He looked out at the line of stalled traffic in front of him. The traffic behind him stretched as far back as he could see. He then glanced across the swampy lowlands to the muddy Stono River. A line of sailboats motored downriver toward Kiawah Island and the Atlantic, a few miles to the south. That was the cause for the traffic backup. The old drawbridge was opened for the boats to pass.

His leg was hurting, but the bleeding seemed to have stopped. He had fashioned a crude bandage out of an undershirt, which seemed to stanch the bleeding. That was the best he could do until he was clear of South Carolina. Real medical care was not in the cards for a while. A stop at a hospital would have cops on the scene before he even saw a doctor. No choice but to grit his teeth and bear it.

DuBois tuned the car radio to a local news station. The story of a shootout up on Rivers Avenue was the lead story with the talking heads waxing long about North Charleston's increase in violence. There wasn't any mention of a fugitive on the run or any police search. Looked like he was in the clear, maybe. DuBois used the wait to reload his Colt Cobra, then slipped it back into his jacket pocket. He stuffed the package into his satchel, alongside his cash.

DuBois jumped when he heard the horn blast, but then he saw the bridge start to swing back closed. The sailboats motored on down the river, out for a day of fun on the ocean, totally unconcerned about the line of traffic they had held up. DuBois eased the Dodge into gear and headed down the Maybeck Highway. His instructions were to turn south on River Road. It was supposed to be the first intersection after the bridge. River Road turned out to be a quiet country lane, completely enshrouded by live oaks branching overhead, covering everything with a cool dappling shade.

Five miles down the road he found the battered old sign for Harley's Pier with an arrow pointing down a rutted dirt road. DuBois eased the Dodge off the road, onto the dirt track. It was a mile of careful driving, with trees on one side and tidal marshland on the other, reminding DuBois of his boyhood haunts in south Louisiana. The track dead-ended at a run-down cinder block building with a rusted tin roof. A ramshackle pier extended fifty yards across the marsh to the river. A battered old shrimp boat sat tied up at the end of the pier.

DuBois turned off the car and grabbed his satchel. The walk across the pier was a balancing act to keep from falling into the mud. The closer he got to the boat, the more battered and rusted it appeared. The name *Sally B* was just visible through the dirt and rust streaks below the gunnel up on the bow.

"You be Henri?" Someone leaned out of the pilothouse and yelled, "Hurry up and get aboard. We need to get movin' a'fore low tide leaves us sittin' in da mud."

DuBois stepped up and over the low gunnel. He had barely landed on the steel deck when he heard the powerful diesel engines roar and felt the boat swing away from the pier. A deckhand shoved him along into the boat's galley.

"You stay in here," the strapping Black deckhand instructed. "Cap'n Bob says you is suppose to stay here so's nobody be seein' you." The deckhand opened a pantry door and then reached up to click a hidden latch. The pantry shelves swung out to reveal a small hidden room. "If'n we be stopped by de Coast Guard, you be getting in heah and stayin' real quiet. Unnerstan?"

DuBois nodded. He was beginning to suspect that the *Sally B* was more than a beat-up old shrimp boat.

Left alone in the tiny galley, DuBois sat and felt the rumble of the diesel engines. He knew that they must be out in the Stono River by now, but there was really no indication that they were moving. He suddenly felt very tired. The long drive and the excitement in Charleston were catching up with him. He sat back and took a nap.

He jolted awake to feel the *Sally B*'s long pitch and heave as she met the open sea. The galley door slammed open. A big, burly man with hair bleached white and skin like old leather, dressed in dungarees and a red flannel work shirt, strode into the space and looked down at DuBois.

"Mister Henri, I trust ya'll be comfortable," he said in a loud, booming voice. He was obviously more accustomed to shouting orders over the sounds of the engines and the roar of the wind. "I'm Cap'n Bob. This be my boat. Billy Joe showed you the *puka* for you to hide in. If'n we get boarded, you hide there an' be real quiet like. Coasties ain't never found it yet."

DuBois nodded. "*Ou'on va tout ca?*"

"You best be speakin' English," Cap'n Bob shot back. "I ain't unnerstanin yer furon gibberish."

DuBois smiled and said, "I apologize. I'm from Louisiana and sometimes speak Cajun. What I asked was where are we headed?"

"Cajun, huh?" Cap'n Bob answered. "I went to New Orleans once to that Mardi Gras shindig. Some party! We takin' you out to a point in the ocean. Supposed to be there at 2300 tonight. Old *Sally B* is gonna have to really hump it to get there on time."

"And then what?"

Cap'n Bob shrugged. "Don't rightly know. I suspect someone is gonna meet us there, but the caller, he didn't say."

Cap'n Bob pulled a first aid kit from a locker under the bench seat. "We best be looking at that leg. I 'spect it be botherin' you some. Shuck them pants so's I can be takin' a look-see."

The rough-and-tumble sea captain was remarkably gentle as he treated DuBois's wound, flushing the entrance wound with peroxide and taping a thick wad of gauze over the hole.

"That be t' best I can do for now. Bullet is still in der. Ain't nothin' I can do 'bout tat." He tossed DuBois a fresh pair of pants. "Best put deese on. For now, why don't you get back in the puka and take a nap. I'll wake you when we get there."

Cap'n Bob left the galley as DuBois climbed into the puka and shut the door. A nap would feel good after a long night.

23

1630Z, 14 April 1983, USS John Jay, GIUK Gap

Darren Walsh stood on the conn and stared at the message that Dale Horton had just handed him. DEFCON THREE! The country had been ordered to DEFCON THREE. The only time that had ever happened before was at the very height of the Cuban Missile Crisis when the entire world teetered on the brink of nuclear war. The world pulled back from the precipice in fear that time. But here we were again, just twenty years later.

"You okay, Skipper?" Stan Wilkins asked. He held up a sealed envelope. "I just got the sealed DEFCON THREE section to Op Plan 2134 from the safe. Permission to open them? It's time to see what the War Plan has in mind for us."

Walsh nodded. "Yeah, XO. I'm okay. Just wondering how we ever got this far. Open the sealed orders."

Wilkins's hands trembled as he tore open the envelope and removed a booklet prominently emblazoned with the Top Secret SIOP stamps at the top and bottom of the cover. It was titled Op Plan 2134, Annex XRAY, War Plan. Together, the pair read through the short document.

"Nav," Walsh called out to Bob Shippley, who was standing beside the

Mark-19 plotter, "plot us the fastest course to seventy north, thirteen west. Point XRAY is the southeast corner of a two-hundred-mile-by-two-hundred-mile box that we have been assigned. We have three days to get there with the clock starting from the day-time group of the DEFCON Alert message, 1600Z. Looks like someone is getting us out of the way while the fast attacks and carriers charge north."

Shippley slapped the parallel motion protractor on the chart and lined it up with the coordinates. "Skipper, looks like course three-four-seven is the rhumb line course."

He grabbed his ever-present nautical slide rule, adjusted it, and read off, "At four knots, I calculate we will be at the point about 1800Z on the eighteenth."

Walsh shook his head. "Not good enough. We have to be there by 1600Z on the eighteenth. What speed do I need to make good?"

Shippley adjusted his slide rule and read out, "Skipper, recommend six knots. Gets us there a day early and allows for baffle clears while we are in transit."

Walsh nodded and turned to the Officer-of-the-Deck. "Eng, come to course three-four-seven and make turns for six knots to conform to Navigator's track. Have all officers and chiefs muster on the mess decks in fifteen minutes."

He turned and walked down the passageway to his stateroom. He shut the door and sat quietly, calming himself and composing his thoughts. Most of the time his thoughts were really thirty-five hundred miles south, in Goose Creek, South Carolina.

Fifteen minutes later, Darren Walsh walked into the mess decks. With all the chiefs and officers present, the space was standing room only. Even the tiny flip-up seats on the ends of each bench were occupied.

Turning to Stan Wilkins, Walsh asked, "Officers all here, XO?"

"All except the Eng and the MPA. They are both on watch," Wilkins replied. "And the Chop. He is babysitting our Russian guests."

Walsh nodded and turned to Max Steuben. "The chiefs, COB?"

"All except Izzy Braxton. He's late as usual."

Chief Braxton came through the hatch from the missile compartment and tried to slip in the back, but Steuben spied him. "We can go now, Skipper. All accounted for."

Walsh looked out over the group. "I wanted to get a chance for all of us to get together and talk out where we are at and what we might expect. As you know, we are at DEFCON THREE. None of us has ever been here before. I don't know what's happening in the outside world beyond what we've all seen on the broadcast, but it must be pretty serious. I know that you are worried about your families back home. I'm worried about mine, and you can bet your men are worried about theirs. The hard, cold fact is, there isn't anything we can do for them right now except do our jobs. And that's just what we are going to do, to the very best of our ability. Talk to your men and make sure they understand that. If they have questions or concerns that you can't handle, have them come talk to the COB, the XO, or me."

Walsh paused for a second to allow his words to sink in. Then he continued. "Right now, we are in the preparation phase for the war plan. Our job is pretty simple. We need to get up north and out of the way of the fast attacks and carrier battle groups that are high-tailing it for the North Cape. The plan expects the Russians to be moving their fleet out toward the Atlantic—at least that part that's not protecting their home waters. We stay alert at Condition 2SQ and stand by for any launch orders. The big difference for us is that we stay out here and stay alert until someone tells us to come home. Or, God forbid, we have launched our missiles. Then we head for a place called Loch Inver, way up north in the Scottish Highlands. The tender should already be leaving Holy Loch for there as we speak."

The room was completely silent. The men looked at each other without a word. The tension was palpable.

Then Walsh went on, "On the brighter side, we won't be having any engineering drills. And, COB, I'm sorry. But field days are on hold, too." That broke some of the tension.

1830 EST, 14 April 1983, Charleston Naval Hospital, Charleston, South Carolina

Joy Walsh woke from a hazy, gray sleep. The brightly lit room was not familiar, and she didn't understand how she got here, wherever "here" was. She felt funny, woozy and disoriented. She hurt all over. There seemed to be tubes and wires running everywhere. She could just glimpse a host of blinking and beeping screens at the edge of her vision. She tried to move, to find a more comfortable position, but that made the pain shoot through her body. She moaned.

"Honey, are you awake?" The voice sounded familiar.

"Mom?" she croaked. Her mouth felt like it was full of bone-dry gravel. There seemed to be a tube or something stuck in her nose that she tried to swat away. Then she saw the IV tubes stuck in her hand, leading off to several bags on a stand beside the bed. "Wha...?"

"Shush, don't try to talk." Her mother's voice was calming, quietly reassuring. "You're in the hospital, in the recovery room. You've been shot, but the doctors say you'll be okay."

"Sam and Pug? Where are the kids? Are they okay?" she whispered, panic on the edge of her voice. The last thing she remembered was rushing them into the motel and then seeing someone with a gun running toward her.

"They're fine. Your dad has them at your house. At last account, he was feeding them pizza and chocolate ice cream for dinner." Her mother chuckled and squeezed Joy's hand. "I suspect that by the time you get out of here, he'll have spoiled them rotten."

"How did you get here so fast?" Joy asked. She really didn't know what time it was, but it seemed that only a few minutes ago she was running outside that motel.

"That nice Admiral Brown," her mother answered. "He called this morning to tell us that you were hurt and that he was sending his plane to pick us up. We got here just as you were coming out of surgery."

A nurse stuck her head in the room. "Oh, our patient is awake. Good, I'll go get the doctor."

She disappeared only to be replaced by a doctor in scrubs and a white lab coat. "Afternoon, Mrs. Walsh. Glad you finally decided to join us. I'm Doctor Shandi. I was your surgeon. You must be sensitive to anesthesia. You've been out for a while."

Joy Walsh tried to nod and say something, but only a groan came out.

"You just lie still. Take some ice chips. That'll help the throat. We had to intubate you during the surgery. I expect it's still pretty uncomfortable. And that oxygen feed in your nose will dry your throat out even more."

Dr. Shandi took the chart from its place on the end of the bed and checked the notes. "Your vitals are looking better now. I want to get your blood oxygen levels up. It's still below where I want it to be. That bullet nicked the upper lobe of your left lung. You had a left-side hemopneumothorax. That's just fancy medical talk for blood and air building up in your pleural space, putting pressure on your lungs. We did a pneumonorrhaphy on your lung. Again, just medical speak for sewing it up. You have a broken rib and a broken scapula. That's where we found the bullet lodged."

"No wonder I hurt." Joy tried to laugh but groaned again.

Dr. Shandi shushed her. "You need to lie quietly. Your body has been through a trauma. You need to reserve your strength to heal."

"How long?" she asked.

"You're going to be with us for a bit. I want to make sure that you are healing and there is no infection. Infection is our worst enemy now that we have the wound all sewed up. We have no way of knowing what the bullet may have rammed into your body. I expect at least a week here on antibiotics and pain meds. We'll move you out of recovery over to the ICU unit in a couple of hours. That'll be a whole lot more comfortable, and we can keep a close eye on you there."

"A week," Joy protested. "I have a family."

It was her mother's turn to shush her. "Now, Joy, dear, don't you worry. Several of your crew wives are out in the waiting area. I talked with that nice Camille Steuben and Annie May Faris. They are arranging to take care of everything. Annie May said that you taught her that's what crew wives did for each other. They're out there with that nice policeman."

"What policeman?"

Her mother shook her head. "I probably shouldn't have said anything. It will only worry you. He said he was here to make sure you were safe."

0700 MSK, 15 April 1983, K-314, *200 kilometers off Charleston, South Carolina*

Captain Second Rank Ilya Agapov stared through the periscope. The message said that he was supposed to rendezvous with a ship here at 0700 Moscow time. 2300 local time. He ordered Anatoly Balakirev, his watch officer, to check the *K-314*'s position once again. It was exactly where he was supposed to be, but there was no one here to rendezvous with.

"Watch Officer, make your depth fifteen meters," Agapov ordered. Maybe a higher look would find the missing ship. It was pitch-black outside; the pale crescent moon had long since dropped below the horizon. He was staring out at an empty sea, not the glimmer of a light anywhere.

"Comrade Captain, should we use the radar?" Balakirev asked.

Agapov shook his head, although he knew that the watch officer couldn't see him in the darkened control room. "No, Anatoly, not a good idea," he answered. "The Americans will immediately identify our radar and pounce on us. We need to stay hidden."

The *K-314*'s Snoop Tray radar was easily identifiable as coming from a Russian *Victor*-class submarine. He would have to rely on his eyes for this mission.

Then the Russian captain saw the barest glimmer of a white light off in the distance to the southwest. If that light was ten meters above the surface, it had to be at least six thousand meters away. Then he spied a red light above the white one. A fishing boat. That had to be their target.

"Anatoly, steer course two-three-zero. Increase speed to twenty-three kilometers per hour."

The increased speed with the periscope raised would mean the sub was leaving a very noticeable feather on the surface, but it was a dark night. This was a chance that Agapov would take to make this mission happen sooner. As it was, he would need to steam toward the light for half an hour just to rendezvous.

When they had closed the range enough that he could see the green starboard running light, Agapov slowed the submarine and dropped back down to normal periscope depth. The fishing boat seemed to be stopped, just floating quietly on the night sea. He made a slow circle around it, warily watching for any sign that this could be some sort of betrayal, a trap.

When he was comfortable that everything was as it appeared, Agapov ordered the *K-314* surfaced. By the time he had men on the bridge, a little dinghy was already motoring away from the fishing boat. In less than thirty minutes, the rendezvous was complete; the fishing boat was motoring away to the west, and the *K-314* had returned to the safety of the depths.

Agapov left the control room and headed for the wardroom. It was time to meet his new guest. He found him sitting at the table, sipping a cup of tea and munching on a biscuit.

"Welcome aboard the Soviet submarine *K-314*. I am Captain Second Rank Ilya Agapov."

"I am Henri DuBois," DuBois said, extending his hand. "Thank you for helping my get-away."

Agapov grasped the extended hand and shook it. "You must be a very important comrade, *Gospodin* DuBois, for Moscow to order us to pick you up and then deliver you back to Murmansk. We will make you comfortable for the next couple of weeks."

1100 EST, 15 April 1983, COMSUBLANT, Norfolk, Virginia

"What an absolute goat rope!" Vice Admiral Rufus Brown growled as he slammed his fist onto the desk, almost spilling his coffee. "Where the hell are we with this Grey Mole business? We have any clue what was in that package? I'm assuming that Grey Mole made off with it."

Ted Strange shook his head. "Skipper, I simply don't know. He gave the Charleston cops and NIS the slip and disappeared. He is in the wind somewhere in South Carolina. The cops have an APB out on him. The FBI is covering all the airports, bus terminals, et cetera. Not a clue what was in the package. Mrs. Walsh didn't open it. Said it was a birthday present from her husband. He left instructions not to open it until her birthday. That's sometime in May."

"What I don't understand is how he got so close to Joy Walsh! Goddamn it! We promised to protect her. What the hell happened with that NIS protection you promised her?"

Strange blushed red. He was almost as angry as Brown. "Turns out the NIS agent in charge down there was having an affair with his secretary. He was treating their safe house as his personal love nest. Thought it would be okay to just send a couple of agents to babysit Joy Walsh and her kids in a motel instead of the safe house. I think you need to have another discussion with Admiral Huxley about how they are doing business."

Brown reached out and jabbed the button on his intercom. "Get me Rear Admiral Huxley on the phone right damn now!" He jabbed the intercom off before his yeoman could even reply.

Strange visibly worked to calm himself. He took a sip of coffee before he continued. "They rushed Mrs. Walsh to the Charleston Naval Hospital. She's in the trauma ICU, but the doctors say that she will be all right. The slug went through her upper body without hitting anything vital, unless you call a lung and a busted scapula vital. Going to be pretty sore for a while."

Brown looked up and shook his head. "Well, we sure as hell ain't telling Darren Walsh nothing. He's got enough to worry about out there without worrying about his family." Then he rubbed his forehead before he added, "Any more than everyone else out there is worrying about their families while the world is going to hell in a handbasket."

"You see the latest on the news?" Strange asked.

"You talking about the Russian ambassador bitching to the UN about how US saber-rattling was going to cause a nuclear war? We need to turn our carriers around and tie up all our submarines or the world as we know it is going to end. He actually threatened that any US warship found east of Bear Island was guilty of unprovoked aggression and would be attacked without any further warning."

Strange nodded. "Yep, that was what I was talking about, and then the US ambassador gets up and shows images of the Russian fleet heading out into the Barents and their empty sub piers. I really got the uncomfortable feeling that they were talking past each other. Not sure how we are going to get over this, but it ain't going to be in the UN."

The intercom buzzed. "Excuse me, Admiral," the yeoman squeaked. "Admiral Huxley is on the outside line."

Brown looked over at Strange. "Excuse me, Ted. I need to rip Huxley a new one, and flag officers do that in private."

24

1705Z, 15 April 1983, USS John Jay, *Norwegian Sea*

The *John Jay* cruised silently, heading north. The sea was strangely quiet. They had not seen or heard another ship in almost a week. Even in the remote regions of the Norwegian Sea, the lack of company was unusual. But steaming in a lonely sea suited Darren Walsh just fine. It was a whole lot easier to stay hidden if no one was around looking.

Walsh headed out of his stateroom and down the passageway toward the control room. He stopped in radio to see if anything had come across the broadcast. SUBLANT had been quiet ever since that DEFCON THREE alertment message caught them by surprise. Walsh was expecting a DEFCON TWO announcement any second but praying for a DEFCON FOUR or, even better, a FIVE. But the message boards contained the usual admin messages, and even fewer of those than normal. He flipped over to the news messages, hoping to find at least some hint of what was going on in the outside world. Not much there beyond the first few baseball scores. It looked like the Sox were off to a good start. Walsh snorted. That wouldn't last.

He stepped across the passageway into the darkened confines of the sonar shack. He checked the BQR-21 broadband waterfall display carefully, but there was nothing except biologics. Even listening on the headphones, all he heard were some distant whale grunts and groans. The BQR-23 narrow-band analyzer was equally quiet.

Walsh shook his head as he stepped out of sonar and into the control room. Everything was all too quiet for the world to be on the brink of nuclear war. It was disconcerting and troubling. He didn't like it.

Stopping at the plot table, Walsh checked the ship's position on the chart. They were about 150 miles northeast of Iceland. Still 230 miles to go to get to Point XRAY. He glanced up at the clock above the plot table. Plenty of time.

Bob Shippley, the Officer-of-the-Deck, hopped down off the periscope stand and stepped over to where Walsh was standing. "Evening, Skipper," he said.

"Evening, Nav," Walsh replied. "Anything going on?"

"Not really. I gave engineering permission to do weekly steam generator water level controls trip and cals a bit ago. They should be wrapping up shortly. And Weps asked permission to back-haul the weapon in tube three. Problem with the tube feeler probe. They want to check it out."

Walsh nodded and said with a grin, "Sounds like another exciting watch."

"Yep," Shippley answered. "Right up there with watching bilge paint dry."

Walsh answered, "Kinda like it that way lately."

The 7MC interrupted their conversation. "Conn, Maneuvering. Machinery one upper level reports of a loud banging external to the hull. Investigating."

At almost the same instant, the 21MC speaker blared, "Conn, Radio, loss of sync on the broadcast. Loss of indication on the BRA-8 buoy."

Loss of sync meant that they were no longer copying the message traffic from SUBLANT. A boomer's number one job, even above remaining undetected, was to be in continuous communications. That was the only way that they were ready to instantly respond to orders from the president. The whole deterrent strategy hinged on the absolute assurance that the missile-firing submarines would shoot their missiles when ordered, and the only way for that to happen was if the president was able to send them the orders. The BRA-8 buoy antenna was the connection that fed communications into the submarine, and now it was gone.

Bob Shippley immediately ordered, "Chief-of-the-Watch, raise the BRA-16 antenna. Dive, make your depth nine-zero feet." Grabbing the 21MC, he said, "Radio, Conn, BRA-16 coming up."

Turning to Darren Walsh, he said, "Skipper, indications that the BRA-8 has departed on independent ops again. Coming shallow and raising the BRA-16."

Walsh merely nodded. Bob Shippley was doing just exactly what he should be doing. The BRA-8 buoy was the ship's primary VLF antenna, but its reliability was low. The cable connecting the buoy to the submarine would, all too frequently, break, and the buoy would simply float away. The main thing right now was to get communications restored.

The BRA-16 was a VLF loop antenna placed on the end of a mast housed in the submarine's sail. The football-shaped antenna could receive VLF signals when the mast was raised, but with the submarine still submerged down to a depth of eighty or ninety feet. It made a good short-term immediate backup when one of the deep-water antennas failed. The only way to safely use the BRA-16 for any length of time was to operate at periscope depth. That was not recommended both because continuously operating in the Norwegian Sea in winter at periscope depth would be extremely uncomfortable and the submarine would be much easier to detect with a periscope and BRA-16 football out in the air.

As the *John Jay* angled up toward the surface, Shippley ordered, "Chief-of-the-Watch, raise the BQR-19 Top Hat." Again, he grabbed the 21MC. "Sonar, Conn, Top Hat coming up."

The BQR-19 Top Hat was a mast-mounted high-frequency active/passive sonar system designed specifically for collision avoidance as the submarine came shallow. To avoid counter-detection, it was only operated in the passive mode. It could detect a ship lurking above the submarine out to a thousand yards or so. The easy rule of thumb was that if a contact showed up on Top Hat, it was too damn close.

"Conn, Radio, in sync on the BRA-16. Taking stations to deploy the BRA-24 floating wire. Request permission to break rig-for-dive and enter the sail trunk."

The BRA-24 floating wire antenna was a thousand-foot-long VLF antenna that deployed from the submarine out the back of the sail and floated up to the surface. The submarine had to go slow enough to keep the antenna floating on the surface for it to work, but that allowed the boat to go back down to 150 feet or so. That was a whole lot better than being tossed around at periscope depth for days on end.

RM3 Milt Schoneman stood at the bottom of the ladder to the bridge trunk carrying a canvas bucket full of tools. RM1 Melvin Yoe, the leading radioman, stood with him carrying an instruction manual and a flashlight. "Request permission to open the lower trunk hatch."

Bob Shippley ordered, "Open the lower hatch, enter the trunk, deploy the floating wire."

It took the radiomen half an hour to get the BRA-24 floating wire antenna deployed and communications shifted over from the BRA-16. With the bridge trunk once more rigged for dive and the hatch shut, the *John Jay* dropped back down to normal patrol depth.

Bob Shippley looked around the control room. He said, "Chief-of-the-Watch, indicate on the status board that the floating wire is deployed. Diving Officer, limit your angles to five degrees and rudder angles to ten degrees."

A major concern with the BRA-24 was to keep the floating wire out of the screw. The big bronze blades would make short work of the wire. That meant the use of both the rudder and stern planes had to be done judiciously to keep from pulling the wire into the screw.

Shippley moved over to the navigation plot. He took a pair of dividers and walked off the distance to Point XRAY and spun his nautical slide rule around. "Skipper, we got a problem."

"Okay, Nav, what's the problem," Walsh asked, although he already had a pretty good idea what the Navigator was going to say.

"With the BRA-24 deployed, we can't go more than four knots and still maintain comms," Shippley answered. "That means we will be six hours late getting to Point XRAY. Skipper, we will be operating out of our assigned area."

Walsh looked at the chart. He used his fingers to approximate the distance and did a rough calculation in his head. The Nav was right. In peacetime this would be serious. They could not operate submerged outside their assigned areas. There was a chance that they could collide with another submarine already operating in the area. They would have to surface and radio back to SUBLANT. It was much more serious now that they were on the verge of war. Surfacing and radioing back home would tell the Soviets exactly where and who they were, so that was a very bad idea. But not saying anything, when all of the fast attacks heading north were racing past them, meant that there was a very real possibility that they would be mistaken for a Russian sub. There just wasn't a good option.

Walsh finally answered, "Nav, head straight for Point XRAY. We still own this section of water for twenty-four hours. Time to figure something out or see what changes."

1500 MSK, 16 April 1983, deep under the National Defense Center, Moscow

The president of the Soviet Union, Vladimar Antonovich Petrov, sat in a high-backed, ornately carved chair that had probably been pulled out of some Tsarist dacha during the October Revolution. He was positioned at the head of an equally old and ornate oak table that ran the length of the room. It stopped just short of a large projection screen that covered most of the far wall. Thick red velvet curtains hid stark reinforced concrete walls and added some grandeur to an otherwise cold functional room six floors beneath the National Defense Center. The drapes were only broken by heavy steel doors that barred access to the room.

On either side of the table sat the brain trust for the defense of the Soviet Union. These old men, dressed in frumpy suits or medal-bedecked uniforms, led the Politburo, Ministry of Defense, the KGB, the GRU, the Soviet Army, and the Strategic Rocket Force. It was highly unusual for these men to all be in one room. It was even more unusual to do so secretly in the bomb-proof and bug-proof emergency national command center.

"Comrades," Petrov started the meeting. "We are receiving very troubling news from the West. I called this meeting to determine if there is a clear picture of what is happening and to get a consensus of what our reaction should be. The Western press is full of stories beating the drums of war. The American president calls us the 'evil empire.' Every week, they announce new weapons and new strategies to 'overcome the Soviet threat.' What must we do to protect the *Rodina*?"

"Dimetri, what do we really know?" The president turned to the Dimetri Olagev, the Minister for State Security, the official title for the head of the *Komitet Gosudarstvennoy Bezopasnosti*, the KGB.

"Vladimar Antonovich," Olagev said as he stood, "our sources in the US tell us that the Americans are bringing their strategic forces to a high state of readiness. They have brought them to a posture that they call DEFCON THREE. That is just short of actual hostilities. Their Strategic Air Command has moved to their underground shelters and have put both their rocket force and their bombers on high alert."

Olagev paused to refer to his notes. "Our assets inside their State Department tell us that their president is taking a very hard line on relations with us. They have canceled several routine meetings with our embassy and have issued more warnings to their citizens about traveling in the USSR."

"Sergi, what does our military intelligence have to offer?"

Sergi Baranov was sitting in for the Director of the GRU, who was currently residing in the Burdenko Military Hospital ICU recovering from a near fatal stroke. "Vladimar Antonovich, as Comrade Olagev has reported, the Americans are coming to a war footing."

Baranov paused to flash up an image on the projection screen. The grainy picture was obviously from a satellite showing a large area of ocean with many ships dotting it.

"Our RORSAT satellites are showing that the American battle fleet is in the North Atlantic, heading toward the Norwegian Sea. All their submarines have deployed. Our source in their command center has told us that their attack submarines, their hunter killers, are heading toward the Barents to attack our missile submarines. Their SSBNs have been moved to their wartime patrol areas."

He cleared his throat and took a sip of tea before continuing. "Our source has also verified that the Americans have a working *maskiruyuscheye ustroystvo* that they call a 'cloaking device' on their submarines. This has been verified with reports from our submarine *K-324*. I don't need to tell you what an advantage that gives the *Amerikanskaya podvodnaya lodka*."

Petrov held up his hand to stop his chief GRU spy. "What is this *maskiruyuscheye ustroystvo?* Do you mean to say that these American submarines disappear?"

Baranov nodded. "The Captain of the *K-324*, Comrade Captain Novikov, reports that when the *maskiruyuscheye ustroystvo* is activated, the American SSBN disappears from our sonars, even active sonars are not effective. He fired one of our most modern torpedoes at the SSBN but achieved nothing."

"Did you say that we shot at an American SSBN submarine?" Dimetri Olagev asked. "It is no wonder they are going to a war footing. Who is the fool who ordered something that stupid? Did this Novikov act on his own? We have a special room in Lubyanka for fools like that."

Baranov hotly retorted, "This is a GRU matter. We will handle any discipline that is needed in this case. Comrade Captain Novikov will be appropriately interrogated as soon as *K-324* returns. It is due into Polyarny in a couple of days. We will have more information shortly after that."

Olagev shot back, "Thanks to your rogue captain, we may not have a couple of days."

Petrov interjected, "Gentleman, enough." He looked at Baranov. "Do you have anything further?"

"I have one last item, Vladimar Antonovich," Baranov replied. "Our agent in the American submarine command center was in danger of discovery. We have extracted him by submarine. He is also on his way to Polyarny."

Petrov looked around the room. "Gentlemen, that still leaves the most important decision to be made. What do we do about the current American military preparations? It is my feeling that we need to bring our strategic forces to a state of instant readiness. Are we agreed?"

He stared at each person seated around the table. Each one nodded and said, "*Da.*"

25

1300 EST, 16 April 1983, Charleston Naval Hospital, Charleston, South Carolina

Joy Walsh pushed the lunch cart away from her hospital bed. She had finally graduated from soups and Jell-O. The sliced chicken and mashed potatoes were so dry that normally she would have shoved them aside, but today just chewing on food was a real luxury that she relished. And a chocolate chip cookie for dessert! She tried to wheedle a second cookie and a cup of coffee from the nurse, but she would have none of it. The prescribed diet was important.

Joy had just reached for her copy of *Good Housekeeping* magazine when she heard a knock at the doorway. She looked up to see two men, one Black and the other White, in business suits and a third one in a police uniform.

"Excuse us, Mrs. Walsh," the Black man said as he flashed a badge. "Do you remember us? I'm Special Agent Jeremy Baldwin."

Joy Walsh smiled. "Of course I remember you, Agent Baldwin, and Agent Johnson. From Norfolk. Come in."

Baldwin nodded. "That's right. And this is Sheriff Beauregard from Charleston County. We'd like to speak with you for a few minutes if you are up to it."

"Certainly, come in and sit down." She reached for the control for her bed. She groaned from a sudden twinge in her side as she raised the bed so she could sit up comfortably. She hurriedly adjusted the blanket in an effort to maintain her sense of modesty. These men obviously weren't medical personnel. "What can I do for you?"

The three lawmen took seats. Chad Johnson started the discussion. "Mrs. Walsh, we'd like to bring you up to speed on where we are with this investigation and to ask you a few questions. Do you remember the spy that we briefed you about when we met at SUBLANT?"

Joy nodded. "I remember you called him the Grey Mole or something like that."

"That's right, the Grey Mole. His real name is Henri DuBois. He ran from Norfolk on the day before the shootings. Looks like he came down here. We think he is the man who shot you and killed our agents."

Chad Johnson pulled an eight-by-ten photograph from a folder and held it up for Joy to look at. "Is this the guy who shot you?"

She looked at the picture and nodded. "Yes, that's him."

"We have one of his accomplices in custody," Sheriff Beauregard interjected. "A local boy named Leland Samson. He's tellin' us how this DuBois guy wanted something from your house."

Jeremy Baldwin interrupted, "Sheriff, Leland Samson is hardly a boy."

Beauregard waved his hand. "Yeah, yeah, I apologize. As I was sayin', this Leland Samson says DuBois hired him to break into your home and steal a package. Evidently, DuBois wanted this package real bad."

Chad Johnson looked over at Joy Walsh. "Mrs. Walsh, do you have any idea what was in the package?"

Joy shook her head. "Darren left a birthday present for me when he left for patrol. He said to open it on my birthday. That's May twenty-seventh, by the way. That's the only 'package' that was in the house, other than all those boxes from our last move that need to be sorted and cleaned out. I had just started on those as a patrol project. I'm guessing that is what they were after."

"You don't know what was in the package?"

"I don't have a clue. We'll have to wait until Darren gets home to ask him," Joy answered.

"That leaves open the question of why DuBois is so interested in a birthday present that your husband bought for you," Beauregard replied. "Well, it was important enough to get three agents murdered and three young thugs killed, too."

Jeremy Baldwin said, "From the way the crime scene laid out, it looks like DuBois was going after you specifically. It's the only reason we can see that he didn't run as soon as he had the package. He must have thought that you had seen what was in it. Good thing you had that little pea shooter."

Joy Walsh shuddered. "Where is DuBois now?"

Sheriff Beauregard answered, "That's really the reason we came by today. We found DuBois's car abandoned at an old fish shack down on Johns Island. The shack is used sometimes by a local that goes by Cap'n Bob. Sleazy lowlife that we been suspectin' o' smuggling an' dope runnin' fer years but could never prove nothin'. Coast Guard caught him as he was tryin' to slip in the Stono River. Tellin' quite a tale o' meetin' some submarine and off-loadin' DuBois onto it. We're holdin' him and his mate in the county jail fer now."

Jeremy Baldwin rose. He handed Joy his card. "We've bothered you enough today. It looks like DuBois has run, and there doesn't seem to be any more reason for you to be concerned. We're going to leave an agent outside just to be safe. If anything comes up or if you remember anything, please give us a call."

The three left Joy Walsh. Her magazine was long forgotten.

0855Z, 17 April 1983, USS Tigerfish, *Barents Sea, 125 nm south of Bear Island*

Roy Blivens stood back and watched as the section tracking party kept tabs on Sierra One-Seven-Six. The Soviet submarine had conveniently established a rigid routine. The *Victor III*–class boat had maintained a course of zero-six-five at just a little over eight knots for the last four days. QM-1 Eric Swarton calculated that Sierra One-Seven-Six was actually making fifteen kilometers per hour, but the tenth of a knot difference wasn't worth the effort. Eight knots was close enough for government work. Every day at precisely 0900Z, Sierra One-Seven-Six would slow to about five knots and go to periscope depth. They would raise a comms mast to copy communications for a few minutes before dropping back deep and resuming their transit.

Blivens noted that Steve Dunn, the Officer-of-the-Deck, had already slowed *Tigerfish* in anticipation of Sierra One-Seven-Six's expected 0900 maneuver. He had the *Tigerfish* well back on the Soviet submarine's port quarter where they would have plenty of time to react if he did something unexpected.

Blivens smiled. The team was thinking ahead, just like they should. When they received the DEFCON THREE alert, seemingly out of the blue, he and George Sanders sat down with each watch section to discuss the different and much more tense situation. Sierra One-Seven-Six had already demonstrated a willingness to shoot first when it tried to blast that MOSS. Now, with DEFCON THREE, they could assume that the Russian would be even more hair-triggered. The only real difference that the alert had caused was that they were now riding with a Mark-48 warshot torpedo loaded in torpedo tube number one, with the tube flooded and the outer door open. It would take only seconds to launch it. *Tigerfish* was steaming around with her gun cocked and ready to shoot.

Blivens looked at the clock hanging above the forward Mark-117 fire control console. 0900. It was time. Almost as if choreographed, Senior Chief Zwarlinski's voice boomed over the 21MC, "Possible contact zig, Sierra One-Seven-Six, contact has slowed." This was followed almost immediately by Eric Swarton announcing, "Possible contact zig on time-frequency, downshift in received frequency." Then Brad Bishop called, "Contact zig on fire control."

Steve Dunn looked at the plot and at the fire control solution, then said, "Looks like his normal PD run. Right full rudder, steady course south. Ahead one-third. We will stay out seven thousand yards just to be on the safe side."

Tigerfish swung around the new course to keep the Russian at a safe distance. The 21MC blasted, "Conn, Sonar, losing Sierra One-Seven-Six as he is going above the layer. Recommend coming shallow so we can follow him."

Steve Dunn looked over at Roy Blivens. Blivens nodded. "Good a time as any to copy the broadcast. Officer-of-the-Deck, come to periscope depth and copy the broadcast."

Blivens watched the paper printout of sound velocity versus depth on the BQH-1 as the *Tigerfish* angled up. Sure enough, there was a sharp change in sound velocity, a layer, at one hundred feet. No wonder Sierra One-Seven-Six had disappeared.

"Conn, Sonar, regain Sierra One-Seven-Six, bearing zero-seven-four. New sonar contacts, looks like at least eight, bearings between zero-four-zero and one-two-zero. Initial evaluation Soviet surface warships. Skipper, receiving Horse Jaw active sonar from at least three of the contacts. Horse Jaw carried on *Kirov*-, *Udaloy*-, and *Kara*-class cruisers. SPL plus thirty-five. Fifty percent probability of detection. Recommend we go deep."

Blivens took a quick look at the BQQ-5 sonar. The little blips of light that represented the surface ships suddenly appeared when the *Tigerfish* came above the layer. They all seemed to be in a line somewhere out east, beyond Bear Island.

Blivens turned to Steve Dunn. "Let's get out of here. Go deep."

Dunn had just opened his mouth when the 21MC blared, "Loud transients from two of the contacts. Sounds like missile launches. They all carry SS-N-14 ASW missiles."

The SS-N-14 ASW missile was fired from Soviet cruisers. It flew out to the submarine's location and then dropped an ASW torpedo on the target submarine. The missile had a range of fifty kilometers and flew just below the speed of sound, so a submarine had very little time to evade.

"Make your depth five hundred feet. Left full rudder, steady course two-seven-zero, ahead flank."

The *Tigerfish* raced down into the depths and away from the unexpected Russian warships. Blivens estimated that they had a minute to run away from the missiles before their torpedoes dropped into the water. That is, if the missiles weren't armed with nuclear warheads. Then the calculation changed to having a minute to live. The thousand yards that they could travel in that minute just didn't matter.

"Torpedo in the water!" Chief Zwarlinski's south Jersey accent jumped an octave. "Two torpedoes! Bearing zero-five-one and zero-six-two. Both active, forty-two-kilohertz sonar, Russian E53-72 ASW torpedoes. Torpedoes going in the baffles."

Blivens looked at the plot and said, "Come around to three-three-zero. That'll keep them just on the edge of the baffles."

The *Tigerfish* snapped around to the new course.

"Torpedoes bear zero-seven-three and zero-seven-five. Skipper, those torpedoes weren't aimed at us."

Blivens looked at the plot again. All the bearing lines for the two Russian weapons converged on the Russian sub. They shot at Sierra One-Seven-Six!

He ordered, "Ahead one-third." No sense charging around the ocean, making a lot of noise when there was no need. It would only draw unwanted attention.

"Loud explosion in the water, best bearing zero-seven-five! Second explosion, same bearing. Breaking-up noises on the bearing."

"Eng, come to course north," Blivens ordered. "I want to snuggle up on the back side of Bear Island to call home and tell them that the Russian fleet is out of the barn, and they are shooting anything in sight. They probably got one of their own."

1200 MSK, 17 April 1983, K-324, Barents Sea, 120 nm south of Bear Island

Captain Second Rank Boris Novikov looked at the clock. It was 1200 Moscow time, time for the *K-324* to come to communications depth and download any communications Northern Fleet had for them. Hopefully, this morning's communications would include their instructions and clearance through the Northern Fleet's strategic bastion east of twenty degrees east longitude and then onward to their homeport in Polyarny. Their last communications from the fleet headquarters had warned Novikov that the fleet was deploying to protect the SSBNs and the northern sea approaches to the motherland. He should not proceed without permission. Unidentified submarines would be considered hostile and treated as such.

Their current instructions included safe clearance only to twenty degrees east longitude. The submarine's *inertsial'naya navigatsionnaya sistema* said that they were already at nineteen degrees and thirty minutes east. If the permissions were not received on this broadcast, they would be forced to circle uselessly south of Bear Island until Northern Fleet headquarters woke up.

"Dmitri," Novikov said to the watch officer, Dmitri Vinogradov. "It's time. Take the submarine to communications depth and copy the Fleet communications broadcast."

Vinogradov ordered the *K-324* slowed to ten kilometers per hour and the depth from fifty meters to sixteen meters. As the boat was passing through thirty meters, the sonar operator reported that he heard active sonar off to the east. It sounded like the *Kirov* and probably one of the new *Udaloy*-class frigates. Novikov looked at the screen. It was unlikely that the surface ships would detect the *K-324* at this range, but even if they did, they were friendly. He signaled for Vinogradov to continue to communications depth.

When Dmitri Vinogradov raised the periscope and looked out to the east, he could see the superstructure of the massive battlecruiser *Kirov* on the horizon. He quickly estimated that the nuclear-powered warship was ten thousand meters to the east. A much smaller ship, probably the *Udaloy* that sonar heard, was a few hundred meters to the port of the battlecruiser.

The communications antenna had just broken the surface when a flash of light grabbed Vinogradov's attention. He saw a second flash coming from the *Udaloy* before he realized that the ship was firing missiles. He wasn't sure what they were shooting at, but he turned to Novikov and reported the missile firings.

Novikov grabbed the periscope and looked down the bearing toward the *Udaloy*. He saw two streaks of bright white light arrowing directly toward them. He slammed the control to lower the periscope and ordered the *K-324* back down into the safety of the deep, but he knew it was already too late.

The missiles dropped their torpedoes a hundred meters behind the *K-324* as the submarine plunged down and raced forward. The race was not a contest. The E53-72 ASW torpedoes were almost twice as fast as the *Victor III* submarine. The first torpedo crashed into the outer hull surrounding the submarine's engine room. The 185-kilogram shaped charge blasted through the outer and inner hulls, sending a jet of liquified metal into the engine room. The searing heat killed the watch standers before the seawater even began to flood in through the gaping hole. The second torpedo struck the *K-324* almost immediately under the sail. The blast instantly incinerated Novikov, Vinogradov, and everyone else in the control room. The third compartment flooded as the submarine settled onto the muddy bottom fifteen hundred feet below the surface.

26

1800 MSK, 17 April 1983, Soviet Northern Fleet Headquarters, Murmansk, Russia

The sun was still midway on its journey from zenith to horizon. This time of year, the far north was blessed with almost twenty hours of sun. But the sun did little to warm a land shrouded by dense, low-lying gray clouds.

Fleet Admiral Dmitri Golubev looked out over the dismal landscape. The piers below his corner window were nearly empty. Only a few unfortunate ships, stricken with mechanical casualties that could not be quickly corrected, populated a few lonely berths. The rest of the fleet was out in the Barents, guarding the *Rodina* from the expected American attack. Golubev longed to be with them, feeling the sea under his feet, but he was stuck here at the Northern Fleet headquarters where he could direct them, and where he was available to receive "guidance and encouragement" from Moscow.

An aide swung open the heavy oak doors and rushed into Golubev's office. "Excuse me, Admiral, urgent priority message from Admiral Andreev. The fleet has detected and destroyed an American submarine. A great victory for the Red Banner Northern Fleet."

Golubev took the message and scanned it. He mumbled, "Vasily, that remains to be seen. We don't know how the Americans will react. Inform Moscow immediately."

He read through the message again. "This doesn't say how our quick-triggered Contre-Admiral determined he had an American submarine in his sights. It is almost too easy for him to find one now when we can rarely detect them any other time. Ask him for positive identification of the American."

"Immediately, Comrade Admiral!" Vasily saluted and turned toward the door.

"And, Vasily," Golubev said. "What have we heard from *K-324*? Captain Novikov should have called in by now."

"No message from *K-324*."

1100 EST, 17 April 1983, COMSUBLANT OPCON Center, Norfolk, Virginia

The Operations Center watch officer, a reserve Navy commander meeting his weekend drill requirements, grabbed the message from the Top Secret message board and read it through carefully. Prior to leaving active duty and joining the Reserves, he had made several runs up to the Barents on the old *Greenling*. There had been plenty of close encounters and near misses back then, but both sides slunk away, licked their wounds, and kept the encounters secret. He had never seen anything like this. According to this message from the *Tigerfish*, the Russian fleet was indiscriminately tossing ordnance and had actually taken out one of their own boats.

This was way over his pay grade. The watch officer picked up the red Secure Telephone Unit, more commonly called the STU phone, and dialed Vice Admiral Rufus Brown's home. He had never used the STU phone before. There was a row of lights on the phone. The red one was lit. The phone chirped for several minutes before it was answered. The red light blinked out while the yellow one blinked on.

"Admiral Brown. I hold you secure."

The watch officer gulped and then noticed that the green light had blinked on. "Admiral, this is the OPCON watch officer. I hold you secure."

Rufus Brown grumped, "Well, get on with it. You're calling me away from Sunday brunch with my wife."

"Admiral, we just received a message from *Tigerfish*. She reports that she is southwest of Bear Island. She says that she saw the Russian Northern Fleet," the watch officer gulped and stuttered.

"Well, get on with it, man," Brown ordered. "Spit it out."

"Sir, they attacked and sank one of their own submarines, a *Victor III* that *Tigerfish* was covertly trailing. *Tigerfish* goes on to report that they have solid sonar contact on at least ten Soviet surface ships. It looks like they are setting up a barrier all the way from Svalbard to the North Cape."

Brown stared at the phone for a second. Well, it had finally happened. They were on the precipice of a shooting war. It was time for action.

"I want you to forward *Tigerfish*'s message to the CINCLANTFLT Command Center and the National Military Command Center. Send it as an *OPREP 3 PINNACLE* message. That should get their attention. Then call the Chief-of-Staff and all the N heads. I want to see them in the SCIF at 1200. Understood?"

An *OPREP 3 PINNACLE* was a flag word that automatically routed messages of extremely high importance to the Chairman of the Joint Chiefs and the National Military Command Authority as well as all the warfare commanders. It was only used for incidents of very high national importance.

"And when you've got that all done, send *Tigerfish* an updated OPORD. I want them tasked to monitor the Northern Fleet. Report any movements and especially any submarine activity," Rufus Brown added before he hung up.

2100Z, 17 April 1983, USS John Jay, *Norwegian Sea*

Darren Walsh stood by the Mark-19 plotter and watched as Bob Shippley laid down the sub's latest estimated position on the navigation chart. A small semicircle enclosed a dot that symbolized the EP. He then grabbed his dividers from their normal spot hanging from the work light and measured the distance to Point XRAY.

"Skipper, we still got eight-point-two miles to get into our box. Won't make it for another two hours," Shippley reported as he replaced the dividers.

Walsh replied, "We'll just have to be real good at playing submarine for the next couple of hours and make sure no one finds us."

"We're going to need a fix to reset SINS in the next couple of hours," Shippley added. "The error plot is right at the edge for launch parameters. If we wait more than a couple of hours, we will fall outside specs and won't be able to launch until we get back. We have a NAVSAT pass in half an hour. Recommend we grab it while we can."

The SINS, or Submarine Inertial Navigation System, used gyroscopically stabilized accelerometers to very precisely measure the submarine's movement in all three axes. Measuring the sub's movement provided a very accurate EP while the sub was submerged and couldn't get an external fix of its position. Always very accurately knowing the submarine's position was vital in updating targeting information to the missiles. They couldn't fly to where they were supposed to if they didn't know where they started from.

Walsh nodded. Coming to periscope depth to copy a NAVSAT pass wouldn't slow them down any in their four-knot dash to Point XRAY. In fact, they could speed up to six knots if there was enough sea state to hide their periscope feather, the plume of white water kicked up by the periscope moving through the water, from any aircraft that might wander into the area. Inputting a good fix to SINS would make sure that the missiles would be ready as soon as they were in the new operating area, and maybe they could get some needed housekeeping done at the same time.

"Sounds good, Nav. Why don't we blow sanitaries, dump trash, and ventilate the ship. Get that housekeeping done now so we are ready to go," Walsh said.

"Yes, sir. I'll have the Aux Forward line up and pressurize the sanitary tanks. The mess cranks report that they have six loads of trash to shoot. Clearing baffles."

Bob Shippley had just stepped up onto the periscope stand when the 21MC blared, "Conn, Sonar, new sonar contact on the towed array. Contact designated Sierra Three-Seven bears two-nine-zero. Ambiguous contact Sierra Three-Eight bears one-zero-zero." There was a pause for a second before the sonar supervisor continued, "Three-hundred-hertz tonal, possible submerged Soviet submarine."

Walsh immediately ordered, "Man battle stations torpedo. Snapshot Sierra Three-Seven, tube one."

The Chief-of-the-Watch grabbed the 1MC and announced, "Man battle stations torpedo!" then yanked the handle for the general alarm. The alarm's *bong, bong, bong* was reverberating when he repeated over the 1MC, "Man battle stations torpedo!"

The fire control technician's fingers danced across the Mark-50 attack console, sending electronic orders down to the torpedo room to flood and equalize torpedo tube one and then to open the outer door to tube one. He then manually cranked in the bearing to Sierra Three-Seven into the angle solver on the Mark-78 analyzer to give the torpedo something to shoot at. In less than a minute, the *John Jay* was ready to send a torpedo out after the Russian submarine. Just in case it suddenly proved hostile. Like many submarine COs had been taught, Darren Walsh called it "cocking the gun."

Walsh stood back, out of the way, as the crew rushed into the control room to take their battle station positions, some wiping sleep from their eyes, others hurriedly zipping up their poopie suits. Stan Wilkins ran down the passageway from the ship's office. He grabbed a set of sound-powered phones that hung above the Mark-19 plotter and slipped the earphones over his ears.

The COB, Max Steuben, slid into the diving officer's seat and reported, "Ship manned for battle stations."

Wilkins mumbled into his sound-powered phone's mouthpiece and then called out, "We have a curve on Sierra Three-Seven and Sierra Three-Eight ready for a maneuver to determine ambiguity." He glanced at the geographic plot where Pete McKay was busy laying out the picture. "Recommend coming right to course zero-seven-zero. Keeps both contacts out of end-fire. It still closes Point XRAY."

Walsh ordered, "Helm, right standard rudder, steer course zero-seven-zero." As the ship swung around to the new course, Walsh looked over at Wilkins and said, "Good thinking, XO. Need to keep heading to Point XRAY if we can. But keep this guy as our priority. Remember, he can shoot at us."

Wilkins held up his hand for a second and then clasped his headphones tightly to his ears. "Captain, Sonar reports contact on the BQR-7. Bearing zero-nine-seven. Correlates to Sierra Three-Eight."

The BQR-7 was the conformal array, three lines of hydrophones that wrapped around the sub's curving bow. Its frequency range was similar to the towed array, but it was not nearly as sensitive. That meant that contacts were almost always detected on the towed array first. Since it was a conformal array and not a linear array, the BQR-7 did not have a bearing ambiguity problem.

Pete McKay threw down the parallel motion protractor and drew a line. "XO, cross bearing range is seven thousand yards. This guy is close."

Wilkins quietly spoke to Walsh. "Okay, Skipper, what do we do? Are we at war, so we shoot this guy, or do we pray that he hasn't heard us and quietly slink away? Or do we just smile and wave as we merrily go by?"

Walsh thought for a moment before he answered. "Nobody has told us that we are at war. We don't shoot unless he shoots first. Let's stay real quiet and see if he goes on past. There are a couple of things we can do in the meantime." Turning to Brett Burns, he asked, "Weps, we still have a MOSS in tube four?"

"Yes, sir."

"Then shut the outer door on tube one, open the outer door on tube four, and make the MOSS ready to launch. Set it on a course to the southeast. And standby the six-inch evasion device launchers. If we need the MOSS, we'll hide behind a wall of noise from them. That'll confuse him. He'll have to decide which target is the real one. We'll stick the MOSS out front so it looks nice and juicy," Walsh ordered.

The *John Jay* was configured so that it could only have one of its four torpedo tubes aligned to shoot, with the outer doors open, at a time. If they were going to shoot a MOSS from tube four, they could not be lined up to shoot a torpedo from tube one.

The six-inch evasion devices were acoustic countermeasures stored in watertight launcher tubes outside the hull and launched by the CSA, the

Countermeasure Set Acoustic, panel. They were meant to fill the water with enough broadband noise to allow the submarine to sneak away in the confusion.

Turning around, he ordered, "Chief-of-the-Watch, load NAEs in both signal ejectors. And stand by with reloads at both ejectors." Turning back to Wilkins, he went on, "I really don't like waiting to take the second shot, but we don't have a choice. If he decides to shoot, maybe this will throw enough shit in the game to keep him confused."

Wilkins nodded, then said, "Skipper, we have a curve. Ready for a maneuver."

"Let's see if we can dance around behind this guy. Left standard rudder, steady course three-five-five."

The *John Jay* slowly maneuvered to slink around behind the Russian while keeping a wary eye on him. The idea was to get back into his baffles and then head away without him ever knowing that the *John Jay* was anywhere in the neighborhood. After a couple of maneuvers, the solution had resolved to a range of sixty-five hundred yards, speed of ten knots, and course of three-zero-six.

"Possible contact zig toward, increasing received frequency," the time-frequency plotter yelled out. The time-bearing plotter yelled, "Possible contact zig, increasing right bearing rate." At the same time, Sonar announced, "Possible zig, Sierra Three-Eight. Zig toward and increasing speed."

Just then the WLR-9 Acoustic Intercept Receiver buzzed loudly. Someone had just lit off an active sonar.

"Conn, Sonar, seven-kilohertz active sonar from Sierra Three-Eight! Plus forty-two SPL. Above fifty percent probability of detection! Blocks-of-Wood fire control sonar! *Alfa*-class submarines."

The Soviet submarine had turned toward them, sped up, and turned on their active sonar. These were all standard precursors to the Russian sub shooting a torpedo. It had found the *John Jay* and was attacking.

"Firing point procedures, Sierra Three-Eight, tube one!" Walsh ordered. Then he said, "Weps, launch the MOSS! Launch the portside CSA!"

Down in the torpedo room, the torpedo watch checked the MOSS presets and punched the button on the MOSS launcher panel. The little submarine simulator's battery energized and sent the ten-inch-diameter mini-sub swimming out the torpedo tube. The MOSS headed off to the southeast, broadcasting the same noises as the *John Jay*.

The torpedo men hurriedly shut the outer doors on torpedo tube four and opened the doors for torpedo tube one so that the *John Jay* could shoot a torpedo.

Brett Burns reached up to the CSA control panel, above the Mark-75 attack director, lifted up the protective covers, and punched the buttons to launch the four portside evasion devices. The gas generators that rammed the noisemakers out into the water exploded with four deafening bangs so loud they caused people to jump, thinking that the boat had been hit. The devices tumbled away from the sub, each putting out more than 250 decibels of broadband acoustic energy.

"Torpedo in the water!" Sonar announced. "Bearing one-two-six! Second torpedo! Bearing one-two-seven!"

"Solution ready!"

"Ship ready!"

"Weapon ready!"

The Russian had just shot at them. There was no doubt now that he was hostile. It was time to shoot back. They might take him out before his torpedoes could catch them. Or at least scare him and keep him busy enough that he wouldn't be able to steer his torpedo for a hit.

"Shoot on generated bearings!" Walsh ordered.

Burns grabbed the brass handle in the center of the Attack Console and threw it over to the left. "Stand by!" Then he yanked it to the right. "Shoot!"

Fifteen hundred psi high-pressure water flushed the four-thousand-pound Mark-48 torpedo out into the water. Its otto-fuel-powered swashplate engine started up and sent it racing toward the Russian sub at better than sixty knots.

"Incoming torpedoes bearing one-two-six and one-two-seven!"

Burns called out, "Indications of a normal launch. Good continuity on the wire."

Walsh ordered, "Dive, make your depth thirteen hundred feet, twenty down, ahead flank!"

The big boat rocketed ahead and down into the depths.

"Chief-of-the-Watch, launch both signal ejectors, reload, and launch again!"

The NAEs, specifically designed to confuse incoming torpedoes, tumbled out into the ocean and began making noise. Four of them would make a lot of noise to hide behind.

"Incoming torpedoes both bearing one-two-six. Forty-kilohertz active sonar. Torpedoes classified Russian USET-80s. Own-ship weapon in active search."

"Helm, left full rudder, steady course three-five-zero," Walsh ordered. He glanced at Pete McKay's plot to see the best way to maneuver. The Russian torpedoes could make better than fifty knots and had a max range of twenty thousand yards. The *John Jay* could barely make twenty knots at flank. He couldn't outrun them. His only hope was to outsmart them and get outside their acquisition cones before either one detected the *John Jay*.

Brett Burns called out, "Loss of wire continuity." Walsh was not surprised. The hair-thin copper wire that connected the *John Jay* to their Mark-48 torpedo would not stand up to the wild gyrations that he had just put the boat through. The torpedo was still out there doing its job, but they couldn't see what it was doing or send it any updated orders over the wire.

"Loss of both incoming torpedoes in the baffles. Loss of own-ship weapon in the baffles."

"Helm, right five degrees rudder, steady course zero-five-zero," Walsh ordered. He needed to keep the incoming weapons just on the edge of his baffles. That was the only way to know where they were and to ease over to the edge of their acquisition cone. He would let the weapon bearings generate back into his baffles and then change course again. That way he would be slowly spiraling toward the edge.

"Regain of one incoming weapon, bearing one-three-seven. We don't hold the second one. Regain of own-ship weapon in active search." The Mark 48 had turned on its twenty-kilohertz active sonar and was searching for the Russian submarine. If nothing else, it would cause the Russian to pucker tightly.

The sub was rocked by a loud blast somewhere astern of them. Either the MOSS or one of the evasion devices had sacrificed itself. That still left the one that they were tracking and that was chasing them.

Walsh looked at the clock above the analyzer. The Russian torpedo had the power to run for about twelve minutes. It had only been seven minutes since they were detected. Could he successfully dance for another five minutes? He felt a trickle of sweat run down the back of his neck.

"Incoming weapon lost in the baffles. Own-ship weapon speeding up." Their Mark 48 had found something and was increasing speed to attack.

"Right five degrees rudder, steady zero-eight-zero," Walsh ordered. "Launch both signal ejectors and reload. Weps, standby the CSA."

"Regain incoming weapon. Incoming weapon is range-gating! Incoming weapon is speeding up!" The sonar report was up several octaves. The Russian torpedo had detected them and was homing.

"Weps, launch the starboard CSAs. Launch the signal ejectors, reload, and launch again."

The banging from the CSA launch was drowned by a larger explosion, and then by an even larger one that rocked the *John Jay*, shoving the big sub over on its side. The blast tossed anyone not seated or hanging on tightly to the deck. Darren Walsh was thrown against the periscope stand, smacking his head into the piping. The lights flickered for a few seconds. Coffee cups and loose debris flew around the control room. The air was filled with dust.

Walsh woozily stood and waited for reports that his ship was doomed. He looked around as people slowly rose to their feet. The Chief-of-the-Watch gathered reports from all the spaces before telling Walsh that, other than a few bumps and bruises, the *John Jay* had not suffered damage.

"Conn, Sonar, no longer hold any torpedoes. Breaking-up noises on the bearing to Sierra Three-Eight."

Walsh's hand came away from the back of his head sticky with blood. Looking over at Bob Shippley, he said, "Nav, get us past Point XRAY. I'm going to walk the boat and see how everyone is doing. And secure from battle stations. Nav, when we are past Point XRAY and slowed down, come shallow and blow sanitaries. Reckon we will need it now. After that little fun, they will be full. And get our spare floating wire deployed."

27

1700 EST, 17 April 1983, Naval Ocean Processing Facility (NOPF), Dam Neck, Virginia

The Naval Ocean Processing Facility at Dam Neck, Virginia, reeked of fresh paint and linoleum adhesive. The building had been completed and operational for only a couple of months. At long last, all of the deep-ocean acoustic data gathered by the various bottom-mounted SOSUS arrays for the Western Atlantic could be processed and analyzed at one location.

Oceanographic Research Watch Officer Steffanie Graham looked out over a broad floor populated with dozens of rows of chart tables with electrodes burning nearly incomprehensible dashes and squiggles on specially treated paper. A troop of Ocean Technicians roamed up and down the rows of tables, watching and deciphering the burnt traces on the paper. Each burnt dot represented some quanta of acoustic energy that an array had detected. The technicians labored to analyze dots, to build them into the detection of a submerged submarine.

One of the technicians, looking at the Nantucket Array, called out that she had a possible contact. The possible contact was in a sonar beam that looked out toward the Gulf Stream. Graham mustered her team to look at the other arrays for similar inputs. The highly manual process took almost half an hour, but by then they knew that they had found a Russian nuclear submarine and named it Case 41171700. It was in an eighty percent ellipse of probability centered a thousand miles east of Cape Cod. The ellipse had a two-hundred-mile major axis and a fifty-mile minor one. That meant there was an eighty percent probability that a sub was hiding in an ellipse of over seven thousand square miles. A big chunk of ocean, but a whole lot smaller than the whole North Atlantic.

Steffanie Graham picked up the STU phone and made a call. It was time to report Case 41171700 and get it verified.

1845 EST, 17 April 1983, P-3C Tail Number 161124, Oceana Naval Air Station, Virginia Beach, Virginia

An hour later, P-3C Orion tail number 161124 roared off the end of the runway at Oceana Naval Air Station and clawed for altitude.

"Navy One-Two-Four, Oceana Air Control, you are cleared to angels ten and vectored direct to op area. Switch to Navy Tactical Control, one-four-three-point-two."

"Oceana, One-Two-Four, roger angels ten, vector zero-seven-five direct to area," Blunt Sharples replied. "Switching to Navy Tactical Control."

The four big Allison turboprops pulled the Orion to the northeast at three hundred knots. Sharples put the plane on autopilot and sat back. They had four hours before arriving on station, and the rest of the crew had nothing to do until then, so they relaxed.

Sharples keyed his intercom mike and called out to Wee Willy Weston, the TACCO, "Hey, TACCO, this scramble caused me to miss dinner. My stomach is growling. Who has ordnance on this trip?"

Weston came back, "We got Miller this time."

Birdman Byrd, the copilot, chuckled as Blunt Sharples cursed. Stu Miller had the reputation as the worst cook in the squadron. It was commonly known that he could and did burn water. But the ordnance man was, by tradition, the crew cook on these long flights. Since he was not involved in the complex search business, he had the time to do the cooking chores.

"What you laughing about, Birdman?" Blunt grumped. "My stomach is growling so loud, it's going to start showing up on acoustics."

"Wee Willy stopped at Luigi's on the way in and bought a dozen pizzas," Birdman Byrd said, still laughing. "Nothing for Miller to screw up. That should keep even you happy."

"Navy One-Two-Four, Navy Tactical," blasted over the UHF radio, interrupting the dinner conversation.

"Navy Tactical, One-Two-Four, go," Blunt answered.

"One-Two-Four, NOPF latest update on mission. Case 41171700 current location fifty-one north, forty-one-point-seven west. Probability ellipse one hundred by thirty. How copy?"

"Tactical, copy all," Blunt answered as Birdman hurriedly scribbled down the number.

"One-Two-Four, Charlie Adams has been diverted to help out. His ETA is thirteen hundred Zulu tomorrow. Good hunting. Tactical out."

Headwinds slowed the P-3C enough as it flew toward the spot in the North Atlantic so that it didn't arrive until after 0300 Zulu. Clouds built into a thick blanket below them, obscuring the entire ocean for as far as they could see. The meteorological report showed a low-pressure center moving down across the Gulf of St. Lawerence directly toward them. Solid cloud layer from a thousand to eight thousand feet with winds gusting to forty knots. It had all the promise of being a typical challenging night over the North Atlantic.

They flew directly over the spot in the ocean and then circled around while Blunt Sharples brought One-Two-Four down to a thousand feet. He dropped below the clouds at fifteen hundred feet only to glimpse a dark and pitching sea. On the first pass over the spot, a single buoy dropped out of the P-3C. The buoy parachuted to the sea surface, where it floated with an antenna protruding clear of the water. The bathythermograph, or BT, buoy released its weighted temperature probe into the depths. Wee Willy Weston used the temperature-depth profile to compute the best listening depth for his SSQ-53 DIFAR sonobuoys.

Sharples swung One-Two-Four around while a precise pattern of passive sonobuoys dropped out of the sonobuoy launcher built into the aircraft's underbelly. Each one released a line of hydrophones down into the deep while its UHF transmitter linked with the computer on the aircraft. Weston verified that all the buoys were live and functioning as they came online. Now it was only a matter of making slow, lazy circles while the sonobuoys listened. Blunt Sharples feathered number one engine to save fuel while they orbited, then he turned to Birdman. "You got the plane for a bit. I'm going to stretch my legs and see if there is any pizza left."

Byrd chuckled. "I got the plane. Boss, you know better. Those chowhounds will have licked the cheese off the boxes."

"Contact," Wee Willy called out. "Have a hot buoy!" A couple of seconds later, he added, "Two more buoys hot. Triangulated. Case 41171700 is up on the Link. Looks like he is on a course of about zero-four-zero, speed fifteen. Confirmed Soviet submarine."

"Okay. Let's make sure we don't lose this guy," Blunt said. He then keyed the radio. "Navy Tactical, One-Two-Four, confirmed sub, posit four-three-point-three north, four-nine-point-zero west. I have four hour on-station time. Request hot turnover."

The UHF radio squawked back, "Roger One-Two-Four. Scrambling turnover. ETA zero-seven-thirty Zulu. Stay with him, One-Two-Four. After turnover, you are being vectored to Keflavik for refuel. Navy Tactical out."

"Birdman, loiter number four engine," Blunt directed. "Need to conserve as much fuel as possible. It looks like it's going to be a long night."

0400Z, 18 April 1983, USS John Jay, *Norwegian Sea, south of Jan Mayen Island*

The *John Jay* had just completed an intensive four-hour search of their operating area. Except for sea noise and biologics, the sonar screens were blank. As far as sonar was concerned, they had the entire ocean to themselves. The Russian submarine that had tried to ambush them didn't seem to have any friends in the area. Still, Darren Walsh was cautious. His job was to hide and be ready to shoot his missiles if ordered, not to go out and play ASW with the Russians. To do his job, he needed to make sure that he owned this piece of ocean.

Walsh leafed through the BQR-21 displays. Nothing there. Then, wrinkling his nose at the smell of burnt paper, he watched the sparking electrode dance across the BQQ-3 LOFARGRAM display. Nothing there either. The hull-mounted passive sonars weren't seeing anything. He stepped into the sonar room and checked out the BQR-20. The towed array was coming up blank. Maybe there really wasn't anyone out there.

Stan Wilkins stuck his head into the sonar shack. "Skipper, radio has the message ready to go."

Walsh stepped across the passageway, into the radio room. The tiny space was crowded with all the radiomen onboard. It wasn't every day that a boomer made a Circuit Mayflower transmission. Built before satellite communications systems were common, Circuit Mayflower was a reliable and nearly undetectable means for the boat to send a short, coded message back to SUBLANT. It relied on a very powerful HF transmitter sending an extremely short pulse of energy. The burst message lasted for only a couple of milliseconds, not enough time for the Russians to detect it and triangulate to where the *John Jay* lay hidden. But to get the system finely tuned and ready to go was a manpower-intensive operation.

RM1 Melvin Yoe looked up from where he was tuning the URT-23 HF transmitter. "Almost ready to go, Skipper. Number two sixty-four-kilowatt motor generator was a little squirrelly on output frequency, but the electricians fixed it. We just broadcast into dummy load, and everything checked out. We're ready as soon as you get up to periscope depth and give us an antenna."

Walsh smiled and answered, "You got it, RM-1."

He ducked out the door and stepped into the darkened control room. This far north, sunrise was still almost two hours away. Dale Horton was the Officer-of-the-Deck and had everything ready to go to periscope depth.

"Officer-of-the-Deck, proceed to periscope depth and conduct a Circuit Mayflower shot," Walsh ordered. He could feel the *John Jay* start to pitch and roll as the boat headed up toward the surface.

Dale Horton raised the number two periscope and started the slow, circular dance, looking in every direction to make sure that no threat waited for them topside. After ensuring that they were all alone, he called out, "No contacts. Chief-of-the-Watch, raise the HF mast."

With the mast raised, he ordered, "Radio, Conn, conduct Circuit Mayflower shot."

Seconds later, the 21MC announced, "Conn, Radio, Circuit Mayflower shot completed. No longer need the HF mast."

Walsh smiled. The whole evolution had gone much smoother than he expected. "Officer-of-the-Deck, secure from Circuit Mayflower ops. Let's clear the area, just in case. Head to the northwest. I'll be in my stateroom. Call me when we get the circuit activation message."

28

0015 EST, 18 April 1983, COMSUBLANT, Norfolk, Virginia

Vice Admiral Rufus Brown had not even bothered to try to return home to West Virginia House, explaining to Ann that things were just too tense. He needed to stay on top of everything going on. He might catch a few winks on the couch in his office. Instead, he had ensconced himself in a corner of the OPCON Center, frequently prowling from desk to desk, seeing what was happening.

The bell on a printer across the center, along the far wall, dinged. The watch officer sat upright and then bolted across the room. "Admiral, we have a Circuit Mayflower activation!" he called out. "An attack report from the *John Jay*. Reports fired upon by a Soviet sub. Counter-fired and sank it. *Jay* reports no damage."

Brown wearily pulled himself to his feet and walked over to the printer. Reading the scripted message, still warm from the printer, somehow made it more real. What was happening with the Russians? *Jay* was over near Greenland, a thousand miles away from the Barents Sea and from Russia. Did the Soviet Union somehow think that they were suddenly in a hot war? As COMSUBLANT, he had over a dozen US boats racing up that way. What were they going to be running into? What should he order them to do?

"Watch Officer, get an *OPREP 3 PINNACLE* off immediately," he ordered. "Then get a message off to all units authorizing weapons free if they encounter any Soviet ships that display hostile intent. And then get a message to *John Jay* acknowledging the report. Got all that?"

"Yes, sir."

"Good, I'll be in the SCIF. Going to call the Joint Chiefs to discuss this." Brown turned and disappeared behind the heavy SCIF door.

The Joint Chiefs were already meeting in the National Military Command Center, deep under the Pentagon. The Chairman came on the line immediately. "Rufus, that was quick. I have your *OPREP 3* in my hand right now."

"Yes, sir. We need to discuss that and decide what to do. We've had two attacks on our boats in one day. I'm issuing orders to all my units to exercise self-defense on hostile intent, not to wait for the first shot."

"Sounds about right, but let's get the JAG readout on that first," the Chairman answered. "SECDEF and the president are on their way in as we speak. I'll brief them both when they get here."

"Sir, I strongly disagree on waiting for some lawyer to tell me when and how to fight. I'm recommending that we up our posture to DEFCON TWO. That will allow all our units to actively defend themselves."

"Rufus, let's just stay cool and calm. I think POTUS is a step ahead of you. He is prepping a statement to the UN Security Council that advises them that in the name of self-defense, any Soviet warships or aircraft detected within a hundred miles of US units will be considered hostile and will be engaged. He is urging restraint and recommending that all warships return to their home waters. The Secretary of State has summoned the Soviet ambassador to deliver the same message."

Brown was nodding as he listened. "Are we getting orders to back that up? Is the battle fleet turning around? Should I order my boats back home?"

"POTUS is on the way here. You should be seeing orders by morning at the very latest. In the meantime, keep your boats doing what they are doing. Get them as far forward as possible. We need eyes on their battle fleet. And I suggest you get some rest. Once this hits the fan, it might be a long time before you get another opportunity."

With the call ended, Rufus Brown suddenly felt very tired. He needed sleep, and preferably in his own bed. After leaving instructions with the watch officer, he called for a driver and official car to take him to West Virgina House.

On a whim, he had the driver enter the Navy base through Gate 5 and then drive along the D&S piers. The piers were strangely empty. The submarine tender *L. Y. Spear* sat there without her normal brood of boats nestled alongside. All of the boats capable of getting underway were already heading out into the Atlantic. All except *Finback*, which still sat, high and dry, up on blocks in the floating drydock, but the number of workers scurrying around at oh-dark-thirty on a Monday morning attested to the maximum effort to get her out to join her sisters.

1115 MSK, 18 April 1983, K-314, 300 nm south of Greenland

Henri DuBois quietly stirred his tea. He had the wardroom on the Soviet submarine *K-314* to himself. The officers seemed to be going out of their way to avoid him. He wasn't sure why, but it suited his purposes to be left alone. His leg was stiff and still bothered him, but at least there was no infection. The submarine's corpsman had poked and prodded the wound, flushing it out with peroxide and swabbing it with antibiotics, before tightly wrapping a bandage around it. Until they arrived in Russia, there was nothing more that could be done. It would take a real doctor to operate and remove the bullet. The corpsman explained through an interpreter that the bullet was too near the femoral artery for him to risk removing the bullet.

DuBois had quickly come to the realization that he hated tea, especially this black Russian concoction. He wanted some good Cajun coffee, heavy with the flavor of chicory, and a plate of beignets. He shook his head and dissolved another lump of sugar into the vile mix. He needed to face reality. There was no coffee on this submarine, nor was he likely to find any in Russia. At least until he had established himself and could access his offshore bank accounts. Then he could afford to drink whatever he wanted.

Captain Second Rank Ilya Agapov walked into the wardroom and sat down. The mess attendant must have seen him approaching. He suddenly appeared from wherever he was hiding and hurriedly filled a glass of tea hot from the samovar and placed it in front of the captain.

Agapov took a sip and sat his glass down. Turning to DuBois, he said, "*Gospodin* DuBois, I trust that you find your accommodations adequate. I'm afraid that we are a little limited in what we can offer, but we will soon have you safely in Murmansk."

DuBois smiled, stretched his wounded leg, and nodded. "Comrade Captain, I am quite comfortable."

"We are now far enough from the American coast that we can radio Murmansk and tell them that we have you aboard," Agapov explained as he sipped his tea. "We are at communications depth now to tell them."

The conversation was interrupted by the announcing system, "Captain, please come to the control room." At the same time, they could feel the deck angling down. Agapov rushed out of the wardroom and headed to the control room. He found Anatoly Balakirev, the watch officer, standing at the navigation station, studying pictures of American aircraft.

"Comrade Balakirev, what is happening?" Agapov asked.

"Comrade Captain, we were over-flown by an American aircraft. It was very low. I fear that we have been detected by this." He held up a picture of a P-3C. "This kind of aircraft."

Agapov immediately recognized that they were in a serious predicament. The American P-3Cs enjoyed a reputation with Soviet submariners of being difficult to lose once they achieved contact. With their sonobuoys and MAD detectors, they were a worthy adversary.

Agapov grabbed the oceanographic charts for the area south of Greenland. If he was going to lose this plane, he would need to use the ocean intelligently. The chart showed that they were on the cold north side of the warm Gulf Stream. There should be several warm-water eddies, huge spiraling masses of warmer water spun off the western wall of the Gulf Stream, sitting there reflecting acoustic energy up and away in the neighborhood. A few kilometers to the west, the Labrador current dumped frigid Arctic water, fresh from under the polar ice, into the Atlantic basin. The extreme temperature and salinity gradients caused by the Arctic waters mixing with the Atlantic only complicated the already challenging environment for any acoustic search.

And to further complicate the P-3C's problems, at this time of year the lower Labrador Sea would be cluttered with icebergs calving a little farther north and then floating out into the Atlantic. Dropping a sonobuoy anywhere near an iceberg was a waste of a sonobuoy. The bergs filled the water with groaning, grinding noises as they broke free and started their journey south, noisily breaking up or crashing into each other along the way.

It was time to do something unexpected and then get lost in all of the clutter. "Comrade Balakirev, come to course three-one-zero. Ahead flank."

The Soviet submarine jumped ahead and raced up into the ice-clogged sea. Agapov waited until they were well into the Labrador Sea and into the vast field of icebergs before he made his next move. Even if the P-3C had tried to chase him here, it would be very difficult for it to seed its sonobuoys, and the grinding, groaning ice would blank out their screens with noise, just like it was doing to his sonar screen.

"Come right, steer course zero-four-five. The winter pack ice should extend out sixty kilometers from the Greenland coast. When you are forty kilometers off the coast, turn and parallel the coast."

Agapov smiled. The Americans would have to figure some way to get through all the ice to track them now. He could follow the pack ice all the way around to Svalbard and the safety of the Barents. It might take a few days longer, but his orders were to deliver his passenger safely to Murmansk, and he would do just that.

0400 EST, 18 April 1983, National Military Command Center, Pentagon

The president sat at the head of the table with the Secretary of Defense on his left and the Chairman on his right. The briefing officer, an Air Force brigadier general, standing at the edge of the projection screen, clicked up the next slide.

"Mr. President, we evaluate that the Strategic Rocket Force has gone to their max state of readiness."

A satellite image of fuel trucks gathered around a missile silo appeared on the screen. "We estimate that over ninety percent of the liquid-fueled missiles in hardened silos have been fueled. Due to the corrosive fuels they utilize, these missiles have less than a week before they must either be fired or defueled and cleaned."

A new image, a map of the USSR dotted with red stars. "The SRF has hardened launchers at these sites. There are over fourteen hundred launcher silos here. They all appear to be active, fueled, and ready to launch."

A new image of a road-mobile ICBM flashed up. "This is an RT-21, or SS-16 Sinner. It is a solid-fuel road-mobile ICBM. We evaluate that the SRF has two hundred launchers deployed on specially constructed roads across the Ural Mountains and selected bases in Siberia. Normally they are housed in hardened garages, but imaging shows them now road deployed."

Another image, a map of Soviet air bases, appeared. "These are the Soviet Long Range Aviation bases. We are seeing Bear G and H squadrons, as well as Backfire squadrons, fully fueled and armed, on strip alert. One squadron of Blackjack bombers appears to be standing by at Olen'ya Naval Air Station in Murmansk. This is the first that we have seen the Blackjack operational."

The president shook his head. "General, this is going to sound like a really dumb question, but the future of the world could hinge on your answer. What is your evaluation of all of this?"

The general put his clicker down on the podium and turned to face the men gathered around the table. "Mr. President, I have, none of us, has ever seen this level of preparedness. They are either planning a massive first strike or they are afraid that we are. I don't know which."

The president looked down the table and thought for a few seconds, then he quietly said, "I don't either. But we have to figure out which. And what we are going to do about it."

29

0945Z, 18 April 1983, USS **Tigerfish**, *Barents Sea, 125 nm south of Bear Island*

The *USS Tigerfish* cruised quietly three hundred feet below the surface on the western edge of the Barents Sea. After reporting the Russians sinking their own submarine and receiving orders to keep tabs on the Soviet fleet, Commander Roy Blivens decided to move slowly to the south while keeping an eye on the Soviet warships off to the east. He would take the *Tigerfish* all the way down to North Cape and reverse course when he got to Norwegian waters. Then they would head north, up to the ice edge. The pack ice in the Barents was reported to be about seventy-five miles south of Svalbard. That meant they needed to search out a line a little over three hundred miles long. Blivens then planned to slip under the ice to the east of Svalbard and search out the hidden Soviet boomer bastions thought to be somewhere between the ice-bound Norwegian island and Zemlya Georga, a forlorn bit of barren wind-swept rock three hundred miles to the east.

Blivens stuck his head into the sonar shack. Senior Chief Zwarlinski sat on his usual tall stool, overlooking his three watch standers while listening on a headset and paging through the displays on the narrowband analyzer.

As usual, Blivens wondered how he could keep all the various inputs clear in his head.

Zwarlinski looked up to see the skipper standing at the door. He removed his headset and stood. "Skipper, we just picked up another skimmer on the TB-16. Sounds like a *Grisha II*. Sierra Two-Zero-Five. Two four-bladed screws, getting turn counts for twenty knots. He's banging away on his Bull Nose active sonar. No threat to us, but it makes for a nice beacon."

Blivens chuckled as he pictured the little thousand-ton Soviet corvette trying to race through the storm-tossed winter seas and still search for the elusive submarines. Life would be rough for the crew on that ship this time of year.

"That makes six surface contacts," Zwarlinski went on. "Not counting two of the heavies that we lost up by Bear Island." He looked at his sonar log. "Sierra One-Nine-Two, broadband contact on the towed array, bearing zero-three-one, probable *Kara*, distant, looks to be past CPA and opening. Sierra One-Nine-Nine, broadband contact on the towed array, bearing zero-six-two, also distant, but closing, probable *Udaloy*. Sierra Two-Zero-Zero, broadband on the sphere, bearing zero-seven-seven, probable *Kashin*, making twenty-two knots by turn count. Sierra Two-Zero-One and Sierra Two-Zero-Two are both *Petya*-class frigates bearing zero-nine-six, both active on their Hawk Screech sonars. You want to feel sorry for skimmers, feel sorry for the guys out here in those old rust buckets."

"Anything to be concerned about?" Blivens asked.

Zwarlinski shook his head. "Not really. They seem to be playing the typical skimmer ASW tactic, steam around fast and bang away on their active sonar. Maybe they'll scare us away if they can't find us."

"Well, they were successful at least once," Blivens noted ruefully. "Sierra One-Seven-Six can attest to that. Let's keep our heads on tight and our eyes wide open." He spun around and headed toward the control room.

Tom Clemont, the on-watch Officer-of-the-Deck, met him at the navigation stand. "Captain, we need to copy the broadcast, and I'd like to get a fix. We haven't had a good fix in almost a week. The dead reckoning error circle is getting pretty big." He looked at some notes he had scribbled. "There's a NAVSAT pass in half an hour. We should be able to pick up the Norwegian,

Paynesville, and La Moure Omega transmitters. Give us a reasonable idea where we really are."

Omega was, at least theoretically, a worldwide radio-navigation system that allowed a ship to determine its position by measuring the received frequency phase difference from two synchronized transmitters. That established the receiver in a hyperbolic band between the receivers. Add in a third station and the intersection of the hyperbolas was the ship's position. Because Omega used VLF, its signals propagated for very long distances.

"What about LORAN?" Blivens asked.

"Last time we were up, we couldn't get in sync on the Jan Mayen station," Clemont answered.

"Give it a try anyway," Blivens directed. "Three sources are better than two. I'd sure like to really know where I am before we go under the ice."

"Aye, sir," Clemont answered.

Loran-C was a radio-navigation system that utilized a master and several secondary HF transmitters. Measuring the time of arrival difference between the master and two secondary stations provided two intersecting lines of position. The intersection point was the ship's position. Because it was an HF system, it was both received over a shorter range and was more accurate than Omega. But there were many parts of the world, including the high north where there were no LORAN stations available.

It took Tom Clemont and his team almost half an hour to clear baffles and determine a good course to come to periscope depth. He finally raised the Type 18 periscope to see a pitching and heaving, gunmetal-gray sea under a gray, cloud-covered sky. The waves made seeing any distance difficult, but it also hid the periscope from being seen by any surface ships.

"One minute till time of rise," QM-1 Swarton called out. In one minute, the Transit satellite would come over the horizon. The BRA-34 antenna needed to be raised to get the NAVSAT fix.

"Raise the BRA-34," Tom Clemont ordered. The Chief-of-the-Watch flipped the switch to raise the mast.

"Conn, Radio, in sync on SSIX," the 21MC announced. It would only take a couple of seconds to receive and receipt for the incoming communications.

"Conn, ESM, detecting Wet Eye radar. Carried on IL-38 ASW aircraft. Signal strength high! Definite detection threat!"

The IL-38 May, the Soviet answer to the P-3C Orion, was a threat to detect them, plus it carried attack weapons. It was time to get out of Dodge.

"Lower all masts and antennas," Clemont ordered as he reached into the overhead to rotate the red scope ring. "Make your depth one-five-zero feet." The scope slid down into the scope well as the sub angled down toward the deep.

"Right full rudder, steady course two-four-zero. Ahead full."

It was important to change course and head off in a different direction just in case the ASW aircraft had detected them. The May used its MAD, magnetic anomaly detection, system to verify a sub contact caught on radar or sonobuoy and to localize a sub after it was detected. The MAD system sensed the localized change in the Earth's magnetic signature caused by a large steel body, like a submarine. Moving on an unexpected tangent lessened the chance the IL-38 would over-fly and find them.

"Conn, Radio, request the Captain come to radio."

Roy Blivens looked around the control room for a second, just to make sure everything was normal. Then he headed aft to the radio room. George Sanders met him at the door and handed him the Top Secret message board.

"Read the top message," the XO said.

Blivens flipped open the aluminum clipboard and quickly scanned the message. Then he turned and walked back to control. He stepped up onto the periscope stand and grabbed the 1MC microphone. "Men, this is the Captain. We have just received a message from COMSUBLANT. I don't know what's happening in the outside world, but the defense readiness position has been raised to DEFCON TWO. As far as we are concerned, *Tigerfish* is now on a war footing. If we are detected or think that we are at risk, we are to shoot first and ask questions later."

1035Z, 18 April 1983, P-3C Tail Number 161124, off Keflavik, Iceland

Blunt Sharples stretched and groaned. The long flight was almost over. He could taste a tall cold one at the Officers' Club. "Birdman," he said to his copilot, "fancy a dinner in town once we get this plane put to bed? After, of course, a couple of brews at the club."

Birdman Byrd smiled. "As long as we keep it simple. We ain't doing any of those exotic things that you always seem to hanker for. No sheep's head or any of that fermented shark. Fish and chips sounds about right. We can get that at the club."

"Where's your sense of adventure?" Blunt shot back. "You need to explore and savor other cultures."

"After the triple pepperoni and salami pizza with hot peppers we scarfed down earlier. No adventure left in my stomach," Birdman answered. "Why didn't the travel agent tell us that beer was still prohibited? Any Nordic country that has outlawed beer can't be normal."

"Did I hear dinner plans?" Wee Willy Weston interrupted. "I'm so hungry that I could eat a whale."

"Navy Flight One-Two-Four, Keflavik tower, you are cleared for immediate landing, runway one-zero. The pattern is clear. Visibility two miles, winds one-five knots from the northwest."

"Navy Flight One-Two-Four, roger, cleared runway one-zero," Blunt answered. He swung the big bird around the landing heading of one-zero-zero.

Birdman flipped a couple of switches before he called out, "Lined up for ILS, you are above glide slope. Five miles out."

Blunt eased the nose down just a bit and trimmed up the aircraft. He concentrated on the ILS display, trying to keep the localizer and glide slope lines centered exactly on the bullseye.

"Three miles out, flaps deployed, wheels down and locked."

"Two miles out, runway in sight."

Blunt saw the sweet sight of the tarmac out the windscreen. The crosswind was blowing him to the south, so he had to adjust, to crab the big plane several degrees to the north of the runway heading. Easing back on the power control levers, he kissed the bird down right in the middle of the touchdown zone.

"Keflavik tower, Navy One-Two-Four. On the ground, request taxi instructions."

"Navy One-Two-Four, take taxiway alpha. Park at Alert Facility."

Blunt Sharples keyed his mike. "Navy One-Two-Four, taxiway alpha to Alert Facility, roger." He steered the bird off the runway, onto taxiway alpha. The joint Air Force/Navy Alert Facility sat at the end of the taxiway surrounded by a broad cement apron that was crowded with Air Force fighter jets. There didn't seem to be any other P-3Cs on the ground here. A signalman stood on the apron with a pair of marshalling wands pointing to where he wanted the P-3C parked. Blunt brought the bird to a stop right where he was supposed to.

A fuel truck pulled up and stopped just off the port wingtip, waiting for Blunt Sharples to shut down the engines. A pickup stacked high with sonobuoys pulled up on the starboard side of the aircraft. Looked like someone wanted this bird ready to go back out.

After shifting the electrical system over to a ground power unit and shutting down the engines, Sharples followed Birdman Byrd out the hatch only to be met by the Navy Detachment CO. "Welcome to Keflavik," he greeted Blunt with a firm handshake. "Don't get too comfortable. Your relief lost contact on Case 4117I700. We need your crew rested, the bird refueled, restocked, and back in the air in six hours."

Blunt looked over at Birdman and Wee Willy. He shook his head and said, "Sorry, guys. Looks like no sheep's head this trip."

1330Z, 18 April 1983, USS John Jay, *Norwegian Sea, south of Jan Mayen Island*

Darren Walsh stood at the back of the radio room, reading the messages as they reeled off the printer. The *John Jay* was continuously monitoring two channels of the VERDIN VLF broadcast, copying all the traffic on each channel whether it was addressed to them or some other boat. Every few minutes, RM3 Milt Schoneman would rip off the scrolling reel of paper from one of the printers, lay it out on the desk/workbench, and cut out each message addressed to the *John Jay*. He would then individually tape each message to a sheet of paper, stamp it with a routing stamp, and place it in the correct message board. The Top Secret board was rapidly filling ever since their Circuit Mayflower shot eight hours ago. It seemed that everyone at every level in the chain of command had something to say.

A ringing alarm bell interrupted the clatter from the printers. Schoneman glanced at the upper printer and grabbed the 21MC microphone. "Conn, Radio, receiving an Emergency Action Message!" Almost immediately, the 1MC blasted, "Alert One! Alert One!"

Walsh grabbed the scrolling printout and quickly read it before heading out the radio room door, where he almost collided with Pete McKay and Dale Horton racing up the ladder to radio. He slid past the pair and stepped out to the control room. There he found Stan Wilkins already pulling out the publications they would need.

"XO, looks like a change in defense posture," Walsh said. "We're going to DEFCON TWO. Let's see what the book says we're supposed to do."

Flipping pages until they found the instructions for Defense Readiness Condition Two, DEFCON TWO, they pored over the words. Reading through it, they found that as a boomer on alert patrol, they didn't need to change anything, just stay undetected and extra vigilant. Whoever was in charge back in the Pentagon thought that war was very likely in the very near future. Boats not on alert and other commands would be scurrying, getting ready for war. The *John Jay* already was.

They had just finished reading the instructions and shaking their heads in wonderment when McKay and Horton walked out of radio. The pair held up the message and said, "Skipper, we have a properly formatted and authenticated message setting DEFCON TWO."

McKay then held up the Top Secret message board and added, "Skipper, we received an OPORD change while we were authenticating the EAM."

Walsh grabbed the message board and read the OPORD change. He walked over to the Mark-19 plotter and looked at the navigation chart. He turned and ordered, "Officer-of-the-Deck, come around and steer course two-two-zero." He then handed the message to the Quartermaster-of-the-

Watch and said, "Get the Nav up here and plot out these new patrol areas. Looks like they want us down by Iceland."

Bob Shippley read through the OPORD change before reviewing the navigation charts. Selecting the right chart, he laid it down on the plotter before swinging the parallel motion protractor around so that the straight edge connected *John Jay*'s current position with the nearest position in the new patrol area. Measuring the distance, he grabbed the nav slide rule and spun it around.

"Skipper, to maintain PIM, we need to make better than three knots good on a course of two-one-eight. I put a five-mile square box around PIM to make sure we get there on time and still have room to maneuver. We will own patrol areas Papa-Two through Papa-Seven and Quebec-Six and Eight. There's a deep transit lane that runs right up through the center for fast attacks heading north. It's from five hundred foot to the basement. In the lanes, we will only own zone shallow, surface to three hundred feet."

Walsh looked at the chart and studied the myriad of colored lines that crisscrossed over it. The patrol areas that the Nav had read off covered the entire ocean from Iceland to Greenland. The overall box was roughly three hundred miles wide by five hundred miles long. They would have over one hundred fifty thousand square miles of frigidly cold ocean in which to hide. A five-mile-wide lane up through it shouldn't present any untoward problem. Particularly since anyone driving through it would be deep and the *John Jay* needed to stay shallow anyway.

Shippley looked up and grabbed another chart from the outboard worktable. The chart showed the expected pack ice edge and marginal ice zone for April. "This new patrol area puts us at the ice edge for this time of year. The MIZ runs right down through the center of areas Papa-Two and Papa-Four."

"Nav, steer us over that way. The MIZ sounds like a really good place to hide," Walsh said. "We'll need to keep out from under the pack ice, though. We don't have any of that fancy under-ice equipment the fast boats carry, and I sure don't want to bend a scope on a bergy bit."

30

1954Z, 19 April 1983, USS Tigerfish, *Barents Sea, 60 nm northeast of Bear Island*

The *Tigerfish* steamed along at periscope depth in the cold, turbulent Barents Sea, sixty miles north and east of Bear Island. They had slipped past the wall of Soviet warships lined up to catch any submarine audacious enough to think they could sneak into what the Russians viewed as their private lake. Senior Chief Zwarlinski's sonar watch could still hear the Russians banging away with their active sonars well off to the west.

The sun was low on the southwest horizon but would not set for another three hours. They were almost at the season of the midnight sun for these latitudes.

Steve Dunn, the Officer-of-the-Deck, stood and slowly walked a tight circle, looking through the Type 18 periscope at an empty gray sea.

QM-1 Swarton called out, "Officer-of-the-Deck, one minute to time of rise." It was almost time to catch the Transit satellite as it soared overhead.

"Chief-of-the-Watch, raise the BRA-34," Dunn ordered as he grabbed the 21MC microphone and punched up radio. "Radio, Conn, raising the BRA-34. Copy the SSIXs broadcast."

"Conn, Radio, aye."

Roy Blivens walked into the control room, sipping on a cup of coffee. "Quiet, Eng?" he asked.

"Yes, sir, real quiet," Dunn answered. "Only sonar contacts are the active intercepts off to the west. Catching a Transit pass and the 2000 SSIXs ZBO. When we're done, I plan to drop down to one-five-zero feet and head to the northeast in accordance with the Navigator's track. As soon as we're clear of the Spitsbergen Bank, I'll drop down to three hundred feet and ahead full."

Blivens nodded and said, "Sounds good. I'll be in radio for a few minutes. Have all the off-watch officers muster in the wardroom at 2000 for officers' training."

As Blivens walked away, he overheard Dunn instructing the Chief-of-the-Watch to send out his messenger and round up the officers.

Blivens saw George Sanders already standing in the radio room door, reading the message board. He handed the board to Blivens. "Skipper, you're going to want to read the top message. Seems SUBLANT has changed his mind about what he wants us to do."

Blivens took the board and read the top message. "Very interesting," he said. "Want to get the Nav and get the track laid out while I get the boat heading in the right direction? Sounds like the topic for wardroom training might have just changed, too."

Blivens retraced his steps back to the control room. He stopped at the Nav center where Swarton had just finished plotting the Transit fix. He grabbed the parallel motion protractor and laid it down on the new fix. He spun the arm around and lined it up. "Officer-of-the-Deck, come right to course one-five-zero. Come to three hundred feet and ahead full."

He could feel the boat drop down and speed up as he headed down to the wardroom.

George Sanders and Tom Clemont already had the navigation charts and the message board laid out on the wardroom table. The other officers, the COB, Senior Chief Zwarlinski, and ETC Greg Lawlar, the Forward ET Chief, stood back, watching.

Blivens walked in, refilled his coffee cup, and sat at the head of the table. He motioned for everyone to sit.

"Gentlemen," he began. "It looks like our mission has changed again. SUBLANT is reporting that *Lionfish* has some kind of casualty and is coming off the I&W station off Murmansk. We are being tasked to go down there and pick up the I&W mission until they can scramble someone else to get up here. I don't think I need to tell you how high a priority this mission is right now."

An I&W mission, or Indications and Warning, was a submarine mission to sit off a hostile country's coast and watch. To look for any signs that the country might be launching an attack, whether that was deploying their fleet, launching their bombers, or launching missiles. The boat on an I&W mission scoured the electromagnetic spectrum for any signals that betrayed what the hostile country was doing while also watching for any visual signs. To do the mission, the sub had to, necessarily, snuggle up close to the hostile country and keep the periscope and intercept masts up and exposed. It was an important and dangerous job.

Chief Lawlar was the first to speak. "Skipper, how are we going to do this? We don't have a DSE team or any of their special gear onboard."

The DSE, or Direct Support Element, team was a group of crypto-technicians, linguists, and intercept operators who came onboard an I&W boat specifically to operate the specialized electronic intercept equipment and to interpret the resulting signals. They were very highly trained for their specific mission but were not part of the normal ship's crew.

Blivens looked up and said, "Well, Chief, we're going to do the best we can. DEFCON TWO is no time to leave the barn door open with no one watching. You got two days to get your gear groomed and ready to go. Once we're on station, I expect you and your team are going to be busy."

Chief Lawlar didn't look happy, but he didn't really have a choice. "Well, both WLR-4 and the WLQ-4 checked out on the pre-underways, but we haven't used them since. My guys and the radiomen will check out everything. But we still don't have any linguists. What good is a comms intercept if no one knows what we intercepted?"

LTJG Brad Bishop, sitting in the back corner of the wardroom, meekly raised his hand. "Skipper, maybe I can help some. I had two years of Russian at the Academy. I'm rusty and never was very fast, but maybe I can catch some of what's said."

Blivens smiled. "Thanks, Brad. That's just what we need. If you got any tapes, you might want to start clearing the cobwebs."

Turning to Clemont, he said, "Nav, let's get the track laid down and up to the conn. The Eng is just following the rough course I gave him before we came down here. Count on a ten-knot SOA. We're going to need to spend some time skirting around all the ASW the Russkies are flooding the Barents with. They're on high alert, and we've already seen that they shoot first and ask questions later."

George Sanders rubbed his jaw and asked, "Skipper, why don't we run over toward Novaya Zemlya and then sneak in the back door going down the coast." He used his finger to trace a track that ran almost due east until it was about a hundred miles from the coast of the barren mountainous Arctic island. Then he swept down along its coast and then the two hundred miles to their station off the Murmansk Fjord. "It's a bit longer, but a whole lot safer than playing bull-in-the-china-shop and just charging straight down there."

Blivens stared at the chart and thought for a few minutes. He walked the distance off with his fingers and then grabbed a nautical slide rule. Spinning it around, he mumbled, "If we make sixteen knots, we get there eight hours later." Looking up, Blivens smiled. "Let's do it. Nav, head straight for Novaya Zemlya. Use a sixteen-knot SOA." He hesitated for a second, staring at the chart, and then continued, "There's a lot of shallow water over there. Be real careful with your red and yellow soundings."

Turning to Master Chief Shaw, he added, "COB, get the crew on board with this and ready to go. We need to be ready to go to war before we ever get to the Murmansk Fjord and stick our masts up. You can bet the Russians are already ready for war.

0430 EST, 21 April 1983, Naval Ocean Processing Facility (NOPF), Dam Neck, Virginia

Steffanie Graham stretched to see over the Ocean Technician analyzing a LOFARGRAM. He was scrutinizing a few faint specs that were printing out from the Nantucket array. The technician's expert eye detected the merest pattern that spelled Soviet submarine. Graham was having a hard time seeing anything beyond random burn marks on the electrostatic recording paper.

"You sure you're seeing something?" Graham asked.

The gruff technician was annoyed. The upstart young woman was questioning his analysis, based on years of accumulated hands-on experience. Even if she was an officer, the question was demeaning. "Ma'am, what you are seeing is the same signature we saw on Sunday. It's Case 41171700 again. He's a whole lot weaker, and there's a lot of background noise masking him, but he's right there." The technician reached out and tapped a very faint line. "Bet my paycheck on it."

Graham laughed and answered, "No one is looking for your paycheck. We seeing this on any other array?"

She looked at the large chart of the Atlantic that filled the far wall. It showed all of the Atlantic SOSUS arrays with the beam patterns that each covered. "How about the Lewes array or the Shelbourne one?" SOSUS arrays terminating in Lewes, Delaware, and Shelbourne, Nova Scotia, looked out into the North Atlantic similar to the array terminating in Nantucket. The multiple arrays could be used to verify a contact and to triangulate a position.

The technician shook his head. "Nothing on the Lewes array. I'm beginning to think that array may need maintenance. It just isn't showing the sensitivity of the others."

"I'll put a memo in with NAVELEX for them to check out the array," Graham answered. "But what about on the Canadian array?"

The technician shook his head again. "The Coasties are reporting a whole lot of ice coming down out of the Labrador Sea. Ice reports are showing way more coverage than normal for this time of year. Reckon those global cooling tree huggers might be on to something. Anyway, according to the Canadians, it's mucking up the picture for the Shelbourne array. But you might want to give them a call. In the meantime, are you going to verify this contact or not?"

Graham looked at the chart again and ran an imaginary bearing line up from the Nantucket array. The line skirted the eastern Greenland coast, up toward Iceland. She mumbled to herself, "If our Russian friend is snuggled up close to Greenland, it would explain the weak signal."

"Well, why don't you call Keflavik or Brawdy, Wales, to see if they are seeing anything," the technician responded. "If he's off the Greenland coast, heading for the GIUK Gap, he will be in Keflavik's backyard and a direct shot across the pond from Brawdy."

Graham grabbed the red phone, a dedicated secure phoneline that connected all of the NAVFACs in the Atlantic and NOPF Dam Neck, installed to facilitate passing information between the facilities. It took a few minutes to get her counterparts at the two facilities on the line. After explaining the situation, Graham waited, holding the phone, while LOFAR-GRAMs at each facility were scrutinized.

Brawdy came back first. They pieced together the data and said that there was a probability that they held contact on something in a beam with a max response axis of three-zero-zero. That beam skirted just south of Iceland. They couldn't confirm contact but were willing to call a possible submarine.

Then Keflavik came back on the line. They had a submarine contact bearing three-two-zero, and it had to be close. It was only three hundred miles to the Greenland coast. They were attempting to pull a blade-rate off the gram now. But Keflavik was worried. They had contact on an American boomer heading southwest that looked to be heading right toward the Soviet sub.

Steffanie Graham was already typing up the RAINFORM message. All US subs would get the RAINFORM message and so would SUBLANT. But with the world at DEFCON TWO and the shooting about to start, she was not about to let the American boomer stumble into a Soviet *Victor III* fast attack. She reached for the phone and called the SUBLANT OPCON Center.

1321 MSK, 21 April 1983, K-314, 370 kilometers west of Iceland

Captain Second Rank Ilya Agapov watched the fathometer. With a layer of seasonal pack ice overhead, the fathometer was his only means to safely navigate through this section along the Greenland coast. He simply followed the two-hundred-meter curve north along the giant island. With the *K-314* keeping a depth of fifty meters, there was 150 meters of seawater between his keel and the bottom. That was plenty of safety margin, and the ice above protected him from the American ASW aircraft and their annoying sonobuoys. If he really needed to go to the surface for some reason, he only had to head east for a few kilometers and he would be back out in the ice-free North Atlantic. In an emergency, he could simply punch up through the ice. His oceanographic charts showed that it would be less than a meter or two thick.

His real worry was American submarines. It was well known that they patrolled what they called the GIUK Gap, searching for Soviet intruders. They were smart and wily, dangerous adversaries, but were they smart enough to patrol under the ice in the shallow waters off Greenland? Agapov was betting that they weren't.

Agapov stretched to ease his aching back. Far too many hours pacing this steel deck. He sent a *michman* down to the wardroom to fetch him a glass of tea. That would ease some of the tension.

"*Kapitan*," the *sonarnny starshina* called out, "I am hearing a contact, bearing zero-four-three. I think it's an *Amerikanskaya podvodnaya lodka*. It's very faint."

Agapov moved over to the sonar controls and looked over the *starshina*'s shoulder. The man was very good. Agapov could barely see the trace developing on the cathode ray tube. He grabbed a set of earphones and listened. To his ears, there was nothing out there except the snapping shrimp and a far-off whale cry.

Agapov watched the trace develop for a few minutes. The bearing did not seem to waver. The submarine was either very far off or coming directly at the K-314.

Agapov gripped the *starshina*'s shoulder. "Very good, Yuri. You have done very well indeed."

He moved back to the navigation chart and drew a line down the bearing to the American submarine. He had lost his bet with himself. It was blocking him from following his track under the ice. The only way around was to move out into the open water of the Denmark Strait and try to sneak past. He laid a protractor down on the chart and read off the scale.

"*Rulevoy*, steer course zero-seven-zero. Make ten kilometers per hour." He then ordered, "Rig ship for silent running. We need to sneak past this *Amerikanskaya podvodnaya lodka.*"

The *K-314* emerged from under the Greenland ice and out into the deep, open Denmark Strait, skirting around the sonar contact but leaving the protection of the ice behind.

1415Z, 21 April 1983, USS John Jay, 200 nm northwest of Iceland

"Conn, Sonar, new sonar contact on the BQR-15. Designate Sierra Four-Nine, bearing one-nine-nine, ambiguous contact Sierra Five-Zero, bearing two-six-one," the 21MC announced. "Possible submerged submarine."

Dale Horton, the Officer-of-the-Deck, grabbed the 21MC and replied, "Sonar, Conn, aye. Send buzz bearing to the plot." Turning to Chief Braxton, the Chief-of-the-Watch, he ordered, "Man the section tracking party."

Horton then grabbed the JA phone and buzzed the CO's stateroom.

"Captain, we have a new sonar contact, possible submerged submarine, ambiguous bearings one-nine-nine and two-six-one. Stationing the section tracking party. I intend to get a leg and then maneuver to determine ambiguity."

Darren Walsh answered, "Very well, I'll be out in a minute."

Chief Braxton rounded up the various roving watch standers who could step away from their normal duties and track the sonar contacts. This much-pared-down version of the fire control tracking party would do the initial analysis of the new sonar contacts to determine if they had a problem needing the first team.

Will Morris, the JOOD, took charge of the section tracking party and started laying out the geographical plot while IC-2 Delvin Brimley started plotting the bearings against time on a large roll of chart paper.

After a few minutes of recording bearings, Will Morris called out, "Officer-of-the-Deck, I have a curve. Recommend a maneuver to course one-two-zero to determine ambiguity."

"Left full rudder, steady course one-two-zero," Horton ordered, then grabbed the 21MC to announce, "Sonar, Conn, coming left to one-two-zero to determine ambiguity."

"Conn, Sonar, aye," the answer came back. "Loss of contact due to array instability."

The *John Jay* swung around and steadied up on the new course. Sonar determined that the array would be stable five minutes after the sub was on the new course.

"Array is stable. Commencing search."

As frequently happened in a sonar approach, nothing. The contact had disappeared while the *John Jay* was turning, not to be regained. There was nothing to do but be extra vigilant while they searched to determine what happened.

31

1800Z, 21 April 1983, P-3C Tail Number 161124, off Keflavik, Iceland

Scott "Blunt" Sharples kicked Tom "Birdman" Byrd's rack. Between missions, the two were sharing a room at the Keflavik BOQ. The spartan room provided little more than a couple of bunks, a desk, and a bathroom, but that was all the fliers needed for those few hours when they weren't up in the air. But they were supposed to have a full day off today after flying for the last four days in a row.

"Up and at 'em, Birdman," Sharples shouted. "You got just enough time for a shower before we're due on the flight line."

"What the heck," Birdman Byrd grumbled as he rubbed his eyes. "Damn it, Blunt. I was right in the middle of a dream. It was just me and Miss January on a beach." He swung his legs out onto the floor. "And you went and ruined it. And what's this flight line crap? We have the day off."

"Flight ops just called," Sharples answered. "NAVFAC has picked up the Russian sub again. SOSUS found him going into the Denmark Strait. We're being scrambled to go say hello. Evidently, we have a boomer at the north end of the strait that the sub jockeys are trying to get out of the way. Now get in the shower. I ain't sharing a cockpit with you smelling like you've been rolling around in a pig pen instead of on a beach with Miss January." He tossed a towel at Birdman. "Hurry up. The wagon and Wee Willy are outside waiting for us."

It took over an hour of briefings and flight plans before the crew finally made it to the P-3C. They all piled out of the crew bus only to meet a cold rain.

"What's hanging on the outboard hardpoints?" Birdman shouted, pointing at missiles hanging from below each wing. "Why're we carryin' Harpoons now?"

Wee Willy Weston, the TACCO, answered, "You really weren't paying attention, were you. COMPATWING has decreed that since we are at DEFCON TWO, we will fly fully armed and ready. That includes strapping a couple of Harpoons on, just in case."

Birdman harrumphed, "I ain't liking it. Anything that we would be shootin' those things at can shoot back. My mama told me to stay away from people that shoot back."

Blunt smacked Byrd on the shoulder. "Get in the plane, Birdman. We all know about your propensity to be a war hero."

"Propensity?" Byrd spluttered. "What's a 'propensity'? You insultin' me with big words again?"

They all laughed as they climbed up into the big bird. Byrd grabbed the preflight checklist and ran down the items as Sharples completed each step.

"Tower, Navy One-Two-Four, ready to taxi," Sharples radioed.

"Roger, Navy One-Two-Four. Cleared to taxiway sierra-four. Hold before entering runway one-zero for inbound flight of four F-4s."

"One-Two-Four, roger. Taxiing on sierra-four. Will hold for inbound flight of four." Sharples released the brakes and moved out onto the taxiway. The four Air Force F-4 Phantoms screamed in and slapped down just as he reached the verge of the runway.

"Navy One-Two-Four, cleared for takeoff runway one-zero. Cleared to angels three, outbound course zero-niner-zero. Shifted to Navy Tactical at angels three."

"One-Two-Four, roger, cleared runway one-zero. One-Two-Four rolling," Sharples said as he lined up with the centerline and reached over to shove the power control levers all the way forward to takeoff power.

The P-3C climbed into the wind and the rain. Sharples banked the bird around and headed out toward their patrol area on the edge of the Greenland ice. With the short run to the search area, there was no time to climb above the rain and fly through clear skies. They would just have to endure the gray skies and bumpy ride.

"Blunt, receiving revised target data. New search box sixty-five degrees thirty minutes north, twenty-nine degrees fifty minutes west," Wee Willy called out. "Revised heading three-two-zero, one-two-five miles."

With less than thirty minutes to fly to the search box, they would need to hurry to be ready when they got on station. The crew had everything ready to rock and roll by the time they arrived and had dropped the BT buoy. Sharples flew a pattern across the search box as they dropped SSQ-53 DIFAR passive buoys to detect the Soviet boat.

The last buoy of the sixteen-buoy pattern had no more than hit the water when Wee Willy called out, "Detection. Buoys three and four are hot. Request you put a DICASS out ahead of buoy four."

The SSQ-62 DICASS sonobuoy was a command-activated active sonobuoy. When commanded, the transducer would drop out to either a shallow (four hundred foot) or deep (fifteen hundred foot) depth and transmit an active pulse at a preselected frequency. This gave the P-3C range, bearing, and Doppler information on the target submarine.

Blunt Sharples swung the P-3C around and dropped the active sonobuoy out ahead of the sub. When the buoy appeared on Wee Willy's UYS-1 acoustic processor screen, he immediately command activated it.

"Positive return. Range seven hundred, bearing two-two-three. Up Doppler. Contact is accelerating," Wee Willy reported.

Blunt Sharples keyed his microphone. "Navy Tactical, Navy One-Two-Four, we have confirmed hostile sub at position sixty-five degrees thirty-three minutes north, twenty-nine degrees forty-seven minutes west."

The voice crackled back almost immediately. "Navy One-Two-Four, Navy Tactical, you are weapons free. You are cleared in hot."

These were words that Blunt Sharples had never heard before. He didn't really believe his ears. "Navy Tactical, say again."

The voice came across again, slowly and with more than a hint of annoyance. "Navy One-Two-Four, I say again, you are weapons free and cleared in hot. Sink the bastard."

"One-Two-Four weapons free and cleared in hot, roger."

Blunt dropped the bird down to two hundred feet and reached over to open the bomb bay doors. "TACCO, prepare to drop two Mark-46 torpedoes on the target. Drop on my order."

Weston checked the solution in the torpedo launch control and lined up two weapons for launch. "TACCO ready to launch. Come to course one-three-six. Stand by to drop."

He watched as Sharples flew the bird onto the launch course. "Stand by to drop. Drop now!"

Sharples called out, "Torpedoes away!" and hit the weapons release button.

The Orion lurched up as a thousand pounds of torpedoes dropped out of the bomb bay. The two torpedoes splashed into the sea a thousand yards behind the *K-314*. Their otto-fueled reciprocating engines immediately started and shoved the twelve-inch-diameter torpedoes up to forty knots as they raced out to search for their submarine target.

2346 MSK, 21 April 1983, K-314, 350 kilometers west of Iceland

"*Kapitan*, active sonar, close aboard!" Yuri Semanov, the sonar *starshina*, called out. "*Amerikanskaya* air-dropped sonobuoy!"

That could only mean that the American P-3Cs were back, and they were ready to attack. There was only one way to escape an active sonobuoy before they dropped a torpedo. That was to run away as fast as they could and get lost before the American aircraft could drop more buoys and track them.

Ilya Agapov ordered, "Ahead flank! Right full rudder, steer course two-nine-zero!"

The *K-314* jumped ahead and spun around, racing back toward Greenland and the protection of the pack ice, picking up speed as they went.

"*Kapitan*, torpedo in the water!" Semanov yelled. "Two torpedoes! Somewhere astern! They are active!"

"Anatoly, how far to the ice?" Agapov asked.

Anatoly Balakirev looked at the chart. "Two kilometers, *Kapitan*!"

It would be very close, but Agapov calculated they had just a small chance of losing the torpedoes in the ice. Maybe their active sonar would be distracted by all the bits and pieces floating at the edge and would lose the *K-314* in their confusion. It was a gamble, but he didn't see any other way.

"Broach the ship," he ordered.

The *K-314* jumped up through the surface and splashed down, shouldering the large shards of broken ice aside as it raced forward. Seconds later they heard two massive explosions somewhere behind them.

Wee Willy Weston stared at the APS-115 radar screen for a second and then shouted, "Radar pop-up, bearing two-nine-zero, range five miles. Two explosions. Blunt, this guy is on the surface, our fish hit something, but it wasn't him."

Blunt Sharples swung the P-3C around to the bearing that Wee Willy had called out.

Birdman had binoculars glued to his eyes as he searched the horizon out in front of them. He pointed out toward the marginal ice zone ahead and yelled, "There he is!"

"TACCO, prepare to launch the Harpoons on him, Bearing-Only Launch!" Sharples ordered. He pulled back on the control yoke to gain altitude. The Harpoon needed at least a thousand feet below it when launched to keep from falling into the drink.

The air-launched Harpoon cruise missile had several search modes. The quickest and simplest to use was Bearing-Only Launch. In BOL, it turned its search radar on right after it was launched and then simply flew down that bearing line until it either found a target or ran out of gas.

Wee Willy's finger danced across the Harpoon missile launch control panel, lining up the pair of missiles to fly straight down the bearing, searching the whole way.

"Harpoons ready."

Sharples watched the altimeter as he clawed for air. When it clicked over a thousand feet, he ordered, "Launch."

Weston pushed the launch order button. They felt the two missiles drop away from the P-3C. As the Harpoons dropped toward the ocean surface, their turbojet engines came up to speed, pushing the missiles up to 0.7 Mach. Their radar seekers energized and almost immediately found the *K-314* and locked on. Both of the Harpoons headed straight for the surfaced submarine.

An alarm chirped in *K-314*'s control room. Anatoly Balakirev looked up and read the panel. "*Kapitan*, American fire control radar."

Agapov spun the periscope around to see the American P-3C low on the horizon, flying straight toward them. He guessed that the plane was ten kilometers away. Then he saw two missiles drop away from the aircraft and come racing right toward him.

Agapov yelled, "Dive! Dive! Make your depth fifty meters."

He kept the periscope up and trained on the incoming missiles, hypnotized by them rocketing directly at him. They seemed to be right on top when the periscope finally dropped beneath the surface.

Agapov was surprised to find his hands shaking uncontrollably when he reached up to lower the periscope. It took several seconds and all of the self-control that he could muster to move the control lever to the "lower" position.

"*Kapitan*, we are under the ice now, recommend coming to course zero-two-zero."

Agapov looked over at Balakirev and said, "Anatoly, slow to ahead standard and come to course zero-two-zero. I will be in my stateroom."

Wee Willy Weston watched the radar track of the two Harpoon missiles as they sped across the pack ice. It looked like the target had gone sinker just before impact. The missiles, with no target to attack, simply raced onward trying to find a new one.

"Blunt, we missed," Weston announced. "The bastard must have seen our launch. He went sinker."

Sharples answered, "Great, so now we've just attacked Greenland. We'll probably get a hit on that. Good thing there's nothing over there but ice and rock. Please tell me you still hold contact on the buoys."

Weston checked his acoustic processor, but he was already sure that they had lost the Soviet sub. "No joy, Blunt. He's gone. Probably up under the pack ice."

Sharples smacked his fist against the steering yoke. "Great! Just great! Guess I'd better report our magnificent success."

He keyed the radio mike. "Navy Tactical, Navy One-Two-Four, conducted attacks on hostile sub with torpedoes and Harpoons. Attacks judged not successful."

0031Z, 22 April 1983, USS **Tigerfish**, *Barents Sea*

"Conn, Sonar, new contact on the towed array." Senior Chief Zwarlinski's voice blasted across the 21MC. "Designate Sierra Two-Zero-Five, bearing two-nine-one, ambiguous contact Sierra Two-Five-Six, bearing three-five-one. Picking up one-two-one-hertz tonal indicating a US *Sturgeon*-class submarine."

Bill Andrews, the Officer-of-the-Deck, grabbed the 21MC microphone and replied, "Sonar, Conn, aye. We can probably drop the ambiguous contact. Novaya Zemlya is fifty miles off in that direction. Think it's the *Lionfish* outbound?"

Andrews could hear Zwarlinski chuckle as he answered, "Unless the Russians got a 637 somewhere, that'd be my bet." Then the sonar chief got serious. "But he's got a problem. I'm picking up broadband noise from him that I shouldn't be hearing. Sounds like he's got a bad rattle someplace."

George Sanders, the midwatch Command Duty Officer, was sitting on a bench locker in front of the Mark-117 fire control panel reading the message boards. He looked up and said, "No reason to spend time doing TMA on him. We need to be down on station ASAP."

He stood and put his paperwork down. "I'm going to go brief the skipper."

Sanders had just knocked and stuck his head in Blivens's stateroom doorway when he heard, "Conn, Sonar, multiple Horse Jaw active sonars to the northwest. Best bearings three-two-zero."

Blivens was instantly awake. "XO, go to sonar and see what's going on. I'm heading to control."

Still clad only in his skivvies, Blivens brushed past Sanders and hurried forward. He stepped up on the periscope stand and read the WLR-9 acoustic intercept receiver. The panel's little CRT screen was showing several bearing lines pointing out toward the northwest. The highest signal was showing a signal strength of thirty-eight decibels. That gave the active sonars a less than fifty percent chance of detecting the *Tigerfish*, but they were off in the same direction as the *Lionfish*. There was a very real probability that the Russians were tracking their sister ship.

"Skipper, what do we do?" Bill Andrews asked. He could see the same picture that Blivens saw. If the Russians were tracking the *Lionfish*, it was only a matter of time before they started shooting.

Blivens was at a loss. He couldn't think of any way to help the *Lionfish*, but at least he could be ready, just in case. "Officer-of-the-Deck, man battle stations."

That would get *Tigerfish* ready and keep everyone busy as the scene played out the way Blivens was sure it would.

The COB had just reported the ship at battle stations when Senior Chief Zwarlinski called over the 21MC, "Contact zig on *Lionfish*. Rapid downshift in received frequency. Loud transients from *Lionfish*. He is coming to flank. Countermeasures in the water."

Then the inevitable happened. "Loud explosions on the bearing to *Lionfish*. Two explosions." Then, "Two more explosions. Breaking-up noises on that bearing. No longer hold the *Lionfish*."

Tears streamed down Blivens's face. He smacked his fist into a locker door in exasperation. There was nothing he could have done to prevent or stop this, and the frustration of it all was maddening.

George Sanders looked around and saw Blivens standing there. He said, "Skipper, why don't you go get showered and dressed. I'll draft up the message to SUBLANT."

32

0500 MSK, 22 April 1983, Soviet Northern Fleet Headquarters, Murmansk, Russia

Fleet Admiral Dmitri Golubev reread the message from Contre-Admiral Andreev. The commander of the battle fleet was claiming that they had sunk another American submarine. This one was found in the middle of the Barents Sea, only six hundred kilometers from the entrance to the Murmansk Fjord.

If Andreev's ships had not sacrificed some errant narwhal and actually sank an American sub at that position, he could only conclude that their ASW barrier was pretty porous. Or else the American submarines were a lot better than the Naval Intelligence had predicted. Either way, he had a million and a half square kilometers of Barents Sea that needed purged of *proklyatyye Amerikanskaya podvodnaya lodki*. It was an impossible task, but otherwise he could not protect the ballistic missile submarines hiding in their bastion up under the ice.

Where was *K-324*? Novikov should have checked in three days ago. He was scheduled to return to Polyarny yesterday. But so far, silence. They had heard nothing.

That was the second submarine that was late to check in. Sergey Vyalitsyn's *K-373* was three days late in making a routine position report. The *Alfa*-class submarine was also transiting back to Polyarny, returning from surveilling the American naval base at Norfolk.

Golubev had his operations center plot the location where Andreev claimed he had sunk the second American sub. It was well outside the submarine safety lanes that Novikov should have been using. Vyalitsyn's *K-373* would still be well to the west, over by Jan Mayen Island.

Then Admiral Golubev asked if they had plotted the position for the first sinking. The operations center was filled with embarrassed faces, but they quickly retrieved the original messages and plotted the location. It was not in an area where *K-324* should have been, but Golubev could see that a navigation error of only a few kilometers could result in a horrible mistake. That could easily explain why *K-324* was missing.

It didn't explain why *K-373* had not checked in. But the *Alfa*'s communications systems were notoriously unreliable. A few days late in communicating was not particularly unusual for the submarine. For now, he would wait and see what developed.

Golubev walked away from the operations center, over to his personal office, deep in thought. By the time he was seated at his desk, sipping a glass of tea, he decided not to raise the question. Better to let Contre-Admiral Andreev claim the glory for sinking a pair of American submarines and for Boris Novikov to die a hero of the Soviet Union.

2130 EST, 21 April 1983, COMSUBLANT, Norfolk, Virginia

"Admiral, wake up."

Rufus Brown slowly came back to consciousness. He blinked his eyes open to find his flag aide shaking his shoulder, trying to rouse him. It took a few seconds to realize that he was lying on the leather couch in his office. His body ached from the discomfort of the couch, but his mind cried for rest. He had not slept in his own bed or even left the OPCON Center for the last four days. The Chief-of-Staff finally convinced him to lie down for a few hours, but he had no more than laid his head down when his aide was shaking him awake.

"Wha...wha...what is it?" Brown stammered. "What do you want?"

"Admiral, we just got a message from *Tigerfish*," the young aide glumly reported. "They are reporting they heard the *Lionfish* attacked and sunk."

"What? Where?" Brown asked, instantly coming fully awake.

"*Tigerfish* reports they are in the Barents, about two hundred nautical miles north and east of Murmansk Fjord. They estimate *Lionfish* was fifty miles west of their position when attacked. Reporting that *Lionfish* had a really loud broadband noise problem that was probably picked up by the Russians. They heard a couple of underwater explosions and what sounded like breaking-up noises."

Brown thought for a second. The location seemed to correlate with where the outbound sub should be, and she had reported a materiel problem but didn't say anything about a noise problem.

Brown stood and started to straighten his uniform. He ordered, "Get over to the OPCON Center. Tell the watch officer to inform CINCLANTFLT and the NMCC that we have a probable sub-sunk in Barents. I'll be over as soon as I splash some water on my face."

Deciding that a shower, shave, and fresh uniform was a good idea, it was half an hour before Admiral Brown walked across the compound to NH-95. The OPCON Center was buzzing with activity when he walked in. The huge map of the North Atlantic that filled the far wall had a dozen submarine icons tracking up the various transit routes to the North Cape and another dozen icons converging on the Strait of Gibraltar and the Mediterranean. These were the fast attack subs heading out to face off with the Soviet fleet. Another twenty color-coded boxes filled up large chunks of the North Atlantic, Norwegian Sea, and the Med. These represented the wartime patrol areas for the boomers. Brown could not remember when he had ever seen so many American submarines at sea at one time.

The Chief-of-Staff, Ted Strange, met Brown at the door. "Boss, the JCS has called for a tele-con." Strange checked his watch. "In ten minutes. They want you on it."

Brown nodded. "Okay. What do we know?"

"I'm afraid not much more than we think *Lionfish* is gone. She is due to check in when she clears North Cape tonight. Until then, we can only hope and pray that Roy Blivens is wrong." Strange handed the Admiral a thin folder. "Here is all the latest intel that we have. The only Russian sub that we hold is a *Victor III*, Case 41171700, hiding under the seasonal ice off Greenland. We think it is trying to sneak back home. The boys have spent a lot of time going over all of the old SOSUS data and rebuilt bits and pieces of its track. They are making a case that this is the boat who snatched Grey Mole out from under us."

"We have anyone in position to make an intercept?" Brown asked.

Strange looked at the map. "Case 41171700 is in *John Jay*'s patrol area, just skirting the landward edge. SOSUS is tracking him out in clear water to the east of Case 41171700. Walsh should have the *John Jay* out in clear water to copy the broadcast. We don't have anybody else we can vector over there to intercept. All the attack boats are on high-priority missions up north. By the time we got anything sorted out and a boat over there, Case 41171700 will be long gone back in the Barents."

Brown thought for a minute. A slight smile creased his face. "It would be poetic justice if we sent Darren Walsh over there to take out the guy who shot his wife. Chief-of-Staff, make it happen while I see what the Joint Chiefs want."

Brown stepped into the SCIF just as the call was connected. Someone on the other end of the line was making a roll call. When SAC and COMSUBPAC were the only other remote members on the call and SECDEF was on the call as the National Command Authority, Brown quickly realized that the discussion was going to be to determine the strategic response to the sub-sunk.

The Chairman opened the call with a short review of where they were, then he asked Vice Admiral Brown, "Rufus, how sure are you that you lost a sub today?"

"General, we are calling it probable," Brown answered. "There is no way of knowing for sure until the *Lionfish* doesn't check in on schedule."

SECDEF chimed in. "There is no way that we're starting World War III based on a probable. Get me something definite."

"Sir, we're talking the Barents Sea," Brown answered. "That's a Russian lake. We just can't steam in and start searching for wreckage. All we're going to have until this settles out is what *Tigerfish* heard. That's pretty damn good, but it ain't paint samples."

"So what do you suggest I tell the president that we are doing?" SECDEF queried.

"Mr. Secretary," Brown shot back, "I'm not in charge of the fleet or for directing our national strategy, but if I were, I'd go to a wait-and-see strategy. Pull the fleet up just short of North Cape. Don't cross over into the Barents but stand nose-to-nose with the Russian fleet. Keep the bombers and ICBMs on high alert. See who blinks first."

The Chairman responded, "Rufus, that makes sense. Mr. Secretary, unless you have a different idea, I suggest we follow Admiral Brown's suggestion. The Joint Chiefs will draft orders to the COCOMs to that effect. Let's just hope the Soviets know the rules to this game of Russian roulette."

0530Z, 22 April 1983, USS John Jay, 200 nm northwest of Iceland

"Morning, Skipper." Stan Wilkins looked up from his plate as Darren Walsh walked into the wardroom. "Sure will be glad when we get home and have real eggs instead of these powdered things."

Walsh poured himself a cup of coffee and sat down. "You and me both, XO."

He looked at the far end of the wardroom where the two Russian fliers had been sleeping. It was all restored to normal, with the bunks lowered and the couch seating back in place.

"Where are our Russian friends?" Walsh asked over the rim of his cup.

Wilkins smiled. "I reshuffled the berthing a little. The COB opened up a couple of racks in the goat locker. It seems that Chief Braxton and Chief Rosecrans volunteered to bunk in torpedo room berthing. So Leonid and Yevgeniy have an around-the-clock watch on them in the goat locker, and we have our wardroom back."

The wardroom mess cook slid Walsh's breakfast in front of him. Walsh took a bite of eggs and chewed for a second. Then he said, "Good thinking,

XO. It was getting hard to get things done with those two always in here. Too many things that they shouldn't hear or see."

A knock at the door interrupted their conversation. RM3 Milt Schoneman, carrying the message boards, stepped into the wardroom. "Skipper, XO, got the boards here. The Officer-of-the-Deck sent me down. Said you should look at the TS board." He handed Walsh the red-striped aluminum clipboard.

Interesting, Walsh thought as he took the board. If this message was important enough for the OOD to route it right away, why hadn't he just called to tell him?

Walsh flipped the board open and read the top message. He slid the board over for the XO to read and then reached under the table to grab the JA handset. He hit the buzzer to get the OOD's attention.

The call was answered almost immediately. "Officer-of-the-Deck."

"Eng, you have any sonar contacts?" Walsh asked.

"No, sir," Pete McKay answered. "Nothing on any sensor. I'm moving over toward the ice edge to see what we find. Based on the last contact info from the P-3 and the SOSUS data, if he is trying to sneak up north using the pack ice, I figure he is making twelve to fifteen knots. At that rate, Case 41171700 should be smack dead in the middle of the Denmark Strait. I'll have us in a position to say hi when he exits the strait."

"Good thinking, Eng. I'll be up in a minute."

Walsh looked at Stan Wilkins as he slid the JA handset back in its holder. "What's your take on this, XO?"

Wilkins shook his head. "This ain't normal. Playing by normal boomer rules, we should be sneaking off to the east, not moving into a position to intercept this guy. Message says Case 41171700 is a *Victor III*. That means we'll be playing him about even up or he might have an edge. I don't like a fair fight."

"Yep, I agree," Walsh responded. "Only thing that makes sense is that SUBLANT wants to keep this guy from getting home real bad, and we are the only one in a position to stop him. Let's go take a look at the charts and see what we need to do."

The two grabbed their coffee cups and headed to the control room, breakfast forgotten. They walked into the control room to find Bob Shippley relieving Pete McKay as the OOD. Walsh waved them both over to the Mark-19 plotter.

The four of them huddled around the plotter and studied the navigation chart. McKay had plotted his best guess on where Case 41171700 was. Walsh stepped off the distance with a pair of dividers.

"If he's doing what we think he is, Case 41171700 should be about six hundred miles to the southwest," Walsh said. "How do we best catch this guy and ambush him?"

After studying the chart for a few minutes, Bob Shippley said, "Skipper, he's hugging the coast, staying under the seasonal pack ice. It's going to be real hard finding him when we are listening to all the ice noise. A whole lot easier if we were landward looking out to sea."

Wilkins nodded but said, "He's going to be hugging shallow water as close as he can get. How do you propose to get inshore of him?"

Shippley put his finger on the chart. "We wait right here. This is Kangertitivaq Fjord. It's the biggest fjord system in the world and plenty deep enough for us. I propose that we slip in there and ambush Case 41171700 as he goes by."

Walsh nodded. "Sounds like the best plan I've heard. Looks like it'll take us about thirty hours to get over to this Kangertitivaq Fjord. Let's call it the 'K Fjord' so I can quit tying my tongue in knots." He stepped off the distance for Case 41171700. "Looks like thirty-six to forty hours for him. Let's see how this works. Nav, get us over to K Fjord. XO, get with the COB and make sure the crew knows to be real vigilant with sound silencing. Eng, get the plant in its quietest lineup."

33

0830Z, 22 April 1983, USS Tigerfish, *Barents Sea*

The USS *Tigerfish* moved slowly though the murky inshore waters only three miles off the precipitous granite cliffs that formed the northern shore of Kildin Island. The lonely, barren bit of rock guarded the eastern approach to the Murmansk Fjord. The submarine appeared to have the sea all to itself. Senior Chief Zwarlinski's sonar team was tracking no sonar contacts except for a pod of minke whales off to the northwest. Steve Dunn swung the Type 18 periscope in a continuous circle, searching for any threat, but the ocean and sky were empty. Not even a seagull interrupted the dull gray, cloud-covered sky.

The radio shack in the *Tigerfish* was an entirely different story. The various antennas embedded in the Type 18 periscope were feeding a near continuous stream of data to Chief Greg Lawlar and his team. Radar signals were routed to the AN/WLR-4 for analysis and mapping. Encrypted data links were sent to the AN/WLQ-4 for further processing. Voice communications were recorded and routed over to Brad Bishop.

LTJG Brad Bishop was struggling to translate the torrent of conversations that he was overhearing. As near as he could tell, most of it was excruciatingly boring. Right now, he was listening to the pilot of Il-38 May describing his current sexual conquest in vivid detail to his ground controller. Bishop shook his head. Pilots were all the same, no matter what uniform they wore.

The radio room printer clattered away almost continuously as SUBLANT used the SSIXS SI channel to feed the *Tigerfish* all of the special instructions and publications that the boat needed but didn't have onboard. Greg Lawlar was reading the instructions as the printer printed each line. Then he would turn and shout instructions to his team. As more and more information arrived from SUBLANT, the intercepted Soviet data started to make more sense.

Roy Blivens paced the control room. It had been only a little over eight hours since they had heard their brothers on *Lionfish* killed. He was concerned. No, he was worried about how his crew was reacting. So far, they seemed to be taking it all in stride and were going about their business in a very professional manner. He couldn't see where they had missed a single beat.

Steve Dunn stopped his continuous revolutions and called out, "I have a lighthouse on this bearing."

The FT-of-the-Watch called out, "Bearing one-seven-six."

QM-1 Eric Swarton swung his parallel motion protractor around on the chart and called out, "Correlates to North Kildinsky Light." He plotted a line from the light and asked, "Officer-of-the-Deck, can you cut a left and right tangent to Kildin Island?"

Steve Dunn swung the scope over and looked to get a bearing just at the western edge of the island. "Right tangent bearing, mark."

"Bearing two-zero-eight."

Dunn swung the scope over to see the northeast edge of the island. "Left tangent bearing, mark."

"Bearing one-four-two."

Swarton looked up and smiled. "Officer-of-the-Deck, I have a good visual fix. Hold us two-point-eight miles off the coast. Course two-eight-five is a good course."

Being able to do visual navigation was a godsend when they were operating so close to an unfamiliar and unfriendly coastline. If the fog rolled in and dropped visibility down to zero, an all too common occurrence up here at this time of year, all bets were off for navigation.

"Conn, ESM, picking up Sheet Bend Coastal Surveillance Radar, not a detection threat," Chief Lawlar reported over the 21MC. "Request you raise the BLD-1 to get a bearing cut."

Steve Dunn answered, "BLD-1 coming up."

The *Tigerfish* carried a couple of specialized antennas. The BLD-1 was a large, trash can–shaped antenna designed to intercept and do direction finding on radar emissions. The BRD-7, another large antenna, was used to DF radio communications signals. Because of their size, these masts were easy targets for a search radar to detect and were thus only raised when needed and then immediately lowered again.

A few seconds later, Chief Lawlar reported, "DF of Sheet Bend completed. Request lower the BLD-1. Detected three Sheet Bend emitters. One bearing south, signal strength very high, estimate system is planted on Kildin Island. Second source, bearing three-two-five, signal strength high, best estimate Cape Tsypnavolok. Third emitter bears one-zero-five, signal strength moderate, probable site on Kolguyev Island. All known emitters."

Eric Swarton plotted each one on the navigation chart.

Roy Blivens had observed the watch team in the control room. Everything seemed to be running smoothly, but he well knew that on a mission like this, that could all change in the blink of an eye.

"Eng, I'm going to radio and watch the ESM team for a bit," Blivens said to Dunn.

Dunn answered, "Yes, sir," but he was already talking to the skipper's back.

When Blivens entered the crowded radio/ESM space, he found Eric Lawlar hunched over the WLQ-4 Sea Nymph screen, clutching a SUBLANT radio message. One of his operators was slowly dialing through the frequencies while they both watched the dancing lines on the screen. Every few seconds, Lawlar would grunt for him to stop scrolling. He would run down the list of emitter characteristics, check what he was seeing on the screen, and then log a new emitter.

Lawlar looked up to see Blivens standing there looking over his shoulder. "Morning, Skipper," he said and smiled. "Havin' fun and keepin' busy.

These Russkies have more radars up than Carter has little liver pills." He read down his list. "We've got Bar Locks, Tall Kings, Spoon Rests, and a couple I ain't figured out yet. That's just the land-based air-search radars. Ain't even got to the airborne stuff yet. And then we need to look at the seaborne, too." He chuckled. "I 'spect it's gonna be a busy mornin'."

"Captain, come to the conn," the 21MC interrupted the discussion.

Blivens hurried forward. "Whatta you have, Eng?" he asked as he stepped up onto the periscope stand. He noted that the WLR-9 was alarming, showing three-kilohertz sonars to the southwest.

Steve Dunn had his arm wrapped around the training handles on the periscope. Without looking up, he said, "Skipper, I have a pair of *Grisha*s just rounding Cape Letinskiy outbound. I'm coming around to get behind Kildin Island as they pass. Sonar just picked them up banging away on their Bull Nose active. Sonar estimates they are twenty thousand yards out."

"Good thinking, Eng. Snuggle up to Kildin until those two steam on past."

"Skipper," Dunn went on, "those guys have to be up on their air- and surface-search radars and probably talking to harbor control on their UHF radio. I didn't get any warning from ESM."

"They're a little busy right now," Blivens replied.

"That's exactly my point," Dunn shot back. "They are so busy finding land-based air-search radars and bearing lines to shore installations, they aren't even looking for the real threats. We're going to get our butts caught if we don't do better."

1715Z, 23 April 1983, USS John Jay, *Kangertitivaq Fjord, Greenland*

The *John Jay* slid under the seasonal ice shelf that now extended almost thirty miles from the rocky coastline. The fathometer was showing more than thirteen hundred feet of water below them, but the idea of several feet of ice above their heads left Dale Horton, the on-watch OOD, with a feeling that he was driving into a confined cave. He steered the *John Jay* for the center of the fjord's fifteen-mile-wide entrance before turning to the south to run parallel the mouth of the fjord.

The plan was to run a series of racetracks with ten-mile-long north-south legs across the fjord's entrance. The boat's high-accuracy bathymetric charts showed that except for the deep, narrow trench that formed the Kangertitivaq Fjord, the hundred-fathom curve was only five nautical miles off the coast. Their quarry should pass by only a few thousand yards to seaward of where the *John Jay* was lying in wait. The latest RAINFORM message said that Case 41171700, or at least the error ellipse that represented Case 41171700, was still fifty miles to the south. They should have several hours to get acclimated to the area before it arrived.

"Conn, Sonar, new contact on the towed array," the 21MC announced. "Designate Sierra Six-Four. Best bearing one-two-four. Three-hundred-hertz tonal, probable submerged Soviet submarine."

With several feet of ice above them, any sonar contact here had to be a submarine, but Case 41171700 was unexpectedly early. Horton ordered, "Chief-of-the-Watch, man battle stations torpedo."

The general alarm's gonging had barely stopped when Darren Walsh rushed up the ladder from middle level and into control. The battle stations team were hurriedly taking their positions around the control room.

"Skipper, contact on the towed array," Horton reported as Walsh stepped up onto the periscope stand. "Designated Sierra Six-Four, probable Soviet sub, based on a three-hundred-hertz tonal. Range of the day is thirty thousand yards for a three-hundred-hertz tonal in these waters."

The COB slid into the diving officer's seat as Stan Wilkins grabbed his sound-powered phone headset from beside the Mark-19 plotter. The COB reported, "Skipper, the boat is manned for battle stations."

Walsh said, "Attention in control. We have a submerged contact, designated Sierra Six-Four on the towed array. He is the contact of interest. I intend to close Sierra Six-Four to broadband range while conducting TMA. We will work to get in his baffles and spiral in on him. I intend to engage him with a Mark-48 torpedo. If he counterfires, we will evade into the fjord. Weps, make tube one ready in all respects. Chief-of-the-Watch, load countermeasures in both signal ejectors. Carry on."

Pete McKay, the plot coordinator, looked at the scatter shot of dots on the time-bearing plot. He eyeballed a straight line through the dots and called out, "I have a curve, ready for a maneuver."

Walsh looked at the chart. With Sierra Six-Four down to the southeast and Greenland blocking any move to the southwest, his only choice was to come around to the north.

"Helm, left full rudder, steady course zero-one-zero."

As the *John Jay* started to swing around to the new course, Sonar announced, "Loss of Sierra Six-Four due to own-ship maneuver."

It took several minutes for the big boat to swing around and steady up on the new course, then several more minutes for the towed array to stabilize.

"Regain Sierra Six-Four, bearing one-one-seven," Sonar announced. "Assigning a tracker to Sierra Six-Four."

Now that they had a continuous feed of more accurate bearing information, the fire control tracking party could solve the TMA problem much faster. They didn't need to wait for a scatter shot of buzzed bearings picked off the BQR-23 screen by the sonarmen to be resolved into a best-guess straight line. The system automatically tracked the contact and sent a continuous stream of usable data.

The *John Jay* maneuvered back and forth across the mouth of the fjord as Stan Wilkins's team slowly teased out the Sierra Six-Four's range, course, and speed. The Soviet boat was plotting arrow straight, seemingly without a care, following the hundred-fathom curve up the coast.

"Skipper, I have a shooting solution," Stan Wilkins announced after they had completed four legs. "Course zero-two-zero, speed twelve, range one-six thousand yards."

Walsh shook his head. "Too long a shot, XO. I want to shoot inside of five thousand yards. Let him get closer."

Pete McKay chimed in, "Skipper, our current solution has a CPA of eight thousand yards at a bearing of zero-eight-zero in thirty minutes."

Walsh looked at the plot. "We need to move closer." He put down the parallel motion protractor, aligned it to where he wanted to go, and read the bearing cursor. "Nav, come to course zero-three-zero, increase speed to standard."

The *John Jay* swung around and accelerated to a standard bell, about twelve knots. The two submarines were on almost parallel courses at almost the same speed. The Soviet submarine slowly drew ahead as the *John Jay* slowly moved into position astern.

"Conn, Sonar, picking up Sierra Six-Four broadband on the BQR-7. Best bearing zero-nine-zero."

Walsh watched the solution develop on the Mark-113 analyzer. They were almost in a position to shoot. He wanted to get another thousand yards closer so that the enemy sub wouldn't have enough alertment time to run away from his torpedo. Everything seemed to be tracking. Just a couple more minutes.

"Possible contact zig!" Sonar called out. "Sierra Six-Four is speeding up!"

"Possible contact zig, upshift in received frequency," the time-frequency plotter yelled at the same time. "Ten knots in the line of sight so far, still climbing."

"Possible contact zig, increase in bearing rate," the time-bearing plotter called. "Plus fifteen degrees per minute and climbing."

Walsh could see the dot stack on the Mark-113 trailing off almost horizontal. Sierra Six-Four had made a radical course and speed change. It looked like he had spun around, sped up, and was coming at them. It was time for action.

"Firing point procedures!" Walsh ordered. He needed to get a fish in the water before the Soviet boat either shot or ran away and was lost.

"Ship ready!" Bob Shippley called out. The ship was in a position to shoot.

"Weapon ready!" Brett Burns answered. The Mark-48 torpedo was ready to go.

"Solution not ready," Stan Wilkins replied. "I don't have a solution after the zig."

Walsh quickly replied, "Damn it, XO! Anchor his range at six thousand yards, give him twenty-five knots, and point him at us. That'll be good enough."

It took only a couple of seconds to spin the dials on the Mark-75 attack director before Wilkins called, "Solution ready!"

"Match sonar bearings and shoot!" Walsh ordered.

The 21MC interrupted the whoosh-bang of the torpedo ejection pump shoving the Mark-48 torpedo out of tube one. "Torpedo in the water! From Sierra Six-Four! Best bearing zero-eight-six!"

Brett Burns yelled, "Normal launch. Weapon running normally in pre-enable."

Walsh ordered, "Right full rudder, ahead flank! Make your depth five hundred feet. Steady course two-seven-zero. Launch both signal ejectors. Reload and launch again."

The big missile submarine jumped ahead as high-pressure steam roared into the main turbines. The shaft accelerated as fast as the throttleman could spin the big chrome throttles open. The boat angled down sharply but then abruptly pulled up at five hundred feet. The solid granite bottom was only a hundred feet below the racing submarine.

A pair of NAEs, small broadband acoustic maskers, tumbled out in the *John Jay*'s wake. The noise they generated echoed off the fjord's granite sides, building a wall of sound to confuse the Russian torpedo. Then a pair of ADCs, equally small torpedo countermeasures, tumbled out and began emitting their torpedo decoy signals.

The WLR-9 acoustic intercept receiver started chirping. Bob Shippley looked at the receiver and called out, "Forty-kilohertz active, bearing zero-nine-zero! SPL plus forty!"

The Russian TEST-71 torpedo had started its search for the *John Jay*. Its forty-kilohertz active sonar was sniffing out the waters to find the evading submarine. With a sound pressure level of plus forty decibels, it was close.

"Heavy cavitation from Sierra Six-Four!" Sonar reported. "He's gone to flank. Incoming weapon bearing zero-eight-six!"

"Loss of wire continuity!" Brett Burns called out. The radical maneuvering had snapped the hair-thin copper wire that connected the Mark-48 torpedo to the *John Jay*. The weapon was now on its own.

"Incoming torpedo lost in own ship's baffles. Last bearing zero-eight," Sonar called out.

Bob Shippley checked the WLR-9. "Plus forty-four SPL! Bearing zero-nine-zero!"

The TEST-71 was running down their trail toward the *John Jay*, but it was directly astern. There was no way to tell how close the incoming torpedo was, only that it was getting closer. At fifty knots, it had a thirty-knot speed advantage. It would not be a long race.

"Nav, get me up close to the ice, make your depth eighty feet," Walsh ordered. "Chief-of-the-Watch, reload the signal ejectors with evasion devices, keep shooting them until we run out."

The *John Jay* angled up and leveled off just a few feet below the thick surface ice. Back here, deeper in the fjord, the ice had piled up all winter, pushed by the wind and the sea. Some chunks projected down more than twenty feet from the surface. With a keel depth of eighty feet, the *John Jay*'s sail was only twenty-five feet below the surface. The TEST-71 torpedo smashed into one of the ice keels only twenty feet away from the submarine and detonated.

The explosion rammed the boat upward, rocking it violently and smashing the sail into the ice. Walsh grabbed the stainless-steel piping that surrounded the periscope stand and held on with all his strength. He saw the depth detectors jump up to read thirty-eight feet. They were on the surface, but they weren't moving forward. He ordered all stop and then reached up to raise the number two periscope. It would not go up. Neither would the number one.

"Chief-of-the-Watch, conduct a normal blow of all main ballast tanks," he ordered.

They could hear creaking and groaning from outside the hull as the boat came up from thirty-eight feet to thirty-two feet. Opening the upper sail hatch proved impossible, something was jamming it down with much more force than the crew could push up.

They were stuck, with no way out and no way to contact the outside world.

"*Kapitan*, sonar contact, bearing three-three-four! Submerged *Amerikanskaya podvodnaya lodka!*" the sonar operator yelled out.

Captain Second Rank Ilya Agapov immediately recognized that he had inadvertently sailed into an American trap. The submarine was sitting there, waiting to shoot the *K-314* as they cruised by. The only way to escape was to shoot and run.

"Shoot the torpedo in tube one on the bearing to the American!" he ordered.

It took only seconds for the weapons officer to send the TEST-71 torpedo on its way. The two-thousand-kilogram wire-guided torpedo might be little more than a very large, expensive, and dangerous evasion device, but it might allow them to escape.

"Ahead flank!" Agapov ordered. "Left full rudder, steer course zero-nine-zero."

The *Victor III*–class submarine heeled over as it leaped ahead and spun an almost complete circle before racing off to the east. The maneuver would leave a large knuckle in the water to confuse any incoming acoustic torpedo. Cavitation sounded like machine-gun fire bouncing off the hull as it sped onward.

"*Kapitan*, American torpedo!" the sonar operator called out. "Bearing three-three-four!"

Ilya Agapov knew that there was very little chance to outrun an American Mark-48 torpedo, but they had to try.

"Launch the evasion device," he ordered. The canister shot out of the submarine. The lithium hydroxide inside the canister reacted with seawater and began generating a wall of sonar-reflecting bubbles as it sank.

"Five kilometers to the ice edge," Anatoly Balakirev said. He turned and read the fathometer. "Five hundred meters under the keel. We are out in deep water now."

"Make your depth two hundred meters," Agapov ordered. At least he could make the annoying cavitation go away. "Bearing to the torpedo?"

"*Kapitan*, the torpedo is in the baffles," the sonar operator answered. Then he yelled, "American active sonobuoy dead ahead!"

Agapov crashed his fist onto the table. The *proklyatyye Amerikanskaya podvodnaya lodka* had driven them directly into the clutches of one of their P-3 aircraft. They were caught in a vise.

"Torpedo in the water! Two torpedoes, bearing zero-nine-zero! American Mark-46 torpedoes!" the sonar operator yelled.

Agapov looked blankly at Balakirev. There was nothing they could do.

Scott "Blunt" Sharples flew P-3C, tail number 161124, in a slow, counterclockwise circle five hundred feet above the water. SOSUS had steered them up to where they were just on the ice edge some thirty miles east of Kangertitivaq Fjord, Greenland.

They had been warned that an American boomer was up in the fjord and Case 41171700 was trying to sneak by under the ice. The boomer would stay in the fjord and not venture out. Sharples's orders were clear. Any submarine coming out from under the pack ice would be Soviet and was fair game. He was weapons free.

Wilbur "Wee Willy" Weston had just guided them in planting another array of SSQ-53 passive DIFAR sonobuoys out ahead of the SOSUS posit and checked the buoys live.

"Blunt," Wee Willy yelled into the intercom. "Got a hot one. And we're getting a big upshift in Doppler! Something really lit a fire under this guy! Let's get a DICASS out there and get ready to drop on this sucker."

Wee Willy vectored Blunt Sharples around to the optimum location to drop the SSQ-62 DICASS active sonobuoy. He gave the buoy just enough time to deploy its active projector down to four hundred feet before he command activated it.

"Positive return on the DICASS," Wee Willy yelled. "He's making better than thirty knots due east. Balls to the wall. He's running from something!"

"Willy, enough with the commentary," Sharples said. "Get me out in front for a drop. Doors coming open now." He reached over and grabbed the handle to open the bird's bomb bay, revealing the Mark-46 torpedoes resting and ready in there.

Weston vectored Sharples around until they were three thousand yards out ahead of Case 41171700 and down to two hundred feet. The big P-3C flew directly at the submarine. When they were a thousand yards apart, the two Mark-46 torpedoes dropped out and plunged into the water.

The two electric fish immediately detected *K-314* and raced toward it. The first weapon hit the submarine almost directly on the bow. The one hundred pounds of PBXN-103 blew the sonar fairing and the cylindrical sonar array away. All six torpedo tubes were mangled beyond repair, but the torpedo did not cause enough damage to sink *K-314*. The second torpedo hit the submarine just forward of the sail, blowing a half-meter-diameter hole directly into the control room, filling the space with superheated gas. No one in the control room had time to even register that something had happened.

Henri DuBois, sitting in the wardroom, had an instant to grab his precious package. He marveled at how incredibly cold the seawater was, just before everything went blank.

The boat had angled down toward the deep when the Mark 48 crashed into the engine room and detonated. Six hundred and fifty pounds of explosives tore the engine room open to the sea. The doomed submarine settled to the bottom.

Wee Willy could hear the destruction over the DIFAR buoys. If he had looked out, he would have seen the explosions bubble gases and debris to the surface.

"Skipper, I just got a weird pop-up on radar," the APS-115 operator called out. "It's way up in the fjord, up by Ivssorigseq."

"What is it?" Blunt Sharples asked. "Shouldn't be anything up there but ice."

"Yeah, I know. That's what's weird. It just showed up in the middle of nothing. Solid return."

Sharples swung the bird around and headed for shore. "Let's go take a look."

Tom "Birdman" Byrd, flying in the right-hand seat was scanning the horizon with his binoculars. "Blunt, you ain't gonna believe this," he said. "Look out at two o'clock. That looks like a sub surfaced through the ice and took a real beating."

Blunt Sharples put the P-3C into a slow circle five hundred feet above the stricken sub. He keyed the radio mike. "Navy Tactical, Navy One-Two-Four. I have a surfaced submarine thirty miles inside Kangertitivaq Fjord, Greenland. Looks like an American missile boat, probably a *Lafayette* class surfaced through the ice. It's badly damaged. I don't see anyone out on the ice. Request instructions."

"Navy One-Two-Four, maintain station over the sub, try to make contact with it. We will route rescue assets to it."

34

2200 MSK, 23 April 1983, deep under the National Defense Center, Moscow

Vladimar Antonovich Petrov, the president of the USSR, listened to his generals and admirals brief the disposition of their forces. He quietly doodled on a sheet of paper as each member of the Supreme High Command, the country's wartime military leadership, listed the forces that they had deployed or put on a war footing. The general commanding the Strategic Rocket Force was just now displaying a graphic that showed all the thousands of intercontinental ballistic missiles that were ready to launch on a moment's notice to rain destruction down on the United States.

"Comrade General," Petrov said as he carefully capped his fountain pen and placed it beside the notepad. "How much longer can we keep our liquid-fueled rockets fully fueled and ready? What do we do when we run out of time?"

"Vladimar Antonovich," the florid, overweight, heavily bemedaled general answered, "we have at most another two days before we must defuel the rockets and flush their systems completely. Otherwise, the corrosion damage caused by the hypergolic fuels will render them inoperable. It will take several weeks to empty and flush all the missiles."

"And in the meantime, those ICBMs will not be available?" Petrov questioned. "They are over half our total launchers."

"That is correct. We will be severely weakened during that time."

Dimetri Olagev, the head of the KGB, interjected, "In that case, we must launch a first strike immediately! If we wait—"

Petrov held up a hand for silence. "Dimetri, your lust for war is well known. But I'm not ready to start a nuclear war because some missiles may rust out. Maybe you can enlighten us on what the Americans are up to?"

Olagev gave a quick bow of acquiescence, barely more than a nod. His position in the Politburo was powerful, but Petrov still held the upper hand. "Comrade President, the Americans remain on a full war footing, but they have been strangely quiet. No saber-rattling speeches or threatening rants at the United Nations. Our agents report that their Congress is in emergency session and their president is meeting in the White House. They have made no effort to evacuate Washington."

"Interesting. It looks like they don't fear an imminent attack." Petrov mused as he rubbed his chin. "Admiral Baranov, what is the GRU seeing?"

Baranov stood down at the far end of the table. He was the most junior person in the room and wielded the least power, but the GRU still commanded respect. A satellite image flashed up on the screen. "Comrade President, the American carrier fleet is just now arriving in Vestfjorden, a large sea fjord in northern Norway. One carrier and its warships are already there, and the other one will arrive in a few hours. They have not attempted any flights over Soviet lands."

The image changed to a map of the Barents and the Norwegian Sea. "We have not detected any American submarines except for the two we sank. We project that they have at least a dozen fast attack submarines that will try to penetrate our ASW barriers in the Barents, but so far, we have not seen anything."

"And their strategic forces?" Petrov asked.

"As near as we can tell, they remain on full alert, but it is difficult to attribute any special war footing to them."

The heavy iron door creaked open. An aide peeked in and said, "Pardon me, the American president is on the hot line, he wishes to speak to you, Vladimar Antonovich."

Petrov waved for everyone to leave the room. When the door had ponderously swung shut, he picked up the handset from the red phone that sat in front of him. There were several clicks and snaps before he heard a voice at the other end. "President Petrov, I am connecting you to the president."

"President Petrov." The twang of a Midwestern US accent was unmistakable. "We need to speak as one leader to another. I fear that we are too near the precipice. One mistake, one misinterpretation and we, both of us, may plunge over the edge and take the rest of the world with us."

Petrov listened carefully and weighed his answer. He knew that several dozen people were silently listening in on both ends of the line and would analyze every nuance of what he said. "Mr. President, I fear that what you say is too true. This is a time when we both must proceed with extreme caution. I trust that you did not call just because you are worried, that you have some proposition to discuss. I am interested in hearing it."

There was a pause on the other end. Then the American president said, "In order to de-escalate the immediate military situation, I will pull our carriers back south of the GIUK line if you return your surface ships to Soviet territorial waters."

Petrov nodded and said, "Agreed. What about your missile submarines?"

"I will surface all of ours and return them to their home ports if you do the same."

"Agreed," Petrov answered. "I propose that we both take our long-range bombers off of high alert and return them to their normal air bases."

"Agreed," the American president answered. "I strongly suggest that we start moving our forces immediately and not wait for our diplomats to negotiate us to death while they prepare the documents for us to sign. I will institute the orders as soon as we finish this call."

"I will do the same," Petrov chuckled as he answered. The diplomats in the Ministry of Foreign Affairs were a constant irritation. It was good to see that he was not alone in that feeling. "I am glad that you made this call, Mr. President. It seems to have been most productive. *Do svidaniya.*"

With the call completed, the Supreme High Command leadership filed back into the meeting room. Vladimar Petrov quickly summarized his discussion with the American president. He ordered the fleet returned to Murmansk and all of the ballistic missile submarines returned to their home ports. There was some mild disagreement and discussion, but Petrov squelched it.

"What about the ICBMs?" the Strategic Rocket Force general inquired. "Should we immediately start defueling and flushing them?"

Petrov shook his head. "No, Comrade General. Those rockets will be our ace in the hole until we see if this is an American trick."

"But they may corrode and be useless."

"Then we will build more."

0800Z, 24 April 1983, USS John Jay, *Kangertitivaq Fjord, Greenland*

The AMR-1 hatch proved difficult to open, but the crew was eventually able to rig up a porta-power hydraulic jack and force it open. They emerged into a cold, empty, white world, surrounded by a flat jumble of pack ice that stretched all the way to high icy mountains in the distance.

The *John Jay* had been badly damaged by the forced surfacing through the ice. Chunks of ice over three feet thick lay piled on the dented and crumpled ruins of the missile deck. Only the missile tubes themselves had been strong enough to withstand the ice. The top of the sail, made of half-inch-thick mild steel, was crushed, jamming all the masts down in their housings. The fairwater planes, unable to stand up to the force and weight of the ice, crumpled and bent down until they folded against the pressure hull.

The *John Jay* would not be going anywhere for a while.

The only sign that they were not alone in this icy world was the P-3C Orion orbiting a thousand feet overhead.

Darren Walsh keyed the handheld walkie-talkie microphone and said, "Navy P-3, this is Navy Unit on channel sixteen, how copy, over?"

The tiny speaker crackled and chirped. Then he heard, "Navy Unit, this is Navy One-Two-Four. Copy you five by five, over."

Walsh smiled for the first time in several hours. At least now the rest of the Navy knew of their predicament. Help would be on the way.

"Navy One-Two-Four," he answered, "we have a bit of a problem down here. We can't submerge, and we can't move. Our antennas are all OOC. This is the only comms we have."

"Navy Unit, roger that. From up here, you look like crap," Blunt Sharples replied. "SUBLANT has been notified. The *Ike* is sending a helo evac of your injured. ETA your location noon Zulu. What assistance do you need?"

The aircraft carrier *Dwight D. Eisenhower*, somewhere out in the Norwegian Sea and heading north, was sending her SH-3 helicopters for assistance. The SH-3 Sea King had a range of about six hundred nautical miles and a speed of about two hundred knots, so it would be several hours before they arrived.

"Copy helos inbound," Walsh answered. "Negative on injured personnel. A few minor bruises and scrapes is all we have. Right now, I need help evaluating how we get out of here and probably some Marines to set up a perimeter around us."

Sharples replied, "Roger that. Relaying your request to *Ike* and to SUBLANT. We will provide comms relay. We have another four hours on-station time with a hot relief by Navy Three-Seven-Six. Navy One-Two-Four out."

1030 EST, 24 April 1983, COMSUBLANT, Norfolk, Virginia

The SUBLANT OPCON center was a beehive of activity. Orders and "guidance" had been filtering down from the JCS, in the Pentagon, and from CINCLANTFLT, across the street, all morning. Even before the president's early morning address to the nation where he announced the unprecedented agreement with President Petrov to step away from confrontation, the orders had already been flowing in torrents.

Rufus Brown and Ted Strange stood back in a corner of the busy room and watched. They kept out of the way as the young junior officers and enlisted personnel worked to get orders out for all of the boomers to surface and start heading to their home ports. As an added twist, the Holy Loch–based boats needed orders routing them to Loch Inver, way up in the Scottish Highlands, instead of to Holy Loch.

Writing orders for two dozen boats and safely routing them back home on quick notice was a mammoth task. And then sending out the orders to the home ports to be ready to receive the boats was even more work.

"What are we going to do with the attack boats?" Ted Strange asked.

Brown grunted, "President didn't mention them. The Chairman didn't say anything, and neither did CINCLANTFLT. And I ain't asking for directions. I'm ordering them into holding patterns west of the North Cape-Bear Island-Svalbard line. That will keep them handy if this whole agreement thing goes south."

"Don't trust the Russkies?" Strange arched his eyebrows as he asked the question.

"Let's just say I'm being careful and hedging my bets," Brown answered. "Just like I'm leaving *Tigerfish* off Murmansk until someone tells me otherwise. Now, what are we doing with *John Jay*?"

"The *Ike*'s helos are shuttling comms gear in so that we can get direct communications with Darren Walsh." Strange referenced a folder that he was holding. "Have a squad of Marines on the way to set up a security perimeter, although there probably isn't anything to worry about except the errant polar bear. The nearest civilization is a native village." He looked at the folder. "Let me see if I can get this right. Ittoqqortoormiit, or something like that. Maybe three hundred people, forty miles from the *John Jay*. No airport or anything. No way to stage out of there."

"Damn, Walsh sure found an out-of-the-way bit of ocean to get stranded in," Brown mused. "What's the word on the Russian sub, Case 41171700, that shot at him?"

"Well, the P-3 that was on-station got a shot at it, and so did Walsh. The P-3 recorded at least three detonations and then breaking-up noises. SOSUS verifies what the P-3 jockey is saying. Looks like our spy met his end."

"Has anyone talked with Joy Walsh or any of the wives on the boat?" Brown asked.

"I was waiting until I got verification that everyone onboard was okay before I called," Strange answered. "Now that I have that and we're pretty sure the crew is going to be stuck there for a bit, I'll make the call. Mrs. Walsh was due out of the hospital today."

Brown nodded, but he was already thinking about the next problem.

35

1800Z, 24 April 1983, USS **Tigerfish**, *Murmansk Fjord*

Steve Dunn stood on the periscope stand and walked a slow circle, swinging the Type 18 periscope around in a continuous clockwise circle. Kildin Island's high bluffs filled his view for half of each revolution, while the dull, gray Barents Sea, empty all the way to the horizon, filled the other half.

To Dunn, it was mind-numbingly boring work, but with the world seemingly recoiling back from the edge of nuclear war, boring was good. Yes, very good. The only noise disturbing him was the intermittent alarms from the WLR-9. Several Soviet surface ships were off to the northwest trying to boil the Arctic waters with their Horse Jaw and Bull Nose active sonars.

"Conn, ESM, intercepting multiple surface- and air-search radars." The 21MC disturbed the quiet that enveloped the control room. "So far, identified Top Plate air-search radars, carried on *Udaloy*, *Slava*, and *Kirov* class. Intercepting Top Pair air- and surface-search radars, carried on the same platforms." Chief Greg Lawlar was reading from a list. "Detecting Palm Frond nav radar, carried on *Kirov*. Intercepting Strut Curve air-search radar, carried on *Grisha*-class corvettes. Detecting multiple Don-2 nav radars carried on just about everyone."

Lawlar took a breath, then he added, "Looks like the whole friggin' Northern Fleet. Request you raise the BLD-1 so we can cut bearings."

Steve Dunn thought for a second and then answered, "Chief, I ain't leaving that trash can exposed for more than ten seconds. Get your bearing cuts done quick, 'cause it's comin' down. Too many people out there looking." He turned to the Chief-of-the-Watch and ordered, "Raise the BLD-1. Leave it raised for ten seconds and then lower it."

The "housed" light had just lit on the BLD-1 mast when Chief Lawlar reported over the 21MC, "Bearing cuts on the Palm Frond and one of the Top Pair radars. Both bear three-five-zero."

Steve Dunn spun the periscope around until he was staring down the bearing. He switched the optics to twenty-four power and could just see the hint of a mast coming over the horizon.

"Mark this bearing," he called out. "I'm seeing the top of a mast, low down on the horizon."

"Conn, Sonar, new sonar contacts, broadband on the sphere," Senior Chief Zwarlinski reported. "Sounds like at least three and probably more. Best bearing three-five-zero. At least one of them is a heavy."

Dunn was just reaching for the JA handset to call the Captain when Roy Blivens walked into control. "What you got, Eng?"

"Skipper, ESM reports several intercepts on Russian warship radars bearing three-five-zero," Dunn answered. "Sonar has several surface contacts on that bearing, at least one heavy. I'm seeing just the top of a mast low on the horizon on the same bearing."

Blivens looked at the navigation plot. He said, "That's about where I would expect the Northern Fleet to be coming from if they were heading home like SUBLANT says they are supposed to."

Blivens stepped back up on the periscope stand and flipped through the displays on the BQR-21 sonar. "You seeing any submerged contacts? SUBLANT says they are supposed to be coming in on the surface, but if I were them, I would run down here submerged and then pop up just off the coast."

Dunn answered, "Nothing yet, Skipper. No submerged contacts, no submarine active sonar. ESM is looking for any Snoop Tray radars, but zilch on that so far, too."

Blivens looked at the nav chart again. "Eng, let's snuggle over here, nice and close to Kildin Island. Don't want to get run over by anyone in a hurry for Polyarny liberty. But we need to count hulls as they parade past and get pictures if we can. From what I can tell, the boss is using us to verify that President Petrov is living up to his part of the bargain."

"Conn, ESM, intercepting Snoop Tray surface-search radars. Request BLD-1 to cut a bearing," Chief Lawlar's voice came over the 21MC.

"Chief, BLD-1 coming up. You've got ten seconds. Chief-of-the-Watch, raise the BLD-1. Lower it in ten seconds."

"Conn, ESM, multiple Snoop Tray radars bearing roughly zero-two-zero. Best guess, at least eight contacts around that bearing, plus or minus ten degrees."

Dunn grabbed the 21MC. "Sonar, Conn, what do you have on between zero-one-zero and zero-three-zero?"

Al Zwarlinski answered, "Nothing, but we'll look closer. Request you come around to something like three-three-zero for best towed array beams."

Dunn answered, "Coming to three-three-zero, but these are going to be short legs. I don't want to get in the way of those surface ships heading home."

Dunn spun the scope around and saw the distinctive pyramidal mast of the *Kirov* appear over the horizon. "Skipper, you need to see this," he said as he turned the scope over to Blivens.

The Soviet battlecruiser, the largest and most heavily armed nuclear-powered surface warship in the world, was steaming right at them. Then Blivens saw a pair of *Slava*-class cruisers, with their eight massive deck-mounted SS-N-12 canisters, appear on the horizon, followed by a smaller *Kara*-class cruiser.

The evening twilight was deepening into nighttime. The Soviet ships' masthead and side lights blinked on. For the next two hours, Dunn and Blivens counted and photographed the Soviet Northern Fleet. The count ended up at a battlecruiser, a half dozen cruisers, thirty assorted destroyers, and another thirty frigates and corvettes.

Dunn shook his head. "Damn, that was a lot of tonnage! If we were weapons free, we would have put Mush Morton to shame."

"Yep," Blivens agreed. "And we still have the boomers to put to bed."

0900 EST, 25 April 1983, COMSUBLANT, Norfolk, Virginia

Vice Admiral Rufus Brown sat back in the leather chair and looked down the worn oak table at the young lieutenant commander who had just plopped his notes down on the lectern to one side of the big projection screen. Brown signaled for the briefing to begin and then reached for the coffeepot to pour himself another cup.

"Good morning, Admiral," the briefer started cheerily. "This brief summarizes the status of the Soviet fleet as of 0800, Monday, twenty-five April."

He pushed a button so that a map of the Kola Peninsula and the Barents Sea appeared on the screen. Other than regional geography, the only thing shown on the chart was a circle labeled "*Tigerfish*" a few miles off the Murmansk Fjord and several circles with American submarine names slightly to the west of North Cape and Bear Island.

"Our latest satellite imagery shows all Soviet warships tied up in various ports on the Murmansk Fjord. *Tigerfish* confirms sighting their return to port and confirms obtaining imagery of each ship. *Tigerfish* also reports eighteen *Delta*-class SSBNs and one *Typhoon* SSBN returning to port. Satellites were unable to confirm all since the *Typhoon* and at least six of the *Delta*s are under covered piers."

Brown looked over at Ted Strange. "Chief-of-Staff, is that everyone?"

Strange looked up from his briefing folder. "Yes, sir. That accounts for all their deployable boomers. But *Tigerfish* didn't report seeing any of their SSNs. I think Admiral Golubev is playing your game and is keeping them hidden."

Brown chuckled. "Sure looks like that's what the clever old goat is up to. But for now, let's pull *Tigerfish* a hundred miles off their coast, just to play it safe. How long until we can get a boat out there to relieve them?"

Strange flipped a couple of pages. "*Spadefish* has completed her deployment certs and is headed that way. She has to stop in Faslane to pick up the direct support team. It'll take a week to get them up there to relieve."

"Good. Make it happen. Now, what about *John Jay*?"

The young intel briefer stammered, "Admiral, I really don't have anything prepared on that."

"That was a Chief-of-Staff question," Brown replied.

Strange answered, "I'm afraid Darren Walsh and his crew are going to be stuck there for a bit. METOC doesn't expect the Kangertitivaq Fjord to be clear of ice until early June. I called the Coasties and asked for help. They have an icebreaker that can help. The *Westwind* can get underway in a week from Wilmington, Delaware. Then two weeks transit to get up to the fjord. Their ice expert figures that it'll take a week to break the *John Jay* free and then tow her to open water."

"Why is it taking a week to break the boat free?" Brown grumbled.

"Well, NAVSEA has a whole bunch of tests that they want to run before they will certify she is safe to tow. They have an oceangoing tug, the *Catawba*, that they need to get certified to tow a nuclear sub. Would you believe there is an eight-hundred-page manual on the requirements to tow a nuclear submarine."

Brown mumbled something derogatory about deskbound engineers before he said, "Of course there is. Just make it happen."

"And Admiral," Strange continued, "the Danish government is asking when we will have the *John Jay* out of their territorial waters."

"Just call over to CINCLANTFLT and give them the timeline," Brown growled. "Let them deal with the striped-pants types at State. But the message is that we are doing the best we can."

Brown did some figuring and then said, "According to my figures, we can have her back stateside in mid-June. Let's plan to tow her to Charleston Weapons Station to off-load her missiles and then to the shipyard to figure out what we are going to do with her. Get N4 working on making that happen. Then get the public affairs people up to speed. This ain't going to stay a secret for long. Get them out ahead of the story."

Almost as an afterthought, Brown said, "And, Chief-of-Staff, work on getting those two Russian fliers off the *John Jay* and sent home. That should make for a nice goodwill gesture."

EPILOGUE

1030 EST, 20 June 1983, Charleston Naval Weapons Station

Two harbor tugs pushed the battered, rusty hull up next to the pier and held the *John Jay* in place against the strong Cooper River current.

Most of the sub's cleats had been too badly damaged by the ice to be used. By the time temporary cleats were welded in place, a large crowd of curious bystanders had migrated from the tender and the boats tied up down at Pier Bravo to stare at what once was a powerful warship. They joined the families that were waiting for their loved ones to finally come home. It took until midafternoon for the crew and the pier-side line handlers to safely secure the boat to Wharf Alpha.

The hot South Carolina sun was beating down when the gangway was finally swung over to allow the crew to rush over.

The Walsh family stood with the rest of the crew families, all dressed in their summer finest. Joy was still encumbered by a shoulder sling and bandages, but Annie May Faris was hovering around to help out. Pug Walsh was tugging on Joy Walsh's "good arm" and hollering, "There's Dad! There's Dad!" as he hopped up and down and pointed at Darren Walsh. Sam Walsh, befitting a proper young lady, stood demurely by her mother's side, but she was smiling from ear to ear.

When the night-rider cables were in place, fore and aft, and the *John Jay* was secured from the force of the Cooper River's current, Darren Walsh finally crossed the brow and stepped onto solid ground. He hugged his wife, being very careful with her injured arm. Then, much to Sam's embarrassment, he grabbed both kids in a big bear hug.

Vice Admiral Rufus Brown stood back and waited until the family greeting had played out before he stepped up. "Welcome home, Darren." He answered Walsh's salute and then shook hands. "Good job bringing your boat home, even if you did ding her up a bit. I want you to turn the boat over to the Gold Crew, take a month's leave, and then give me a call. I have a job I want you to do."

Operation Golden Dawn
by George Wallace

When a Chinese spymaster uses an Islamic terrorist to attack Western interests in the Pacific, a US Navy submarine is sent in to prevent disaster.

Mustafa al Shatar, one of the world's most dangerous terrorists, lives only for vengeance.

Indonesian Navy Admiral Suluvana plans to overthrow the government and establish an Islamic state.

And Liu Pen, spymaster for the People's Republic of China, plans to use them both to solidify China's grip on power.

From a secret island base in the Java Sea, Liu Pen's research team is developing a genetically engineered version of smallpox. A dangerous biological weapon to be unleashed upon the West.

But when US intelligence catches wind of the plans, Commander Joe Hunter and his crew aboard the USS SAN FRANCISCO are deployed to neutralize the threat...before catastrophe strikes.

Get your copy today at
severnriverbooks.com

ACKNOWLEDGMENTS

Putting together a Cold War submarine story has been on my list for a long time. For nigh on fifty years, America's submarine force maintained a highly successful struggle that kept the world protected from the horrors of nuclear war while keeping us safe and free. That fight was accomplished mostly in darkness and stealth. We aren't called the "Silent Service" for nothing. In this story, I wanted to give the reader a feeling for what a "boomer" patrol was really like and some of what the fast attack crews were dealing with. The day-to-day operations, the mechanical and technical challenges, the camaraderie of a submarine crew. Most of those details in this novel are taken from real life. To keep the reader from being bored senseless, I wrapped a techno-thriller/spy plot around this.

There are several people that I need to acknowledge and thank in writing this story. First off is Andrew Watts and Severn River Publishing for having the trust in me to make this happen. Cate Streissguth, publisher, and Kate Schomaker, copy editor, made sure the whole process was smooth and painless. I need to thank a couple of personal friends for lending their knowledge and expertise. Col Doug "Smash" Yurovich, USMC (ret), provided the insights to make the P-3C details realistic, and CTTC Mike Varone, USN (ret), did the same for the submarine EW mission.

And, finally, but most importantly, I want to thank my wife, Penny. She gave me the insights about family life while we on the boats were out boring holes in the ocean. The families were the unsung heroes of that time. Hopefully, I did them justice.

ABOUT GEORGE WALLACE

Commander George Wallace retired to the civilian business world in 1995, after twenty-two years of service on nuclear submarines. He served on two of Admiral Rickover's famous "Forty One for Freedom", the USS John Adams SSBN 620 and the USS Woodrow Wilson SSBN 624, during which time he made nine one-hundred-day deterrent patrols through the height of the Cold War.

Commander Wallace served as Executive Officer on the Sturgeon class nuclear attack submarine USS Spadefish, SSN 668. Spadefish and all her sisters were decommissioned during the downsizings that occurred in the 1990's. The passing of that great ship served as the inspiration for "Final Bearing."

Commander Wallace commanded the Los Angeles class nuclear attack submarine USS Houston, SSN 713 from February 1990 to August 1992. During this tour of duty that he worked extensively with the SEAL community developing SEAL/submarine tactics. Under Commander Wallace, the Houston was awarded the CIA Meritorious Unit Citation.

Commander Wallace lives with his wife, Penny, in Alexandria, Virginia.

Sign up for Wallace and Keith's newsletter at
severnriverbooks.com

Printed in the United States
by Baker & Taylor Publisher Services